THE
PIPER'S
TUNE

THE
PIPER'S
TUNE

—

Dallas Miller

WILLIAM MORROW AND COMPANY, INC. · NEW YORK

Library of Congress Cataloging-in-Publication Data

Miller, Dallas.
The piper's tune.
I. Title.
PS3563.I379P5   1987   813'.54   87-11283
ISBN 0-688-06476-0

Printed in the United States of America

First Edition

1 2 3 4 5 6 7 8 9 10

BOOK DESIGN BY LINEY LI

Oh, the days of the Kerry dancing
Oh, the ring of the piper's tune . . .

ONE

1960

"This is Andrew Sinclair with the Molloy Company in New York, and there's a little something we'd like you to do for us."

As a rule, housemothers at Radcliffe College are anything but obliging when asked to perform the duties of an answering service for the young women living in their dormitories. But there was something about Sinclair's request—gentle but magisterial—that immediately commanded Mrs. Amy Foxworth's attention. She had no idea who or what the Molloy Company was, but would soon make it her business to find out.

"We've sent the company plane to Boston this morning for Kathleen Molloy," he resumed. "With luck, it should be setting down at Logan Airport shortly before twelve noon, where our pilot has been instructed to wait until Miss Molloy arrives for the return trip. Could you see to it that she receives this message as soon as she gets back to the dorm from morning classes? It's very important. And also ask her to call me at her grandmother's place in New York before leaving for the airport."

"Her grandmother's place?"

"The River House apartment."

Even Mrs. Foxworth, the widow of an impoverished schoolteacher in western Massachusetts, had heard of that exalted residence on New York's Sutton Place, reputedly the most exclusive, most expensive address in all of Manhattan.

"Yes, of course. I'll tell her the minute she comes in. I hope that nothing serious has—"

"Thank you," he said, terminating the conversation. "You've been most helpful."

After Andrew Sinclair hung up, Mrs. Foxworth continued to sit at her desk, intrigued by the second message of the morning she had been asked to deliver to the Molloy girl. Only minutes before, the switchboard had transferred a call from a woman identifying herself as Caitlin Phipps, Kathleen's aunt. When the housemother explained that her niece was attending a class—"Puritan Literature from 1636 to Emerson," she read from a duplicate class schedule—not due to adjourn until twelve, the Phipps woman pondered the matter momentarily, then suggested, "I wonder if we should send someone to fetch her. Perhaps I could call Nathan Pusey."

The *president* of Harvard? Mrs. Foxworth couldn't imagine President Pusey dashing from his office simply to run an errand for a student's aunt, no matter how important or influential she was. Instead, she reminded her caller that it was now eleven-fifteen, and by the time a messenger reached Kathleen's classroom in Emerson Hall, in all probability she would already be on her way back to the dorm for lunch. So in the end, Caitlin Phipps was satisfied with a pledge that her niece would return the call the minute she arrived.

Of all the young women under the housemother's charge, none was more mysterious or alluring than Kathleen Molloy. With her sea-green eyes and long tawny hair, she could have passed for a West of Ireland colleen or perhaps a scholarship student from South Boston. But there was a good deal more to her than that. How could Mrs. Foxworth forget her arrival last September in a dark gray Rolls-Royce Silver Shadow with New York license plates, or the immaculately uniformed chauffeur who carried her baggage to her room? Accompanying her was a stunningly attractive woman wearing an old-fashioned wide-brimmed straw hat and a navy-blue silk dress, a dazzling double string of pearls around her neck. Even in a college town as jaded by displays of wealth as Cambridge was, the spectacle drew a certain amount of attention, although the Molloy girl herself seemed oblivious to it. In the confusion surrounding the beginning of term, Mrs. Foxworth hadn't been able to introduce herself to the woman she supposed was Kathleen's mother. Yet only a week later, another woman appeared, this one wearing country tweeds and low-heeled shoes and driving a station wagon with Connecticut license plates. In a languorously patrician voice, she asked for directions to Kathleen's room, then identified herself as her mother, Nancy Romily.

Mrs. Foxworth liked to believe that she wasn't unduly impressed by money or caste, but there was something so irresistible about the two women—the glamour of the one, the sureness and serenity of the other—that she consulted a dog-eared copy of the Social Register she'd acquired at a garage sale the year before. Sure enough, she found the Romilys listed with a Greenwich, Connecticut, address, and noted that Nancy Romily had been born a Delano, an ancient Hudson River Valley family that had been ornamenting history books for centuries and ranked socially with the Van Rensselaers, Schermerhorns, and Roosevelts—into which latter family, in fact, they had married. But what was baffling was that no children were included in the entry. Then how was it possible for Nancy Romily to be Kathleen Molloy's mother?

As for the other woman, Mrs. Foxworth didn't like to ask outright, but one evening in the dining hall she happened to mention the episode to Kathleen's roommate, who revealed with schoolgirl candor, "Oh, that must have been her grandmother, Nora Molloy, from New York."

It was all the housemother could do to finish dessert before rushing back to her office to see what the social arbiters said about the woman. But to her astonishment, she found that although several Molloys were listed in the New York area, there was no listing at all for a Nora Molloy.

At the time it had seemed to Mrs. Foxworth something of a contradiction—did such obvious wealth often go unrewarded?—and now to learn that the grandmother lived at the River House made it all the more perplexing, because that cooperative apartment building on New York's East Side was a bastion of old money and respectability, where nouveau types and rich celebrities seldom got past the doormen. If the Molloys were shunned by the editors of the Register, then how had they managed to charm their neighbors?

As always when faced with questions regarding a student's family, Mrs. Foxworth picked up her telephone and dialed

Carrie Whittemore, who worked as a secretary in the Dean of Admissions' office and was—or at least claimed to be—a direct descendant of both William Bradford and Cotton Mather.

The minute her friend answered, Mrs. Foxworth asked, "So what do you know about some people named Molloy who live at the River House in New York?"

The reply was instantaneous. "Never heard of 'em. They sound *Irish*."

Mrs. Foxworth couldn't help but be amused at her friend's lack of charity toward people whose pedigrees she considered less distinguished than her own. Just as the worst snob at Radcliffe was invariably a small-town rich girl from some obscure corner of the Midwest—one year it was a girl whose father owned a soda pop bottling franchise in Toledo—nothing equaled the arrogance of former members of the gentry, like Miss Whittemore, who now had to work for their living.

"Then what about the Molloy Company of New York? Or haven't you ever heard of that either?"

"Oh, but of course I have! Who hasn't? It's either the largest construction firm in America, or the world, I forget which. Larger than Bechtel. Larger than Brown & Root. I read about them recently in *For-tee-yune* magazine. They're sinfully rich. Do you mean to say you know those Molloys?"

"It seems that I have one of them living here in the dorm. What do they do anyway, the Molloys?"

"What don't they do? They build airports and bridges and pipelines and dams and entire cities in the desert for Arab sheiks. They're so cute and cagey, I wouldn't be a bit surprised if they have the exclusive contract to pave the streets of heaven—if there is a heaven. If there isn't, the Molloy Company could probably build one. Charles Molloy is boss. He's one of the most powerful men in America."

"Then why is it I've never heard of him?"

"Because when you're as rich as Charles Molloy, it's not convenient to be the subject of notoriety. In fact, the less people know about you, the better. Rumor has it that Molloy is one of the men who put Dwight Eisenhower in the White House."

Mrs. Foxworth was aghast. "But I thought we elected him."

"Figuratively, I meant. You see, he helped bankroll Ike in his race for the presidency, and they're also the best of friends. They play golf together, which must be excruciating for Molloy if Ike's golf game is no better than his repartee." She waited, then asked, "So what's the girl like anyway?"

The housemother was ashamed to admit that she scarcely knew. "She seems very sweet and unaffected." She searched for truer, apter words. "Clean-cut and nice."

"Well, that's certainly a novelty. Half the girls I see around campus look like airline stewardesses after a forty-hour flight from New Delhi. Tired and shopworn. You know what I mean? I've almost forgotten what a nice, clean-cut girl looks like. I wonder what's happening to the Molloys of New York that's so important they're sending a private plane to Boston in the middle of the week just to bring her home. I'm dying to find out. Promise me you'll call the minute you learn something."

Mrs. Foxworth promised. After she hung up, she wrote two notes: one to be stuffed under the door of the girl's room, the other to be placed in her mailbox. But then it occurred to her that Kathleen might very well go directly to the dining hall without stopping for her mail or going upstairs to her room, so on second thought she decided to station herself in the hall next to the main entrance.

At shortly after noon, she was standing inside the huge oak doors, and as girls entered she asked them, "Have you by any chance seen Kathleen Molloy? I have an urgent message for her."

Some had, some hadn't. A fair number, however, took note of their housemother's newfound deference to their classmate, and more than a few guessed the reason. "I was wondering when Old Pruneface would finally figure out who Kathleen is," one of them remarked acidly as she sailed down the hall.

"It's remarkable what money can buy."

"Isn't it? But what I've never been able to understand is why it's thought to be contemptible for the rich to buy people, while the poor, who allow themselves to be bought, expect nothing but our pity."

As the girls' high-spirited laughter filled the hall, the

housemother anxiously peered through the windows of the door for the first glimpse of the Molloy girl as she rounded the corner. The second she came into view, Mrs. Foxworth would hurry down the steps to tell her . . . tell her what?

That something momentous had happened in New York. Or was about to.

Kathleen was late because she had bumped into a Harvard senior named Ted Birmingham as she was leaving Emerson Hall on her bicycle. Literally bumped into him. Collided with him.

Her head was bent into the fierce wind blowing off the Charles River, so she hadn't seen him dart onto the sidewalk from between two parked cars, and the front wheel of her bike caught him in the leg.

"For Christ's sake, can't you watch out where you're going!" he thundered, then recognized her and added more gently, "Oh, it's you."

They'd met the January before at an Eliot House dance. Kathleen's date was an impeccably well-bred but excruciatingly boring member of the varsity tennis team. Ted Birmingham struck up a conversation with her at the refreshment table, and they got along so well that he asked for her telephone number. But it was now mid-March, and he had yet to call.

Today, he was sheepish, apologetic. "I've been meaning to get in touch. How have you been?"

"Fiendishly busy," she answered. "Writing papers, studying for tests."

"Me too," he sighed. "Have you been home recently?"

Upon meeting someone for the first time, Kathleen seldom volunteered anything except the barest biographical details, having learned from experience that to reveal too much tended to put something of a strain on relationships. Being the granddaughter of the great Charles Molloy often impressed people she didn't particularly want as friends, and intimidated those she did. So at their first meeting she had told Ted Birmingham that her father was dead—killed during the Second World War—and that she lived in Connecticut with her mother, whom she liked, and stepfather, whom she didn't, but spent a great deal of time with her father's family in New York. Because Ted was New York-born—in Greenwich Village, of all places, he boasted, adding that not everyone in that hedonistic part of town was contraconceived—they immediately had something in common, since Kathleen was born at Lenox Hill Hospital on Manhattan's East Side.

Now in front of Emerson Hall, she told him, "I have to be in New York this weekend, because I'm hosting a birthday party for twin cousins of mine."

Jake and Molly Phipps would be twenty, a year younger than Kathleen, and since both were away at college—Jake at Princeton, by the skin of his teeth; Molly, who was uncommonly pious, at Manhattanville College of the Sacred Heart in Purchase, New York—their birthday would be celebrated in town over the weekend.

"I'm going home this weekend too," Ted informed her. "I'm driving, in case you might be interested in a lift. It'd save you train fare."

Ordinarily, Kathleen caught a late-afternoon Eastern Air Lines flight because it took less than an hour, and a car was always sent to the airport to collect her. If anything, it would be an inconvenience to accept Ted Birmingham's offer, because even if the weather didn't turn nasty, it was a long drive, and if they ran into snow, it could very well become interminable. Still, she'd been drawn to him at their first meeting and had been disappointed when he hadn't called.

One of the advantages of accepting his invitation was that they'd be able to get to know one another better during the trip south. So she said brightly, "All right. Provided that you let me pay for half the gas."

"You've got yourself a deal." The color rose in his face. "Actually, the reason I haven't called is that I had a bit of trouble getting my tuition money together this term, and I also had to pay to get the brakes relined on my Chevy. So I'm about two months behind in all my social activities. I couldn't even afford to take someone to the movies."

Kathleen had scant personal knowledge of poverty, and it simply hadn't occurred to her that he might be poor. She remembered that he was a scholarship student from the Bronx

High School of Science—"I was the token goy in my graduating class," he'd said—and also had a long haul in front of him because he was pre-med. She imagined that Ivy League tuition could put a definite strain on an average income, and she seemed to recall that he had a pack of little brothers and sisters at home and a widowed mother who worked for a living.

Everything considered, there was something refreshing about a Harvard man who unashamedly confessed that he'd been stone-broke. More often than not, they tended to put on great airs.

"When's your last class on Friday?" he asked.

There was no way in the world she could skip her three o'clock in Hellenic sculpture, because the professor always gave quizzes on Fridays and didn't allow makeups.

"I've got a three o'clock in chemistry," he volunteered, "then I have to get some books out of the library. So why don't I meet you at four-fifteen or so on the steps in front of Widener?"

That would be fine. She could sign out for the weekend before leaving her dorm for class, and would carry her small overnighter with her.

"There's only one thing, and you're going to hate me for it," he began with obvious embarrassment. "I remember your first name—Kathleen, isn't it?—but I can't remember your last name. I wrote it down somewhere after we met at the dance, then I must have lost the slip of paper."

Far from hating him for it, she was delighted. Too often she'd seen the shock of recognition, the cowed look of adulation on the faces of people who would never *forget* her name.

"Molloy," she answered simply, and his expression was unchanged.

"Molloy!" he repeated. "Got it now." Suddenly he was grinning. "See ya on Friday in front of Widener. I'm glad I ran into you, Kathleen Molloy."

"You mean you're glad I ran *over* you."

Laughing, they parted, and while he rushed off in one direction, she peddled her bicycle in the other, buoyed at having encountered him when she least expected to.

* * *

Once, when Kathleen was still a student at Rosemary Hall in Greenwich, her mother persuaded her to visit a local psychiatrist because in a fit of rebellion she'd demanded that her name be stricken from the Social Register, even going so far as to threaten legal action if her wishes weren't carried out.

The psychiatrist attempted to reason with her. "But Kathleen, being listed in the Social Register is generally thought to be something of an honor."

"It's nothing more than a stud book," she said, dismissing it, "more appropriate for horses than for people."

"And is that the reason you've insisted that your name be removed, bringing embarrassment to your mother and stepfather?"

"My mother and particularly my mother's *husband*," she corrected him, "are terrible snobs, although they pretend not to be. They're not the least bit annoyed that my Grandmother Nora doesn't quite measure up to the Register's standards because she worked as a domestic servant when she first came to this country from Ireland. You see, members of society enjoy eating well, but they don't like the idea of sharing a page of the Social Register with one of their former cooks."

"But Kathleen, everyone can't be a member of society."

Defiantly, she replied, "My grandfather says that society is piffle. Nothing but a lot of silly twits who think they're better than someone else, as compensation for not being too bright. He's *above* society."

The psychiatrist couldn't conceal his amusement. "Oh, he is, is he? And who, might I ask, is your grandfather?"

She watched his face fall as she answered, "Charles Molloy."

In the end, he gave her a clean bill of health, merely noting that contentiousness was a phase that most youngsters went through in their teens.

Kathleen's mother, however, knew better. By now she was convinced that contentiousness was an inescapable, ineradicable characteristic of all the Molloys. Whenever she and her daughter had a difference of opinion, which was often, Nancy Romily would remind her that she defied comprehension. "I simply can't understand you, Kathleen, I really can't. You're not at all like me or anyone else in my family, living or dead. You're like . . . I don't know what. One of *them*."

One of *them*, as if referring to satanic forces too horrid to be identified more fully, not the merry, gentle Molloys of New York, a family she'd once adored.

It was Charles Molloy who said that if he'd learned nothing else about life during his seventy-six years, it was that people change. Like strychnine that can be tolerated in small doses but is lethal in large ones, being alive has a cumulative effect that sometimes packs a terrible wallop. And it was his contention that Nancy Romily would never, never forgive the Molloys for the sorrow they brought into her life.

More than anything else, what had altered Nancy's personality—and formed Kathleen's—was the death of Tom Molloy at the age of twenty-three while piloting an RAF Spitfire over Dunkirk at the outbreak of the Second World War. Less than a year after her marriage, Nancy found herself a widow with a tiny baby to raise. Understandably, the Molloys were grief-stricken, and when they saw the fatherless baby, in their grief they rushed in to become her father, every last one of them.

Thus, Kathleen had a most unusual childhood. For five days of the week, she lived with her tearful mother, her morose Grandfather Delano, her stone-deaf Grandmother Delano, and a succession of cross, frustrated governesses in a huge, melancholy house in Millbrook in Dutchess County, New York, but every weekend she was permitted to visit the Molloys, who at that time still lived in a townhouse on East Seventy-first Street. The contrast was stunning. At Millbrook, her only companions were adults, somber and silent except for her mother's quiet sobbing and the long fulminations her Grandfather Delano delivered against Harry Truman and his Democratic party. But in New York, the Molloy house was always brimming with children and filled with laughter and noise, so she had to shout above the din to be heard at the dinner table. In Dutchess County, she was required to return her playthings to their proper places the minute she finished with them, but at the Molloys' house the first-floor hall was always littered with ice skates and sleds, baseball bats and tennis rackets, and puppy dogs ran helter-skelter over rare antique Bokhara rugs in the living room.

At the beginning, Nancy was relieved that Tom's family had volunteered to help her bring up her daughter, but when Kathleen was ten, a crisis arose. Nancy decided to marry a stockbroker named George Romily, who was variously described by the Molloys as being kind or dull, depending upon who was doing the talking. In fact, he was a very decent, ordinary man who also happened to be rich, and the only mistake he made was to propose that he adopt Kathleen and give her his name.

All hell broke lose at the Molloy house. Charles Molloy went so far as to threaten to put him in jail for attempting to alienate his granddaughter's affection. Tom's surviving brothers and sisters plotted ways to have him shot on the front lawn of his home in Greenwich. Not even a hyphenated name, which Nancy in desperation finally suggested, was acceptable. So in the end, Kathleen was allowed to make her own choice, and not surprisingly, she decided to remain a Molloy.

Had no choice, the Molloys said. How could she be anything other than a Molloy? Utterly forgetting all the distinguished Delano genes that had also gone into making her.

Since then, in order to preserve peace in Greenwich, Nancy had become more or less estranged from the Molloys. When it was necessary to plan Kathleen's holidays from school, she would make all the arrangements by telephone, but politely decline Nora's invitation to dinner, knowing that to accept would offend her new husband. Kathleen was the bridge between the two families, sometimes stretched to the utmost. Every summer, she accompanied Charles and Nora Molloy on their annual trip to Europe—she was the only grandchild afforded the privilege—and dutifully sent postcards back home to her mother and stepfather, painstakingly avoiding any reference to her traveling companions. Only recently, she had spent part of her Christmas vacation with them at their winter home in Palm Beach, but when she spent the remainder with the Romilys, all she dared tell them was that she'd had a lovely time at a number of parties and had met several young men who seemed quite interesting.

But not interesting enough to get serious about.

It was her mother who warned her that one of the hazards of having a grandfather like the legendary Charles Molloy was that when the time came for her to get married, she might not be satisfied with someone less awesome, and there just weren't that many truly galvanizing men around.

Another problem—much greater—was that if anything should ever happen to her grandfather, the very rock on which her life rested, there would be a terrible void in her world, almost too terrible to imagine.

And who would fill it? The Molloys? Nancy Romily? Or perhaps someone Kathleen hadn't even met yet?

As she steered her bicycle toward the bike rack in front of the dorm, she looked up and saw Mrs. Foxworth tripping down the icy walk, arms waving. Even before she reached her, the housemother called out breathlessly, "You're to telephone your Aunt Caitlin in New York at once."

Kathleen had spoken to Caitlin only a few nights before about this weekend's birthday party, so she supposed that the call was somehow related to that. But when Mrs. Foxworth delivered her second message, this one from Andrew Sinclair, she knew that something much more important than a birthday party was involved.

By the time she got to her room and placed the call through the switchboard, her hands were trembling and her mouth was dry. Her aunt picked it up on the first ring.

"Aunt Caitlin, I just got your message. Also one from Andy Sinclair. Is something wrong?"

Guardedly, Caitlin Phipps inquired, "What exactly . . . did Andy's message say, darling?"

Kathleen repeated more or less what her housemother had told her, and when she'd finished, her aunt observed, "I'm afraid that nothing is being synchronized at this end. I wasn't aware that they were sending the plane to Boston for you, but I think it's a very good idea." She paused to take a breath. "We want you home as soon as possible, Kathleen. I'm afraid I've got some bad news—about your grandfather."

Kathleen was grateful for the chair behind her, and suddenly she was cold even though she still had her coat on.

"But you mustn't worry, darling. He's had a . . . minor stroke, but he's already making remarkable progress."

"A stroke? Is he paralyzed or anything? Sometimes that happens when you have a stroke."

"It's nothing like that, Kathleen. I assure you, he's out of danger now. But we all want you home as soon as possible. When will you be able to leave for New York?"

"But Grandfather's in Southampton, isn't he?" She'd spoken to her grandmother on Sunday night, and Nora had mentioned that they were having Senator Callahan out to the house on Long Island for a midweek break.

"Well, he was," Caitlin Phipps explained, "but he insisted on being brought into the city as soon as his doctors said it was safe enough for him to travel. He's at . . . Columbia-Presbyterian Hospital uptown. You'll probably remember that he gave them some money several years ago to help build a new wing after someone accused him of never helping anyone except the nuns. So he said he wanted to be taken there to see if they were giving him his money's worth. When will you be able to leave Cambridge?"

Kathleen's skull was throbbing as she tried to collect her thoughts. All she had to do was pack a few things, mostly books—she had duplicates of almost all her clothes at the room she kept at the River House apartment—write a quick note for her roommate, sign out with Mrs. Foxworth, then take a taxi to the airport. "I can leave in five or ten minutes," she said. "The plane should be here by now. Could you call Andy and tell him I'm about to leave for the airport?"

Caitlin would do that immediately. "Jean-Claude will be at the airport to meet you, darling," she said, naming the Molloys' chauffeur cum butler. "Just remember: You're not to worry about anything. Your grandfather's out of danger now."

By the time she hung up, Kathleen's forehead was wreathed in perspiration. She rang the switchboard and asked them to order a cab for her, then tossed some books into an overnight bag. She scribbled a hasty note for her roommate, Carolyn

Biddle, then propped it up against the lamp on Carolyn's side of the double desk. She was just about to leave the room when she realized that she wouldn't be able to meet Ted Birmingham in front of the library on Friday, and she didn't want him to wait for her.

But when she called Eliot House and asked for him, the young man who answered said, "I'm sorry, but I can't find a Ted Birmingham listed. Are you sure you've got the right house?"

"But of course I'm sure. I met him at an Eliot House dance."

"And you're positive you've got the right name?"

"Yes, I am. It's Edmund—spelled with a *u*"—she remembered from their first meeting—"Birmingham. B-i-r—"

"I'm awfully sorry, but he's not listed as a resident."

Good God, how was that possible? Surely the other boys from Eliot House seemed to know him. Well, she had done her best. She thanked the young man, and even before she was able to replace the receiver, the switchboard operator downstairs broke in to say that she had an incoming call.

Kathleen waited a second or two, then said, "Yes, hello? Who is it?"

She listened as her mother's eternally serene voice asked, "Kathleen, have you heard?"

"Yes, just this minute. Aunt Caitlin called."

"Your father rang up from his office a few minutes ago. Apparently the news is just reaching Wall Street. When will you be able to get home?"

Kathleen explained that she was about to leave for the airport, where the company plane was waiting for her. "I wish they hadn't gone to all the trouble and expense. I could as easily have gotten a commercial flight."

"I'm sure they meant it as a kindness, dear, because they didn't want you to sit with other passengers who might want to chat. Will you be going directly from the airport to the apartment, or will you be coming out here first?"

"I think I'll go straight up to Columbia-Presbyterian Hospital."

In the silence that followed, Kathleen thought momentarily that they'd been disconnected. But then she heard her mother ask, "But why on earth would you be going up there?"

"Because Aunt Caitlin said that's where they took Grandfather as soon as he was well enough to travel."

Nancy Romily was clearly under a strain. "Kathleen, your grandfather is dead. He died last night in Southampton, and they brought his body to New York first thing this morning. Caitlin should have told you. You're old enough to face these things."

As her mind began to reel, Kathleen let the telephone slip from her hand into her lap.

Each of them, her mother and her aunt, had reacted to death very much the same way they reacted to life: Caitlin with merciful Irish delusion, her mother with remorseless adherence to reality. Each was a prisoner of her genes and breeding, as Kathleen was too, because she was both the one and the other, grateful that Caitlin had attempted to protect her, but at the same time angry at herself for not having perceived how absurd the tale was. She should have doubted it at once. Why hadn't she? Because deep down she knew it was a lie, but desperately wanted to believe otherwise.

"Kathleen, are you all right?"

It was an effort to pick up the fallen receiver. "Yes, I'm all right."

"I'm sorry I had to be the one to tell you. I was sure they'd already done it. But pretending it never happened isn't going to help matters. I know you loved him a great deal. So did I, once upon a time, long ago, and I'll always remember him the way he was back then. Right now, my heart goes out to Nora. I know you'll want to be with her at the apartment for the next few days, so I won't get in your way. Call me when you get settled in."

"I will, Mother."

"There's something else you should know. The very last time I spoke with your grandfather, he told me what his intentions were insofar as you're concerned, although I advised against them. You're to get Tom's share of the estate, and also your Uncle Robbie's. So you're now a very rich young woman, Kathleen, and it's going to make an enormous difference in your life."

Almost inaudibly, Kathleen asked, "Why does it have to make a difference?"

"Oh, but it does. Maybe not to you, but to other people and the way they perceive you. It always does."

TWO

*A*ll morning long, ever since arriving at the apartment from Long Island, Nora Molloy had been trying to reach her son Lee, but it was beginning to look as if he had disappeared from the face of the earth.

She had called his home on Beekman Place and spoken to his wife, Sally, who informed her that Lee had left shortly after dawn to drive to Southampton, a fact that scarcely needed repetition because Nora had been with him while they arranged for the medical examiner to release her husband's body. Afterward, she had driven into town with John and Caitlin Phipps, fully expecting Lee to follow and join them at the River House. But that was over three hours ago, and he still hadn't appeared.

Moreover, he wasn't at the offices of Molloy and Company on Park Avenue at Fifty-first, closed today as a mark of respect for its founder and chairman. While the switchboard wasn't in service, Nora had dialed Lee's private line, then Charles's in his office down the hall, and either Lee wasn't there or he simply wasn't answering.

Although she'd had a sleepless night, Nora was unable to rest until she had clarified a matter of some importance. Before leaving Southampton, she had asked Lee if perhaps his father had called him the evening before, and her son had replied that he hadn't spoken to him at all the previous day. But just a short while ago when she was speaking with Lee's wife, Sally volunteered the information that Lee had excused himself from his dinner guests sometime after ten the night before to accept a telephone call, and when he returned he was visibly upset. She supposed that it was Charles on the other end, because he often had that dramatic effect on his son.

The evening before, Nora and her husband were also entertaining guests, Senator Marcus Aurelius Callahan and Mrs. Callahan of Oklahoma, who were spending the night. Like Charles, the senator was a prominent Republican and close friend and confidante of President Eisenhower's, and it was Charles's hope that they might discuss Ike's successor as leader of the party now that his term of office was about to end. Rumors had been flying in Washington for some time that the President might not endorse Vice President Nixon for the nomination—in fact, it was said that he had a very real aversion to the man—and liberal Republicans like Charles Molloy were of the opinion that this might result in an open convention and perhaps the nomination of Governor Nelson Rockefeller of New York.

But early in the evening Senator Callahan had dashed Charles's expectations by announcing that Ike, after all, had been persuaded that it would be foolhardy and inimical to party interests not to endorse Nixon, so for the sake of unity he had agreed to work for the election of his Vice President.

After dinner, the Molloys and their guests adjourned to the living room for coffee and brandy. It was there, sometime between ten and eleven—Nora was unsure about the exact time—that Jean-Claude walked up behind Charles's chair and whispered, "The gentleman from Galveston is on the line, sir."

Jean-Claude had standing instructions never to accept business calls at the Southampton retreat unless Charles requested him to do so. So when her husband jumped up from his chair and hurried to the study to take the call, Nora supposed that he'd been expecting it.

Senator Callahan was, if not a spellbinding raconteur, at least a persistent one, and during Charles's absence he continued to drone on and on about the various experiences he'd had during his lifetime with, of all things, Texas chili. Personally, Nora considered chili a thermal condition rather than a culinary treat, more suitable for insulating walls than for human consumption. The senator had arrived at chapter three or four of his gastronomical memoirs—this one having to do with chili he'd been served in Tokyo—when Nora realized that Charles had been gone for an unusually long time. It wasn't like him to desert her, so when Marcus Callahan paused momentarily in his oratory, she excused herself and went in search of him.

At first, the study appeared to be empty, although Charles's aromatic cigar smoke still lingered in the air. Nora had just about decided that he had concluded his call, then perhaps left to go upstairs, when she noticed that the telephone on the desk was off the hook.

As she stepped toward it to replace it, she felt an eerie premonition. So that by the time she reached the desk, she knew what she would find behind it, slumped on the floor.

She must have cried out, because suddenly Jean-Claude was in the room, then the senator and his wife, and as they lifted Charles's huge frame to the leather sofa, Marcus Callahan began to gasp and Nora thought that he was about to have a seizure.

Charles was still alive, but his face was cruelly misshapen, one eye opened, one closed, his mouth agape. While help was summoned, Nora sat with him, doing what little she could, and in the background Senator Callahan was panting, struggling for breath. Within minutes, an ambulance had arrived, and Charles and Marcus Callahan were carried off, sirens wailing, while Nora, Mrs. Callahan, and Jean-Claude followed.

It was after midnight by the time they arrived at the hospital, and as her husband and the senator were rushed into the emergency treatment area, Nora decided that no good would come of alarming the rest of the family at that time of night. So as they worked over Charles's almost lifeless body, she sat in the hallway and prayed.

Charles was much older than Nora—at their marriage, she was eighteen, he thirty-three—and she had tried to anticipate this event and prepare herself for it. Often, late at night, as they sat reading, he would fall asleep, and she would sit across from him, watching his silent, slumbering face, and say to herself, This is what it will be like. Accept it.

For all that, she'd somehow expected last farewells. But Charles never regained consciousness, not even when the priest annointed him for the last sacraments of the church.

At three in the morning, it was all over.

While Mrs. Callahan remained at the hospital with her husband, who was responding well to treatment, Nora and Jean-Claude went back to the empty house and waited for dawn before notifying the rest of the family. It was after she had finished making the calls and while she was still seated at the desk in the study that she noticed the memo pad next to the telephone.

For a man who could recite construction specifications with dizzying fluency, Charles made it a habit never to commit what he called trivial numbers to memory, claiming that they merely cluttered the mind. Instead, whenever he placed a telephone call from home, he would first locate the number in his personal directory, then transcribe it to a memo pad, writing the digits prominently because his vision had begun to fail.

On the pad, Nora found three numbers.

The first was written diagonally across the page in a slap-dash sort of way, as if perhaps he had written it with one hand while holding on to the telephone with the other. It was an out-of-town number, but Nora was unable to find it listed in his personal directory. She wasn't sure, but it seemed to her that it might have been the number given to him by last night's caller—"the gentleman from Galveston"—in the event that it would be necessary to return the call.

But this morning at the New York apartment, when curiosity finally drove her to dial the number, Nora reached an answering service, not in Galveston but in Los Angeles, and the manager couldn't name the party who had engaged the service. When Nora then contacted the offices of the Pacific Telephone Company, she was informed that the subscriber couldn't be identified because the number was unlisted—a moot point since a request had been made that very morning for the service to be terminated.

The information left Nora uneasy.

The second number she recognized at once as that of Lee's townhouse in Manhattan. But he denied ever having received a call, although Sally's suspicions seemed to contradict him.

The final number also had a New York exchange, and it took Nora only a few minutes to find it in Charles's directory. It was the home of Mathew Rowley.

Charles had alwasy described Matt as his indispensable administrative assistant, but Lee, who made no secret of disliking him, called him nothing more than a glorified secretary, a mother hen. It was Matt who screened all of Charles's visitors and incoming calls, and who supervised his correspondence, made his travel arrangements, planned the menus in the executive dining room, chose birthday gifts for the Molloy children and grandchildren and anniversary gifts for Nora— although she wasn't supposed to know—and even dusted Charles's desk every morning, a task no one else was permitted to do.

Some found him prissy and overbearing, but Nora had always been fond of him because he'd made life easier for Charles. She had been trying to reach him on the telephone for the past half-hour, but the line was busy. At last, she heard it ringing.

When a woman answered and Nora identified herself and asked to speak to Matt, loud music playing in the background was suddenly switched off.

In another minute, Matt was saying in the easy Georgian drawl that fifteen years' residence in Manhattan hadn't been able to shake, "I'm simply devastated by the news, Mrs. Molloy. Devastated."

As both a Catholic and a mother who had lost children, Nora had long ago learned not to quarrel with death. "Charles had a very full and bountiful life, and was strong and vital right up to the minute he died. Who could ask for more?"

"Still, I'll miss him terribly."

"We all will, I'm sure." She paused momentarily. "Could I ask you something, Matt? Is it at all possible that Charles spoke to you late last night?"

He seemed temporarily confounded. "Did Mr. Molloy speak to me last night? Why, no. The last time I talked to him was . . . oh, about three o'clock yesterday afternoon when he called in. Apparently he had just arrived at the house in Southampton from the city. But wait a minute. He could have called me last night, but I was out. You see, my wife and I were attending a concert at Carnegie Hall and didn't get home until . . . I'd say about twelve-thirty or so."

"Then you would have missed the call, because it was probably made between ten and eleven."

"It's possible, of course, that he might have left a message for me on my machine. I have one of these new answering machines that you attach to your telephone. I haven't checked it yet this morning because of all the confusion. If you like, I could do it now."

"Would you please, Matt?"

Nora listened to a click as she was placed on hold. She was surprised to learn that Matt was married. No more than six months before, at a party for a retiring vice-president, he'd been alone. And only a few weeks ago when she and Charles were being driven downtown, as they passed through Chelsea, Charles remarked that Matt had recently purchased a house on West Twentieth Street, the Seminary block, but he hadn't mentioned a new wife.

Another click. "Mrs. Molloy? I just played back the tape, and I'm awfully sorry but there's nothing on it from Mr. Molloy. Of course, he may have called and simply not left a message when he heard the recording. A lot of people are intimidated by these machines."

Nora was about to say that her husband had never been intimidated by anything in all his life, but thought better of it. Clearly, she was disappointed that Matt was unable to give her some indication of Charles's state of mind before he was stricken.

"Could I ask you another thing?" she continued. "Would you have any idea who the gentleman from Galveston might be?"

"I didn't quite follow you. Would you repeat that please, Mrs. Molloy?"

She did so, explaining how last night's telephone call had been announced by Jean-Claude.

When she finished, Matt replied, "I can't for the life of me figure out who in Galveston would be calling Mr. Molloy."

"I've just learned that the call was made from Los Angeles."

"Of course, we have an office in L.A., and it's more than possible that someone out there might be able to clarify things.

But I can honestly say that as long as I've been working for the company, I don't think I've ever placed a call for Mr. Molloy to someone in Galveston, and I handled all his incoming and outgoing calls at the office."

"Well, all right, Matt. Thank you anyway."

"I'm sorry, Mrs. Molloy. Perhaps . . . the younger Mr. Molloy might know something about it."

"I intend to ask him."

She would, that is, if Lee ever surfaced. But at the moment he was still missing, either getting drunk at a Third Avenue bar or praying in a church, and for the same reason.

He was afraid.

From the four corners of the globe, members of the clan were converging on New York to pay their final respects to the beloved patriarch, the fallen suzerain.

The family was large, and once had been even larger, but time and circumstances had reduced it. At forty-one, Caitlin was oldest by default, ever since Tom's death in 1940. She and her lawyer husband, John Phipps, a partner at Sullivan and Cromwell, one of the city's most lustrous legal firms, lived with their children, Jake and Molly, in a large apartment at Park Avenue and Seventy-first and summered in Southampton at a house not too far away from the original Molloy "cottage"—a vast, sprawling place of twenty-five rooms, more or less.

Lee, who was christened Liam but quickly Americanized, was next at thirty-nine, and he and his fashionable young wife, Sally, were members of New York's smart set, frequently entertaining at their Beekman Place house. Characteristically, when the time came for them to choose a summer retreat, they rejected Southampton, which they considered stuffy, and instead built a strikingly modern house at East Hampton, about which Charles once said that it deserved to be washed away in a hurricane. Both in prep school (Portsmouth Priory) and college (Yale), Lee had been very popular, always serving as class president and either captain or co-captain of the football team. Intellectually, he was no great shakes, but managed to get a degree in engineering from Yale, then an MBA from Harvard Business School, combining the two skills his father considered essential for success in the construction industry: engineering know-how and business acumen. The two teachable skills, that is. The unteachable ones—being a prophet and visionary, a never-losing gambler—either one had, or one hadn't.

Robbie, had he lived, would have been thirty-seven, but the Second World War had dealt the family two cruel blows, one after the other, when less than two years after Tom's death, he was killed in the Pacific when the destroyer on which he was serving was sunk. Of all the boys, Robbie was the sweetest, gentlest, and although Lee and his younger brother Paul were often at one another's throats when they were growing up, both had loved Robbie, so his death was deeply felt. Had he been spared, it was more than possible that Paul would not now be estranged from the family.

People who knew both of them could scarcely believe that Lee and Paul were siblings, they were so different temperamentally. Lee was always the center of attraction, surrounded by adoring friends, while Paul was generally alone but never seemed to be bothered by loneliness. As Nora once said, Paul had the richest interior life of anyone she'd ever met, and Lee sometimes seemed to have none at all. Paul had rejected engineering over his father's protests and instead studied architecture at Yale, saying that any fool—casting a significant glance at his brother Lee—could erect a building, but only a poet could build one that would set people dreaming. Refusing to do graduate work at a business school, as his father had hoped, he reluctantly joined the firm—on a temporary basis, as he described it, just long enough to prove to his father that he was unsuited for it.

But to everyone's astonishment, he did exceedingly well, and more often than not it was Paul's counsel and judgment that Charles Molloy sought out, not Lee's. "Let's go somewhere and have us a chat," his father would say to him, "before your brother comes in tossing that damned football of his around."

Just a little over two years ago, however, after a quarrel with his father that lasted most of a day, Paul resigned from the firm and left New York. He now lived near Santa Rosa in California, where he had set up shop as an architect with an old Yale colleague, and although Nora had visited him and often spoke to him by telephone, Paul refused to see or speak with his father. "Not until he apologizes," he said, and now that Charles was no longer able to do that—apologize for what, Nora never learned—it was altogether possible that Paul wouldn't even show up for the funeral.

Next in line was raven-haired Mary, thirty-three, the brood mare of the family. She and her broker husband lived in Lake Forest, Illinois, and during the twelve years of their marriage they had produced nine children. Caitlin's son, Jake, once calculated that if she continued to procreate at that dizzying rate until menopause set in, she might mother as many as sixteen. When informed of this, far from being dismayed, Mary clapped her hands together and cried joyfully, "Oh, how lovely!"

Deirdre, thirty-one, had always defied convention. Instead of attending Manhattanville College of the Sacred Heart, as her sisters had done, she elected to go to Bennington College in Vermont, and during her senior year shocked the family by living off-campus with a Dartmouth dropout. Nora was almost relieved when she called one night to report that she had just gotten married, then added triumphantly that the groom was Jewish. Charles was nearly apoplectic, but Nora took it quite well, and after they met Ben Stein they realized that she had made a splendid choice. Not only was Ben kind, generous, and decent, but he was also smart as blazes, and as Charles admitted, the family could certainly use a good genetic shot in the arm—although what he meant, of course, was in the brains, an obvious reference to Lee's wife, Sally, who was very beautiful but vapid and who had produced two blond, blue-eyed vapid children. Deirdre and Ben lived in Paris, where Ben was a cardiologist on the staff of the American Hospital, preferring to live in France because, as he put it, even when they were ill the French were the most civilized people on earth.

Eddie, at twenty-nine, was still in the process of finding himself, he maintained, although Nora was beginning to wonder if anything was findable. He had done very badly at prep school and was admitted to Brown University on probation, but he lasted only until his sophomore year. He had little aptitude for academic studies and none at all for business. If

Paul resented being rich, Eddie resented being born. Eight years out of college, he was now a ski instructor in Colorado— a ski bum, Lee called him disparagingly—and virtually the only time he ever got in touch with his parents was when he needed money. When it was sent, he never bothered to thank them.

When the children were younger, Nora always felt that Eddie was a preparation for Megan, because while he was partly alienated from the family, her alienation was total. She wasn't particularly pretty—in fact, she was the only one in the family who wasn't good looking—she had just average intelligence, and she was fat, incorrigibly, irredeemably fat. She'd been a fat baby, a fat child, a fat teenager, and was now a fat woman, but unlike the stereotype, she wasn't the least bit jolly. She was mean and black-hearted. At the age of nineteen, she was expelled from Manhattanville College for using drugs and now lived in the East Village with a man who wrote incomprehensible poetry and had a long series of drug convictions. She no longer attended family gatherings, which, everything considered, was a blessing. The last time she had, she said she hated them all. Nora still visited her from time to time in the squalid St. Mark's Place apartment, and each time she left, she wondered at God's mystery for having given her a child so unattractive and filled with rancor, so whining and self-destructive.

In short, it was a typical Irish-American family, including one genius—Paul, his teachers always claimed—and at least one quare one. It lacked only a drunkard and a priest or nun to make it complete. Some said that Lee, who'd been arrested in East Hampton the summer before for drunken driving, might well make up for the former deficiency. And as for the latter, there was little doubt but that Nora could command as much of God's attention as any nun or priest, perhaps even more because she was so persuasive.

And there was Kathleen.

To be sure, she was a granddaughter, but she occupied a special position in the family, more favored than that of the Molloy daughters. There was a sweetness and gentleness about her that was absent in the other children and grandchildren. A sadness too, even in her merriest mood, as if she were gripped by some half-remembered sorrow. Charles had said that it was very Irish. If kept under control, it added depth and gravity to one's character. But a surfeit of sorrows could send one reeling. Make one bewildered.

Sometimes the rich merely squander their lives in the pursuit of pleasure, but Nora was sure Kathleen would never become the sort of woman her Aunt Sally was, who did little except give parties or attend them. What Kathleen would become she herself would have to decide. But now that Charles was no longer available to provide her with emotional support, there were bound to be rocky times ahead.

Her grandmother had insisted that news of his death be withheld from Kathleen until she reached New York, where Nora herself could gently break it. How Kathleen was going to bear up under it, Nora had only one clue. If a man or woman is weak to begin with, the death of someone beloved will generally make them weaker.

But if they're strong, such a death will make them stronger.

There was a gentle tapping on the door, and in a second it was opened by Andrew Sinclair, hair disheveled, eyes red from fatigue. Ever since he'd gotten the first call from Southampton at dawn, he'd been on the go, rushing into town from Westchester in order to handle all the necessary details. He had supervised the travel arrangements for members of the family, dealt with the staff at the Frank E. Campbell Funeral Chapel, prepared press releases, and worked out funeral arrangements at the Church of St. Vincent Ferrer, where Francis Cardinal Spellman, a close personal friend of the Molloys and often a dinner guest at their apartment, was expected to deliver the mass.

"Mrs. Molloy," he began, voice husky from grief, "Mr. Potter just arrived, and I've shown him into the small drawing room. But are you absolutely sure you're up to seeing him right now?"

Quentin Potter, of the Wall Street firm Potter, Stevenson, and Potter, had been Charles's personal legal counsel for as long as Nora could remember. Shortly after she'd arrived at the apartment from Southampton, he called and requested a few minutes of her time, and because she supposed that it was somehow related to the estate or the firm, she suggested that he attempt to talk to Lee instead. But he was insistent. "No, it's you I have to see," he repeated..

She now said to Andrew, "I'll see Mr. Potter in a few minutes," then smiled warmly in spite of the heaviness of her heart. "Come sit down, Andy. Have I told you how grateful we all are for what you've done for us? I don't know how we could have borne this without you."

His eyes misted over as he sat across from her in a matching loveseat in the small sitting room off the master bedroom. "There's nothing I wouldn't do for Mr. Molloy. I loved him more than I did my own father. I'd always meant to tell him, but I never got around to it."

It was perhaps appropriate that Andrew had been called upon to serve the family at this time, because ever since Lee had brought him home from Yale for Thanksgiving dinner when both were gangling freshmen, he'd been inseparable from the Molloys. The first time Charles met him, he had prophesized about the well-mannered, self-possessed youth from New Mexico, "That young man will be a good influence on Lee."

As always, Charles's assessment of character was correct, for during the next four years of college, then grad school, not only did Andrew prepare Lee for all his exams, but once he even took one for him, saying afterward that it was the only service he would never perform a second time. He made certain that Lee got out of bed for classes most mornings and that he got into it at night. On more than one occasion, he cleaned up his vomit after Lee had had too much to drink, and always made certain that there were no used condoms in the back seat of Lee's car when they drove to Southampton for weekends. After they graduated from Harvard Business School—Andrew near the top of the class, Lee near the bottom—it was only natural that the two of them would join the firm. Now both were vice presidents.

"What news of Lee?" she asked him.

He shrugged his shoulders helplessly. "I'm still trying to track him down. I just don't understand what's happened, Mrs. Molloy."

"Is he drinking again?"

It was obviously painful for him to admit it. "It's possible. I've left word at all his hangouts along Third Avenue in case he shows up. The other thing that occurred to me is that he might be over at the Racquet Club playing squash or swimming or soaking up steam in the steam room. Lee's a very physical man, not an intellectual one. Sometimes when he has trouble coping with things, he has to work his body until it collapses. You see, he's not sure he's ready to step into his father's footsteps. I don't think I have to tell you, do I, who Mr. Molloy had chosen to do that."

Nora knew full well. The errant Paul, who was so much like his father, had been singled out for that honor. Until a little over two years ago, Lee had been vice president in charge of personnel. Paul was head of operations. Not until Paul resigned in a huff and fled the city was Lee transferred to the operations division.

"What *was* the dispute between Paul and his father?"

Andrew sighed. "I was never made privy to it, nor was anyone else so far as I know. I do remember, however, that we had recently signed a contract with one of the Arab countries, and as part of it, we'd agreed not to employ any Jews on the site. Paul found that morally repugnant. But whether or not that precipitated the quarrel, I can't say."

"Did my husband or Lee have any such qualms?"

"A businessman can't afford to have a conscience. Do you know who said that? Mr. Molloy did. And in a way, I suppose, he was right. A corporation as large as ours can't possibly please everybody. So Mr. Molloy's goal was always to build the best bridge or the best pipeline, and leave moral considerations to others. Paul disagreed. Lee went along with his father. But when Paul left, we all expected Mr. Molloy to start priming Lee to take over—when the time came. But he kept holding back. Right up until yesterday, Mr. Molloy was still in charge of everything at the firm—up to and including the kind of stationery we used and the brand of soap in the washroom dispensers. Lee was never allowed to make a single decision without first getting clearance from his father. Now I think he's worried because Mr. Molloy won't be here anymore to help him. So he's out somewhere trying to shore up his confidence."

Please God, Nora hoped, he wasn't drinking himself into a stupor. Until last summer when he'd been arrested for drunken driving, she hadn't been aware of the problem. And when he was released from the drunk tank at the town jail, his first concern was that his father must never know of it. Nora had agreed only on condition that he stop drinking entirely, a condition she was not sure Lee had met.

"What will happen," she now asked, "if he's unable to find the confidence?"

He took a deep breath. "There's a chance—a remote one—that the company might be in trouble."

The Molloy Company was owned entirely by the family and its chief executives, accountable to no one but themselves. It never issued annual reports and never announced its earnings. Yet its present and future customers, and more particularly its competitors, would be watching with great interest the manner in which the company reacted to the passing of its dynamic founder. If there was uncertainty, mischief could take place.

"Last year," Andrew resumed, "our billings were close to three billion dollars. That's *billion*, Mrs. Molloy, not million. So by no stretch of the imagination is anyone on the way to the poorhouse. But our profits were down considerably from the previous year because we lost close to four hundred million dollars on the two natural gas processing plants we built in the Ruwali Emirate shortly before the coup, when everything was nationalized. We'll no doubt get some of it back, but not all of it, and a temporary setback is the sort of thing that competitors like to take advantage of. So we're very vulnerable now, and any number of things could happen."

Nora didn't have to have them spelled out. Worst of all was that present and past executives of the company, who owned close to 50 percent of its stock, would force a change of management, naming someone other than a Molloy as president.

To Nora, it was unthinkable. The Molloy Company was Charles Molloy's lasting testament. When, at the age of twenty-one, he had bid on his first street-paving contract, he didn't even own a truck or a steam roller and had never laid pavement in his life. When he built his first subway beneath the East River, critics said that people would never use it for fear that the walls would cave in. When he constructed his first dam, scientists predicted that it would crumble during the next earthquake. When he piled floor after floor of the world's highest building over one hundred stories into the sky, theologians called it an affront to God that would be reduced to cinders by lightning bolts. Nearly every project he began was thought to be impossible or unbuildable—until he finished it.

It was legend in the family that on their fourth birthday, each of his children would be taken to the world headquarters of the Molloy Company, first on Nassau Street in the financial district, now a towering skyscraper on Park Avenue, for what Charles called "a tour of the premises." But before entering, he would stand with them on the sidewalk in front and point to the name incised in gray marble over the entrance. "Tell me what that says," he would urge them.

"But I can't read, Papa."

"Then consider this your first lesson." He would then recite each letter until he had spelled the entire name, repeating it several times until the child whose hand he held had committed it to memory. "M-o-l-l-o-y. That is your name, and this firm is your heritage. Never dishonor either of them, for one day you'll be bringing your own children to stand here and teach them what I've taught you today."

No, Nora would never permit the presidency of the company to pass into the hands of a stranger. Never.

"I must speak to Lee. And also to Paul," she promised.

After Andrew left, she made her way down the long hall to the smaller of the two drawing rooms in the vast apartment overlooking the East River. In contrast to the larger room— the size of a ballroom, two huge fireplaces at either end, its walls covered with paintings of saints and madonnas collected over the years: a Rubens, a Tintoretto, a Murillo—the smaller room was cozy and cheerful, with chintz-covered furniture and photos of children and grandchildren on every tabletop.

As she entered, Quentin Potter jumped to his feet. Consolingly, he began, "I just can't believe that Mr. Molloy is dead. I'm sure we all thought he would live forever."

As she extended her hand, she replied, "There's evidence that Charles thought so as well. But all living things must come to an end, Mr. Potter." She sat in a comfortable armchair and invited him to do the same. "You mentioned, I believe, that there was something you wished to discuss with me in private."

Potter squirmed, visibly distressed. "I don't know where to begin." He faltered momentarily, as if to prove it. "It's more than possible that I've overstepped my authority in even broaching this subject, Mrs. Molloy, but because I've served you and your husband for more than forty years, I feel that it's my duty."

Nora sat up with sudden interest.

A thin line of perspiration broke out on Potter's upper lip. "You're aware, I'm sure, that I've drawn up several wills for Mr. Molloy over the past few years. But perhaps you aren't aware that just a few months ago, he insisted on writing a new one. There will be few surprises in it—as there were few surprises in Mr. Molloy himself. There is, however, one little matter that might . . . cause embarrassment, so I thought it best to speak to you personally before the contents of the will become generally known."

Potter withdrew a linen handkerchief from his pocket and wiped his forehead. "For the past eight years, I have been sending a check for fifteen thousand dollars on the first day of every month to a person who is neither a member of the family nor connected with the firm. The last check was mailed on the first of March. And in the will that Charles had me draw up in early December, he has provided a very handsome settlement for her."

"Her?" Nora asked incredulously.

"A Christine Lawrence, who lives on East End Avenue."

Nora's mouth fell open. For one of the few times in her life, she was at a loss for words.

"For nearly a half-century I've known you, Mrs. Molloy," he resumed, "and I would do anything humanly possible to avoid bringing pain to you or members of your family. Who this other woman is or how she figured in Mr. Molloy's life is beyond my speculation. But it seemed to me that whatever the relationship was, no matter how profound or how frivolous, it might possibly bring sadness to you. And that is why I've taken this most unusual step to alert you, so that perhaps you might plan a course of action should questions arise upon the release of the will from probate."

Nora recovered sufficient composure to ask, "Are you saying what I think you're saying?"

If he was, Potter was unable to be more explicit. With embarrassment, he cast his eyes down at the Oriental rug at his feet.

At last Nora broke the silence. "I believe that what you're trying to say, Mr. Potter, is that for all these years, it appears that my husband has had a mistress."

THREE

*I*n San Mateo County, California, Father Joseph Cassidy peered through his dusty windshield and suddenly had the distinct feeling that he was out of his turf.

God knows, he'd had tantalizing glimpses of the local rich before—at Pebble Beach in Carmel, and Ross and Belvedere in Marin County—but even in those storied places, their style of life was unmistakably Californian. Rambling, shake-roofed houses were built around sky-blue swimming pools, if they lived inland, or around Mercedes and Jaguars if they were on the fog-bound coast. They partied, barbecued, meditated, even copulated—he had it on hearsay, much more than he cared to hear—out in the open, all with disarming naturalness.

But the minute he turned off Route 280 south of San Francisco and began to follow the twisting road toward Hillsborough, he became aware that California was being left behind. He might as well be in the rolling hills of Tuscany or Devonshire for all the palazzos and Tudor manors behind the high hedges and ivied walls. The air was heady with new clover and horses, and the benign sun shone so brilliantly it hurt his eyes, but little of nature's honest smells or primal light was able to penetrate those leaded glass windows. It was almost as if the people living there had turned their backs on the present, saying, "What a vulgar age this is!"

Well, everyone to his own tastes. He wouldn't have half minded owning a little retreat of his own in this lush countryside, but was sure it wouldn't be a house designed three hundred years ago for England's damp, sunless climate or a fortress meant to surmount an Italian hillside. Who wanted to live in Elizabethan splendor or Renaissance magnificence anyway, particularly if it was counterfeit?

Apparently Ada Babcock did, because her house was in these fabled hills, and it was Father Joseph's destination. Earlier in the day when he'd talked to Aaron Golden at his motel in Palo Alto, Golden had said that he hoped to finish his business there—trying to persuade Adlai Stevenson diehards among Stanford's eggheads that their cause was hopeless—by late morning and would arrive in Hillsborough in time for lunch. "Ada is laying out a big feed for us, I understand, so I intend to have a Spartan breakfast here, then gorge myself at her table. Needless to say, I'm on an expense account, and despite the fact that everyone thinks that old man Kennedy is spending a fortune on this campaign, he likes the hired help to travel on the cheap."

"What precisely is the purpose of this gathering in Hillsborough, Mr. Golden?"

"Mrs. Babcock wants her rich neighbors to meet an honest-to-God Democrat, and since there's apparently a shortage locally, I've been imported."

"Perhaps I should warn you: California isn't always hospitable to exotics. Someone tried importing camels here about a hundred years ago, and they all perished."

"I'm a damned sight tougher than any camel. Hell, where I grew up in New York City, we used to think that Harlem was a nicer neighborhood. I got the ass beat off me by the Irish kids on my block almost every day on the way home from school."

"Don't you find it a bit ironic now to be working for an Irish-American presidential candidate?"

"We Jews have always shown gratitude in most peculiar ways. Actually, it's astonishing what you can learn while you're being thrashed. And what I learned was that the Micks were beating me up out of frustration because they were despised by New York's Anglo-Saxon Protestant establishment almost as much as Jews were. Presto! We had something in common. So I talked them into going downtown with me after school and beating up the posh WASP kids who went to the Buckley School!"

"Being hated by the same party can be a surprisingly strong bond."

"Exactly what I'd like to talk to you about, Father Joe. I hear that you have friends in Oakland and the barrio, and it's essential that we get Negroes and Latinos in our camp for this election. Sheldon Hawkins brought up your name last week when I spoke with him in Sacramento, and Rafael Banuelos down in Salinas thinks very highly of you."

Sheldon Hawkins was the flamboyant Negro assemblyman from Oakland who drove around the ghetto in a white Cadillac and was partial to expensively tailored suits, hand-cobbled shoes, and beautiful women of all shades. His lifestyle offended many of his fellow Democrats, but he defended it by saying that people craved majesty. "Hell, you don't see Queen Elizabeth taking the bus to do her shopping, do you?"

It was rumored that what paid for his fancy cars and Russian Hill penthouse were his close ties with California realtors and developers, who considered him one of their staunchest supporters in the state capital. To be sure, he worked on their behalf with evangelical zeal, but at the same time sponsored worthwhile legislation for his constituents in the ghetto. Father Joseph had mixed feelings about him, because even though the poor of Oakland were somewhat better off than they would have been without him, it was nothing compared to the opulence enjoyed by land and property speculators. During the past five years, vast areas of Northern California had been plundered, often with the aid and consent of Sheldon Hawkins.

As for Rafael Banuelos, it was doubtful that any man could have been more saintly without running the risk of beatification. He was a deadly earnest, dedicated ex-migrant worker who was attempting to organize the field hands of California, and in doing so had aroused the wrath of rich ranchers, who looked upon him as a revolutionary—as he no doubt was, if it was revolutionary to want to improve the working conditions of people at the very bottom of the economic heap, doing backaching work that gringos refused to do. For his efforts, he was often hauled off to jail. When freed, he lived little better than the men and women he represented, as poor as they were and sometimes as hungry. Father Joseph would never forget the first time he visited Rafael's small stucco house near Salinas.

In the living room, serving as a sofa, was the backseat stripped from an old car. Yet he had never been shown such warmth and cordiality as when he sat next to the gentle Rafael on that battered car seat. He couldn't help but compare it to the lavish parties that Sheldon Hawkins gave at his lofty penthouse on Taylor Street.

"And do you actually believe that you're going to get Shelly Hawkins and Rafael Banuelos together for this campaign?" he asked Golden.

"They're very influential among their people, and Jack Kennedy needs a huge ethnic turnout at the polls in November if he expects to win."

"Negroes and Hispanics seldom vote. In fact, most of them aren't even registered."

"That's one of the things we'd like you to do for us, assuming that you agree to do anything at all: Help get them registered."

"Using what argument? In the long run, they know it's not going to make much difference who they vote for."

"That's the argument! This time, it is."

Father Joseph wasn't convinced. He had listened to promises from sweet-talking politicians before, and the fact that this time they were coming from a Harvard professor working for the Kennedys of Massachusetts didn't make them any more believable. What could Aaron Golden offer that others hadn't?

Father Joseph was on his way to Hillsborough as a direct result of having had dinner the evening before with his father, Patrick Cassidy. "We're being fed by my parishioners tonight," he explained when he issued the invitation. "A young fellow I helped when he had a drug problem went diving this morning near Bodega Bay and about an hour ago dropped five abalone on top of my desk. With them, we're having fresh artichokes. A Mexican-American near Watsonville sent me a whole bushel basket for christening his new baby boy."

"Don't the faithful ever pay you in anything but edibles?"

"But haven't you been telling me for years that money corrupts?"

It was his housekeeper's day off, so Father Joseph prepared the meal himself, first gently pounding the sinewy flesh of the abalone until it was tender, then sautéing it. Patrick had brought a bottle of California chardonnay as his contribution, and while they ate and sipped, they chatted about family matters, spiritual matters, and inevitably, because it was an election year, political matters.

At one point his father asked, "So who will you be supporting at the Democratic convention this time?"

"The party can't possibly find a more accomplished candidate than Adlai Stevenson."

"He's certainly an accomplished loser, I'll grant you that."

"But he has a tremendous talent for turning phrases. Even if he can't win an election, we're bound to hear some damned fine speeches."

During the past eight years, it seemed to Father Joseph that being a Democrat had become little more than an abstract intellectual position because the party had been unable to field a candidate capable of countering Dwight Eisenhower's almost universal adoration. No one expressed the frustration and idealism of the average Democrat better than former governor Adlai Stevenson of Illinois, who spoke with a felicity unmatched since William Jennings Bryan. But for many, particularly members of the intelligentsia, oratory had become almost as important as winning an election. Some party luminaries— Eleanor Roosevelt and Herbert Lehman, to name two—seemed so entranced by their hero that it was beginning to look as if they might prefer to succumb with him once again rather than shift their allegiance to another candidate.

"You realize, of course," Patrick warned him, "that if you stick with Stevenson and he wins the nomination at the convention in July, you might as well hand over the election to Richard Nixon."

"Some people think that he has great gifts."

"Some people thought that Oliver Cromwell had great gifts."

Father Joseph was well aware that Vice President Nixon was a consummate politician, but as a rule he had nothing but disdain for politicians. In fact, the chief reason he was attracted to Stevenson was that the man was so politically inept, always speaking his mind, even when it cost him support.

Richard Nixon's mind was largely uncharted, even perhaps by himself.

After topping off his father's glass of wine, Father Joseph collected the empty plates from the table and carried them into the kitchen. In another minute, he could be heard splashing water over the dishes in the sink.

Over the sound, Pat called out almost casually, "Bobby Kennedy slipped into town earlier this week and gave me a ring."

Instantly, the rinsing stopped. "So what did your old friend on the McClellan Committee want?" he asked cautiously over his shoulder.

In point of fact, Robert Kennedy had been Pat's bitter adversary before becoming a friend. When they met for the first time, Kennedy was chief counsel for the Senate Permanent Subcommittee on Investigations looking into labor racketeering, and Pat was leader of the West Coast Longshoremen's Union and object of his scrutiny.

"The Mob is breathing down your neck, Mr. Cassidy," Kennedy had warned him. "I'd suggest that you turn around and confront them now, before it's too late. When they get that close, it's not only their breath that can be annoying. I assure you that they've also been known to throttle people."

Pat remained unswayed, but subsequently discharged two high-ranking union officials for having accepted kickbacks from shipping agents. One night shortly afterward, he was set upon in the parking lot outside union headquarters and savagely beaten. Upon recovering, one of the first things he did was send a wire to Kennedy.

BODY DAMAGED BUT SCRUPLES MORE OR LESS INTACT. IT LOOKS AS IF YOU WERE RIGHT. WHILE WE LIKE TO BELIEVE THAT WE'RE ALL GOD'S CHILDREN, IT'S NOW APPARENT THAT THE DEVIL HASN'T EXACTLY BEEN PRACTICING BIRTH CONTROL. THANKS FOR THE REMINDER.

In time, Pat came to esteem the younger Kennedy. Although on occasion he was moody, even abrasive, he was unyieldingly high-minded. So when he called a few days before and suggested that they get together when he was passing through San Francisco, Pat knew it wouldn't be for small talk.

"We met for drinks at the Union Club," he answered as his son returned to the dining room with two perfectly polished apples and a wedge of Camembert.

"Surely Kennedy can't be a member of the P.U.C."

"He was using guest privileges, I believe, through his New York club. He said that he always likes to drop in when he's in town because he's amused by the fact that San Francisco's most exclusive social club occupies the home of a former Irish saloon keeper."

"It's a wonder both of you weren't thrown out."

"We created quite a sensation. I've never seen so many disapproving Republican eyes."

The Pacific Union Club on Nob Hill was where the city's gentry met to look down, literally and figuratively, on the rest of mankind. Built by James Flood after he struck it rich in silver, it was the city's most palatial residence, and Bobby Kennedy couldn't have been the first to remark that its original owner would now be ineligible for membership.

Pat sliced the tart Rome Beauty apple, then chewed on it. "Kennedy doesn't think that Stevenson is going to get the nomination in Los Angeles."

Father Joseph sat back in his chair and sighed. "Are you now going to ask me to guess whom he's promoting? It couldn't by any chance be his older brother, could it? If so, it's absurd and impossible."

"Why?"

Father Joseph folded his arms against his chest. "Do I have to remind you that the Kennedys are Catholics, and in the event it's escaped your attention, nothing could be more fatal for a presidential candidate. Can't you remember what happened to Al Smith in 1928? This is a nation of Protestants, and although they're generally the nicest, most decent people in the world, they get downright irrational at the thought of a Catholic in the White House. They're terrified that the Pope may be invited to sleep in the Lincoln bedroom or become a guest member of the Cabinet. And I'm the first to admit that there's probably justification for their suspicion. Historically, the Catholic church is anything but blameless. So most Protestants simply wouldn't vote for John Kennedy out of fear. Catholics constitute something like twenty to twenty-five percent of the population, and even if every single one voted for a fellow Catholic—which is most unlikely—Kennedy still couldn't win the election."

Pat made no effort to conceal his confusion. "I don't understand you. You're a Catholic priest, but you're telling me that you won't support a Catholic candidate because he's going to lose. Instead, you intend to support Stevenson, even though we both know damned well that he can't win the election either. What's the difference?"

What *was* the difference? Father Joseph struggled for words. "The difference is that if Stevenson loses, it'll be for political reasons and he'll accept the loss graciously, as always. But if Jack Kennedy loses"—he paused—"it'll be because of bigotry, and he'll be very hurt. So will I."

Sadly, Pat conceded the point. Few people knew more about bigotry than he did, because he had often been its victim. When he fled Ireland in 1916, he'd done so with a price on his head for his part in the failed Rising, leaving behind him a father and brothers murdered by British soldiers. In no other nation in the world were ancient hatreds caused by religious differences more pronounced than in his native Ireland, but now that he was an American, Pat was able to look upon the tragedy with greater understanding. Men weren't inherently evil. They were simply selfish or deluded. In the Old World, a Christianity that preached love and tolerance sometimes became perverted, but one of the tenets of American democracy was the right to worship in the manner one pleased. Surely, in America, Protestants no longer hated Catholics. Surely Catholics no longer hated Protestants.

Or did they?

"The older I get," Pat began, "the more I question faith. Maybe the Greeks were closer to the truth than we are, and maybe all we can hope for is a god of thunder or a god of fire. Is it possible that we were mistaken in ascribing love and forgiveness to a deity, or to man himself? What do you think, Father?"

Smiling, Father Joseph replied, "I never discuss shop while I'm at home."

Expectedly, Pat laughed, then became somber again. "What would you say if I told you that the Kennedys think they can win the election—in spite of bigotry?"

"I'd say they're mad. How do they intend to do it?"

"Through a coalition of minorities: Catholics, Negroes, Hispanics, liberal Jews, and former Stevenson supporters like you who might be willing to forsake fine speeches for honesty and resolve."

In a democracy, it was difficult to know with absolute accuracy just how many of "this" or "that" was around. Father Joseph knew, for example, that Jews represented a comparatively tiny minority—less than 5 percent of the population—but were articulate and influential, having learned from experience that it was the only way to survive. As for American Negroes, probably no more than 10 percent of the population could be classified as such, and many of them lived in the South and were deprived of the vote. At the very most, Catholics comprised 25 percent, but no one knew better than Father Joseph that there were poor Catholics and rich ones, and while the former tended to be Democrats, the latter were generally Republicans. The Hispanics? Well, who could even guess? Perhaps between 5 and 10 percent, but like Negroes, many weren't even registered to vote.

As for former Stevenson supporters, as Pat described them, they represented the liberal branch of the party, but a very feisty Hubert Humphrey was hoping that they would transfer their allegiance to him. On the other hand, the more conservative branch of the party was being wooed by Stuart Symington and Lyndon Johnson, and during the coming primaries it was more than possible that they might all devour each other in internecine war.

Added to that the fact that many of them—Negroes, Stevenson and Humphrey liberals, Johnson and Symington conservatives—were Protestants, how in God's name could a Catholic bring them all together in order to win an election?

"It's an interesting notion," Father Joseph said at last, "but I don't think any man can do it."

"Most men couldn't. But then the Kennedys aren't like most men. There's something—I don't know what—about them. Such magnetism and youth and hope. I honest to God think they just might be able to carry it off."

"They? Just how many of them are running for President?"

"All of them!"

Pat's eyes shone with an excitement that Father Joseph hadn't seen there for a very long time. When Eva Cassidy died four years before after a fierce struggle against cancer, something had died in him, too. It was almost as if he'd decided to put himself out to pasture, to retire from life. Not only had he lost a loving wife, but at the same time he seemed to have lost his usefulness, because his job at the Longshoremen's Union no longer required much of his attention. Back in the 1920's, he said, there were essentially two classes of people in America, a working class and a mandarin class, and although the labor movement was often vilified, sometimes with justification, it was doubtful that a strong, vibrant middle class would ever have emerged without it. Yet in helping to create that class, the very heart of American society, Pat and others like him made themselves redundant. Workers no longer needed unions to protect them from their bosses. If anything, now they needed to be protected from themselves. But that wasn't Pat's job.

So Father Joseph was gratified to see the old gleam in the warrior's eyes once again.

"I take it that Bobby Kennedy didn't get together with you merely to be convivial. Have you been conscripted to work for him?"

"I told him I'd do everything humanly possible to help his brother win the nomination and the election. I still have a fair amount of clout here in the city." He waited, sipping his wine. "But I also told him that what influence I have doesn't extend to Oakland and the East Bay."

Father Joseph lifted an eyebrow. "You mentioned Oakland?"

"*He* mentioned Oakland."

"Apropos of what?"

Pat took a deep breath, then exhaled. "Apropos of asking me to suggest the name of someone to head the Citizens for Kennedy office in the East Bay." He looked down at the apple core on his plate. "I proposed you."

Father Joseph's mouth fell open. "You did *what?*"

"I told him that you're the best man for the job."

Without another word, Father Joseph leaped from his chair and fled to the kitchen, where Pat could hear the angry rattling of a kettle, then water being splashed into it. Well, at least that was a good sign, an act of Celtic civility. If his son were truly offended, he'd make Turkish coffee bitter enough to extract teeth. A cup of tea would soothe his ruffled feelings.

Joseph Cassidy had always shied away from the limelight surrounding his famous and controversial father. Pat was a born brawler, more comfortable on a soapbox inflaming a crowd than he was in an easy chair. He'd been pitched into jails and more than once called a Communist. When Joe was growing up, it seemed to him that he first began to perceive his father through the newsreels or on television with such cronies as John L. Lewis or Walter Reuther, and with such respectable friends as Franklin D. Roosevelt. Once, when he was still living at home, he answered the telephone one evening only to be told that it was the White House calling and that President Truman would like a word or two with Mr. Cassidy—*if* Mr. Cassidy was available.

It was a tough act to follow, so Joe didn't even try. But at the seminary, then later at Berkeley, he smarted with embarrassment whenever someone mentioned his famous father. Quiet, reflective, unaggressive, Joe probably became a priest in order to avoid comparisons. If Pat Cassidy chose the soapbox, his son would choose the pulpit.

Now as he leaned against the archway between the dining room and the kitchen, waiting for the kettle to come to a boil, he looked at his father and said, "I'm a priest, not a ward boss. My concern is the salvation of souls, not who wins or loses an election. If I took the time to help the Kennedys in the East Bay, I'd have to neglect my parishioners."

"But in the long run, you'd be helping them, Joe. Most of the people in your parish are Hispanic or colored, and if Kennedy's strategy proves correct, this will be the first time in American history that Negroes and Latinos will play a crucial role in a presidential election."

Almost cynically, Father Joseph demanded, "And what will they get in return?"

"What do you mean, what will they get?"

"Just what I said. If John Kennedy hopes to reach the White House by climbing there on the backs of Negroes and Hispanics, what does he propose to do for them in return? Do I really have to remind you that his voting record as a senator on civil rights legislation was anything but admirable?"

"As a senator, he represented the people of the state of Massachusetts, and if you'll forgive me for the exaggerated underestimation, there may be no more than a dozen blacks or Hispanics in the state, and half of *them* are on the faculty of Harvard. But as President, he'd represent all Americans, from each and every one of our states, many of whom are members of minorities. And this time he won't fail them. You have my word for it."

"How can you be so sure?"

Pat set his lips firmly. "Because his brother won't let him."

First surprise, then amusement gripped Father Joseph's face. "Did Bobby tell you that?"

"He didn't have to. I know the sort of man he is. He's the conscience of that family."

If that was the case, why not try to elect Robert Kennedy to the presidency and leave his older brother in the Senate? Father Joseph knew, however, that politics was much more complicated than that. If Bobby Kennedy had a rock-hard conscience, he also had a serious flaw: He didn't seem to care if people liked him or not. By no stretch of the imagination did he attempt to charm or seduce. On the other hand, his older brother, John, could charm the pants off almost everyone—including a fair number of women, if rumors were to be believed, at least while he was still a roistering bachelor on Capitol Hill. He had a dazzling personality and magical good looks. Bobby didn't dazzle. Instead, he had the quiet intensity of an altar boy.

Steam began to hiss from the kettle behind him, but Father Joseph ignored it. If he had a quarrel with his church, it was its attitude of resignation and acceptance when faced with injustice. As a priest, he was expected to deal with spiritual matters, and leave worldly matters to others. But when others were indifferent, injustices remained. If priests didn't attempt to correct them, who would?

Bishop Moriarity would not approve. But was this something between Father Joseph and the bishop of the archdiocese, or between Father Joseph and God?

Pat must have perceived that he was weakening. "I didn't propose your name simply because you're my son, although no family in the world has greater clan loyalty than the Kennedys. What they admire more than anything else—they're enthralled by it!—is talent, and that's why I suggested you for the job. I'm convinced that no one else in this section of California can serve their interests better than you. If anyone is able to bring Latinos and Negroes into the Kennedy camp, you can, because they trust you. In fact, at the moment, they trust you a hell of a lot more than they trust the Kennedys."

Father Joseph stared silently into the air. If Kennedy's strategy proved correct, there was a very good chance that this time the Democrats might be able to wrest control of the White House from the Republicans. To be sure, there were good men and bad men in each party, men with honor, men without, opportunistic scoundrels and bright-eyed idealists. Surely the nation would survive, perhaps even flourish, if Richard Nixon were to win the election. But Father Joseph had a feeling that his parishioners would be worse off. Not necessarily victimized, but ignored. Under those circumstances, wasn't it folly to remain with old Cap'n Adlai Stevenson on his perpetually sinking vessel merely to hear one more burst of fine language?

"No one expects you to make up your mind immediately," Pat continued, "and I'm sure you have questions you want answered before you commit yourself. Aaron Golden, a Harvard fella the Kennedys have recruited to help in the campaign, is in the Bay Area, and he'll be getting in touch with you. He's in Palo Alto now, but he's going to be in Hillsborough tomorrow at a fund-raiser given by a woman named Ada Babcock. Have you ever heard of her?"

"If she's a Babcock of the Hawaiian sugar and pineapple fortune, I'm surprised that she's a Democrat."

"So are the Kennedys. But she wanted to throw a party for them, and how could they say no? Golden is going to be in Palo Alto most of the morning—enlisting supporters among the eggheads, pulling them away from Stevenson by the scruffs of their necks, if necessary—but he's due in Hillsborough by noon. Why not arrange to meet him there?"

Already, Father Joseph felt that his life was being turned topsy-turvy. In order to be in Hillsborough by noon, his entire schedule for the morning and early afternoon would have to be rearranged. Confessions would go unheard, hospital visits to the ill or dying would be delayed.

Was it worth it, just to help a rich boy who wanted to be President?

A moonlighting state highway patrolman halted Father Joseph's five-year-old Ford in front of the huge wrought-iron gate that led to the Babcock estate, peering suspiciously at the Roman clerical collar.

"I may not be on the guest list," Father Joseph explained after he'd given him his name. "I'm here to see Aaron Golden."

But as he was soon to learn, Golden seldom left anything to chance, his mind a vast repository of details that ordinary people forgot, and he had already notified the attendants at the gate that there was an addition to the guest list.

At the end of a long, white-graveled drive stood an immense white Palladian-style house that looked as if it had been transported, stone by stone, from the English countryside. Stretching the length of its facade was an ornamental pool with tritons and *putti* ecstatically splashing water from their mouths, and Father Joseph half expected to hear harpsichord music spilling out of the long, many-mullioned windows, but instead he heard animated voices and the clinking of glasses.

After parking his car under the shade of a gnarled live oak, sandwiching it between two Mercedes, he made his way into a circular, domed entrance hall. After the drive, the first thing he wanted to do was to find a bathroom, so he intercepted a tray-carrying Mexican-American maid and asked for directions. She pointed down a long gallery before scurrying away.

Since all the doors leading off it looked similarly imposing, he tried the first one he came to.

It wasn't a bathroom but a book-lined library, and it was occupied. A man's back was turned toward the door, and he was holding a young woman by her shoulders, shaking her.

"If you ever do that again, you silly bitch, I'll slug you right in front of everyone, so help me God!"

The man hadn't seen or heard the door open, but the woman had. As Father Joseph was about to step into the room to help her, her eyes implored him not to.

"It's all right," she said with remarkable composure, then, noticing his turned collar, added, "Father."

She had long black hair, creamy white skin, and huge violet eyes brimming with tears. The dress she was wearing—or was it a cardigan and matching skirt?—was probably the most romantic and beautiful color Father Joseph had ever seen. A heathery kind of color.

Slowly, giving her time to reconsider, he backed out of the room, and as he did the man removed his hands from her shoulders.

It was reassuring that the rich had squabbles, just as the poor did. Still, he didn't like to see a woman bullied.

At last, he found the bathroom, used it, then washed up at a marble basin with gold-plated fittings, wiped his hands on monogrammed towels, and returned to the foyer. As he passed the library, the door was open and the room was empty.

At the entrance to the immense living room, he stood and surveyed the crowd that had come at Mrs. Babcock's invitation to contribute a little something to the Kennedy coffers. For the most part, they were middle-aged or elderly country squire types, dressed stylishly but comfortably. Most were standing, eating from plates they had filled at a buffet that had been set up at one end of the room.

Father Joseph recognized the hostess from photographs

that had recently appeared in the *Chronicle* at the opening of the Ada Babcock Cultural Center in San Francisco, honoring not her husband, who had amassed the fortune that had made it possible, but herself. Self-effacement was apparently not the lady's forte. She was in her late sixties, he guessed, and her face was brown and leathery from relentless tanning. Her eyes were narrow, black as a pirate's and almost as mean.

A hand grabbed Father Joseph by the crook of the arm, and when he looked up he saw a short, chunky man with watery eyes behind thick hornrimmed glasses, his skin cratered from old acne scars, his jaw blue under its heavy beard, although a speck of blood indicated that he had recently shaved.

"Hi ya, Father Joe. Glad you could make it. Jesus, aren't these people rich? Back east, people have no idea how rich you can be in California."

"Or how poor either."

Aaron Golden flashed a winning smile, revealing teeth that were crooked and uneven. A calcium-deficient Depression baby, Father Joseph supposed. He didn't look—or sound—the least bit like a Harvard professor. More like City College of New York, that breeding ground for geniuses on Manhattan's Upper West Side.

After introducing himself, he fixed his eyes on Father Joseph. "So what exactly is it that you want from Kennedy before you'll work for us?"

"A strong pro–civil rights statement before the convention."

Suddenly, Golden looked agonized, as if an ulcer had hemorrhaged, flooding his stomach with blood. "Why do you have to spoil my day, Father Joe? Don't you know by now that in politics you spend most of your time avoiding issues, not confronting them? It would be downright suicidal for Jack Kennedy to come out with a strong civil rights statement before the election. Because if he did, he'd lose the only block of voters we're reasonably confident are going to support him: the Catholics."

Father Joseph frowned, then laughed. "You know, I'm beginning to think that God may have a sense of humor after all."

Golden cocked his head. "Sorry, Father. I miss the transition."

"Well, apparently you people have decided that Protestants aren't going to vote for Kennedy because he's a Catholic, and to compensate he's decided to ingratiate himself with Negro and Hispanic voters. But he can't ingratiate himself too much, or too publicly, without losing support among the Catholic voters."

Smiling wanly, Golden nodded. "Yeah, it's crazy, isn't it? It makes you wonder. A couple years ago, I considered becoming a Buddhist just to get away from it all, but I didn't like their holidays. I tell ya, Father, there's nothing like the bleating of a shofar at Yom Kippur to bring out the religion in you. It's terrific theater, terrific. Almost as good as scattering incense around the church, the way you Catholics do. I guess a man has to believe in something. Otherwise, why the hell bother getting out of bed in the morning? Right? As for wanting Kennedy to reassure minorities before the election, all I can say is that you have our honest pledge that in a Kennedy administration, the Department of Justice will enforce the Civil Rights Act of 1957, and that's a damned sight more than President Eisenhower has done. But there are limits to what you can expect in the way of a public announcement *before* the convention and the election, because Kennedy simply can't afford to lose the support of the inner-city Catholic vote, and they're the ones who feel threatened by block-busting and school integration. In a real crunch—if they're forced to choose between a candidate who might move a black family onto their block, or one who won't—they'll vote against their coreligionist and give their support to Nixon, who doesn't even know that there *are* Negroes or Hispanics. I don't understand. Maybe it's human nature to be wary of someone who isn't exactly like you. A presidential candidate can't be expected to change human nature. Hell, you theologians have been trying to do that without success for two thousand years."

What he'd said was incontestable, but Father Joseph was doubtful that it would be acceptable to Northern California's Negroes and Latinos, who had become impatient and were no longer willing to listen to traditional arguments.

"And what if Kennedy is *forced* to make a public commitment before the election?" he asked the Harvard professor.

Golden's face became ashen. "Oh, God! You know something we don't know! But if any of your minority friends are planning a public confrontation between now and November, will you please ask them to cool it?"

"They've been cooling it for over a hundred years."

"Okay, so will another couple months kill them?"

"From our point of view, probably not. From theirs, quite possibly."

In fact, it was conceivable that the momentum couldn't be halted. After having slumbered in neglect for nearly a century, American Negroes were demanding the rights guaranteed them by the Constitution, and the Supreme Court was now upholding their demands. In 1954, public schools were ordered integrated, and in 1957 Negroes at last affirmed their right to vote in primary elections in the Deep South. Largely because of Martin Luther King's successful boycott of buses in Montgomery, Alabama, the Court was now considering the legality of segregated waiting rooms and rest rooms used in interstate commerce. Their decision was expected to be handed down before the year was over.

Father Joseph challenged Golden. "For the last hundred years, Negroes have been dying to sit in a Whites Only waiting room in the South. It would be convenient for John Kennedy if they could remain standing—or sit in the Colored section—until after the November election, but it's not going to happen that way. With or without the permission of the Supreme Court, they're going to sit down where they want to sit, and they're going to be arrested by some brute with a pistol on his hip and a pack of German shepherds on a lead. So what's Senator Kennedy going to do about it?"

In despair, Golden snapped his eyes shut. "You *do* know something we don't know! The Reverend King is going to embarrass us, isn't he?"

"I have no idea, but he probably has reason to. You can't very well expect him to deliver a block of votes to your candidate without making certain that he gets something in return."

"We're not even counting on King's support. He's a Stevenson man, and if Stevenson doesn't get the nomination, he'll probably sit this one out."

"It's not just the Reverend King I'm talking about. I'm also talking about myself. You're asking me to help generate support for Kennedy among the people in the ghettos and barrios here in California, but what if one of their brothers or sisters gets arrested in Mississippi or Alabama for sitting in a Whites Only waiting room? What do I tell them? To vote for Kennedy anyway, even though you say he'd prefer to duck the civil rights issue entirely? They'd be fools to vote for him under those circumstances. And I'd be a fool to work for him."

Golden moaned softly. He shifted his ample weight from foot to foot in his suffering, and tears brimmed in his eyes. "Okay," he began reluctantly, gulping for air. "I hope to God it doesn't happen, because if it does, it could make things very, very messy. If there's a confrontation between colored people and whites in the South between now and the election, it'll cost us plenty, because Nixon will exploit it and win more white votes as a result. I assure you, it'll bring out the worst in most people."

"But maybe the best in some."

"Maybe, maybe not. But you're asking what Kennedy would do should such a confrontation take place, so that you can assure your friends that he means business. And the answer is: I don't know. I wish I did. But he's only human. A Christian, yes, but also a pragmatist. If it becomes necessary to make a choice between supporting one Negro who's testing the law in the Deep South, and losing the election as a consequence"— he shrugged his shoulders inside his ill-fitting suit jacket—"I don't know. But he *is* Irish, and for centuries being Irish was just another way of being hated. So I would hope that his conduct would reflect that."

"If I'm not mistaken, Richard Nixon is also Irish."

Suddenly, Golden was convulsed with laughter. "By God, I think you're right. But there *is* a difference. We know with reasonable certainty what Nixon's attitude would be. But there's no way of guessing Kennedy's. His response is unknown. Perhaps it's offensive to you, but in this case it seems to me that the unknown is preferable to the known. Is that good enough?" He waited, then demanded, "So are you with us or aren't you?"

"I'm with you."

Golden had to leave early because he was due in Santa Barbara by late afternoon, but he instructed Father Joseph to stick around and thank Ada Babcock for having made it possible for some of her rich neighbors to contribute to the Kennedy campaign.

"A lot of people think that old man Kennedy's money is inexhaustible and can't understand why we're passing the hat," he explained. "The fact of the matter is that Richard Nixon is going to have so much dough behind him in this election that by comparison Joseph Kennedy's fortune is chicken feed. Big business helped put Dwight Eisenhower into the White House, and they like the arrangement so much that they'll spend anything to preserve it for Nixon. Anyway, we got pledges for about six thousand bucks today, so it was worth the effort. The chow was pretty good, too. You should have some before you leave."

Father Joseph said that he would try to.

"I was told that Roger Grainger's daughter would be here and that she'd probably be good for a thousand, but I haven't seen her," Golden continued.

"Grainger, the department store tycoon?"

"Yeah. They live around here somewhere. She's his only daughter, the apple of his eye, and understandably she gets a very handsome allowance. Her father's a big wheel in the state Republican party, but Susan defected when she went to UCLA. She's very interested in the Kennedys."

Father Joseph said that he'd keep an eye out for her.

"Do. Also tell Mrs. Babcock how grateful we are. I looked all over for her a couple minutes ago to say good-bye but wasn't able to find her." He extended a damp hand. "We'll keep in touch, Father Joe. I'll be based in Washington, but part of my responsibility is to bring in the vote in the Rocky Mountain and Pacific Coast states, so I'll be out here a couple times a month. I'll call you once or twice a week, but remember: We'll be operating on a shoestring, so I always call after nine at night to get the cheaper rate."

Father Joseph had to smile. "How are you getting down to Santa Barbara? Hitchhiking?"

"Oh, Jesus! I'm glad you reminded me. I didn't want to spend money renting a car. I borrowed one from a Stanford egghead and I'm leaving it off in L.A. at his girlfriend's house. But I'm almost out of gas." He dug into his pants pocket for a rumpled dollar bill and some loose change. "I couldn't possibly hit you for a fiver to help cover my expenses, could I?"

"I thought you collected six thousand today."

"I did, but it's all in checks. Anyway, it's reserved for more important matters. If you're short now, I'll just stop at the first gas station I come to and try to appeal to someone's patriotism. Kids who pump gas are almost never Republicans. Someone told me to use the Coast Highway between here and Santa Barbara—Big Sur and all that—but I don't dare run out of gas, because there's nothing there but water."

Father Joseph opened his well-worn wallet and withdrew a five. "I have a feeling you could talk gasoline out of a mermaid."

Golden flashed a gut-wrenching smile. "Unless she's a registered voter, it wouldn't be worth my trouble."

Only a few guests remained when Ada Babcock sailed across the living room and seized Father Joseph's hand. "I think I met your father once," she announced after introductions. "Back when my husband was still living. If I recall correctly, they weren't particularly fond of one another."

"That's more than possible," Father Joseph conceded.

In fact, there'd been no love at all lost between them. Horace Babcock's shipping line had been struck on several occasions by Pat Cassidy's longshoremen, and Mr. Babcock once went so far as to suggest that the elder Cassidy should be hanged from a lamppost on Market Street.

"Has Mr. Goldman left yet?" his widow asked.

"Golden. Yes. He couldn't stay because he's due in Santa Barbara by four. He looked all over for you to say good-bye."

"Well, I've certainly enjoyed this lovely little party. One

meets such interesting people at political gatherings. I had no idea there were so many Democrats in Hillsborough."

"We wish there were more."

"I'll be sure to say a kind word on Senator Kennedy's behalf whenever the opportunity arises. But you must understand that my first choice remains Douglas MacArthur. It's the crime of the century that a man of his towering intellect and experience hasn't yet been summoned to the White House— either by you Democrats or by the Republicans."

"Well, ah . . ."

She handed him an envelope, then lowered her voice. "Since Mr. Goldman has left, I suppose you're the one I should give this to."

Father Joseph opened the envelope and extracted a slip of paper. He expected to find a check made out to the Kennedy Campaign Headquarters, but instead read an itemized bill from the Peninsula Catering Service for the buffet lunch just served. Including drinks, it came to a little over three hundred dollars.

"I'm afraid I don't understand, Mrs. Babcock."

"But surely I made things perfectly clear to Mr. Goldman when I volunteered the use of my home. I've always been most interested in other people's points of view, and I had no objection to you Kennedy people meeting here, but I see no reason why I should have to pay for your food and drinks. You don't think that's unreasonable, do you?"

At that moment, Father Joseph didn't dare tell her what he thought. Providentially, he was spared the embarrassment because there was a sudden rustling of silk behind him, then a soft voice said, "I'll take that," and the bill was lifted from his hand.

When he looked up, he saw the young woman he'd seen earlier in the library, only now she was opening her purse and withdrawing a checkbook. On a tabletop, she quickly wrote out a check, signed it with a flourish, handed it along with the bill to the hostess, then walked away without another word.

"Who was that?" he asked.

"That was Susan Grainger."

Father Joseph had to hurry to catch up with her. She was

already out of the house and on her way to the few remaining cars in the parking area when he finally reached her.

"I want to thank you for picking up the tab. That was very generous of you."

"I had a feeling that old frump would do something like that. I heard she gave a party for Nixon last week, and one for Hubert Humphrey the week before, and each time she charged them through the nose."

"Why does she do it?"

"Surely you must know by now that the rich expect the rest of the world to entertain them, and the reason they're rich is that they keep their entertainers on short rations."

"I guess I haven't known all that many."

"Consider yourself lucky." Her eyes plumbed his, then turned away. "It was nice of you not to make a scene, Father, back in the library a little while ago." She laughed shortly, perhaps at herself. "When you study for the priesthood, do they teach you how to save souls?"

"In this world, people save their own souls. Or lose them. All a priest does is try to guide and counsel."

"So you have no magical recipe for salvation?"

"No. I wish I did. But I remember, when I was a boy, my father telling me that the best way to cure sadness is to do something for someone who's worse off you than you are. There are thousands. Millions. I've got a couple hundred in my own parish, St. Brendan's in Oakland."

Almost defiantly, she said, "I don't think, in all my life, I've ever done anything for anyone except myself."

"You just wrote a check."

"Anyone can write a check—as long as you have a rich father."

"If you really want to, you could help us register voters in Oakland. You don't need a rich father to do that."

A burgundy Daimler drew up behind her, and the young man who'd been with her in the library said sternly through the open window, "Susan." It was a command.

"I'm afraid I have to go now."

"Well, if you ever change your mind . . . about helping us, we're in the telephone directory. I'm at the parish house."

"I wouldn't count on it, Father."

"In my vocation, we're eternally hopeful." Before she left, he added, "Could I ask a question? I don't think I've ever seen a more incredible color on a human being than the color you're wearing. It's heather, isn't it??"

"Yes. It's my favorite."

"It's very beautiful."

After he'd said it, he could feel his face flush slightly, because what he meant to say but couldn't was that *she* was very beautiful.

It was almost with relief that he watched the car disappear down the narrow avenue toward the gate.

FOUR

*F*ather Joseph indulged himself and took the long way home over the twisting mountain road, confident that his pink-cheeked, cherubic assistant, Father Declan from County Sligo, would be able to perform the parish duties until late afternoon.

It was always a dramatic, scalp-tingling experience to reach the summit of the road, then catch the first glimpse of white-capped blue sea far below. As he began the dizzying descent, he couldn't help but once again revel in California's beauty. Little wonder there were so many mystics lurking behind the redwood trees. If Christ had been born in Santa Cruz County, would he have been a Druid?

Father Joseph was himself a priest not so much because he'd been drawn to the spiritual life as because he had rejected the worldly one. Originally, his intention was to become a Franciscan monk, emulating the gentle Francis of Assisi, but before he knew it, the Jesuit teachers at his high school had seized his mind. He had always been the nun's darling, the holiest boy in the parish, as they described him. How to express that holiness was decided as much by his teachers as by Joe himself.

He enjoyed his work, although he was the first to admit that he was at heart a Franciscan monk wearing the turned collar of a Jesuit priest. Ceremony itself—or theater, as Aaron Golden had called it—interested him far less than serving people in distress, confused or alone.

Bishop Moriarity, however, believed firmly that a priest in his archdiocese should above all things serve the church, and because he was an infirm and crotchety old man, often that meant serving *him*. So as he followed the narrow Coast Highway north to San Francisco, Father Joseph pondered how to break the news to his superior that he'd agreed to engage in political activity in the East Bay among his disadvantaged parishioners.

He knew with certainty that Bishop Moriarity would disapprove, even forbid him to undertake the assignment. If such resistance was inevitable, should he even mention his plans? Or should he seek counsel directly from God, who didn't suffer from the aching rheumatoid joints or bilious digestion that soured Bishop Moriarity's disposition?

It was after four by the time he reached the parish house in West Oakland, and he at once recognized the white Cadillac parked at the curb. Inside, Father Declan was puttering around, lifting objects from tables and dusting—it was astonishing how caponlike men became after years of celibacy—and announced with agitation, "Mr. Hawkins is in your study, Father Joseph. I told him you might not be back until quite late, but he insisted on waiting."

Father Joseph wasn't unduly alarmed. From experience, he knew that the Negro assemblyman from Oakland spent most of his life insisting. He didn't mean to be rude by arriving unannounced or commandeering someone else's office, but simply had an aversion for appointment books and closed doors, and couldn't imagine why people let such obstacles to spontaneity interfere with their lives.

"Hello, Padre."

Enthroned in Father Joseph's chair behind the desk, Sheldon Hawkins looked like a fashion plate that had been rejected by *Esquire* magazine and published as a centerfold in *Ebony*. He was wearing a stylish double-breasted navy blue suit, a white shirt with a button-down collar, and a rep tie, and flung on top of the desk was a tan cashmere polo coat.

"It's always a pleasure to see you, Sheldon—and might I add, always a surprise."

After they shook hands, Father Joseph opened his briefcase and removed the picnic lunch that Mrs. Esposito, his housekeeper, had packed for him that morning before he set out for Hillsborough. For reasons he didn't quite understand, he'd been too busy to partake of the buffet.

"Do you mind if I have a late lunch?" he asked his guest.

Hawkins watched as Father Joseph laid out his lunch on one edge of the desk: a Monterey Jack cheese sandwich on a sourdough roll, a thermos of tomato soup, and a pear. Grimacing, he remarked, "Why don't you let me take you down to Trader Vic's instead?"

"Because if you did, it would make the gossip column in the *Chronicle* tomorrow, and my character would be impugned. Last week, the columnist reported that you and Dolly Maguire had lunch together at Tadich Grill, and in view of the fact that Miss Maguire has recently acquired a huge parcel of ocean-front property in Sonoma County, wasn't it a strange coincidence that you'll be voting in the Assembly this month on the new Coastal Preservation Bill?"

Shelly Hawkins reached out and grabbed the pear. "It *is* a strange coincidence. Dolly Maguire and I never talk about her business interests when we get together. We talk about grapes and wine-making. You see, she owns a large vineyard near Napa, and of course I've always been extremely interested in the finished product."

Father Joseph bit into his sandwich. "I'm sure you're aware that Miss Maguire evicted a lot of nice people from the apartments she owned on Russian Hill and Telegraph Hill so that she could convert them into condominiums and make herself a bundle. That's what paid for her Napa vineyard."

Dolly Maguire was one of the new crop of high-powered real estate speculators who had drifted northward to San Francisco after having plucked much of Southern California dry. She'd begun by buying apartment houses in the North Beach district, performing modest cosmetic jobs on them, then offering her tenants the choice of buying their apartments or moving out. In most cases, they were forced out. Recently, she'd been quoted in the *Chronicle* as saying that renters were an undesirable element, contributing nothing to San Francisco.

"I take it that you don't think much of her," Hawkins observed.

"I don't like what she and her conniving friends are doing to this beautiful city of ours. Pretty soon, only the rich will be able to live in San Francisco because she's decided that renters add nothing to the quality of a city's life. Well, may I remind you—and Miss Maguire, too—that in Portsmouth Square there's a memorial to Robert Louis Stevenson, who lived in a humble boardinghouse nearby when he graced our city with his presence, and here in Oakland we have a square named after Jack London, who was also a renter. It's very doubtful indeed that anyone will ever go to the trouble of erecting a memorial or naming a square after Messrs. Grubb and Ellis, Mr. Century 21, or Miss Dolly Maguire for that matter."

The assemblyman's laughter filled the small study. When he finished, he said, "You know what I like about you, Padre? You're the most indignant preacher I've ever known. That's why I drop by from time to time to shoot the breeze with you. You see, on occasion it's necessary for me to meet with people like Dolly Maguire, and they're so goddamned charming and ingratiating, it's tempting not to hate them. But you won't let me, will you?"

Father Joseph challenged him. "If that's the way you feel, Sheldon, why do you accept campaign contributions from her?"

"How else can I survive? If I didn't receive help from the real estate industry, it's doubtful that I could get reelected. In return, I admit that I sometimes do small favors for them in Sacramento, but if anyone suffers as a result of those favors, I assure you they're not *my* people. Yes, you're right. The Coastal Preservation Bill comes before the Assembly later this month, and I'll probably vote for limited development. Do you know why? When was the last time you saw a Negro on the beach at Aptos or Capitola? And how many of my colored constituents do you think can afford vacation homes on the dunes north of Monterey? So why should I break my neck protecting the view of some rich doctor who lives in an expensive oceanfront home? No way, Padre."

Father Joseph squinted at his guest. "There's one thing I've never really been able to figure out, Sheldon. Do you like white people? Or do you hate them?"

Hawkins sat up straight in the chair. "Let's say that experience has taught me that the only way to survive is to imitate them." He waited, placing the half-finished pear in an ashtray. "Do you want to hear a morally instructive story? Well, I'll tell you one. Back when I was a kid, growing up here in the flats of Oakland, my Momma used to have troubles . . . with her nerves. She took in washing, she cleaned white folks' houses, and she raised six kids all by herself, so it was probably understandable that she was nervous. Anyway, once every two weeks, she went to see a white psychiatrist on Pill Hill, and the fees were paid by welfare. My Momma always took my two little sisters and me along, because she didn't have anyone to look after us and she didn't want to leave us alone. We waited for her in the waiting room, while the fancy psychiatrist wrote out a prescription for her. Well, the first time I ran for the Assembly, ten years ago, some journalist came up with an exclusive story that I'd had a psychiatric history and he could prove it." Even now at the recollection, the assemblyman's face was filled with rage. "Do you know what that white psychiatrist did? He billed the state of California for *four* patients: my Momma, my two sisters, and me."

It was a minute before Father Joseph could respond. "Not all doctors are dishonest."

"Of course not. And not all white people exploit Negroes. But a lot of them have during the past two hundred years, and all I'm doing is turning the tables. I use whites to get what I want, Padre. Some people think that Dolly Maguire has me in her pocket, but they're dead wrong. She's in mine."

Father Joseph was willing to admit that being colored in a white society could be a painful, humiliating experience. As late as the Second World War, American Negroes weren't even permitted to fight side by side with white troops but instead were forced to serve in segregated units, sometimes giving up their lives to help preserve a democracy that had excluded them.

It wasn't so much the Constitution that had betrayed them, but men. More specifically, men who should have known better: the justices who sat on the Supreme Court. Until the 1950's, the judges continued to uphold the principle of "separate but equal" facilities, the foundation on which segregation was built. But then the Court began to perceive that their interpretation of the Fourteenth Amendment had served only to keep Negroes in bondage. Not only were facilities offered colored people seldom equal, but there was something repugnant about their being separate. Until then, southern Negroes attended segregated schools, traveled on segregated buses and trains, and ate in segregated restaurants. But now, at last, largely as a result of agitation on the part of northern Negroes like Sheldon Hawkins, the Court had begun to issue decisions calling for integration.

But no one knew better than Father Joseph that for some, it was too late. They were unable to free themselves from the legacy of poverty and neglect. Violence and crime had become their way of life. He would never forget the jail interview he'd had with the young colored boy in Washington, D.C., who had stolen the car that killed his niece Sara Conroy, Mimi Cassidy Conroy's only daughter. It had happened in the middle of the afternoon while eight-year-old Sara was walking her puppy in the Georgetown section of the city, and out of nowhere a speeding car careened out of control onto the sidewalk, killing her at once. Father Joseph hated the boy, but as a priest tried to forgive him.

He was twenty years old and lived in a society where the automobile was king, but he had never learned how to drive one because no one in his family had ever *owned* one.

As Father Joseph saw it, there were two victims: Sara, whose life was lost, and the boy, whose life was squandered because he'd stolen something he couldn't afford to buy.

Perhaps four victims. Because Mimi and Robert Conroy, who until then had been liberals sympathetic to minority causes, now feared and distrusted Negroes more or less indiscriminately. If Mimi even saw a colored man walking down her fashionable block, she would call the police and report it— even if the man in question was the ambassador from Ghana with a degree from Oxford University.

"Well, Sheldon," Father Joseph said wearily to his visitor, "I gather that you didn't drop by just to discuss the deplorable state of mankind. What can I do for you?"

"I've come for some advice."

Father Joseph arched his eyebrows. "That's something of a novelty. As a rule, you're very generous in dispensing it."

The assemblyman reached for one of the potato chips Mrs.

Esposito had included with Father Joseph's lunch. "You know, Padre, I'm not a rich man," he began. "My car is being paid for by installments, and I rent my apartment on Taylor Street, I don't own it. I spend more money than I should on clothes, I suppose, but that's because I wore rags when I was growing up. No member of the California Assembly can hope to live on the miserable stipend we're given by the state. I live on my salary as an attorney." He took a breath. "I mention all this because I've been offered a very substantial retainer by a prospective client who has interests in the Oakland waterfront."

Father Joseph could never hear the word "waterfront" without an emotional response. He'd virtually grown up on San Francisco's Embarcadero, where his father was president of the West Coast Longshoremen's Union. But since the end of the Second World War, Oakland's waterfront had captured most of the shipping business to and from the Orient that had formerly gone to San Francisco. Where booms and winches once thundered twenty-four hours a day, there was now nothing but boarded-up piers tumbling into the bay.

As if reading his thoughts, Hawkins said, "Do I have to tell you why San Francisco's waterfront is moribund, if not dead?"

No, he didn't. "Because my father and others like him were betrayed by the city's bankers, who'd decided that the future of San Francisco lay in tourism, not shipping, and they didn't want dirty old piers interfering with the tourists' view."

While San Francisco had spent huge sums of money trying to induce tourists to visit, Oakland had invested in new docking facilities across the bay. Now the Embarcadero was virtually deserted except for people from Omaha aiming cameras at seagulls, while Oakland's waterfront was thriving.

"But your old man let it happen," the assemblyman accused him.

"The decision was made by bankers and realty interests, not by him. I assure you, no one solicited his opinion."

His visitor sighed. "I'm disappointed in you, Padre. I gave you more credit than that. Even a nigger like me from Oakland knows that bankers and realtors don't ask for the opinions of people like your old man and me. We have to lay our opinions in front of them—then rub their noses in them. Patrick Cassidy didn't do that. He accepted their decision."

Yes, it was a mistake. It had happened so quickly that it was all over before Pat Cassidy realized that San Francisco's once dynamic shipping industry was lost.

"And now after that lengthy introduction, I take it you're going to tell me who your client is?" Father Joseph urged.

"Prospective client," Hawkins corrected him, then left his chair and walked to the window overlooking the quiet garden behind the parish house. His back toward Father Joseph, he said, "The Teamsters Union has asked me to help them in smoothing out any obstacles they might encounter while attempting to reorganize the labor force on the Oakland waterfront"—he turned to face his host—"in a breakaway from your old man's union."

Father Joseph felt as if someone's head had just butted into his soft underbelly. "Then your client is Jimmy Hoffa."

Hawkins admonished him with a shaking finger. "Prospective client, Padre. I haven't accepted the job. I wanted to talk to you first to see if you could give a Baptist like me some sound advice."

Father Joseph exploded, "You know damned well that Hoffa is little more than a gangster!"

"Surely I don't have to remind you that your old man's good buddy Robert Kennedy has tried to prove those allegations, but without success. And in this country, a man is innocent until proved guilty—unless, of course, he happens to be colored."

It was becoming obvious that Sheldon Hawkins hadn't come for advice. He wanted something else. In another minute, he put his cards on the table.

"Could you tell me how many Negroes your old man has in his union?" he asked.

Truthfully, Father Joseph answered, "It's my understanding that membership isn't tallied on the basis of race or religion."

"A goddamned good thing it isn't, because if it was, Pat Cassidy would be embarrassed all to hell. The fact of the matter is that the West Coast Longshoremen's Union is dominated by you Irish and by the Italians. It's nearly impossible for a Negro to get a stevedoring job."

"But, Sheldon, there are reasons for that. When the union was organized, there just weren't very many Negroes living in the Bay Area. It took the war to bring them here from the South. Some of the men in my father's union are fifty-five or sixty years old. Are you suggesting that he fire them in order to give jobs to your people?"

Hawkins fixed his eye on him. "What if I told you that Jimmy Hoffa has promised to do just that?"

Father Joseph leaped from his chair. "The only thing Hoffa can promise you is graft and corruption on the waterfront. If you're willing to pay that price to get jobs for your constituents, then go ahead and do it. But as for my father, he's ashamed to be part of the same labor movement as that scoundrel."

If Father Joseph was angry, so was the assemblyman. In an emotion-filled voice, he began, "Listen, Padre. You whites complain that we litter your streets and dirty your parks and steal your cars and"—he faltered—"even kill your children. But nothing's ever going to be corrected unless you get us out of the ghetto. If people are forced to live like animals, why should you be surprised when they behave like animals? There are only two ways of getting us out of the ghetto. You can ship us out in cattle cars, the way they did in Nazi Germany, or you can give us jobs and we can call Atlas Van Lines and move out ourselves. What's wrong with you, Padre? Have you forgotten what it's like to struggle? I thought you Irish knew what it's like to live under the yoke of slavery."

"My sympathies are with you, Sheldon. But aren't you talking to the wrong Cassidy? Shouldn't you have gone to see my father instead?"

"No, because I know you and I don't know him."

"Well, if you're asking me to intercede on your behalf for a quota system in hiring, forget it. My father will throw me out of the room. He hires the strongest, most dependable men he can find. Period. He doesn't look at your face; he looks at the muscles in your arms. And as for you joining Hoffa and his henchmen to try to get the Teamsters onto the Oakland waterfront, my father would tell you to go ahead and do it. He'll meet you head-on, and he'll stop Hoffa—even if it kills him."

For a moment Hawkins remained quiet in his chair. "Why is it that you consider it your God-given mission to keep me an honest man, Padre?"

A smile lifted Father Joseph's lips. "Because we want as many Baptists as possible with us in heaven."

"To do the cleaning?"

"No. Everyone makes his own bed and does his own cleaning in heaven."

The assemblyman reached over and patted his friend on the arm. "You're a good man, Father Joseph. I wish you were colored, because we could use men like you." He stood up and picked up his cashmere coat. "I didn't drop by today for advice. I wanted to warn you to expect trouble on the waterfront in the near future. Tell your old man to be very careful, because Hoffa plays dirty."

"Then you're not accepting his retainer?"

"I already turned it down." He slipped into his elegant coat even though the mild weather scarcely warranted it. He cocked his head in puzzlement. "There's one thing I don't understand. When I was approached about the job, I asked Hoffa's emissary if my services would also be required for the port of Seattle. And he said no, Seattle wasn't a target. Only Oakland."

If the Teamsters were about to launch an attempt to re-unionize West Coast ports, why had Hoffa decided to concentrate on Oakland?

"That's most peculiar," he conceded. "It doesn't seem consistent."

"One thing's for sure: If Jimmy Hoffa is a crook, as you and Bobby Kennedy allege he is, he's a very consistent one. So something out of the ordinary is in the works here. Better tell your old man."

"I will, Sheldon."

Father Joseph's visitor lingered in the doorway. "Maybe you can even do more than that. You just said a minute or so ago that your father gives preference in the hiring hall to men who are strong and dependable. I don't have to remind you, do I, that we're mighty strong people. That's why we were brought here from Africa in the first place—not to sing or dance or play our banjos, but to work. It's true we may not be quite as dependable as you whites are at this stage, but keep in mind that most of us were still living in a plantation society until about twenty years ago. But we're ready to change. We've got yearnings. So maybe you could mention to your old man that the next time he's measuring men's strength and dependability, he might also consider measuring their yearnings. You think so?"

Their eyes met with tacit understanding. "I'll speak to him. You have my word on it, Sheldon."

After Hawkins left, Father Declan tapped on the door, then entered the room. "While Mr. Hawkins was here, you had a telephone call," he said. "It was your sister, Mrs. Conroy. I'm to remind you that you're expected at a concert of some sort at Grace Cathedral tomorrow night."

Father Joseph stifled a groan. He'd quite forgotten the promise he'd made to Mimi.

In a somewhat unusual arrangement, Mimi Conroy and her son, Owen, lived in San Francisco full-time, while her husband, Democratic congressman Robert Conroy, lived in a Washington, D.C., apartment, commuting home on most weekends.

It was an expensive way to live—the airlines were the real winners—but deemed necessary. It was Mimi who had rushed to the window that day when she heard the screeching of brakes in front of her Georgetown house, only to see her daughter, Sara, flying through the air. As Robert later said, Mimi began to scream even before she reached the front door, and it was a year before she finally stopped.

After Sara's funeral, the congressman's office explained Mimi's absence from Washington's social whirl by reporting that she was in the south of Ireland supervising the renovation of a vacation house they'd purchased the year before. In fact, she was a patient at the Menninger Clinic in Topeka, Kansas, suffering from depression so deep as to be almost bottomless.

When at last she was judged well enough to leave, her doctors advised against returning to the Georgetown house, so it was sold and a handsome house purchased in the Pacific Heights section of San Francisco.

Robert Conroy's family had been members of the luckless Donner Pass party a hundred years before, but survival had cost them their Catholicism. They became Episcopalians, and so did Mimi when she married into the family.

Owen was in his final year at the Cathedral School and also a member of Grace Cathedral's choir. An organ and choral concert was scheduled for the next night, and since Owen's father was in Washington, his grandfather and uncle had been called upon to pinch-hit.

"If there's one thing I abominate more than organ music," Father Joseph complained, "it's the voices of adolescent boys in the process of changing. They all sound like castrati to me."

"Perhaps you could tell your sister that you have a bad cough. No one likes coughers at concerts."

Father Declan was about to leave the room, but paused at the doorway. "I almost forgot. You had a second call, from a woman who wouldn't leave her name. She wanted to know when you'd be available tomorrow, and I told her that you'd be taking confessions between three and four. But she said that what was wrong with her was far beyond confessing. Wasn't that a peculiar thing to say? She said that she's decided to do something for someone else, for once in her life, and that you'd know who she is. Do you, Father Joseph?"

FIVE

As Paul Molloy hurried down the long corridor at Idlewild Airport, he caught sight of his father's chauffeur waiting in the crowd in the main terminal—cap in hand, shoulders bent from a lifetime of kowtowing—and the second he saw him, he ducked into a nearby telephone booth, sweat pouring down his neck.

If there was one symbol of wealth he despised above all others, it was that damned Rolls-Royce, even now illegally parked in front of the Arrivals building, blocking the progress of taxis, buses, cars, and a fair share of the rest of mankind simply to allow Jean-Claude to pluck the cheap canvas bag from Paul's hand, then escort him through the throng like an Oriental potentate being led through lepers.

Would they never learn?

In fact, to avoid being met at the airport, Paul had been deliberately vague when Andy Sinclair called earlier in the day to confirm travel arrangements between San Francisco and New York. After being given the flight information, Paul had said, "Listen, Andy, better not count on me showing up for the funeral. There are a lot of things I have to sort out in my head."

"Your mother's expecting you, Paul."

"Mother is well aware of my feelings. Tell her that I may come—then again, I may not."

"We'll send the car to the airport to meet your plane."

"For God's sake, no! I'd take an airport bus before I'd set foot in that obscene car."

Andy sighed, then said softly, "Paul, you don't have to fight him anymore. Remember? Your father's dead."

But in spite of his threat, there was Jean-Claude standing

at the end of the corridor, scanning the faces of arriving passengers. In another minute or two, the last would enter the terminal, and Paul was sure that he would then report to Andy and almost certainly be instructed to return to the city alone. Until then, Paul would simply have to sit it out in the cramped, malodorous telephone booth.

It had taken all of his resolve just to get this far.

Even as a child, Paul had hated being driven around in his father's cars—first ostentatious Cadillac or Lincoln limousines, then when they became too "common," as Charles Molloy had described them, a series of Rolls-Royces, each more opulent than the last. Unlike his brother Lee, who never seemed to worry about the impression he made, Paul was acutely conscious that there were an astonishing number of people in the world who resented you if you had money and they didn't. Sometimes they could be cruel. Once while still in short pants, he was about to step into the waiting Rolls after his compulsory weekly trim at the barber shop in the Plaza Hotel when a hackney driver nearby pointed at him, then jeered derisively, in a thick brogue, "Look at that rich little gob-shite!"

Paul had no idea what a gob-shite was exactly, but the words sent him into unstoppable tears. Then and there, he vowed to avoid a repetition of such gratuitous abuse, and the easiest way was simply to eschew all the gaudier trappings of wealth.

Thus, when he and Lee were home on vacation from prep school, they sometimes went to baseball games at Yankee Stadium or matinees of Broadway plays, and if the car was available, Lee always insisted on being dropped off and collected, loving the drama of it all. But Paul suffered excruciatingly, crouching in the backseat as low as he could to avoid being seen. And more often than not, he slipped away before the game or play was over so that he could either walk home or take the subway.

Once he arrived at the River House apartment sopping wet after having walked in pouring rain all the way from Broadway and Forty-fifth, only to find Lee waiting for him in the hall.

"You know what your problem is, buster?" his brother said accusingly. "You're ashamed of the old man's money."

"I just happen to think it isn't . . . nice to drive around in a car like that when there are so many poor people in the world."

"Oh, crikey! Listen to 'im! New York's youngest self-appointed saint has just made another pronouncement. Well, I got news for you. If you offered the old man's car to the first poor guy you met on the street, he'd take it like a shot and then he'd run over you."

One winter's day when they were on their way to ice-skate in Central Park, Lee nudged Paul's elbow and began hooting and howling as a chocolate-brown Rolls passed them, the Negro singer Marion Anderson regally enthroned in the backseat.

"There!" he exclaimed. "That proves my point, doesn't it? If she can get away with it without guilt, why the hell can't you?"

"I bet it doesn't belong to her," Paul answered apologetically. "Someone probably let her use it."

"But it's brown! For God's sake, who else would buy a brown Rolls!"

"Well, even if it is hers, it's not the same thing, you dumb jock. She has a lot to compensate for."

"Don't call me a dumb jock, you ball-less little do-gooder!"

And the next minute, they were rolling in the snow, pummeling one another—more or less what they'd been doing ever since they were old enough to stand up straight and clench a fist.

By the time they were in their late teens, Paul was ready to concede that on some occasions water was thicker than blood. Two creatures from the same loins couldn't have been more different. While at Yale, Lee was always in demand as an escort at debutante balls—he'd also married the prettiest deb of the 1947 season, or the dumbest, as Paul claimed—while his younger brother refused even to attend a dance. Lee was a member of the El Morocco crowd, sometimes picking up the tab for a party of ten elegant, decorative young people who danced the night away. Paul had never once stepped into the place and never intended to. It seemed to him that there was only one thing sillier than dancing, and that was tossing a football around, as his brother did well into middle age.

Lee was a member of the Racquet Club, the Yale Club, and the New York Athletic Club, but Paul declined membership in all three, saying that the dining room at the Racquet Club set a very mediocre table for the money it charged, the Yale Club pool was underchlorinated and overpopulated by elderly bankers, and he had no intention of ruining his health by exercising at the Athletic Club. In fact, Paul was so unclubbable that his name no longer even appeared on the mailing list of Yale graduates, having been stricken ten years after graduation because his annual contribution to fund-raising drives never exceeded ten dollars, which Yale officials considered an affront in view of the Molloys' vast wealth. But it wasn't so much that he was opposed to charitable donations. He simply didn't want his money contributing to the education of obfuscating lawyers and scheming brokers, which, he insisted, was all that Yale seemed to be turning out anymore. Instead, he gave substantial contributions to such un-ivied institutions as Brooklyn College and Queens College with the proviso that the money be used for needy students—but only if they promised never to become lawyers.

So wary was he of members of the legal profession that after having read somewhere that in a recent graduating class at Harvard College, nearly 50 percent planned to enter law school, Paul at once telephoned his brother-in-law John Phipps, himself a Harvard Law man, to complain about what he called "this tragic state of events in Cambridge," then tried to induce John, who was on the board of overseers, to resign in protest.

Needless to say, John thought that Paul had flipped. Become a leftie. A Bolshevist.

Not in the least. In fact, one thing Paul had in common with both his brother and his father was that all three were conservative Republicans. Like Charles Molloy, who often boasted that Dwight Eisenhower would still be languishing in his office as president of Columbia University if it hadn't been for him, Paul considered Ike to be one of the greatest of

American presidents. Not because of his towering intellect or magnetic personality, but because of his unshakable integrity. After the nightmares of the Great Depression and the Second World War, Eisenhower inspired boundless optimism. Everything seemed possible. Under his administration, America prospered, and so did the Molloy Company.

Like the President, Charles Molloy and his sons believed firmly in the free enterprise system, simply because, in the long run, it worked. A welfare state didn't. The function of government, they felt, was not to create a society in which whole classes of people were supported from cradle to grave—a new form of slavery—but to nurture a healthy business climate that would improve the lot of everyone, rich and poor alike.

Well, maybe the rich a little bit more than the poor.

But while the Molloys agreed on that premise, they disagreed, often violently, on what kind of restraints, if any, should be placed on American businessmen as they went about producing universal prosperity.

It was because of this, two years before, that Paul resigned from the family firm and fled New York.

During an interview with a *Time* magazine reporter, Charles Molloy once admitted that it was the Second World War that had propelled his small East Coast engineering and construction firm into an international conglomerate so huge, so diversified, that only a few outside the inner circle at Molloy Company headquarters on Park Avenue knew exactly how many pies its corporate fingers were deep into.

It all began with Liberty ships.

During the war, Molloy shipyards constructed hundreds of Liberty ships to carry supplies from the New World to battlefields in Europe and Asia, and after the war was over, the ships lay idle, destined to become floating graveyards. Seizing an opportunity, Charles Molloy bought a fleet of them from the government for half nothing and suddenly found himself in the shipping business. Apart from a few enterprising Greeks, there was little competition on the high seas, and as a devastated, war-torn world slowly began to rebuild, Molloy ships were ready to transport desperately needed goods.

As Europeans erected new factories to work in, houses to live in, offices and shops, they also began to produce automobiles for the first time since the outbreak of war. Staggering numbers of them. And the chairman of the Molloy Company at once perceived that automobiles would everlastingly change the way people lived in a postwar society. But automobiles required fuel, and half a world separated the one from the other Tankers were needed to carry the precious oil from the Middle East, and Molloy shipyards along the Gulf Coast had already begun building them. Because the family was experienced at shipping, in no time at all they owned the largest fleet of tankers on the high seas.

The profits were mind-boggling. But more than that, Charles Molloy found that he was among the very first Western businessmen to have his foot planted firmly in the rich sands of Arabia. So when pipelines had to be strung between the oil fields and refineries, it was only natural that the sheiks turn to their old friend in the shipping business—who just happened also to own a huge engineering and construction firm. Soon new refineries had to be constructed, then gigantic new gas-processing plants, then cities to house the workers, then universities to educate their children, then airports, then . . .

As the Arabs became immensely rich, so did the firm. They liked and trusted each other, the sheiks and Charlie Molloy. Both were simple, earthy people, cut from humble fabric, born in poverty. The founder of the Molloy Company was but one generation removed from Brooklyn shanty Irish, while the new princes of the desert had been little more than nomadic shepherds until a few years before. To be sure, there were some things they couldn't share. Paul's father liked rashers of bacon for breakfast and several scotches and soda at sundown, while the Arabs were sometimes given to pinching the buttocks of beardless youths. But on the whole, they were much alike. For the one, the making of money was a challenge; for the other, the spending of it. So when it became necessary to build even more cities, more universities, more airports, once again the sheiks turned to their old Irish-American friend in New York, knowing that he would give them good value for their money and would never be too censorious when they delivered their inevitable diatribes against their archenemies, the Israelis.

In the end, it was the Israelis who brought about the estrangement between father and son.

A little over two years previously, the firm had been awarded a contract for the design and construction of a new city in southeastern Saudi Arabia over a period of ten years, the entire project estimated to cost a staggering six hundred million dollars, give or take a million or two.

Paul was trained as an architect, not an engineer. For all the money they generated, pipelines and refineries failed to stir him. Shapes and forms were his passion, along with the way a structure lay on the land. So when he was invited to help conjure up an immense new city rising from the desert wilderness—each and everything to be designed from scratch, nothing left to chance—he was bedazzled.

To be sure, he knew his limitations. At most, he was a workmanlike practitioner of his trade. But he had a knack for bringing out the best in others, and as he began to assemble a team of the most imaginative architects and city planners he could find to work on the scheme, he was never happier. The Saudis had placed no design limitations on the project in the hope that the end result would somehow bridge Islam and the West.

For several months, Paul and his team labored on the project. Then, and only then, did he learn of one important qualification the Saudis *had* placed on the construction of the new city.

No Jews could be employed to work on it.

As soon as he discovered this restriction, he confronted his father. "You don't actually mean to say you're going to let other people tell us who we can and can't employ!" he shouted.

Charles Molloy attempted to soothe him. "Paul, in the long run, does it matter who carried the stones to build the Pyramids or carved the columns of the Parthenon, or what their political or religious views were? All that matters is that these timeless monuments were built. It so happens that the Saudis are highly sensitive to Israelis—not entirely without reason—

and since it's their money that's financing this project, I can't for the life of me see why we can't accommodate them on this little matter."

Paul was nearly speechless. When he recovered, he cried, "*Little* matter? It's a very *important* matter. We're an American firm operating under American laws, and not only would it be immoral for us to give in to the Arabs in this way, but it's also illegal."

His father bristled. "Could I ask you, Paul, when was the last time the Molloy Company was invited to submit a bid on a project in Israel?"

"You know perfectly well what the answer to that is. We've never been asked to submit a bid, because the Israelis have their own expertise. They don't need to import it."

"And do the Israelis employ Arab engineers on their projects in Israel?"

"You know the answer to that one, too. It's exceedingly unlikely. After all, Israel is a Zionist state."

Charles made no effort to conceal his exasperation. "Yet you're taking me to task for agreeing to the Saudis' demand that we employ no Jews in constructing a Saudi-financed project within Saudi Arabia. Quite frankly, I find your reasoning harebrained, if you don't mind my saying it."

Angrily, Paul rose from his chair. "A foreign government is dictating to an American firm, asking us to do something that's morally repugnant. That's what I'm protesting about, Father. If we sell out to the Saudis on this one, we'll be vulnerable for selling out to others in the future. What's more, if the Department of Justice finds out what we're doing, they'll haul our asses to court."

His father squinted disapprovingly. "And who would tell them? You?"

Both Paul and his father were sufficiently Celtic to have nothing but contempt for that particularly Irish weakness, betrayal of one's own, which the British had so successfully exploited over the centuries.

"No," Paul replied. "I wouldn't do that. But if you persist in proceeding with the contract, then I have no alternative but to resign from the firm."

Charles jumped to his feet, scarlet-faced. "You're asking me to turn down a six-hundred-million-dollar contract over a matter of principle! Have you taken leave of your senses?"

"No, but I think you have of yours. To be perfectly honest, I'm revolted by what you're doing."

"If you think so little of me as that, I see no reason for us to continue this conversation."

"Or begin any other," Paul answered sharply. "I quit, and I'll never come back until you're willing to admit your mistake." With that, he turned on his heel and stormed from the room.

From the telephone booth, Paul peered through the accordion door as Jean-Claude entered a booth in the main terminal, dialed a number, spoke for a few minutes, then made his way toward the exit.

He waited before following him, and by the time he reached the pickup area in front of the terminal, the Rolls was nowhere in sight. Taxis lined the curb, and an enormous Carey bus was spewing carbon monoxide into the air. Paul was a rarity among New Yorkers, having long ago decided that the wisdom and charm ascribed to local cabbies was pure fabrication and that most of them drove like escaped patients from Rockland State Mental Hospital. So he walked toward the bus instead.

As he approached it, a mud-splattered white Mercedes pulled up in front of the bus, and a familiar voice called out to him, "Hey, chief, you need a lift?"

Paul knew that voice almost as well as he knew his own. "I don't believe it," he muttered to himself, then bent over to look at the figure behind the wheel whose head seemed to be hooded in either a monk's cowl or a sweatsuit. "How did you know I'd be here?"

"Easy," Lee Molloy replied as his younger brother slid into the passenger seat. "I checked in with Andy Sinclair about an hour ago, and after he gave me hell for disappearing—"

"Disappearing?"

"You know me, Paulie. Whenever something happens that throws me for a loop, the only way I can cope with it is to flog myself physically until I drop. Get it out of my system, like poison. So I went for a long run along the beach at East Hampton. Andy thought that I'd gone over the edge. Anyway, after I reassured him that I was still whole and entire, he told me you were due in town about now and he'd sent Jean-Claude out here to meet your plane. I said, 'Oh, Andy, no way! Paul will *walk* into town before he accepts a ride in the old man's car!'" He looked over at his brother. "And was I right?"

It was hard not to notice that his breath reeked of whiskey. "You've been drinking."

"Not have been. I *am.*" As he put the car in motion, he reached under the seat for a bottle of Jack Daniel's and offered it to Paul, who shook his head. He then unscrewed the cap, lifted the bottle to his lips while steering with the other hand, and took a healthy swig.

"What's an Irish wake without a little gargle?" he said after stuffing the bottle back under the seat. "If we believe all that bushwa about an afterlife, shouldn't we give the deceased a merry send-off? I understand that back in Ireland, wakes sometimes got to be so riotous that they took the corpses off the cooling boards and danced around the room with them."

Paul remarked dryly, "One more reason I'm glad I have no talent for dancing."

Lee reached over and massaged Paul's kneecap. "Good old Paul! You haven't changed a bit."

Paul was tempted to say that Lee hadn't either, but thought better of it. With very real concern, he suggested, "Don't you think it would be a good idea to let me drive into town? You wouldn't want to be stopped by the police."

To question Lee's ability at anything that required manual dexterity was to provoke antagonism. Now, to prove his virtuosity behind the wheel, he glanced in the rearview mirror, pressed on the gas pedal, then shot into the passing lane. He zoomed past a half-dozen slow-moving cars, sounded his horn violently for a car in front of him to hurry up, and when it didn't, he effortlessly moved back into the slow lane, passing the car on its right, then flew back into the fast lane.

"Dazzling, as always," Paul observed.

"I'm a better driver than you are, Paul, even with half a

bottle of booze under my belt. And do you know why? Because driving a car bores you, that's why. It's not creative. Well, I'm just simple-minded enough to get a kick out of it." He grinned at his brother. "But as a concession to you, I'll slow down and drive like a spinster schoolteacher, okay?"

He pulled back into the slow lane, then wrenched his head from the hood of his sweatshirt. "So what are your plans, Paul?"

Without hesitation, Paul answered, "First, I plan to attend a funeral. Then I plan to go home. Those are my plans."

"Home? Does that mean you now consider California your home? Jesus, I don't know how anyone could live out there. The smog alone would kill me."

"You're thinking of Los Angeles and Southern California. I live in Northern California. There's a difference."

"Where are you, exactly?"

"I work out of Santa Rosa. But I live in a place called Kenwood. I built my own house there."

"You mean you designed it?"

"No, I built it. Everything except the plumbing and some of the electrical work, I did myself."

It had been one of the most pleasurable experiences of his life. He'd cleared the rocky site himself—high on a hill overlooking the Valley of the Moon—laid the foundation, erected the frame, roofed it, sheathed it in redwood, laid the floors, plastered the interior. Not bad for a dilettante carpenter out of Yale.

Lee asked, "So what have you proved?"

"I guess I've proved I can build a house that so far has stood up under a five point five on the Richter scale."

"And you don't aspire to anything else?"

"Well, I'm third man in a three-man architectural office in Santa Rosa. Pete Linden, who was in my class at Yale, is another. And a guy named Steve Nakamura, who went to school in Berkeley, is the founding genius. And I mean genius. He's doing some of the most beautiful stuff on the West Coast, and I feel privileged to be part of the team."

"What do you do?"

"Private residences, shopping centers, dentists' offices, that sort of thing."

Lee turned to scrutinize his face. "And you're happy doing that?"

"Very." He waited, then added, "So don't even consider asking me back to the rat race here in New York."

"Can't blame a guy for trying." He shrugged his shoulders. "I was hoping that you and the old man could have made your peace before . . . well, before he died."

"Wasn't it Mother who said that there's only one person in the world who could hold a grudge longer than Father, and that was me?"

"We've missed you, Paul. He never talked about it, but I think the old man did, too."

"All he had to do was pick up the telephone and call me. He knew where I was."

"You just would never forgive him over that Saudi deal, would you? Well, you'll be interested in knowing that the project is coming along beautifully. Just beautifully. You'd be proud of us."

"I doubt it."

Lee laughed robustly. "You and the Justice Department. Did you know that they fined us two hundred thousand dollars for unfair hiring practices? We're appealing the case on the grounds that what we do outside territorial U.S.A. isn't subject to U.S. laws."

"I hope you lose the case."

This time, Lee's laughter rocked the car. "Ah, nothing like family solidarity. I'll tell you this though, Paul. You may not think much of what we're doing, but I happen to think it's a helluva lot more important than building an office for some . . . some two-bit dentist."

Paul's face smarted. The truth of the matter was that the dental clinic he'd designed in Napa was adequate but would never win any architectural awards. Apart from economy, there were limits to just how attractive you could make a clinic where teeth were filled or pulled.

"These are going to be very exciting times for the firm," Lee resumed. "A whole new world is about to open for us, and I have a feeling that during the next couple of years, our gross income will at least double. It'll be fun to be part of all that, I guarantee you. And if you come back, I can promise you that you won't have any problems with your conscience."

"Oh, yes, I would," Paul retorted. "The last time I spoke to Father, I told him I'd never work for the company again unless he admitted his error over that Saudi deal. He had two years to reconsider his position, but he never did. As a result, I'm not coming back."

"But for God's sake, Paul, you can't ask a man to apologize to you from the grave!"

Almost wistfully, his brother replied, "Most men, no. But Father wasn't an ordinary man. If he's prepared to apologize, he'll find a way, even from the grave. If not, then my intentions are to return to California immediately after the funeral."

It was a bad day for Jean-Claude.

After reporting to Andrew Sinclair that Paul wasn't on board the flight, he was instructed to drive to Teterboro Airport to wait for the arrival of the company plane carrying Kathleen Molloy from Boston.

Nora Molloy's plan to keep Kathleen in the dark about her grandfather's death until she herself could personally break the news had been scotched by Kathleen's mother. Unintentionally, Nora was sure. Maliciously, Caitlin Phipps believed.

Thus, it was Eddie in snowy Colorado who was last to be notified. He was hosting a private party for a blond bank teller he'd been trying to get into bed for some time, so he hadn't bothered picking up his telephone. It had been necessary to send a member of Aspen's police force to knock on the door of his chalet. As the girl later complained, it proved to be costly, because between seeing the policeman standing on his stoop and learning of his father's death, Eddie flushed a month's supply of marijuana down the toilet.

Except for him, Kathleen, and Megan—the latter missed the funeral entirely because all the telegrams left at her East Village apartment were stolen by locals looking for welfare checks—everyone else in the family was winging homeward by first light.

However, there were problems involved in dispatching the

company plane to Boston, so it was almost two in the afternoon by the time it taxied down the runway toward the Molloy hangar at Teterboro.

As Kathleen left the plane, she found a somber-faced reception committee waiting for her. Not only was Jean-Claude there, looking tearful and fatigued, but also Nancy Romily.

And behind them, unshaven and disheveled, wearing yesterday's rumpled button-down collared shirt and a tweed sport coat that looked as if it had been slept in on more than one occasion, was Jake Phipps, whose relationship with Kathleen's mother was almost as frosty as the nippy March air.

As a consequence, although Kathleen had been prepared to throw herself into someone's arms and have a good cry, she realized at once that it would take all her powers of diplomacy to prevent an embarrassing scene. Quite obviously, she could be driven into Manhattan by only one of them, and somehow the other two would have to be dismissed without hurt feelings.

"Poor baby," Nancy Romily purred into her ear as she enveloped her in her arms. "I was worried that there might be another mix-up and no one would be here to meet you, so I drove down from Greenwich."

As Kathleen was hugged, she looked over her mother's shoulder and saw Jake roll his eyes disdainfully.

"I've brought some suitable clothes for you," her mother continued, "because I had a feeling you'd arrive with almost nothing. And I see I was correct. You can't very well wear a tartan skirt and Shetland sweater to a funeral. I searched through your closets at home and found two or three dresses that aren't too frivolous. They'll do until we can get something more appropriate for you from Altman's or Peck & Peck."

"Thank you, Mother. That's very kind."

My God, at a time like this, she was thinking about shopping! Couldn't she unbend, even once? Was it possible, as Jake uncharitably suggested, that she never showed emotions because she had none? Or did she simply consider it bad form?

But all of Kathleen's sympathies now went out to Jean-Claude, whose face was drawn and colorless, showing every one of his seventy years. He'd been far more than a mere valet and driver to Charles Molloy. Ever since Kathleen's grand-father had first discovered him waiting tables at a hotel in Brussels and commandeered him on the spot, he'd made life easier for his employer, knew all of his prejudices and pecca-dilloes, anticipated his every need. Now that his old friend was gone, he looked stunned.

Kathleen held his hands consolingly in her own. "How will we ever manage without Grandfather, Jean-Claude?"

With a sigh, he answered, "Ah, I shall soon be joining him, Miss Kathleen."

It seemed cruel that he should have to work at a time like this. Quickly, Kathleen took charge. "I'm sure that whoever sent you out here couldn't have known how close you were to Grandfather. I don't want you to be doing any work for the next few days. I'll speak to Mr. Sinclair as soon as I get to the apartment, but right now I want you to go home and rest."

As he turned to leave, his face was filled with gratitude. In fact, he was far too old to be performing his duties any-more, and Kathleen had more than once listened to her grandparents discuss his inevitable retirement. But Charles couldn't bear adjusting to a replacement. His solution was to humor his trusted servant and friend, never letting him drive more than thirty-five miles an hour, even on expressways, and pretending not to notice when he got into the brandy in the evenings and was unsteady on his feet.

Jake Phipps now stepped forward and held Kathleen in his arms. "Oh, boy, what a lousy birthday this is." Kathleen had almost forgotten that today was his birthday. "I've always hated them, and now I've got one more reason. How are you bearing up, Kit?"

"Better than I would have thought. How did you get here anyway?"

"Drove. I'm parked next to your mother's wagon."

Now came the hard part. Kathleen preferred to drive into town with her cousin, but at the same time didn't want to of-fend her mother. "Mother," she began softly, "since Jake is going to be driving into the city anyway, wouldn't it be more convenient for you if he dropped me off at the apartment? That way, you could go home by way of the George Washington Bridge and avoid all the traffic. I know how you dislike driving in midtown traffic."

To Kathleen's relief, her mother immediately welcomed the suggestion. "That might be a good idea. I just wanted to make certain that you had something decent to wear. Yes, that's an excellent idea. The Buick is so long, and I can never judge distances in city traffic. Rush hour begins in no time at all."

When they reached the Buick station wagon, her mother removed the dresses from the backseat and heaped them into Jake's arms with elaborate care. "I pressed everything, so try not to get them wrinkled, Jake." As he stuffed them into the small space behind the seats in his MG, she watched with disapproval, then said to Kathleen, "Do you want me to try to choose a few dresses for you tomorrow, or do you think you'll have time to join me?"

It was the last thing in the world Kathleen wanted to do, but she didn't want to offend her mother. "Why don't you stop by the apartment at two o'clock or so and we can go to Peck & Peck?"

"All right. I can take the noon train into town. That way I won't have to worry about driving in traffic. But I'd just as soon meet you in front of the store at, say, two-fifteen? Would that be all right?"

It had been a number of years since Nancy Romily had stepped foot into the Molloy apartment at the River House, and this didn't seem to be the right time to try to mend fences. Kathleen told her that she would be standing in front of the main entrance at Peck & Peck the following afternoon at a little after two.

"And thanks for coming to meet me and bringing me the clothes," she said, then kissed her mother through the open window of her car. "I'll see you tomorrow."

As they watched the station wagon drive away, Jake said, "You handled a potentially sticky situation very adroitly, Kathleen."

"Would it really have been sticky?"

"Oh, yes, no doubt about it. Your mother doesn't even pretend to like me. She thinks I drink too much and whore around and will never graduate from Princeton."

Compassionately, Kathleen offered, "That's because she doesn't know you well enough, Jake."

He shook his head in disagreement. "Un-unh, she knows me too well."

As Kathleen looked into her cousin's face, she saw that his bottom lip was trembling, and with a start she realized that he was very close to breaking down.

"I've really made a mess of things this time," he confessed. "There's something I have to tell you. You'll find out sooner or later. Everyone will. I haven't been at Princeton this year. I got axed at the end of spring term and never went back."

Kathleen attempted to grasp what he was trying to tell her. "But I don't understand. You *have* to be at Princeton. I've been sending you letters there since last September, and you've answered them."

"My ex-roommate forwarded them to me. You see, the thing of it is was that I was on probation most of last year and I needed a C average for spring term to stay in college. But I flubbed up, so I was suspended."

"But that's impossible! I was talking to Aunt Caitlin just a few days ago about the birthday party I was supposed to be giving you and Molly this weekend, and she didn't even intimate that you were anywhere but at Princeton."

Darkly, he answered, "She doesn't know. Neither does the old man. You see, the dean sent a letter home last spring, but I got there first and intercepted it. No one knows, not even Molly."

"But your mother and father have been paying your tuition. And your room and board. How can they possibly not know?"

He sighed eloquently. "The old man has always been very big on self-reliance, so I've got my own checking account. He's always put enough money in it in September to cover my expenses for the year. I've been writing checks like mad, but not for Princeton."

"But if you're not at college, where are you, Jake? And how did anyone get in touch with you to tell you about Grandfather?"

"I've got an apartment in the Village. West Thirteenth Street. The arrangement I have with my ex-roommate is that if my mother or the old man tries to get in touch with me at college, he's supposed to say that I'm attending a class or something, and I'll call them right back. Then he calls me at my apartment."

"Oh, Jake!" she cried.

"There's worse," he added solemnly. "My ex-roommate tells me they've apparently sent a telegram to the dean of students to explain why I'll be missing classes for the rest of the week. It won't take too long for the dean to figure out what's been going on. So this time it looks like I'm really in trouble."

Kathleen marveled at her cousin's talent for mischief, and her sympathy went out to him. But at the same time, at the back of her mind, she half wondered if this weren't merely more Irish trickery to distract her from her own grief.

President Eisenhower didn't disappoint his old friend.

Two hours before Charles Molloy's funeral mass at the Church of St. Vincent Ferrer, Secret Service men swarmed into the venerable structure or stationed themselves across the street in preparation for the President's arrival, and although Cardinal Spellman requested that they remain unobtrusive, it was difficult not to notice them peering into the crowd, craning their necks every which way.

It was an awesome gathering of governmental and corporate power, come to pay homage to the legendary businessman and fellow suzerain. In addition to the President, there were three senators, two governors, a number of congressmen, and the chairmen of some of America's largest corporations, among them U.S. Steel, the Texas Company, the Aluminum Company of America, and Pan American World Airways, on each of whose boards Charles Molloy had at one time or another sat.

It was perhaps understandable that among the mourners, these leaders of men and tycoons of business were most prominent, just as they had been during Charles Molloy's lifetime. Years before, he had chosen as his motto that ancient Turkish proverb: *Caress the favorites, avoid the unfortunate, and trust no-*

body, and it could be said without exaggeration that he hadn't known many unsuccessful men. Or if he had, he had had little time for them. Now the favorites he'd so assiduously caressed had come to pay their last respects.

If there were unfortunates in attendance, they were in the minority, seated in dark corners of the church. Here and there were aging men wearing small, valiant Irish tricolors on their lapels, friends of the deceased from the time he was a substantial contributor to the Irish Republican Army, whose goal it was to abolish partition in that country. But over the years, Charles Molloy had lost his zeal for noble causes, particularly unwinnable ones, and toward the end of his life even had to be reminded when St. Patrick's Day was once again about to be celebrated. When a member of the Frank E. Campbell mortuary establishment suggested that a tricolor be placed on his coffin to honor a revered son of Hibernia, Lee exploded with anger. "What the hell are you talking about? It's been years and years since my father was Irish!"

But he had remained resolutely Catholic. Perhaps the funeral mass that followed seemed interminable and often unfathomable to the President, and that was why he was seen to nod periodically, his head sinking onto his chest.

The minute the mass was concluded, the President and his gray-haired cronies roused themselves and quickly departed, rushing to their limousines, where the first thing they did was reach for the telephone. It was a Friday morning, and while the wheels of government and business could pause momentarily out of respect for a fallen comrade—and remind the mourners of their own mortality—much had to be done before the close of day.

Interment at the family plot near Southampton was to be private, and as members of the family waited near the church steps to be assigned to cars, a foreign-looking gentlemen in a cashmere greatcoat stepped forward, removing his hat.

"Mr. Olivari," Nora began as she accepted his hand. "How good of you to come."

"My debt to you and your husband is, and always will be, inestimable, Mrs. Molloy. I was in Paris when I heard the news, and I canceled everything just to be here."

"Will you be coming to Long Island with us?"

"I wish I could, but I'm due back in Milan this evening. I go directly from here to the airport." As he glanced at the young woman standing next to her, he looked as if he'd seen an apparition.

"My granddaughter Kathleen," Nora said, then to Kathleen, "This is Stephen Olivari from Milan, one of your grandfather's dearest friends."

As his dark eyes surveyed her, Kathleen had the peculiar feeling that he wasn't looking *at* her so much as he was looking *over* her and into the past.

"You're Tom's daughter," he declared. "I'd know you anywhere."

Even now, twenty years after his death, the very mention of her father's name caused Kathleen to catch her breath. But how was it possible, she wondered, for Stephen Olivari, an Italian businessman, to have known Tom Molloy?

Nora was quick to explain. "Mr. Olivari and your father were classmates at Harvard."

With sadness, Olivari added, "But I'm sorry to say that events beyond my control forced me to leave before graduation."

Kathleen's father had been in the class of 1938, so if Olivari had left in order to return to his homeland, he would have arrived just in time to participate in the Second World War—but on the opposite side from Tom Molloy.

In the distance, John Phipps stood scowling. He was also class of '38, but if he knew Olivari, he clearly had no intention of acknowledging it.

"The next time you're in New York," said Nora, "I hope that you have more time and that the circumstances that bring you here will be less distressing. Please call on me, Stephen. It would be so nice to talk to you."

"I shall, Mrs. Molloy. I promise." He grasped Nora's hand once again, then before he turned to leave, his eyes met Kathleen's.

In all her life, she'd never seen such loneliness before. It set the very roots of her hair tingling.

After he left, and as Nora entered the first car in the

procession that would drive them to Long Island, John Phipps remarked acidly, "Why the devil did that buccaneer have to come?"

As the others joined her in the backseat of the limousine, Nora said with annoyance, "Charles thought very highly of him, and so do I. Once we were the best of friends."

"He should have been thrown into jail after the war, just like Baldur von Schirach, that other distinguished son of Harvard the alumni association doesn't dare mention anymore!"

Innocently, Kathleen asked, "What did they do? Mr. Olivari and that other man."

"Von Schirach went home to become a Nazi, and Olivari left school in his senior year to become a member of Mussolini's Palace Guard, that's what. Then when things started going sour for his beloved Duce, he made a dash for it across the border into Switzerland carrying bags of money—none of it his own."

Nora sighed at the repetition of old accusations. "You're forgetting that much of that money belonged to Charles and had been frozen in the company's Rome accounts since the outbreak of war. Charles was convinced that the Communists would seize control of the government once Mussolini was dead, and he persuaded Stephen to risk his life getting our money out of the country for us."

"But for a commission!" John sneered, as if it were a filthy word.

Caitlin took the seat on one side of Nora, Kathleen the other, while Caitlin's husband and Lee sat in the jump seats. Nora said, "But may I remind you, John, that with that modest commission, he acquired a bombed-out factory, and with a staff of three, he formed what is now Olivari Industries."

Kathleen recognized the name at once. It was one of the largest producers of automobiles in Europe.

But John protested, "No matter how much money Olivari makes, it doesn't alter the fact that he was never the right sort for Harvard. As hard as he tries, he'll never be a gentleman."

Suddenly, Kathleen blurted out, "But neither was Grandfather."

Caitlin gasped, and from the jump seats Lee and John looked apprehensively across at Nora.

Charles Molloy had been the son of illiterate Irish immigrants, and his native Brooklyn accent never entirely left him. Often, he'd peppered his speech with colorful obscenities—though never in the company of women—and he had a weakness for telling ribald stories to shock his stuffy friends at the Union Club, where he'd bought membership, cash on the counter, by enlisting the support of hard-up members willing to sponsor him for a price. To people he didn't admire he was sometimes rude and abrupt, but to a friend down on his luck he would give his last dollar. In his office, furnished with nineteenth-century nautical antiques—among them a desk reputedly from Commodore Vanderbilt's yacht—he generally worked in his shirtsleeves, and sometimes if, as he put it, his old bones ached, he padded around on the carpet in his stocking feet. He was natural and unaffected, earthy and real. He distrusted prudes, toadies, phonies, and most of all, men who claimed to be gentlemen.

As Kathleen rested her head on her grandmother's shoulder, Nora touched her hand reassuringly, confident that her remark would have earned a good, hearty laugh from Charles, who would have been the first to agree that, yes, thank God, he was no gentleman!

The morning after the funeral, *The New York Times* carried a three-column article in its financial pages headlined:

WILL THE GIANT OF THE CONSTRUCTION INDUSTRY
FOUNDER AS A NEW GENERATION REPLACES ITS LEADER?

When she read it, Nora was in her bedroom at the Southampton house, the summer "cottage" where she had been taken as a bride more than forty years before, now enlarged to include twelve bedrooms and seven bathrooms. It was in Southampton that the family traditionally gathered to observe Thanksgiving, Christmas, Easter, and the Fourth of July, and it was only natural that they should converge here after the death of the leader of the clan, the man who had almost single-handedly discovered the Hamptons in the first place, building his summer cottage on the south shore when it was still considered unfashionable by New York's *ton*.

Members of the family were parceled out among the three Molloy houses. Kathleen, Paul, and Mary, along with five of her immense brood from Lake Forest, were staying with Nora, while Deirdre and her family from Paris, along with Eddie from Colorado, were with Lee and his family at East Hampton. In the Phipps's house, near the original cottage in Southampton, were Mary's husband and the rest of their children, who were being shepherded by Molly Phipps.

Jake, Molly's twin, was in bad odor, not because he was a counterfeit Princeton student but because he hadn't made an appearance the night before when calling hours were observed at the funeral home. Instead, he'd sat in the White Horse Tavern in the Village till almost midnight, then gone home with a forty-year-old divorcée he'd never met before and would probably never see again. When he showed up at the church for the funeral mass, he was wearing the same shirt—no tie— that he'd worn when he met Kathleen at the airport.

"*We* are going to have a talk," his father had said, scarcely able to conceal his rage.

"Well, that will certainly be a novelty," replied Jake, then contritely explained to his grandmother that he couldn't stand being among strangers—he clearly indicated his father—at such a time as this, which was why he hadn't appeared at calling hours.

Nora couldn't help but be fond of Jake. He was sometimes ungovernable, but he had genuine feelings. She told him that she understood.

As for Lee, since his reappearance, his strength was an inspiration to everyone, and Nora was angry with herself for having doubted his reliability. The reason for his temporary disappearance—his long jog along the beach—was so characteristic that she was surprised she hadn't thought of it herself. And after Lee picked up Paul at the airport, on the way into town he stopped at a church, still dressed in his sweatsuit, and went to confession.

Paul stayed in the car.

Later, with Nora and the rest of the family, Paul remained slightly aloof and wary. To be sure, he was kind to Nora, and she leaned on him emotionally almost as much as she leaned on Kathleen, but she had the feeling that he was deliberately holding back, unable or unwilling to become too involved in family matters because of the unhealed quarrel with his father. Along with the grief he was feeling, there seemed to be a sense of disappointment, even resentment that his father hadn't made an attempt to reach out to him.

Nora realized that the task would fall to her, and she had no inkling how she should go about it.

And at the same time that she was saying her last farewell to the man she had faithfully loved, and trying to hold together a family and a business that seemed to be disintegrating, she could not entirely forget Quentin Potter's astonishing revelation.

In the social set in which she and Charles had traveled, it wasn't unknown for men in the twilight of their years to be smitten by sweet young things in their twenties. In fact, both Nora and Charles had personally known several. But Charles had always been scathing in his condemnation. Only months before, he'd said about a banker friend who'd left his wife for an actress half his age, "Damned old fool! Ought to be shot for taking up with a silly young twit like that."

Yet somehow he himself had become ensnared. For men, sex was more of a biological necessity, she supposed, like eating or sleeping, and had to be attended to periodically for reasons of health. When they were younger, Nora had shared his ardor, but as they grew older, she saw it gradually decline in him. Often, a gentle touch or a hurried kiss was enough to communicate the depth of his feelings. But now to learn that during all that time he'd been sleeping with someone else hurt her to the very core of her womanliness. If only he'd been honest about it and confessed, "Look, Nora, forgive me, but I'm a randy old goat, doing something utterly preposterous." But he hadn't. And truly, it was the deception that pained her most.

Yet out of allegiance to him—she owed him that much—

she decided that until there was incontrovertible evidence, she would withhold judgment. If necessary, she would confront the woman herself, this Christine Lawrence.

And in the meantime, no one else in the family must know of the allegation. Charles's children and grandchildren must continue to think of him as he'd always appeared to be: a kind, gentle, loving, and—most of all—faithful man.

This morning, however, another matter engaged her attention, and she was almost grateful that *The New York Times* had taken the occasion to express its concern about the future of the Molloy Company.

The article spelled out the problems succinctly. If Charles Molloy had a serious fault, it was that he hated to delegate responsibility. As a result, although the firm employed more than three thousand men and women worldwide, he himself made most of the decisions. In an earlier *Times* interview, he'd been quoted as saying, "I've got so many Ph.D.'s working for me, I couldn't even begin to tell you how many. They're smart as blazes, and they cost me an arm and a leg to keep on the payroll. Funny thing, though. They never seem to know what to *do*. I'm the gent who has to tell them."

The evening before, Nora had asked Lee, Paul, and Andy Sinclair to join her this morning, and she hoped that they'd read the article at the breakfast table.

Lee was first to arrive, ruddy-faced from his morning run. He strode across the room, bent over her chair to kiss her on the forehead, then said, "Paul and Andy will be here in a few minutes. They're finishing breakfast."

"Before they come, Lee, could we try to clarify something?" She waited for him to take a seat across from her. "You'll remember that when I spoke to you early Wednesday morning, I asked if by any chance your father had called you the night before. You said he hadn't, but when I happened to mention it to Sally, it was her impression that Charles *did* call you sometime between ten and eleven on Tuesday evening."

He furrowed his forehead. "Sally said that? I can't imagine what could have given her that idea . . . unless . . ." He snapped his fingers together. "I bet I know what it was. Do you remember Tony Fleming from Yale? He lives in New Orleans now and planned to be in New York last Thursday. We were going to get together for lunch, but something came up so he called me. Yes! It was Tuesday night, sometime after ten, I believe. So that's what Sally must have been thinking about. Yes, it was Tony Fleming."

Nora wasn't quite satisfied. "But I told you, I think, that I found your number on a memo pad on your father's desk."

"No, you didn't," he said with surprise.

"Then I must have forgotten. But your home number was there, as well as an out-of-town number, and also Matt Rowley's. Why would your father have made note of your number if he hadn't tried to get in touch with you?"

Lee pondered it momentarily. "Well, there's always the possibility that he *did* call. But if I was talking to Tony Fleming, he would have gotten a busy signal. Another possibility is—I hate to say it—he could have been stricken before he placed the call."

Yes, of course. In fact, that seemed to Nora the most logical explanation. She told him so. "That must be what happened, because Matt didn't receive any call either. Or at least there was no message on his answering machine."

Lee seemed puzzled. "Why would Father want to get in touch with Matt Rowley at that time of night? I mean, to be brutally honest—and in spite of what *he* thinks—Matt is just a high-paid secretary. Whatever it was, it couldn't have been very important if Matt was involved. Hell, maybe Father didn't like what Matt had chosen for the menu in the executive dining room for the next day. That's about the most crucial decision Rowley's ever made." His expression clearly indicated the low esteem he had for his father's administrative assistant. "Speaking of whom," he went on, "one of the first things I intend to do on Monday is to give that bastard his walking papers."

"Your father was devoted to Matt."

"Too devoted, if you ask me. The truth of the matter is that Matt has just gotten too damned big for his britches. I've got my own secretary. I don't need anyone like him to tell me where I'm supposed to be and what I'm supposed to be doing."

"If you have no need for him, can't another place be found for him at the office?"

Lee leaned over to confide in her. "You know what a one-man dog is, Mother? It's a dog that serves one master and no one else. Sometimes when their masters die, they have to be put down because no one else can retrain them. Well, that's the trouble with Matt. I couldn't work with him, and I doubt that anyone else could either. My suggestion is that we offer him early retirement and give him a generous settlement."

It seemed an extreme measure. "He's not that old. Late forties, I'd say."

"So he'll be able to enjoy a long retirement. If he wants to get another job, he can. If he doesn't, he can live very nicely on the pension we'll give him."

"Don't make any decision until we've spoken with Paul and Andy. Would you do that for me?"

"Paul has no intention of returning to work for us. I've already asked him."

Nora was keenly disappointed. "When?"

"On the way from the airport on Wednesday. He's got a return ticket to San Francisco for tomorrow night, and so far as I know, he plans to use it."

"Perhaps if I appealed to him."

"I doubt it. Once his mind is made up, nothing budges it."

"At least I can try."

Just then there was a tapping on the study door, then it opened. Paul entered the room, followed by Andy Sinclair.

"If this is going to concern business," Paul said at the door, "I'm not sure it's appropriate for me to be here."

"Please, Paul, let me be the judge."

As the two pulled up chairs next to hers, Andy noted the *Times* on her lap, still opened to the main financial page.

"I see," he began, "that the members of the Fourth Estate are predicting our possible demise."

Scornfully, Lee stated, "Saturday is a light day for financial news, so the *Times* felt compelled to create some. There's nothing in that article that everyone hasn't known for months. Our profits were down this year, but we're on the move again, no doubt about it."

Nora turned to Andy for confirmation. "Would you agree?"

"Provisionally. You see, if I can allude to the matter that brought about Paul's resignation . . ." He watched Paul stiffen in his chair. "That *did* make a profound impression on Mr. Molloy. He didn't like doing business with anti-Semites any more than Paul did. The reason he refused to alter his position on the Saudi project was that it seemed to him that there was so much hatred and prejudice in the Arab world—the Holy Land, if you'll pardon the sarcasm—that the best bet was merely to do the finest job we could, then get out pronto. Over the last year or so, Mr. Molloy had become weary of the ever-present risks involved in doing work for the Arabs. So increasingly his attention had been turning to another part of the world. And that's what Lee is referring to when he says that we're on the move again."

Until now, Paul had looked bored and uncomfortable. With sudden interest, he repeated, "Another part of the world?"

Andy answered him directly. "It was your father's belief that sooner or later, the sheiks would start running out of money and the company would have to find new areas for development. I don't think I have to tell you how remarkably prescient he was. That was why we were the first major American firm to do business with the Arabs. He also wanted us to be the first to exploit the huge new market in Asia."

"Asia?" Paul said doubtfully. "I would have thought that the Japanese had that market all wrapped up."

Andy shook his head. "Your father saw two Asias, Paul. One is composed of islands and at the present time is under the Japanese sphere of influence. The other—much larger, almost limitless—is mainland Asia. Chiefly, the People's Republic of China."

In spite of the gravity of the discussion, Paul couldn't resist smiling. "*Father* doing business with Red China?"

Lee took up the argument. "Andy just said that Father was exceedingly prescient. Among other things, he had a feeling that once Mao Tse-tung is no longer in power, the Chinese will develop a more Oriental version of Marxism. Dad used to say that the Chinese make the best and shrewdest businessmen in the world, and that as soon as Mao passes from the scene, that Chinese genius for business is going to make itself felt.

Karl Marx didn't know or understand Orientals. Dad surely did. It was his conviction that in time the People's Republic would begin to welcome help from capitalistic nations to develop their country."

Almost reverentially, Andy remarked, "Your father used to think of China as one billion people just waiting for the Molloy Company to come along and yank them into the twentieth century."

"But Mao Tse-tung is still firmly in control," Paul reminded them, "and will be for some time."

"Exactly," his older brother agreed. "And in the meantime, the company has to establish a beachhead in Asia, just as we did in the Middle East. We have to be there when the huge new market opens, because the Chinese are going to need dams and power plants and irrigation projects and airports. The whole works. We have to be there, ready to serve them."

"On mainland China?" Paul asked in disbelief.

"In Southeast Asia," Andy answered. "That's where we intend to begin, and why we've been working our butts off trying to win a Defense Department contract for the construction of a huge new military installation in that part of the world. It will be the largest construction contract ever awarded during peacetime."

"Where?" asked Paul.

"South Vietnam."

Paul liked to believe that he wasn't geographically illiterate, but he knew next to nothing about the Vietnams, North and South, except that the former was Marxist-oriented and the latter a corrupt government supported by the United States.

Nora was more candid in admitting her ignorance. "I'm not even sure that I know where Vietnam is, but I associate it somehow with the French."

"The French would have preferred to keep it that way—Vietnam was a French colony—but they were defeated by insurgents at the battle of Dien Bien Phu. Afterward, the country was divided—a Communist government in the North, a not always benign dictatorship in the South, shored up by U.S. aid. That was the situation until recently, when the Vietcong from the North began to make incursions into the South. On the theory that if one nation in Southeast Asia falls to Communism, others will follow, the United States intends to do everything possible to prevent the collapse of the Saigon government."

"A heating up of the Cold War," Nora observed.

"It never cooled down," Andy replied.

Since the conclusion of the Second World War, few Westerners had any illusions about the Russians' intentions. The Cold War had been both real and relentless. From the building of the Berlin Wall and the Berlin blockade, to the savage crushing of the Hungarian uprising, the Russians left little doubt as to their aims: to impose their system of government on the weak, then to squash any attempt at resistance.

Less was known about the Red Chinese, but because they were also Communists and were supporting the Vietcong, most Americans looked upon them as a threat. Everything considered, it was a legitimate fear. That they were a threat to the South Vietnamese was considerably less important than that they were a threat to Americans, because a victory in Vietnam would inevitably mean a lessening of American influence in the area. And a lessening of influence would result in the reduction of power. America would be weaker, and the Communists fed on the weak.

Thus ran the argument. Paul was not unfamiliar with it. He was, however, surprised that the American involvement in the quagmire of Vietnam was about to be increased.

"You mentioned that the immediate fate of the Molloy Company rests on the acceptance of our bid on a Defense Department contract that you've called the largest ever in peacetime," Paul began. "What precisely does the project involve?"

"It will be a staging area," Lee replied. "At the present time, much of it is still on the drawing boards, but it's expected that there will be a new port, airfields, barracks, hospitals, roads, a new U.S. embassy, and military headquarters. A huge undertaking. And if we win the project, and General McFadden of our staff is confident that we will, we'll be spending about forty million dollars a month, which will make us the largest employer in Asia."

"General Mc who?" Nora asked.

"McFadden," her eldest son answered. "He joined us about a year ago. We have several other ex-military biggies on the payroll too, including Admiral de Lacey, U.S. Navy retired, and Chick Fleetwood, former brigadier general, U.S. Marines." He explained to Paul, "Since you left, Father thought that our managerial board needed strengthening in that area if we were to compete on military projects. But frankly, I also think he just plain liked the company of military guys, the camaraderie."

"I'm very impressed," Paul said with sincerity. "It sounds like fun. Too bad I can't be part of it. But I'm all tied up—building dentists' offices in California."

Contritely, Lee replied, "All right, I apologize. I didn't mean to question your contribution to the world of architecture, but I happen to think that designing an office for a dentist seems pretty damned trivial compared to what we're about to embark on at the firm. We've always worked together remarkably well, you, Andy, and I, and I'd like to see you back on the team, Paul, and help us win the contract for Project Galveston."

"*Galveston?*" Nora cried.

"Why, yes, Mother. That's the working name we've given the South Vietnam installation."

"But I don't understand. Galveston is in Texas."

Andy stepped in to explain. "That's probably why Mr. Molloy chose it as a code name for the project in Southeast Asia. It's classified Top Secret, and the fewer people who know about it the better. When we needed a name for the South Vietnam installation, Mr. Molloy simply pulled a folder from his files and said, 'Here, we'll use this. It'll confound everybody."

It certainly confounded Nora. More particularly, she was troubled because Mathew Rowley had told her that he knew nothing that would clarify the identity of "the gentleman from Galveston," as Jean-Claude described the telephone call Charles had received Tuesday night.

Now she asked, "Just out of curiosity, would Matt Rowley be familiar with this project, the one you're calling Galveston?"

"I don't know why not," Lee replied bitterly. "He pretends to be an authority on almost everything else. But why do you ask?"

Suddenly—instinctively—Nora was reluctant to elaborate. "It really isn't important. I was just curious."

"Well, speaking of Matt," Lee resumed, "since we're all here, this seems to be as good a time as any to discuss him. As I was saying to Mother just a few minutes ago, I'll have no use for his services. He was Father's secretary, although he prefers to call himself an administrative assistant. The two of them had a good working relationship, but frankly, he's always rubbed me the wrong way. I'd like to terminate his services as soon as possible. Are there any objections?" He addressed the question to his younger brother.

"Can't he be transferred to some other department?"

"I'm sure Matt wouldn't like it, and neither would I."

"I always thought he was extremely competent, but I can see why you might not feel comfortable working with him."

"Andy?"

"I'm afraid that we all like to believe we're indispensable. Matt certainly performed a valuable service for Mr. Molloy, but he's not indispensable. So I would defer to your judgment on this, Lee. If you don't want to work with him, then I think the kindest thing would be to let him go—but on very generous terms."

"Okay, we've agreed on that. Now all we have to decide is whether or not my little brother here"—he reached over and tousled Paul's hair—"will swallow his pride and come back. What say, Paul?"

"Before you answer," his mother interrupted, "I'd like a few words with you in private, Paul."

Paul was reluctant to remain alone with his mother because he knew precisely what she intended to do. So after Lee and Andy left, he steeled himself against any argument she might present.

"I'm a man of my word, Mother. I can't go back on it," he began the minute they were alone, taking the initiative.

"Yes, I know. I also know that if your father had had any inkling of how little time was left him, he would have reached out to you. I'm convinced of that, Paul."

"But the fact remains that he didn't. He had a choice. He had to choose between money and my fealty. He chose money. There was plenty of time to reconsider, but he didn't."

She met his eyes straight-on. "What would you say if I told you I thought he was trying to tell us something the night he was killed?"

"*Killed?*" Paul repeated incredulously.

"Something or someone killed your father. I know it. I've known it from the night he died, but I've confided in no one. That night, he received a telephone call from a person identified as 'the gentleman from Galveston,' and that call caused his death. Until a few minutes ago, I thought it was someone in Texas, but now I know otherwise."

Calmly, Paul urged her, "You'd better start from the beginning."

SIX

*D*uring the morning, Father Joseph Cassidy traveled a veritable Via Dolorosa through the streets of West Oakland, making sick calls on parishioners too infirm to attend church services.

Even at the best of times, it was a sobering experience, but today a winter storm was blowing out of the Gulf of Alaska and striking the coast of Northern California with a vengeance. By midmorning Father Joseph was chilled to the bone and soaked from the bottom of his decidedly unclerical yellow slicker—the only protection he could find in the parish house closet—to the soles of his feet.

His first call was at the home of an aged Mexican-American whose cancerous esophagus had been replaced recently by a plastic one and who now croaked and gurgled his prayers like a drowning man. He then visited one of his few regular colored parishioners—long ago he'd decided that Negroes preferred the participatory sport of the Baptist Church to the spectator sport of Catholicism—and found her inconsolable because a son had committed suicide the very day he'd been released from a psychiatric hospital, ostensibly cured.

Then, as if things weren't bad enough, his third call brought him to a Polish-Irish widow whose daughter was suffering from leukemia, and even though the woman didn't actually come out and say it, it seemed to Father Joseph that her faith might very well die with the girl.

And he could offer no argument to draw her back to the church. The old arguments simply had no relevance as he stood next to the grieving woman watching life ebb from the golden-haired little girl.

St. Brendan's parish was a mixed neighborhood, and his

morning calls reflected its ethnic diversity. Whites continued to live there either because they couldn't afford to move or because they were waiting for more advantageous prices for their homes once their blocks were broken by realtors. At one time, before the war, 90 percent of the area was white and of European origin, but now it was largely Negro and Latino, and while the Mexican-American population seemed static, the Negro population was increasing dramatically. But as whites fled and coloreds moved into their houses, the Negro congregation didn't grow.

Someday, in the not too distant future, St. Brendan's would be a boarded-up, unconsecrated building, having outlived its usefulness. Or, if it was really unlucky, it would be sold to one of the more exotic religions that flourished in California—barefooted monks in flowing robes, or astrologers who worshiped the stars, or plain old con men who fed on people's weaknesses.

After he finished, Father Joseph decided to play truant from his parochial duties for the next few hours, having nothing pressing until he was scheduled to hear confessions at three. Instead of going home and sharing a hot lunch with Father Declan, he drove through pelting rain over the Bay Bridge into the city in search of the address Aaron Golden had given him.

The man certainly had an eye for locating office space out of the high-rent district. Folsom Street was by no stretch of the imagination fashionable or even trendy, unless one happened to be a down-and-out wino. Through cascades of water, Father Joseph peered through his windshield at various casualties of life huddled in storefronts for shelter, and he wondered what could have possessed Golden to set up a Citizens for Kennedy office on San Francisco's Skid Row. But upon reflection, it seemed to him that it might have been a judicious choice after all, quite apart from the low rental. If indeed it was Kennedy strategy to enlist the aid of the disenfranchised to help put a Democrat in the White House, what better place to seek them out than here?

At last, he spied the address he was looking for, between a saloon and an army and navy shop, pulled over to the curb, cut the engine, then dashed into the vestibule. A directory on the wall, behind shattered glass, indicated that the Citizens for Kennedy office was two flights up. He trudged up the creaky staircase, past a printing shop on the second floor that smelled of ink and grease, to the third floor. There he found two doors. One had no identification at all. The other contained a typed notice that read EUREKA PHOTOGRAPHIC STUDIOS. BY APPOINT-MENT ONLY.

Father Joseph opened the unmarked door and entered a large, uninviting room containing six or seven olive-green desks, obviously army surplus, perhaps purchased at the shop next door; a dozen or so of what he generally referred to as funeral home folding chairs; two or three battered filing cabinets; and a single ancient typewriter that only slightly postdated the San Francisco earthquake of 1906.

Standing on one of the chairs, her back to the door, was a young woman in Levi's and a sweater, hammering a tack into one corner of a gigantic poster of the candidate.

Without turning, she said, "If you're looking for the place where you photograph naked ladies, that's across the hall."

She pounded at the tack, then stepped down. "Goodness!" she exclaimed as she saw the Roman collar beneath his slicker. "I'm sorry, but I've been here since early morning, and you're just my third visitor. The other two were carrying cameras and *said* they were amateur photographers."

Father Joseph stretched out his hand and introduced himself. "Consider me an amateur theologian."

Her engaging smile nearly closed her eyes. "I'm Vinnie Chan," she announced, then added, "Now I remember. Mr. Golden said that someone named Cassidy would be using one of our desks, but he didn't tell me you were—ah, a priest. Should I call you Father or something?"

"I also answer to Joe."

"Terrific. I already have one father, and that's enough. He's driving me up the wall, he's so old-fashioned. If he had his way, girls would still have their feet bound. He doesn't approve of me being here at all."

"Why are you here?"

"I'm in my last year at Berkeley, majoring in political science, and until now the only scientific thing I've learned about politics is that most politicians are crooks. They're in the racket for themselves. What I like about John Kennedy is that he's already so rich, he doesn't need to steal from the rest of us, and I really think he cares about serving the people. Does that sound cornball?"

"I don't think that's at all cornball. Partisan, yes." He looked around the vacant room. "But I wish there were more people on our side. Are we the only ones working here?"

"Well, at the moment, it's just you, me, and the naked ladies across the hall." She grimaced. "We have to share the rest room at the end of the hall with those . . . models at the Eureka Photographic Studios."

"Next time you run into one, ask her if she'd like to be a Citizen for Kennedy in her free time."

"You know, that's a very good idea. I didn't even think of that. What's really beautiful about democracy is that someone like a Rockefeller has one vote, just the same as those models. It's really all very—well, inspiring, isn't it?"

"It would be even more inspiring if we had a few more people here to help us out."

"Oh, we will. Later this afternoon. We've got kids from San Francisco State and Berkeley and even Stanford coming in."

"Don't adults also vote in California?"

"Sure, but they're not very gung-ho—if you'll pardon the Orientalism—about John Kennedy. You see, they're so used to presidential candidates who look as if they've just been wheeled out of the geriatric unit at San Francisco General Hospital that they don't know what to make of Kennedy. They're suspicious of him."

"If they're suspicious of a candidate because he's forty-three years old, what are they going to think when a twenty-year-old college student like you knocks on their door and asks them to vote for him?"

"I suppose they'll slam the door in my face. In fact, that's one of the things Mr. Golden said we really have to work on. We have to find some more mature Citizens for Kennedy. The problem is, once you're mature, all you care about anymore is yourself. You don't care about other people. In San Francisco, if you're over forty, you're either a Republican rolling in dough, or you're an Okie from the Central Valley who's retired here to get away from all the heat, and even though you've been voting a straight Democratic ticket since Dust Bowl days, you wouldn't vote for a *Catholic* even if the only alternative is for Union Square to be under six feet of dust by next Christmas."

"That's because most of them have never known Catholics, Vinnie. If they did, they'd realize that Catholics don't take orders from Rome on political matters any more than a Chinese-American takes orders from a—well, a Buddhist temple in Peking."

Her smile widened. "Thanks for noticing that I'm not Japanese. You'd be surprised how many people can't tell the difference. I don't think they've ever taken the trouble to look."

Father Joseph had grown up with San Francisco's Chinese-Americans. After the war, the Cassidy family moved from North Beach to the Richmond District—or the Richmond, as it was called locally—and they arrived at the same time the first Chinese families began to buy houses there. Until then, many had lived in squalor in Grant Street cellars, often with no plumbing except a bucket, but they worked like demons in their small shops or restaurants and saved money. As soon as they'd assembled enough for a down payment, they bought a house on the avenues, one of the pleasant streets running from Golden Gate Park to the Presidio.

And once they'd saved a bit more money, instead of putting it into an elegant car or expensive furnishings, they bought a second house as an investment in order to use the income to put their children through college. As a group, they were dizzyingly smart. In a single generation, they'd progressed from being cooks or cleaning women to holding Ph.D.'s in physics from Berkeley.

But still, more than any other of the ethnic slices that went into making up the population of the Bay Area, they preferred to remain in the city rather than follow the Anglo-Saxons, the Irish, and the French into the hills of Marin or Alameda counties. They liked sidewalks and pavement under their feet. And a tiny backyard garden on Eighth Avenue could contain more horticultural variety than could be found at huge spreads in Ross, where anything more elaborate than grass was thought to be vulgar and ostentatious.

Father Joe genuinely liked California's Chinese. If he had his way, thousands more would be admitted as immigrants. But what was truly astonishing was that until just forty years before, they were held in such scorn—along with the Japanese—that citizenship was denied them.

"Well, Vinnie," he began, pulling up a chair and sitting across from her, "I think it will be fun working with you. So where exactly do we start?"

"I was hoping you'd tell me. I've never done anything like this before."

He wished now that he had spent more time with Aaron Golden on the methods of popularizing a candidate. But then it occurred to him that Golden, who taught history, probably knew no more than he did. What was happening was unique. Until now, the machine, as it was called—party hacks and strongmen—did most of the work, but there was no machine in California, and even if there was, it was doubtful that it would be supporting John Kennedy.

"Well, this is just a guess," he proposed, "but I'd say the smartest thing for us to do is to try to identify the registered Democrats here in the Bay Area and convince them that we've got a good candidate. Then after that, we can concentrate on unregistered voters who might have . . . well, Democratic tendencies."

"Sounds swell. Except that Governor Brown isn't going to like it much if we start tampering with his supporters."

"Who says we have to tell him?"

"Unless I'm mistaken, the registrar of voters is a political appointee, which means that he's probably already pledged to support Governor Brown at the convention in Los Angeles. And he's the only one who'd have a list of registered Democrats."

"I hadn't thought of that."

"But I've got a cousin who works at City Hall," she continued brightly, "and maybe I could ask her to steal the list for us."

Father Joseph shook his head in disapproval. " 'Steal' is one word we must never use in this office, Vinnie."

"I stand corrected."

"On the other hand, if it's the only way we can obtain a list that we're entitled to, then I think it's not inappropriate for us to ask your cousin to borrow it."

"I see the distinction."

"Then once we're in possession of the list, we should try to contact each and every name on it personally."

"You mean call them on the telephone?"

"No, it's too easy for them to hang up. If we have enough volunteers, we can send them into the various neighborhoods to make a personal appeal."

"But didn't we just say they'd probably shut the door in our face?"

"They won't do that if we have the right kind of people making the appeal. Let's try to use the Beatnik crowd in the Beatnik areas, for example. We don't want them out in the Sunset, where they'd scare hell out of everyone. By the same token, in places like Pacific Heights, we need Pacific Heights types to go from door to door."

"I don't think Democrats are allowed to live anywhere between Van Ness Avenue and Arguello Boulevard. It must be in the deed or the lease when they move there."

"Not everyone in Pacific Heights is a Republican. My sister lives there, and she's a Democrat. Not that she has much choice in the matter. She's married to a Democratic congressman."

"Not Congressman Conroy!" Vinnie exclaimed. "Oh, I adore him. He's so cute."

It certainly wasn't the first time that a politician's career was aided by cuteness. At one time, right after the Second World War, Robert Conroy was the bright young hope of the Democratic party. There seemed to be no limit to how far he would go. Several years later, he very nearly gave up his seat in Congress to run for the Senate, but somehow he just wasn't able to get a campaign going. By the time he was in his early forties, his career had run out of steam. Granted, he was an influential Democratic congressman because he had seniority over many others, but he never really distinguished himself.

Cuteness fades fast, Father Joseph knew. Something of more substance was needed—intellect, charisma—and Conroy wasn't able to arouse the enthusiasm of his electorate as he once had. Recently, just within the last month or so, the *Chronicle* hinted editorially that it might be time to step down, that new blood was needed.

For his part, Father Joseph would be happy. Not especially because his sister, Mimi, was now living in San Francisco and saw her husband only two or three times a month when Congress was in session, but because Robert lived by himself in an apartment in Washington, and he was a healthy, virile man who needed companionship. And Father Joseph was terribly afraid that he might do something that would hurt Mimi.

She wasn't strong enough to bear such a setback. It had taken all the skills of a superb staff at the Menninger Clinic to heal her after the death of Sara, and another breakdown might be her undoing. The sooner Robert could extricate himself from his congressional duties, the better.

Father Joseph said to Vinnie, "I'll be seeing my sister tonight. I can ask her if she'd like to help us out in Pacific Heights."

"That'd be terrific."

"But if we have to rely on the handful of Democrats in Pacific Heights to elect our candidate, we might as well call it quits. Did Aaron Golden talk to you about the importance of getting new voters registered? That's going to make a tremendous difference, he thinks. You kids will be a great help in that department, because being young is a minority, and we particularly want to register as many other minorities as possible. Colored people, Hispanics."

"Then we definitely need Spanish-speaking volunteers here to help us, because a lot of the people in the Mission don't speak English."

"If we can talk to them in their own language, they'd be more inclined to listen. I'll need help down in Monterey County, too. I told Aaron I'd give Rafael Banuelos a hand in setting up a voter registration drive down there."

"Okay, I'll put a notice on the bulletin board saying we

need more Spanish speakers." She surveyed the room. "Except we really can't afford a bulletin board. Maybe I could put a notice on the wall instead."

Just then, the telephone began to ring and she jumped up to answer it. "First call all day," she announced. "Maybe the word is getting out that we need volunteers." She picked up the receiver and said into it, "This is the Citizens for Kennedy office. Can I help you?"

As she listened, first puzzlement, then something like horror swept over her face. At last, she removed the receiver from her ear and held it at arm's length so that Father Joseph could hear what was being said.

A high-pitched, hysterical voice was ranting, ". . . so you and your goddamned Pope better get out of town, sister, if you know what's good for you. We don't need trash like you to tell us folks how to vote. And you can take all those Jew boys Kennedy has working for him with you and you can . . ."

Slowly, Vinnie pushed down the button on the cradle and replaced the receiver.

For a minute, neither could say anything, so shaken were they by what they'd just heard.

At last, she asked, "Why are people like that, Father?"

If only he knew.

There was no rational way to account for intolerance, any more than there was a rational way to account for religious beliefs. Both occupied dark corners of the mind where the sunlight of reason seldom ventured.

Why were there religions anyway? Because of all living creatures, man alone saw the precipice at the end of his life, and either feared death or loved life so much that he couldn't bear the thought of relinquishing it. Almost without exception, every primitive society created two things to make earthly existence more endurable. They learned how to brew intoxicating spirits to annihilate consciousness and give the illusion of happiness. And they looked up at the sky and saw heaven beckoning to a world of everlasting life.

Father Joseph knew that it all boiled down to that. Whether one worshiped Jesus Christ, Allah, Buddha, or Krishna was secondary. Every religion promised a better life, a paradise, to the believer, and they differed mainly in the way man was to prepare himself for it. One faith scorned shellfish, another abjured alcohol. One venerated plaster replicas of divinities, another repudiated such practices. One preached the accountability of one's acts, another offered forgiveness for one's sins. One considered life precious, another found it trivial. One worshiped Brahmin bulls that roamed the streets, and so on and on.

Most of all, virtually every expression of faith insisted that it was the only true one, and that others were wrong. Thus, sharing with faith that corner of the mind—black as the caves where early man huddled, terrified of thunder—was intolerance. Because for one religion to succeed, another had to be despised and reviled.

That was why people were like that. But Father Joseph had no intention of delivering his thumbnail sketch of religion to his new friend. Instead he said, "We'll probably be hearing a lot worse before this campaign is over, Vinnie, because if John Kennedy gets the nomination, a lot of old fears are going to be rekindled. By the time it's all over, you and I may have learned a thing or two about promoting a presidential candidate. But we're going to learn much, much more about ourselves."

It was nearly three when Father Joseph finally returned to the parish house in Oakland. Having missed lunch, he brewed himself a pot of tea and made a sandwich, enough to tide him over until this evening's supper at the Conroys' house before the choir concert at Grace Cathedral.

As he ate his sandwich, Father Declan briefed him on the day's events. Nothing spectacular had happened except that the children in the neighborhood were still managing to pitch stones through the metal latticework that had been erected to protect the church's stained-glass windows.

Their persistence confounded Father Joseph. "Maybe we should erect a window on the front lawn and invite them to throw stones at it," he suggested. "They might leave the others alone."

"It wouldn't be a challenge."

"Well, I'll call Fred Witherspoon and ask him to make an announcement from the pulpit next Sunday." The Reverend Witherspoon was minister of the Baptist church three blocks away, and a very likable fellow. They'd discussed the matter once before and agreed that the children, who were not members of St. Brendan's, had no ulterior motives. All they wanted to do was practice their skill at tossing stones.

"Anything else?" Father Joseph asked his assistant.

"Only that you're scheduled for three o'clock confessions. Or would you prefer that I take it for you?"

"No, I can manage." He was almost grateful for the reminder that he had spiritual matters to attend to. Perhaps it would help atone for his secular work done on Folsom Street. He wolfed down his sandwich.

As a young man just out of the seminary and assigned to his first parish, he'd looked forward to hearing his first confession, sure that it would be an ennobling experience to listen to a fellow human being bare his soul. But he soon discovered that confessions often mirrored the monotony and banality of life. Either confessors dissembled and concealed the worst of their sins, or they were much less wicked than was commonly believed.

And from three to four in the afternoon, confessions tended to be hurried recitations from children on their way home from school. Their sins were remarkably modest. Today, a boy confessed that he'd looked at someone else's paper during an arithmetic test. A girl had had a fight with her best friend. Another had broken a plate the night before while washing dishes and had hidden it from her mother. Three young lads each confessed to impure thoughts, but were mercifully vague about them.

At four o'clock he was just about to leave when once again he heard the door open and someone sit down on the other side of the partition.

"I really shouldn't be here," a woman began rather nervously. "I'm not a Catholic. In fact, I'm nothing at all."

He recognized the voice at once. "I'm glad you came, Miss Grainger."

"I've been sitting at the back of the church waiting for the little children to finish. Did all those boys and girls confess evil things to you?"

"To them, they seemed evil."

"And afterward, did you—what's the word I want?—did you absolve them?"

"Yes, I did."

"Do you always do that, without exception?"

"When the confessor is truly penitent, yes."

He heard her move restlessly. "That's what I can't understand about you Catholics. No matter how sinful you are, you're forgiven."

"Would it be better if we punished people for their candor? I'm not sure that anyone has ever done a scientific study, but offhand I'd say that forgiving people for their transgressions is probably just as good a deterrent as punishing them."

"Would you forgive . . . a Mafia boss who'd murdered someone?"

"I've never had the occasion to listen to the confession of a Mafia boss, but if I did, and if he expressed genuine contriteness for what he'd done, I'd be obliged to absolve him."

She laughed softly. "That's really remarkable. There may even be hope for a bitch and a whore like me."

"I'm sure you exaggerate, Miss Grainger." He waited, then added, "You have a very low opinion of yourself."

"I assure you that hundreds of people share it. I've done things so terrible that if I told you about them, you'd ask me to leave at once."

"I doubt it."

She began to tick off her faults. "I'm disloyal and untrustworthy. If you do me a favor, there's a good chance that you'll wind up with a kick in the groin. I have no feelings for anyone. None at all. I'm lucky enough to have a rich father, so when I want something I buy it. And when I want someone, I buy him, too. Are you shocked yet?"

"Not yet."

"One Christmas, I was stopped at the entrance to I. Magnin by a young woman with a baby in her arms. She told me that neither of them had eaten for two days. I walked right past them and into the store because I had an appointment at the beauty salon. I didn't give them a second thought."

"But you must have. Otherwise you wouldn't be telling me."

She dismissed his attempt to find redeeming qualities in what she'd done. "My mother was an actress named Marisol Rivers. You've probably never heard of her," she went on.

"Yes, I have." It would have been impossible for anyone growing up in the 1940's, as Father Joseph had, not to have heard of the famous Argentine actress. She was a kind of Latin version of Dorothy Lamour or Hedy Lamar, and at one time or another had been paired with all of Hollywood's leading men: Cary Grant, Humphrey Bogart, Clark Gable.

"Whatever happened to her?" he asked.

"She was married another three times after she divorced my father and also had problems with booze and drugs. She died at the ripe old age of forty-two of Alzheimer's disease, if you know what that is."

Indeed, he did. It was almost indistinguishable from senile dementia. The victim became as helpless as a baby. It was very hard to reconcile it with the beautiful actress he remembered from movies he'd raptly watched when he was a youngster.

"I was ten years old when she died," Susan Grainger resumed. "My father came to me and told me that the end was near, then asked me if I wanted to see my mother one last time. And do you know what I said? I said no." She waited. "Have I shocked you yet?"

"There might have been reasons for not wanting to see her."

"But of course. At the age of ten, I was a cold, black-hearted child. Now that I've grown up—*if* I have—I'm a cold, black-hearted woman."

In spite of the gravity of it all, Father Joseph couldn't help but smile. "I'm very impressed at your self-denigration. Rarely have I met anyone who hates herself so much. I take it that someone's been prompting you. It wouldn't by any chance be the fellow I saw you with at Mrs. Babcock's, the one who threatened to use you as a punching bag?"

"That was just a friend," she answered. "I would have introduced you, but it's an effort to remember his name. He's a professional escort. He's failed at virtually everything he's ever attempted—automobile salesman, scriptwriter, film producer. Now I'm all he has left. I'm his career. He helps me spend my father's money. He's very good at that."

How could a woman so young, so beautiful, be so burned out?

"If he makes you unhappy," Father Joseph suggested, "why don't you leave him?"

"I'm afraid to. He has a terrible temper, as you saw at Mrs. Babcock's. He says he'll kill any man who takes me away from him, and I believe it." She laughed stridently. "So you see, I'm a proper mess. I had nowhere else to go but here. When I woke up this morning, I said to myself, 'Well, Susan, what's on the boring old agenda for the day? Should we try to kill yourself again? Or should we drive up to Oakland and see that young priest with those haunted-looking eyes?' You won by a hair."

Suddenly, he was aware that he'd never in his life listened to a confession like this. It was a cry for help. "I'm glad you decided to come, Miss Grainger. But since you're not a Catholic, and apparently have no intention of becoming one, why don't we get out of this box and go next door to the parish house and just talk?"

Mrs. Esposito was out doing her afternoon shopping, so they had the kitchen to themselves. While Father Joseph measured out the coffee for the percolator, Susan watched from the table.

"What do you priests do," she began, "when you're not giving absolution?"

"Well, some of our critics say that all we do is hold bingo games." He turned to gauge her reaction and was pleased to find that she was smiling.

"Then maybe you have a function after all."

"Oh, we have another, much more important one."

"More important than bingo?" she asked irreverently. "I can't believe it. What is it?"

He stood at the end of the table before answering. "We bring comfort to the sorrowful."

He heard the sharp intake of her breath, as if she'd been slapped. It was a few seconds before she said anything. "But you also believe in all that other malarkey."

"Which malarkey is that?"

"Well, miracles for one. Do you actually believe in miracles?"

He had to choose his words with care. "Let's say I understand the need for people to believe in them."

"Ah, but you don't believe in them yourself? You don't think that God creates miracles?"

"I think that man does."

"Doesn't that make you a bit of an oddball as a priest?"

"I'm sure that the same thought has occurred to my superiors in the archdiocese."

"You mean your bosses?"

"They prefer to be called bishops."

He was frequently at loggerheads with the archdiocese office and particularly with some of Bishop Moriarity's more outlandish pronouncements. To Father Joseph's unorthodox way of thinking, Catholicism had suffered two tragedies since the crucifixion of Christ. The first was that Rome became the seat of the church, and Italians were too passionate, too hotheaded, and too devoted to ritual and luxuries to supervise a religion founded by a simple Jewish carpenter. The ensuing abuses—the selling of indulgences, Popes frolicking with mistresses, and the Latin idolatry of the Virgin Mary, who was no more than a plain old fertility symbol borrowed from earlier faiths—led inevitably to the Reformation and the cruel division of Christianity. The second tragedy—as anyone who ever visited Ireland soon realized—was that the Emerald Isle exported only three things: priests, nuns, and greyhounds. And the sad fact of the matter was that Irish priests, as Bishop Moriarity was, tended to be mother's boys who never wanted to rock the boat or offend the Mother Church. Innovation was not merely frowned upon. It was met with a severe rap across the knuckles.

But Joe Cassidy was a homegrown product, 100 percent

American. Not only that, he had a Jewish mother—which, as he remarked during bull sessions in his seminary days, was one thing he had in common with Jesus Christ. Eva Cassidy was a Jew who converted before her marriage.

"You're very interesting," Susan said from the table.

"I also make a good cup of coffee." He had allowed it to percolate for five minutes, then settle.

"You're probably thinking I should be wasting a psychiatrist's time instead of yours," she continued as he poured coffee into two mugs.

"Who said you're wasting my time?" He placed a mug in front of her, along with a pitcher of cream and the sugar bowl, then sat down across from her.

"I've been through all that. Psychiatrists, I mean. I've worn out five or six, I can't remember, and all I've succeeded in doing is spending a lot of money."

"So why are you here?" he asked at last.

"I thought I'd already told you. I've run out of other places to go. And, when I spoke to you at Mrs. Babcock's, you said there was one sure cure for sadness. And that was to do something for someone worse off than I am."

He sipped from the mug, watching her from over the rim. "So what are you doing next week?"

"Same thing I did this week. I'll wake up each morning and wonder how I can get through the next twenty-four hours."

"You said your mother was Marisol Rivers. Would that mean you can speak some Spanish?"

"I used to be fluent. I'm pretty rusty now."

"Next week, I'm driving down to Salinas to see a man named Rafael Banuelos, who's been trying to organize the field hands there."

"The name rings a bell. Not too long ago, he was trying to get us to stop eating grapes or strawberries or artichokes, I can't remember which."

"Well, if you're available sometime next week, perhaps I could help jog your memory. I have to go down there to help set up a voter registration drive. It would be a big help if I had someone with me who could speak the language of the people we're trying to register. What say?"

Momentarily, she studied him with her icy blue eyes, as if she were trying to puzzle out his angle. "All right," she agreed at last, "but on one condition. I may be able to help them, then again I may not. But I don't want you to do any missionary work on me. Do you understand? I'm not interested in salvation."

"Fair enough," he replied. "But I'm afraid you misunderstand. I can't offer you salvation. That's something you have to work out for yourself."

"Then next week will be fine."

Patrick Cassidy could never quite understand why it was that in New York City the Victorian Age was celebrated by the building of block after block of somber brownstones, as dour and cheerless as terrace houses in Welsh coal mining villages, while at the same time in San Francisco, exuberantly beautiful palazzos in wood were being erected, as joyful as bordellos.

No doubt the climate and scenery had something to do with it. But more than that, it was the audacious and playful California state of mind, quickly absorbed even by newcomers. The citizens of San Francisco had rejected English Victorian architecture, in which all dwelling places looked like vicarages or workingmen's cottages, and instead lined their streets with glorious examples of Italianate Victorian, both gracious and whimsical.

But for spacious Van Ness Avenue, which blocked the spread of devastating fires following the quake of 1906, Pacific Heights would have been gutted. That wide street had served as a fire lane and preserved some of the finest domestic architecture in the world—the Beethoven's Ninth of the humble home, as Pat Cassidy once said.

It was always a pleasure for Pat to walk down green and leafy Pacific Avenue, marveling at all the splendid houses, washed in the warm, sensuous colors of the Mediterranean. It was here that Mimi settled after leaving Georgetown, and style and charm did not come cheap. She and Robert had paid far more for their new house than they'd intended to, but in the end were swayed by their realtor who predicted—correctly, as it would turn out—that it would be worth a million or more in a decade or two.

Pat sometimes jokingly referred to Mimi as "my rich daughter," and it was only partly hyperbole. Robert's family were old Californians who had amassed a fortune in timber and ranching almost a hundred years before. Originally, there was a great deal of money, but much had been spent and little had been added to it. As more than one financial adviser counseled Mimi and her husband, no family could remain indefinitely rich on money made a century ago unless a great deal of time and effort was spent to ensure that they were getting the best return on it. Robert preferred to leave that task to others, generally old college friends, and of all perils facing the rich, none is more potentially dangerous than permitting well-meaning friends to serve as one's brokers and accountants.

Still, in spite of recent small economies since purchasing the house, the Conroys lived exceedingly well. As a congressman, Robert was expected to entertain his more influential supporters in both Washington and San Francisco, but the strain and expense of maintaining two separate residences, as well as a third house in the south of Ireland, sometimes showed. Their return to California was worth it though, Pat was convinced. It had saved his daughter's life. It was almost impossible to believe that the hollow-eyed, gaunt-faced woman he'd visited at the Menninger Clinic was the same confident, self-assured woman he was having dinner with tonight.

As much as Pat loved his priestly son, Joe, he adored Mimi. So unbounded was his adoration that it once led to the only lie he'd ever told his wife, Eva, during their long, blissful marriage.

And it was over Robert Conroy, who was Patrick's trusted friend.

Mimi was still a schoolgirl of seventeen when Robert entered the Cassidys' lives that balmy, innocent prewar year of 1939. He was then a Californian assemblyman, ten years older than Mimi, and had delivered a rousing speech to the longshoremen on the Embarcadero, urging America to enter the war that had just broken out in Europe. It was an unpopular view among the longshoremen, many of whom were America Firsters and dyed-in-the wool isolationists. But Conroy's magnetism had carried the day, and he was given a tumultuous reception.

Afterward, Pat brought him home to have dinner with the family, the first of many such occasions. If Mimi was dazzled by the handsome young legislator, it seemed no different from the crushes she had on movie stars. Later when Robert visited again and again, sometimes two or three times a week, it was Pat whose company and conversation he ostensibly sought. Seldom did he say more than a few words to Mimi.

Thus, it came as a tremendous surprise for Pat to be told by one of his union members that Mimi was seen regularly entering and leaving an apartment building on Leavenworth late in the afternoons between being dismissed from school for the day and suppertime. Pat's informant asked if perhaps he had relatives living in the building.

One afternoon shortly before four, Pat stationed himself in a saloon across the street from the address he had been given. He sat by the front window from which he had a good view of the street and the sidewalk and at a quarter after four, he saw Mimi hurrying down the walk toward the building, her schoolbooks under her arm. She didn't buzz anyone but instead used her own key to open the door.

At four-thirty, Pat had just about decided to walk across the street to check the mailboxes when a cab stopped in front of the entrance and Robert Conroy stepped out. He rang an apartment, the front door opened, and he entered.

Pat was not a heavy drinker, but during the next hour and a half he had three Irish whiskies.

At six o'clock, the door across the street opened and Mimi emerged with Robert Conroy holding her arm. They quickly embraced, then Robert turned to walk in one direction while Mimi, still clutching her schoolbooks, hurried off in the other.

And that night at the dinner table, she still looked like the same chaste and innocent girl she'd always been.

The next day Pat made a special trip to Sacramento to confront Robert in his office.

"What would you think of a man who would ravish the

young daughter of a close friend, then later the same day accept the hospitality of that friend and his family?"

Wisely, Robert said nothing. Pat's rage was too huge to be assuaged by words.

"What would you say to anyone who would abuse friendship and trust, and lie with a man's daughter only minutes before sharing that man's bread?"

Conroy was prepared for almost any kind of abuse. Resigned to it. He waited for Pat to yank him from his chair by the scruff of his neck and pummel him.

Suddenly, Pat's face was awash with tears. "Why did you do it to her, Robert? She was such a sweet, innocent girl. Why did you take advantage of her? Why?"

Conroy sighed, "You don't understand, Patrick. I couldn't stop it. She wouldn't let me."

Through watery tears, Pat studied Mimi's seducer. "What the hell are you talking about?"

"Mimi gave herself to me. Freely. I did everything humanly possible to stop it. But it was Mimi who insisted."

"Mimi?"

"She knew you wouldn't let us marry because she's so young and there's such a difference in our ages. She's the one who picked out the furnished apartment. Did everything. I didn't want to, but I couldn't stop it. I love her. She loves me. She *gave* me her gift of love. I didn't seize it."

Pat didn't know what to say. Mimi was just a little girl. Or was she? Had she changed and become a woman without his ever having noticed?

"She doesn't know herself," Pat said in misery. "She's just a child."

"No, you're wrong. She does know herself. You're the one who doesn't know her."

"I never want you to touch her or see her again."

"It makes no difference, Pat. You can tell me that and maybe even scare me off because you're a stronger man than I am. But if you give that ultimatum to Mimi, she'll walk out on you. You'll lose her, I know you will."

"So what do you suggest?"

Robert waited before replying. "I suggest that this meeting between us never took place. Tonight—if I'm still invited to your house for dinner—I'll ask for Mimi's hand in marriage. Mrs. Cassidy will object, for the reason you've just given me: Mimi is too young. Since you and I both know better, it will be your task to persuade your wife not to oppose what's going to happen anyway, inevitably, with or without your consent."

Pat ached from hurt and disappointment. Of all the things he knew about the world—and he readily admitted that he knew very little—one thing he knew with certainty was that any relationship founded on flesh alone was doomed from the beginning. He'd seen instances of it far too many times. A bed was an overrated symbol of marriage. A kitchen table would be much better. Even two chairs, side by side on a front porch.

"All right," Pat said at last, "but if you ever let her down, so help me God I'll cut out your heart with a rusty can opener—and I warn you, I'll make a mess because I don't know a heart from a Bulova watch."

Robert relaxed, smiling easily now. "Well, if I stay in politics, as I intend to, I have a feeling you won't have any trouble locating it. The mark of almost any politician is a small, shriveled heart and an enlarged liver."

Twenty years later, Pat was surprised but relieved that the marriage had held up so well. Robert had turned out to be a dutiful husband, even going so far as to agree to their most unusual living arrangements—Mimi and son Owen in the house in San Francisco, he in a bachelor's apartment in Washington—for the sole purpose of trying to restore Mimi's health. It was a considerable sacrifice, both financial and emotional, but Robert hadn't balked.

Shortly before six-thirty, Pat mounted the steps of the Conroys' house and rang the bell. Later in the season, the front door would be surrounded by flaming bougainvillea and sweet-scented jasmine, and birds of paradise would be in bloom beneath the windows. But now the trailing green vines glistened in the wintry rain, the shrubbery swaying in the brisk breeze blowing off the bay.

Mimi herself opened the door.

"As always, you look marvelous," Pat declared without exaggeration—excepting her stay at the clinic. "How is it possible that every time I see you, you get more beautiful?"

"Well, I hate to disillusion you, Dad, but one of the reasons is that I spent most of the afternoon and over eighty dollars at the beauty parlor undergoing total reclamation. Robert's due home tomorrow, and I wanted to look my best. He'll be scandalized when he gets the bill."

"Preserving works of art is always justified."

"Oh, you old flatterer! Come on in. You'll have time for a drink before dinner, won't you? Joe's running a bit late, he says. Saving souls, no doubt."

As Patrick entered the large, high-ceilinged living room richly furnished with overstuffed furniture, mellow old Oriental rugs, and priceless Chinese antiques, he replied, "A Jameson with a little water would be very tolerable." As she poured the drink at a liquor cabinet, he added, "Too bad Robert has to miss Owen's performance tonight."

"There was no helping it. He has an important committee meeting that will probably last till midnight, he says. He's taking an early flight tomorrow morning."

As she handed him his drink, he said, "Aren't you having anything?"

"From long and sad experience, I've learned that there's one rule that the successful hostess must always observe: The cook never gets a drink until the meal is on the table. But sit down, Dad. Everything's under control in the kitchen. I've got two splendidly plump Petaluma chickens roasting in the oven."

"A sound choice."

"We won't be able to linger at the table because Owen is due at the cathedral by eight, and the concert begins at half past. Did you drive, by the way?"

He shook his head. "Took the California Street bus. I figured I'd have trouble finding a parking place around here."

"Joe will be driving in from Oakland. Either we can all go in the station wagon or we can use the two cars. By the grapevine, I've heard that you've induced my little brother to work for the Kennedys. How ever did you do it?"

"I gave him no alternative. It'll be good for him, Mimi.

The trouble with most priests is that they get so wrapped up in ceremony and symbols that they forget people. Joe is a very, very human sort of guy, and that humanity cries out for expression. The time has come for priests to come down from their pulpits anyway."

His daughter smiled guardedly. "I'm not sure the hierarchy would agree—not that I'm an authority anymore, having been banished from my convent school, then marrying out of the faith."

The year before she first met Robert, Mimi had been asked to leave her school by the mother superior because she refused to conform.

"Joe and I have discussed this at great length. From the very first day that he came to your mother and me and said that he wasn't entirely sure but thought he had a vocation for the religious life, I warned him that he'd be up against an unenlightened hierarchy. You remember the time, Mimi? That was when he'd go backpacking by himself in the Sierra Nevadas for a whole month during the summer, and he'd have no one to talk to except chipmunks and the occasional doe. He'd come home looking like an advertisement for Charles Atlas, he was so healthy, and I'd say, 'But, Joe, weren't you lonely?' and he'd look at me in the funniest way, as if he found it difficult even to grasp the notion of loneliness. Joe is the most . . . serene guy you'll ever meet. Self-contained, sure of himself. It's a gift, and I think the main reason he wanted to be a priest was to help people who were less self-contained, less sure of themselves. It would be a pity to waste his strength and calm on all that foolish gimcrackery those Italians have imposed on the church."

"It is, may I remind you, the *Roman* Catholic Church, and obedience is one of its chief tenets."

"You call it Roman if you prefer. I'll call it the Italian Catholic Church. The Vatican may speak for other Italians, but the sooner they realize that they can't speak for Americans, the better. No American worth his salt, priest or otherwise, accepts the doctrine of blind obedience, whether it's an edict on birth control or on the indissolubility of marriage. We Americans know that to found a faith on such things alone is to miss the point." He gulped from his glass of Jameson. "Joe is a new kind of priest, the wave of the future. He's going to surprise all of us, I'm sure."

Gravely, she cautioned him, "Don't manipulate him, Dad."

Pat seemed offended. "Who said I am?"

"It's just . . ." How could she explain it? "You've always been the firebrand, the revolutionary. The only reason you fled from Ireland was that British soldiers were chasing you."

"Yes, and I'm pleased to say that they, in their turn, have been chased out of Ireland by the Irish. Everywhere except in the North, and that day will come."

There he was, inciting the mob to violence again! He couldn't help it. It was second nature to him.

"I'm not sure I would agree," Mimi replied, "but that isn't what we're talking about. All your life, you've defied the status quo and called for change. How many times have you been thrown into jail while you were leading strikes against the shipping lines? Or can't you even remember anymore?"

"Twenty. Twenty-five. Something like that. But in the end, the shippers lost and we won."

"Yes, and now you're over sixty and headed for retirement. You have nothing to do anymore. You don't even much care for the Longshoremen's Union you helped create. So rather than relax and start putting yourself out to pasture, the way most people would do, you've decided to take on the Holy Roman Catholic Church—through Joe."

"I resent that, Mimi. Joe is his own master and always has been."

"No, he isn't. He submitted himself to the church when he took holy orders, and you didn't like that because you've never submitted yourself to any authority. Now you're setting Joe up to defy the church."

"Merely by suggesting that he work on behalf of John Kennedy during this election campaign? I don't follow you, Mimi."

"You know as well as I do that it's going to be more than that. He told me himself that he'll be organizing a voter registration drive in Monterey County among the Chicanos. I don't have to remind you what kind of person Joe is. If you think he's going to witness suffering down there in those camps set up for migrant workers and come away unchanged, then you're kidding yourself."

"Joe passionately loves people."

"But he also loves the church. Don't force him into a dilemma where he has to choose between the two. It would torture him. All he ever wanted to be was a kindly begging friar, but he became a priest to please Mother. I wouldn't want to see him hauled off to jail for inciting a revolution just to please you."

"You overestimate my influence. Joe will do what he wants to do, no matter what I say."

They were interrupted by the ringing of the doorbell. "There he is now," Mimi said, rising from the sofa. "Could you let him in, then call Owen, who's upstairs resting his vocal chords. I'll attend to our chickens."

With such a Celtic name, Owen Conroy should have had carrotty-colored hair and a face full of freckles. Instead he had curly black hair and piercing dark eyes, which had led more than one of his classmates at the Cathedral School to ask, "Are you sure you're not a Jew?"

The fact of the matter was that he *was* partly Jewish—Eva Cassidy was, of course, until her marriage—and his grandmother's features were stamped on his face. It was a lovely little genetic surprise, though both Mimi and Robert were a bit dismayed at not having contributed very much to his appearance.

Whenever Joe looked at Owen, as he did now while seated in a pew at Grace Cathedral, listening to his nephew and other members of the choir perform a rousing rendition of a Bach cantata, he could see his mother's face again, Eva Cassidy incarnate. It was uncanny. For almost five years she'd been in her grave, yet here was the same wise smile, the same tilt of the chin, the same sad eyes with bluish smudges beneath them. Not for the first time, he wondered if perhaps this wasn't what was meant by everlasting life—death and rebirth—and all the rest was merely symbolic. Or malarkey, as Susan Grainger had described it. Men and women lived briefly, procreated, then perished, yet lived perdurably in their children, their children's children, their children's children's children . . .

Unless, of course, one was a priest, sworn to celibacy and cold showers.

The vow of purity had never really bothered Joe as much as it had some of his fellow seminarians. Some had fallen by the way, unable to endure the prospects of a life without carnal expression. As he often enough explained during bull sessions in those days, the fact that he was half Irish was something of a blessing in this respect. Being unmarried and celibate was not considered an aberration in Ireland. In fact, marriage was. Of his grandfather's six brothers, only one other had married. All the rest had remained bachelors until their death.

"But aren't you horny all the time?" a friend would ask.

"Sometimes," Joe would serenely reply, "mostly at night, but I don't consider it . . . relevant."

For all that, Father Joseph always questioned his motives when he befriended a woman, as he had this afternoon when Susan had shown up in the confessional box. Had he offered to help her because he was truly moved by her suffering? Or was he drawn to her for another reason?

As he listened to the choir, he pondered it again.

No, Susan would be no problem, he was sure of that. Suffering had rendered her genderless. Next week, he would introduce her to Rafael in Salinas, and if their chemistry was right, perhaps they might be able to work together. If not, at least he had made an effort to engage her in life. As for his own efforts to register new voters in Monterey County, he would have to keep a very low profile. Bishop Moriarity would definitely not approve.

Somehow, between now and the end of the evening, Joe would have to apprise his father of Sheldon Hawkins's warning about the possibility of a Teamsters takeover of the Oakland waterfront. Before dinner, he'd just begun to broach the subject when Owen came bounding down the stairs. Perhaps Joe and his father could leave immediately after the performance. Mimi had mentioned something about refreshments in the parish house for members of the choir and their families, but he would just as soon pass them up.

There was a glittering turnout at the concert, not the sort of people Father Joseph would ordinarily run into at *his* church in Oakland. He'd recognized former secretary of defense Lester Robinson, now chairman of the board of the giant Jordon-McVittie Corporation, which manufactured airplanes and missiles. He was seated several pews in front of Father Joseph next to his huge, bovine wife wrapped up in natural mink because of the evening's chill. Not too far away was a former assistant attorney general who had returned to San Francisco as a senior partner in the city's most respected law firm. Both had spoken to Mimi before the performance and had asked after Robert, whom they had seen in Washington within the past two weeks, which was more than Mimi herself could say.

Ah, music did indeed soothe savage breasts or beasts, whichever it was, but it also put to sleep aging union officials. As Pat's head lolled onto his shoulders, his son nudged him sharply with his elbow.

"Is it over yet?" Pat whispered rather too loudly.

"It will be shortly."

"I'll certainly be glad when Owen graduates and goes off to a school where they do less singing."

Neither Patrick nor Father Joseph could be induced to partake of refreshments—"Any strong liquor?" Pat asked doubtfully and got the anticipated Episcopalian response—so after commending Owen on his performance, they left mother and son to the cakes and ginger ale and went off in search of Joe's car.

"Where did you park it?" Pat asked, having been dropped off in front of the cathedral with his grandson earlier in the evening while Mimi and Joe disposed of the two cars.

"I followed Mimi into the parking lot behind the Pacific Union Club," Father Joseph explained. "I pulled my raincoat over my Roman collar so as not to agitate the guard."

"Probably the first time an RC has spent more than five minutes on that plot of ground since Jimmy Flood passed away," Pat said, roaring with laughter.

Indeed, Robert was a member of the Pacific Union Club, primarily because his father and grandfather had also been members. Whether by accident or design, there were very few Catholic members and no Jews at all, so far as Pat knew.

The guard at the parking lot gate challenged them and they explained they were with Congressman Conroy's party. "Literally and figuratively," Father Joseph added.

"Not that Robert is much of a Democrat anymore," Pat complained as he slid into the passenger seat of Joe's well-worn Ford.

"Oh, I think he does a fair job," his son replied, setting the car into motion. "After nearly twenty years at the job, I'm sure he's beginning to feel a little jaded."

"Yes," his father observed rather wistfully, "the more you try to change the world, the more it stays the same. I guess there's reason for Robert to have lost interest in government."

As Father Joseph turned onto California Street, he braked gently every now and then during the descent to lively Polk Street.

"There was something I wanted to mention earlier," he began, "but didn't have the chance. Sheldon Hawkins dropped by to see me the other day, and he has a message for you. A warning, really."

"Is Sheldon in the soothsaying racket nowadays?"

"Not too long ago, he was contacted by someone representing the Teamsters Union and was offered a very handsome retainer if he agreed to help them with any legal problems they might have—are you holding on to your seat?—in trying to reorganize the Oakland waterfront."

Patrick appeared to be confounded. "Why the hell do the Teamsters want Oakland?"

"Sheldon posed the same question. Apparently they're not—for the time being anyway—interested in San Diego, Long Beach, Seattle, or Portland."

"That's most peculiar."

"Sheldon thought so. What sort of relationship do you have with Jimmy Hoffa?"

"Mutual hatred. I hate him because he's a crook, and he hates me because I've made my views known publicly."

"What's his incentive? Why does he want your long-shoremen?"

"The obvious answer would be money. You know as well as I do, Joe, that union pension funds are gold mines. Millions upon millions of dollars. I can say with absolute confidence that while I've served as president of the Longshoremen's Union, not one penny has been misappropriated. I'm afraid that Hoffa can't make a similar boast about Teamsters' funds."

"If he just wants more money to play around with, why is he restricting his takeover bid to Oakland?"

"I don't know, and it worries me."

"It worried Sheldon as well."

Patrick deliberated carefully before speaking. "Why did Sheldon tip you off, and not me?"

"His constituents are my neighbors and members of my parish."

"Is he going to work for Hoffa?"

Father Joseph turned to look at his father. "What do you take him for?"

"I've never been able to figure him out, exactly. Sometimes I think he's a bounder, a Mississippi riverboat gambler who just happens to be a California assemblyman. Then other times I think he's God's gift to colored people."

"I think he may sometimes have the same ambivalent feelings himself. But on the whole, I'd trust him. What are you going to do?"

Patrick sighed. "There isn't much I can do, until Hoffa's goons make a move. So far as I know, at the moment nothing but peace and concord reigns on the Oakland waterfront. I'll check first thing in the morning to see if anything is stirring."

"Good idea. But be careful. Hoffa is mean."

"So am I."

"Not as mean as you used to be." Father Joseph laughed shortly. "In fact, Mimi was saying the other day that she thinks you've mellowed a bit with age."

"That's downright calumny!" Pat thundered. "And to think that my own daughter would spread such vicious rumors."

"You *have* become gentler since Mom died."

Almost inaudibly, Pat answered, "That's because I miss her so."

"So do I. Just tonight, at the concert, I was looking at

Owen and I saw Mom. They're so alike. And it was all I could do not to start bawling."

"Death is the one thing we can never truly prepare for. Our own perhaps, but never the death of someone we love. It's an astonishing and soul-wrenching thing."

"So astonishing and soul-wrenching that faith alone enables us to get through it."

"Faith alone? Oh, I would add memory, too. Not a single day goes by that I don't think of Eva. But not in a morbid sort of way. I remember all the fine and wonderful ways she enriched my life. And I feel so lucky for having known her. So lucky."

At the end of Sacramento Street, Father Joseph turned onto Arguello, then continued on to Lake Street toward his father's house.

"Would you be opposed to a nightcap?" Pat asked.

"I thought I'd have to prompt you."

As Father Joseph parked the car in front of the brown-shingled Edwardian house, he thought he heard a telephone ringing in the front hall, and as they hurried to the front door, the sound was more insistent.

Father Joseph had his key in the door before his father could locate his own, and he quickly opened it, then dashed toward the telephone.

"Is that you, Pat?" a voice asked. "I was just about ready to give it up as a lost cause."

"No, this is Joe Cassidy, but my father's here, if you'd care to speak to him. Who's calling please?"

"Joe, this is Cornelius Murphy down at police headquarters. I'm on duty tonight, and something just came in that I thought your father might want to know about."

"Here he is now." He handed the telephone to Pat. "It's Con Murphy at police headquarters."

With unconcealed apprehension, Patrick said, "Yes, Con? What can I do for you?"

"Well, Pat, I don't want to alarm you, but we just got a report about five minutes ago that Congressman Conroy's car has been in an accident at the corner of Van Ness and Union. I gather that no one was seriously injured, but I thought you might want to know and maybe go down there and give a helping hand if necessary."

Pat protested, "But my daughter and grandson planned to stay at Grace Cathedral for at least the next hour. I don't understand."

"It's not Mrs. Conroy's car," Lieutenant Murphy explained. "It's the congressman's car."

"But that's impossible! Robert is in Washington."

"I don't know who's driving it, but it's definitely the congressman's car. That's what alerted me. As soon as the patrolman down there called in the license number—it's California-four, isn't it?—I decided to give you a ring."

"Of course, Con. Many thanks. I'm on my way."

Joe had already reopened the front door and was on his way to the car when his father caught up.

"It can't be Robert," Pat insisted. "Robert's in Washington."

"That was my impression, too."

Rain hurled against the pavement as a patrolman funneled northbound traffic into a single lane on Van Ness Avenue near Union. Behind him, standing next to a small foreign car that had been struck from the rear, was a second patrolman questioning a young man wearing a Berkeley sweatshirt, water streaming down their faces.

A gray Mercedes sedan had pulled over to the curb behind the Volkswagen. Its hood was damaged but its engine was still purring, and its wipers rose and fell across the rain-washed windshield.

Inside, Robert Conroy turned to his companion. "I'm asking you as a favor to try to be a little more civil to the police. You'll only antagonize them by being snotty, the way you just were."

Luckily, no one had been hurt, although the Berkeley student complained, no doubt with justification, that he'd been shaken up. The fact of the matter was that his Beetle had stalled in the lane without taillights and was waiting, hood up, for a tow when the Mercedes plowed into it. Robert had been going very slowly because portions of the pavement were flooded by the torrential rainstorm, but nonetheless the nose of the Mercedes had driven the most desirable part of the VW's engine into its rear seat and scared hell out of its driver, who thought he was about to be killed.

With exasperation, the woman seated next to Robert suggested, "Why can't we simply give the police a little something, and that young man too, so they can forget this ever happened and we can get out of here and let the insurance people handle things?"

"You don't bribe policemen and Berkeley students the way you bribe headwaiters."

"But I thought you said that everyone in the world had a price."

Nearly everyone. But it took extraordinary skill to determine exactly what it was, and the utmost diplomacy to deliver the payment. A hundred-dollar bill in an envelope stuffed casually into a pocket while patting someone on the back was rarely returned. But the same hundred-dollar bill dropped into the palm of a hand—bare money meeting bare flesh—stood a good chance of being rejected, because people liked to believe they had scruples even when they didn't. They hated to give up their illusions about how incorruptible they were. Sealed in an envelope, money was a gift. In the palm of one's hand, it was an outright bribe.

Robert's primary concern was that when the accident was reported he had been identified by name, and perhaps some hungry journalist—was ever a journalist not hungry?—was even now rushing to the scene. Impatiently, he consulted the Rolex on his wrist. The patrol car had arrived almost ten minutes before, only a few minutes after the collision. Someone on the police beat at the *Chronicle* or *Examiner* could appear any second.

"Listen carefully," he began urgently. "If any newspapermen show up, we'll have to get our stories straight. Why don't we just say that you're an old college friend of mine I happened to bump into at the airport tonight and I offered to give you a lift to your hotel."

"Where did you go to college?"

"Stanford."

"But how lovely! That means I'm getting up in the world. I had to settle for the University of Akron."

At any other time, Robert would have been tempted to say that it showed. Not that he had anything against graduates of the University of Akron, but he had suddenly taken an immense dislike to the woman next to him. If a photographer from the *Chronicle* snapped her picture, he could well imagine what it would look like in the morning's paper. In person, she was very attractive. But he had a feeling that she'd photograph hard and brittle. Cheap.

Suddenly, he could wait no longer. "Dammit, I'm going to pull rank and try to get out of here. You stay here in the car, will you, and if any newspaperman comes snooping around asking questions, simply tell him that you went to Stanford with me."

"What class?"

"Nineteen thirty-eight."

"Oh, God, that means I graduated when I was twelve years old. I'm a prodigy!"

Angrily, he pushed the door open and stepped into the pouring rain. Hatless, he pulled up the collar of his raincoat to cover his neck, then hurried to where the police officer was questioning the student.

To the young man in the soaked sweatshirt, he began, "Mr. Ashley, I have your address and phone number, and someone from my office will be getting in touch with you first thing in the morning. I'm just terribly relieved that you weren't injured."

"That makes two of us," the youth replied sharply.

Robert turned to the policeman. "Could we conclude this now, Officer Martinez? My car is still in operating condition, and I can't see that I'm accomplishing anything by remaining here. With your permission, I'd like to leave."

Before the patrolman could answer, however, they both turned to watch a car weaving in and out of backed-up traffic, its lights blinking, its horn honking. In a minute, it pulled up behind the police cruiser and two figures dashed from it.

"Then it *is* you, Robert," Pat cried as he bore down on his son-in-law. "Are you all right?"

Robert's face fell. "It's nothing serious. But for God's sake, how did you find out about it?"

"A friend down at police headquarters gave me a ring, soon as he heard." Pat's face reflected the confusion he felt. "But I don't understand. Mimi said you were in Washington and weren't due till tomorrow."

"I finished my business earlier than I expected and managed to get space on a flight tonight. I didn't have time to tell Mimi about the change of plans."

Pat was about to ask what the Mercedes was doing at the airport, but then recalled that it was standard procedure. The day before Robert's arrival, his secretary always picked up his car at the Pacific Avenue garage and left it at a reserved parking place in the airport parking lot. It was easier for her to drop it off sometime before his arrival rather than wait for him, because Robert never seemed to know until the very last minute which flight he'd be on. On too many occasions in the past either Mimi or Miss Rennick, his secretary, had waited hours at the airport. This way, he could make his way home even at three in the morning without disturbing anyone.

Robert again turned to the patrolman at his side. "Would it be all right if I left now, Officer Martinez?"

"I guess you're free to go, sir."

Robert gripped his hand and shook it manfully. "I want to commend you for the professional way you've handled everything. I'll be sure to bring it to the attention of the chief of police the first chance I get."

The words of praise had the desired effect. A smile lifted the young Hispanic's lips. "Thank you, Congressman."

At the mention of the title, the Berkeley student's eyes narrowed. Perhaps because of the downpour, he hadn't been able to get a good look at the man whose car collided with his. Or perhaps he'd just been too rattled to hear the name correctly when Robert volunteered it. But now as he looked at the Mercedes in the distance and read its license plate, bent but legible—California-four—he had all the confirmation he needed.

"And Mr. Ashley," Robert continued, "let me assure you

that you won't be out of pocket as a result of this. My insurance company will contact you in the morning, and I'm sure we'll be able to work out something to your satisfaction."

He stretched out his hand, but the student declined it. Instead, he looked once more in the direction of the Mercedes and said, "I just hope that someone is going to see the young lady home, Congressman."

Until now, neither Patrick nor Father Joseph had perceived anyone in the car. But as the garish revolving light from the cruiser's roof flashed into its front seat, they saw a figure seated there, face averted. She was platinum blonde and smoking a cigarette.

Without a word, Father Joseph turned on his heel and walked back to the Ford.

It was well past midnight and all the lights in the Conroy home on Pacific Avenue had been extinguished by the time Robert steered his damaged Mercedes into the driveway, then drew up alongside his wife's station wagon in the garage. As he cut the ignition, he saw the rosy glow of a pipe in the front seat of the Buick, then caught a whiff of Pat Cassidy's aromatic smoking tobacco through the open window.

Pat asked, "Can you spare a minute or two for one of your constituents, Congressman?"

With tired resignation, Robert left his car and slid next to his father-in-law in the Buick. "How did you get here?"

"Joe dropped me off on his way home."

Robert spat out the words, "Joe is so goddamned self-righteous."

"If a priest can't be self-righteous, who can be?" Pat puffed contentedly on his pipe, leaning back in the seat to stretch his legs. "You know, Robert, what you're doing could be very, very damaging to your career."

His son-in-law made no attempt to conceal his annoyance. "Smoking a pipe can be damaging to the mouth and throat. Drinking champagne can be damaging to the liver. Making love can be damaging to the prostate. Did you come over here just to deliver a tiresome homily?"

In the darkness, Pat turned to face him. "No, I came as your wife's father, and grandfather to your only son, to ask you who that woman was in the car with you this evening."

Robert exhaled his breath before replying. "Dammit, I knew that you and Joe would jump to conclusions! I just knew. Well, you'll be relieved to learn that it's a perfectly respectable relationship. She happens to be an old friend of mine from Stanford I bumped into at the airport tonight, and since she's visiting here for a few days, I offered to give her a lift to the Fairmont."

"Mimi wasn't expecting you till tomorrow," Pat reminded him.

"I was able to cut out from a meeting earlier than I'd expected. I went directly from the Hill to the airport and took my chances as a standby. I don't even have any luggage except my briefcase. I was put on standby for two flights but lost my seat on both occasions when passengers with confirmed reservations turned up. I didn't call Mimi to tell her about the change of plans for the simple reason that I didn't know when I'd be pulling into town. End of explanation—not that I owe you one. Am I now free to go to bed, or hasn't this inquisition adjourned?"

Pat's judgments were always intuitive, not intellectual. Until Robert's strident protest, he'd been quite prepared to accept his account of the evening's events. But now there was something about it that didn't quite ring true.

"Robert," he began firmly, "I'll never forgive you if you hurt Mimi."

"I just told you, it was all perfectly innocent."

"Perhaps it was. But do I have to remind you that it didn't appear that way. A happily married man simply doesn't share his car with a beautiful young woman late at night—unless she's a friend of the family. It just doesn't *look* good."

"What am I supposed to say? How can I prove that it's not what you and Joe thought it was?"

"Well, for one thing, you can make damned sure that it never happens again."

"The likelihood of my ever bumping into someone like that again—someone I haven't seen for over twenty years—is very, very slim. And I assure you that it could never happen a second time."

"All right, then we'll leave it at that." Pat touched the door handle, preparing to leave. "Whether or not you mention it to Mimi is no concern of mine. I certainly won't." He waited, his hand poised over the handle. "But I want you to remember, Robert, what a long haul it's been, bringing her back to life after Sara's death. I couldn't bear to see her reduced to that misery again. But I'm afraid it could happen if . . . well, if she jumped to the conclusions Joe and I did tonight."

"I'm aware of that, Patrick. This hasn't been easy for me either, these last few years. I'm lonely in Washington, I kid you not. I would have done anything to keep my wife and son near me, but when her psychiatrists at Menninger suggested it would be a good idea to get Mimi out of Washington, I didn't protest. I was one hundred percent behind her. Why would I let her down now?"

"Because we're all human," Pat answered. "You are and I am. As much as we would like not to be, sometimes we're ruled by passion, not reason. You're a comparatively young, virile man, and it's only natural that you might crave the company of women. And isolated as you are from your family, it's even more understandable—"

"Patrick! For the last time! It isn't what you think. I never touched that woman in my car tonight."

Pat felt the tension drain from his muscles. "All right, Robert. I believe you. I won't tarry. I'll leave you now and you can go in and surprise Mimi."

"But how will you get home?"

"The walk will do me good." Pat at last opened the door and stepped out, then scanned the sky as he left the garage. It was starry now. "Storm's over, so it'll be a pleasant walk. Most of the time I'm too busy to look at the sky, but tonight I intend to give it my full attention. Good night, Robert."

SEVEN

*T*hree days after returning to Cambridge, Kathleen Molloy had just left her eleven o'clock class and was about to remove her bicycle from the rack when a husky voice said behind her shoulder, "Is it a habit of yours to stand guys up? Or did you make an exception just for me?"

It was a frigid twenty-two degrees, and Ted Birmingham was bundled up in a sheepskin jacket, his chin half buried in a long crimson and white muffler. Under a black knit cap rolled down partly over his forehead, his eyes were baleful.

"I'm terribly sorry," Kathleen began. "I really did try to get in touch with you. You see, I had to leave campus suddenly last Wednesday—it was an emergency—so I couldn't meet you in front of the library. But when I called Eliot House to let you know, they said you didn't live there."

"What gave you the idea that I did?"

She refreshed his memory. "But that's how I met you. At an Eliot House dance. Don't you remember?"

His expression softened as he began to grasp what had happened. "I get it now. You thought I lived at Eliot because I went to the dance. Actually, I just saw it announced on the bulletin board there last January, so I crashed it. But I don't live there. I *work* there—in the dining room. I guess I should have told you."

Now it was her turn to be embarrassed. "I should have figured something like that. It's my fault for jumping to conclusions."

A boyish grin lifted his lips. "We sure are full of apologies today, aren't we?"

In spite of the sadness she felt, still reeling from the events of the past week, Kathleen found his smile infectious. "I hope you didn't wait in front of the library too long."

"Only about *two* hours," he answered with exaggerated hurt feelings, "in *freezing* rain, getting madder and madder by the minute. By the time I called it quits, I think I'd probably used every curse word in my very extensive vocabulary."

"If you'd telephoned my dorm, chances are that they would have told you I'd signed out on Wednesday."

"I considered that. But there was always the possibility that you'd just decided you didn't *want* to ride to New York with me. Like maybe you thought I was a sex maniac or something. My self-esteem couldn't cope with that, so instead I preferred to believe that you just probably forgot or got a lift from someone else."

"I *am* sorry."

He took the bicycle from her hands and guided it from the rack. "How about starting all over? What would you say if I asked you to have lunch with me?"

"But I thought you work at Eliot House."

"Only at suppertime. And even then I don't work very hard. I wear a little white jacket and pick up plates and silverware from the tables, and for that I get a free meal. But I almost always have lunch at the apartment. You see, I petitioned the dean of students for permission to live outside the residence halls for senior year, and he was only too glad to get rid of an irritant. Today I was thinking about toasted cheese sandwiches and tomato soup. How does that sound? Or do you have to eat at the dorm?"

It wasn't compulsory. But if she didn't make an appearance, it was more than likely that her rommate, Carolyn Biddle, would fret. Ever since Kathleen had returned to campus, Carolyn had been very helpful—almost excessively so—and so had everyone else in the dorm. In fact, it was difficult to step into the hall without running into someone gushing well-intentioned words of condolence. The problem was, they only succeeded in making her feel worse.

But apparently Ted Birmingham never read the newspapers—God knows, her grandfather's death had received an enormous amount of publicity—or if he did, he simply hadn't made the connection. Whichever, Kathleen considered it a kindness.

"On a cold day like today, I can't think of a nicer lunch than tomato soup and toasted cheese sandwiches," she heard herself say.

"Terrific. I don't live too far away. Just off Brattle Street." He began to wheel her bike down the sidewalk, steering its handlebar with one hand. "But there's something I'd better tell you. I mean in case you have any problems in that department. My roommate's a Negro."

How could Kathleen have any problems in that department? She'd never *known* one before. Except for a Negro doorman who used to work at the River House when she was a child, she couldn't recall ever having spoken more than a few words to one either. And several years ago, the cheerful colored man had been replaced by an unsmiling Central European, for what reason she couldn't say. As for knowing any Negroes at Harvard, she was surprised that there *were* any. She'd never seen one in any of her classes. Ted must have combed the campus to find a colored roommate.

"No, I don't have any problems in that department," she answered truthfully, never having been tested.

And suddenly she was more intrigued than ever by this strange fellow next to her. And she couldn't help but wonder what her mother would make of him.

Who was he? Nancy Romily would want to know. Had he gone to Groton or St. Paul's, and if not, why not? Was he a member of the Porcellian Club? And if he wasn't, why wasn't he?

And above all, why in the world would anyone seek out a Negro roommate except as self-punishment?

Ah, a dangerous young man to know, Kathleen imagined her mother saying. And somehow, the strangeness of Ted Birmingham, even the peril she felt, made him all the more irresistible.

Ted lived in a faded yellow early-Victorian house whose chief architectural features were elaborate gingerbread at the eaves and a rickety wooden staircase that climbed the outside wall to his second-floor apartment. The treads were worn thin, the banister shaky from having supported generations of students when they came home reeling after a night's debauch at Jim Cronin's bar.

"Clayton?" Ted shouted as he opened the door. "I hope you've got some clothes on, because we have a guest for lunch."

"What the fuck did you say?" a resonant voice answered over splashing water from the shower in the bathroom.

"Pardon the language," Ted said as he showed Kathleen into the living room. "I mean, in case—"

"I have problems in that department?"

"Exactly. We don't often get to entertain a Cliffie for lunch. And Wednesdays are peculiar days anyway because Clay doesn't have any morning classes, so he stays up all night Tuesday, catching up on his work, sleeps late, has lunch, then runs off to a one o'clock in zoology."

"You don't have to apologize for him."

"Yeah, I know. I just want you to like him. And around here, nice guys aren't supposed to say 'fuck' in front of Cliffies."

"You'd be surprised at some of the things you can hear in my dorm."

"No, I doubt that I would be. But I have a feeling you are."

He had a point. Prudery was something that was hard to grow out of, and sometimes the salty language of the girls in her dorm shocked her. The most popular girl in her class swore like a drunken sailor. Kathleen had long ago decided that obscenities were used by people with feeble imaginations, and as a result she seldom resorted to swear words herself.

The living room furniture consisted of two tattered armchairs and a lumpy sofa, both of which had Salvation Army written all over them, the sort of things that students used for a few years, then hauled back to the shop for resale when they graduated. The floor was uncarpeted except for two or three small rugs in need of vacuuming, and two oak desks had been pushed together in front of the twin windows overlooking the street. There were books scattered everywhere: on the desks, the floor, the sofa, the chairs, and heaped in terrible disorder on shelves of pine supported by bricks.

Over the shelves were huge posters. Kathleen at once recognized Albert Schweitzer and Mahatma Gandhi, but a third man, a colored man with a gentle expression and luminous eyes, she couldn't place, so she asked Ted who he was.

"That's the Reverend Martin Luther King, Jr. He's a hero of Clay's and mine."

"Martin Luther King," she repeated, savoring the name. "Wasn't he involved in a bus boycott or something down South a few years ago?"

With scarcely concealed condescension, he replied, "That bus boycott or something, as you call it, just happened to be the beginning of one of the three most important events in American history! Don't they teach you anything about history at Radcliffe?"

"I'm an English major," she said apologetically. "Mostly eighteenth and nineteenth century."

"Well, that doesn't mean you have to lock yourself out of the twentieth century. Come help me fix lunch and I'll fill in the gaps in your education, okay?"

She followed him into a small kitchen, where he extracted two cans of Campbell's tomato soup from a cupboard—"one of the glories of American cuisine," he described it—then handed her an opener and a saucepan. "How about if I put you in charge of the soup?" He arranged six slices of whole wheat bread on the counter, then spread them with a light coating of mayonnaise before going on. "There are three, and only three, truly important events in American history." He arranged thick slices of cheddar over the mayonnaise, then placed two rounds of dill pickle on top of each, covered them with a slice of bread, then buttered them on both sides.

"The first significant event was when the American colonies broke away from the Old World and established a new nation with liberty and justice for all. That's spelled a-l-l. It was an incredibly novel idea. Until then, the world was divided between the well-off and the starving, the rich and the poor, lords and ladies and the lackeys who served them. Now, for the first time, the framers of the Constitution said that all men were created equal. The only problem was"—he lifted the sandwiches onto a large skillet, covered it, then set it on a burner—"that even while the Founding Fathers were writing the Bill of Rights, slaves were being conscripted in Africa and brought against their will to work on the plantations of the South. The contradiction never really bothered most people until the middle of the nineteenth century, when abolitionists in the North began to wonder how there could be slavery if everyone was created equal. Are you following me so far?"

"Raptly," Kathleen answered, stirring the soup.

"So the second important event in American history took place," Ted resumed, picking up the cover and turning his sandwiches. "That was the Civil War. Some people will try to tell you that the war was fought to preserve the Union, but that's a lot of baloney. There could *be* no Union with slavery. The whole idea of America was that everyone here had equal rights. Slavery had to be abolished, and it was. But then the problem was—"

"Do there always have to be problems in history?"

"Always."

"Then I'm glad I'm an English major."

"The problem," he went on, "was that after the slaves were emancipated, everyone forgot about them. Almost without exception, the freed slaves stayed in the South—millions of crude, uneducated people whose level of civilization wasn't much greater than it had been in Africa. Having lost a war because of them, southerners were understandably reluctant to invite them into their parlors. Or their schools. Or their rest rooms. Or their lunch counters. They established Jim Crow laws to keep them separate. Then"—he turned to her—"are you ready? Then came that 'bus boycott or something,' as you called it. In December 1955, a very brave woman named Rosa Parks boarded a bus in Montgomery, Alabama, and took a seat. When a white man got on, the bus driver ordered her to give up her seat and stand at the rear of the bus. And do you know what she did? They should put that woman's face on a postage stamp! She said no. And after all, why should she relinquish her seat? She was equal, wasn't she? And that was the beginning of the third most important event in American history: the civil rights movement. Before it's over, we'll know once and for all what this country is really about. Whether it's a nation of free men or a nation of racists."

From the doorway came the sounds of gently clapping hands, and when Kathleen looked up, she saw a strikingly good looking brown-faced young man wearing tan cords and a crimson sweater emblazoned with a white *H*.

"I like it," he said as he entered the kitchen, "but isn't it sort of early to be delivering a sermon? Anyway, I didn't know we had company."

"I yelled when we came in, but I guess you didn't hear. Kathleen, this is Clay Gibson. Clayton, Kathleen Molloy. She's having lunch with us."

"Oh, sure. You're the one who stood Ted up last week."

"Not exactly. I think we've thrashed that out by now. It's nice to meet you, Clay."

"Same here." He lifted the cover of the pan in which the sandwiches were grilling. "Ah, good. You remembered to snitch some cheese from Eliot House."

Ted explained, "This is an unofficial annex of the Eliot House kitchen. The cook was going to throw out about three pounds of cheese because I told him I saw some weevils near where it's kept."

"Weevils!" Clay exploded. "I draw the line at weevils."

"Don't get excited. I just told him there were weevils because I knew he'd want me to throw the cheese out. So how about making yourself useful, Clay, and setting the table while Kathleen and I attend to our chic little lunch."

As Ted's roommate scooped up a handful of silverware from a drawer and began to arrange it on the table, Kathleen asked, "Where did you two meet each other anyway?"

"At a CORE meeting in Boston last spring," Ted answered.

Kathleen wasn't sure she had heard correctly, so she repeated, "Corps? As in esprit de?"

"Listen to her!" Ted complained, nudging Clay with his elbow. "Now you know why I delivered the lecture." Then to Kathleen, he said rather indignantly, "You don't know what CORE is? Where have you been for the last ten years?"

Sheltered was where she'd been, but she decided not to go into it. "Now that you mention it, I think I do know what it is. It has something to do with the NAACP, doesn't it?"

Clay sighed, "This can't be true. I must be hallucinating."

"It's true," Ted groaned. "What we have here is that rara avis, an English major from Radcliffe who can probably recite verbatim all the fifth-rate poetry written by a Puritan metaphysical poet named Edward Taylor—"

"How'd you know I've been studying Taylor?" Kathleen asked in surprise.

"Snuck a look at your lecture notes while I was making the sandwiches," he explained. "You can do *that*. Then you say that the Congress of Racial Equality has something to do with the NAACP. I mean, I don't believe it. What do you Cliffies talk about anyway?"

Ruefully, Kathleen had to admit that the conversations at her dorm rarely went beyond recapitulations of last weekend's date or complaints about sadistic professors. Briefly, after Charles Van Doren's fall from grace on the *$64,000 Question*, they'd discussed public morality, but private morality—was so-and-so actually sleeping with so-and-so?—soon replaced it.

In self-defense, Kathleen replied, "I don't think there are any Negroes in my dorm."

If she'd expected to win approval, she was mistaken. Vehemently, Ted said, "*I* knew about CORE long before I met Clayton. Didn't anyone tell you that you're in college to broaden your outlook?"

Clay came to her rescue. "I think you're being tough on her. I'm sure her parents didn't send Kathleen to Radcliffe to become part of a revolution." Sympathetically, he explained, "The difference between the National Association for the Advancement of Colored People and CORE, Kathleen, is in the interpretation of the word 'advancement.' Most NAACP people are patient, willing to advance very, very slowly. CORE members tend to be younger and much angrier. We want to be advanced right *now*."

"Clay and I are also members of SNCC, the Student Nonviolent Coordinating Committee. But I suppose you've never heard of that either."

Yes, she had. "Just recently, SNCC tried to desegregate a lunch counter somewhere. North or South Carolina, I forget which."

"There's hope for you yet. It happened at Greensboro, North Carolina, and it's just the beginning. This year, we hope to do the same thing all over the Deep South. Clay and I plan to go down to Georgia over spring vacation."

Kathleen was undeniably impressed. At spring break, it was traditional among Ivy League undergraduates to make their great escape to Bermuda or Fort Lauderdale. There, under the tropical sun, they slept too little, drank too much, and were very, very silly. At the end of their bacchanalia, they returned to campus and showed off their new suntans for the benefit of their luckless classmates who'd been left behind.

And now to discover that two Harvard seniors weren't interested in sunshine and surf but in joining a lunch counter demonstration in Georgia!

"Won't it be dangerous?" she asked.

Ted answered. "It shouldn't be if the southerners follow the rules. You see, our protest will be nonviolent, and we're hoping that the response we get will also be nonviolent. That lesson we've learned from Gandhi. Very often, it's easier to shame people into correcting injustices than it is to force them. But southern whites are feeling very beleaguered right now, so there's no telling what they'll do."

"We expect resistance," Clay contributed. "And I for one can understand why a lot of those crackers down South aren't going to be too happy when a bunch of smart-alec college kids from up North tell them what to do. I sympathize with southern whites. After the Civil War, northern abolitionists said, 'Okay, the slaves are free. Now they're *your* problem.' For a hundred years, white southerners have been trying to cope with one of the worst social messes in history, and now we're going to tell them that they did it the wrong way, and they'll have to do it our way. It's not going to be easy."

When the sandwiches were done, Ted scooped them from the pan and placed them on plates while Kathleen emptied the soup into three unmatching F. W. Woolworth's bowls, adding a dollop of butter on top.

"Okay, let's dig in while everything's hot," Ted suggested.

Kathleen was grateful that no one had helped her into her chair. It seemed such an artificial gesture for someone perfectly capable of sitting down by herself. In spite of the badinage directed at Radcliffe women, they were treating her as an equal. Almost.

"It's all very hard to understand," she said at last. "This race business, I mean. My whole family is . . . well, pretty conservative politically. They're all very patriotic, mind you."

"There's only a very short step between patriotism and fascism," Ted reminded her. "The perfect example is Nazi Germany."

"Yes, I suppose you're right. But what I'm trying to say is that most members of my family think that . . . well, that social change can't be legislated. I know this may offend you, Clay"—she turned to him—"but take American Indians. I once heard someone in my family"—actually, it was her grandfather—"say that what's happened to them hasn't been genocide, as they claim, but suicide. Because look at all the immigrants from Europe, who started out with virtually nothing and now have everything. I mean . . ." She stopped in embarrassment.

"What she means, Clay," Ted began, coming to her aid, "is how come Negroes, who've had three hundred years to get to the top in America, are still at the bottom? That's what you're trying to say, isn't it, Kathleen?"

Apologetically, she offered, "I warned you I'd probably offend you."

"No, you haven't," Clay answered, putting his soup spoon down. "I can see why it doesn't make much sense. Here you have all these other people being dropped into the melting pot—illiterate Russian Jews, ignorant Italian peasants, penniless Irish, Polish, Germans, the works—and, presto! they come out one hundred percent Americans in no time at all. Business tycoons, leaders of society, mayors, governors. So how come it doesn't work for Negroes? Right?" He waited for her to nod. "The answer, Kathleen, is that color is one thing that can never be melted down. If you're black when you go into the pot, you're still black when you come out. So we look different in a society where everyone else looks pretty much the same. You following me? I went to high school with some of the dumbest white kids you could imagine who lived in rundown old houses on the edge of town. I was the smartest kid in my class, or at least I had the highest average. My dad works for the post office, and he takes pride in his house. Here I am at Harvard. I even own a J. Press suit. But when I go home to Hudson, New York, I'm just another nigger. Those kids I went to high school with can play golf at the country club, if they can afford it. But I wouldn't be allowed to." He picked up his spoon again. "After a couple hundred years of that, you give up trying. Because no matter how much you change—even if you have a Harvard degree—you can't change the one thing that's unforgivable in this country of ours. You're *different.*"

His plea for understanding was impassioned, but quiet and well reasoned. Until now, Kathleen had always looked at the race problem through her grandfather's eyes. If people wanted to advance, let them pull themselves up by their own bootstraps, he often said. But what perhaps he failed to understand was Clay's argument that for a Negro, there was no "up" to advance to, even if they tried. So why bother?

She wanted to know more about him. "What brought your family to Hudson, New York?" Depending upon how you looked at it, it wasn't too far from her maternal grandparents' place in Millbrook—or it was a universe away.

"My father's people had been there since the 1860's. First one was an escaped slave who was taken in by an abolitionist family in town. One of his sons opened a barbershop and cut white people's hair. That was my great-grandfather. My grandfather was also a barber. My father probably would have been a barber, too, except for the Second World War. He was drafted and served in an all-Negro outfit, and after the war he decided he didn't want to cut people's hair. So he got a civil service job, working for the post office. A decent job that wasn't demeaning, and a regular salary. That's all it took to move the family up a few notches in the social stepladder. My papa thought that all it would take was for me to get a college degree, and I'd be at the very top. He was wrong. My grandfather had his barbershop across the street from the best hotel in town, but he never once went into it for a dinner, and neither has my papa. I tell myself I have every right to try it, but I'm not sure I ever will. Because I am afraid they might throw me out."

"Which is why," Ted interrupted, "we need a lot of people to help us this spring in trying to desegregate lunch counters down South. The white supremacists could get very nasty. It's a helluva lot easier to tolerate abuse if you've got somebody's hand to hold on to."

"Which is why you're going along," Kathleen said.

"Exactly. I don't think Clay should have to do it by himself."

"I wish you guys could also help me pass my course in zoology," Clay said, looking at his wristwatch, then jumping up. "But you can't, so I'd better get hopping or I'll miss my class." He wiped his mouth with a paper napkin. "It was real nice meeting you, Kathleen. I won't say good-bye because I've got a feeling I'll be seeing a lot of you around here."

So he had felt the rapport, too, sensed her excitement. "I'm sure of it," she said.

After he grabbed his jacket and book bag and disappeared down the outside staircase, Kathleen said truthfully, "I like him."

"I knew you would. Clay's one of the most galvanizing people I've ever met. He's so . . . I don't know what . . . vivid and alive. Smart as blazes, too. Harvard's lucky to have him. One of these days he's going to be governor of New York, maybe even the first colored President."

"This will probably sound patronizing, but I think it's a terrific idea for you two to be roommates. I don't think I've ever heard of anything like that before around here, but it's so right."

"I've learned a lot more from Clay than he's learned from me. My freshman year I was in Holworthy, and during my first week there, everyone I met asked me two questions: where I was from, and what my old man did for a living. It was as if they couldn't judge me unless they knew how much money my father made a year." He paused. "At first I told them the truth—that my father owned a bar on Eighth Avenue and was broke most of the time. You should have seen the faces fall when I said that! After I got tired of being cut dead, I told them he was a corporation lawyer. What a difference. Immediate success. They courted me, couldn't get enough of me. But then I decided I didn't want them as friends if they couldn't accept me for what I was."

"Does he really own a bar?"

"He did. Until his liver wore out. He had that fatal weakness, common among saloon keepers, of pouring one for himself every time he poured one for a customer. He died when I was a sophomore. He was a mess when he was drinking, but I loved him. I couldn't have asked for a finer father. Mom has the bar now. She's turned it into a restaurant. She threw sawdust on the floor, dressed up her waiters in straw hats, and charges almost twenty dollars for a filet mignon. It's very successful. Shane's Wife, it's called."

Kathleen had heard of it. Her uncle Lee and aunt Sally and their fashionable friends often ate there, before or after the theater. "Shane?" she repeated. "Does that mean your father was Irish?"

"As Irish as you can be. Don't let the name Birmingham fool you. They arrived in Ireland in the twelfth century. But my mother's Italian. So I'm your typical American hybrid. How about you?"

"Irish on my father's side, Yankee on my mother's. My father was killed during the war."

"Tough break."

"And my mother married again. I don't much care for my stepfather. I adore the Irish side of my family and spend most of my time with them, when I'm not here at school."

"Any brothers or sisters?"

"None. I wish I had."

"I've got six. I'd be happy to share them."

"Six brothers and sisters! But how marvelous!"

"Hah! Try growing up in a small apartment with six brothers and sisters. We were always getting in each other's hair. I'm the oldest, so after Dad died, I had to assume his role. Everything but the drinking. I worry about them while

I'm here in Cambridge. I have one brother who's had some trouble in school—in fact, he was suspended for a while, and that's one of the reasons I like to get down to New York every couple of weeks. To help Mom ride herd. So that offer to drive you down there some weekend still stands."

"I promised my grandmother that I'd come home this weekend." Actually, Nora had tried to dissuade Kathleen, telling her that it was more important for her to resume her life at college than to comfort a widow. But Kathleen wouldn't hear of it. The first few weeks living alone would be very difficult, and Kathleen wanted to help all she could.

"So let's make it a date," Ted suggested. "Only I don't see why we have to wait till Friday to see each other again. I know the lunch was pretty awful—I burned the goddamned cheese sandwiches!—but how about having lunch here again tomorrow?"

It was absolutely insane. There were hundreds of reasons for her to decline. But somehow, after having lunched with Ted and his roommate, it was hard to generate much enthusiasm for breaking bread with a pack of girls who would probably talk about nothing but parties and dances.

"Why not?" she heard herself reply. "But tomorrow, why don't we give the generous chef at Eliot House a rest and let me provide the lunch? How do you feel about sloppy joes?"

"I could kill for them."

So it was settled. On the following day, Ted would once again meet her in front of Emerson Hall after her eleven o'clock class. Only this time, she'd be carrying an old gym bag filled with provisions for their lunch, shopped for before class.

Ted helped her tidy up the kitchen—she washed the dishes, he dried them—then he hurried off to use the bathroom. She could hear him urinating into the john and couldn't help but compare it to her stepfather, who generally flushed as he urinated in order to hide that most human of all sounds.

Afterward, when she went into the bathroom herself, she was amused by its masculine disorder. Layers of dried soap encrusted the tub under the shower head, and pubic hairs half clogged the drain. The toilet bowl was muddy, and only a few leaves were left on the roll of toilet paper. She reminded herself to include some Dutch Cleanser and john paper in her marketing tomorrow.

As she rejoined him in the cluttered living room, she remarked, "I'd say you're in need of a mother's love."

"Make that a woman's love, and I'll agree with you."

Kathleen had to turn away in embarrassment as a warmness flooded through her body. She felt giddy. And later as they made their way down Brattle Street toward Harvard Square, when his bare hand accidentally brushed against her gloved one, she nearly cried out.

Her mouth was dry, and it was an effort to swallow. Either she was coming down with a cold or she was falling in love.

By the time she reached her class on the Lake poets—my God, how trivial poetry was, all of a sudden, in contrast to real life!—the professor was already droning away at his lectern at the front of the room, and Kathleen had to scrape past a dozen or so kneecaps to reach her seat next to Carolyn Biddle.

As she slipped out of her coat and opened her notebook, she heard her roommate whisper, "Where were you at lunch? I looked all over for you."

Could she tell her? Carolyn was probably her best friend and most loyal confidante. Had been since they were prep school students at Rosemary Hall. But Carolyn's family also lived in Greenwich, and her mother saw Kathleen's mother socially. If Kathleen told Carolyn about Ted Birmingham and Clay Gibson, it was more than possible that her roommate might mention it to her mother, who in turn would probably pass it on to Nancy Romily. And of all her mother's qualities—and she had some very good ones—tolerance of rebellious or unconventional people simply wasn't one of them.

So Kathleen replied—was it treachery or the beginning of maturity?—"I skipped lunch today and studied at the library instead. Chances are I'll be doing it again tomorrow."

EIGHT

*P*aul Molloy was seated in his old office on the thirty-first floor of the Molloy Company's Park Avenue headquarters, wondering how he had ever been induced to remain in New York to help "clear things up," as his mother euphemistically called it, when a secretary deposited a letter on his desk, hand-delivered by a messenger only minutes before. The envelope bore the Wall Street address of Potter, Stevenson, and Potter.

In wonderfully archaic English, Quentin Potter begged to inform him that he was a beneficiary of Charles Molloy's estate. In addition to the income from the trust fund set up years before—which was more than enough to meet the needs of any prudent, level-headed Christian, Mr. Potter couldn't help but remind him—he was to receive "the late Mr. Molloy's Brooks Brothers dress shirts, heavily starched."

Paul rocked with laughter.

He was still laughing when Lee entered, holding an identical envelope. "I see you got one too," his brother observed, "but what's so funny?"

Wordlessly, Paul handed him the letter, then watched as he painstakingly read it. "His goddamned dress shirts? What the hell is that supposed to mean?"

"It's Father's parting shot. He wanted to tell me precisely what he thought of me for having butted horns with him over that Saudi deal. I am, not to mince words, a *stuffed shirt*!"

Lee seemed to be a good deal more offended than Paul was. In a curious sort of way, he was the gentleman his father never had been. Or, if not that, he was more gentlemanly. Good form was a matter of great importance to him. That his father had pointedly insulted Paul was a serious lapse in manners. A gentleman would have concealed his feelings.

"Don't forget that the old man was already sick when he executed that will," he volunteered sympathetically. "He didn't mean it, Paulie."

"Oh, I think he did. But it doesn't bother me, really it doesn't," Paul retorted, perhaps too heartily. "In fact, I'm almost relieved that he cut me out of his will without a penny, because now I don't feel so guilty about not having made any overtures to him during the last two years."

"Will you be hard up, Paul? Because if you will be, you know the family will always stand by you."

"I don't even spend the money I get from the trust fund. What I haven't given away is just piling up in the bank. As a matter of principle, I live on the salary I make as an architect."

He could have added, but didn't, that he lived very precariously on an extremely unpredictable income. So unpredictable that there was a good chance the check he'd written to cover his plane ticket to New York might bounce.

"Suit yourself," Lee said, "but you know where to come if you're ever in need."

Paul glanced at his brother's envelope. "I take it that Father has left you a handsome percentage of his holdings in the firm," he remarked.

"More than I'd expected. I thought it would be ten percent, because that's what Caitlin got. Deirdre, Mary, and Eddie each got five. But I got a whopping twenty percent, same as Kathleen."

There was little doubt that the additional ten percent had originally been destined for Paul. As that fact dawned on Lee, he added with genuine feeling—or what passed for it anyway; he was such a master of artifice that Paul never really knew what his feelings were—"I'm sorry, Paulie."

"Don't apologize. You're top banana, so it's only reasonable for you to have a substantial holding in the company. I gather that Megan got nothing?"

"Correct. In his will, the old man described her as 'my brain-damaged daughter who lives in the East Village.' "

"He did have a way with words, didn't he? I'll miss that."

More than that, Paul wanted to say but didn't.

"Listen," Lee began, "Sally wants you over for dinner one

of these nights. She has a list of eligible girls she's still trying to pair you off with, so she needs a few hours to set you up for the kill. How about tonight?"

"Tonight I promised to have dinner with Caitlin and John."

"Then what about Friday?"

Good God, Paul had been back at the office for almost a week! Time had passed much more swiftly than he'd thought possible. "That'd be fine."

"Swell. We'll try to get Kimberly Winant over. Do you remember her? She's still a knockout. She's divorced, so she's back on the market."

Paul stiffled a groan. All the Kimberlys and the Courtneys, the Hilarys and the Hollys in that set! Jesus, where did they get those pretentious names anyway? The women were all slight variations of Lee's wife, virtually indistinguishable from one another.

How could Paul explain to his brother that Sally's matchmaking skills were being wasted? He was already spoken for. So why didn't he simply tell Lee that he'd been living with a woman in California for more than a year and planned to marry her?

He didn't for the simple reason that he was afraid to share her. When they were growing up, whenever Paul shared a toy or precious possession with Lee, in the end his oldest brother had always appropriated it, then broken it.

No, he would keep Emmy for himself, for the time being anyway. And when he decided to go public, he was sure he'd create a sensation.

"Emily *what*?" he imagined his ever so proper brother saying.

"Emily Nakamura."

"She's a *foreigner*?"

About as foreign as Paul and Lee were, having been born in California. But in an only marginally American place called Manzanar, where her Japanese-American parents were interned during the Second World War, so she was not exactly the girl next door. Particularly if you lived on Beekman Place, as Lee did.

But Paul resisted the temptation to say that Kimberly

Winant might as well have dinner at home on Friday night, because just then Mathew Rowley appeared at the doorway.

"I'm sorry, Paul," he said, backing out. "I didn't know you were busy."

"Come on in, Matt."

Charles Molloy's former administrative assistant looked at Lee as if to ask his leave and was met with darkened eyes and a scowl. "I won't hold you two up," Lee said, clearly disapproving of Paul's hospitality toward a man he obviously didn't like. "What about lunch today, Paulie?" he said before leaving.

"I'm having lunch with Mathew. Why don't you join us?"

This time, it was much more difficult to retain his equanimity. "Maybe I will. Tell you what. If I don't get back to you by twelve, then something has come up."

Nothing would induce Lee to share a luncheon table with Matt Rowley, Paul knew, even at gunpoint.

"All right, Lee. Thanks for coming in." After his brother strode out of the office, Paul said to Matt, "Sit down, Matty. Have you been able to come up with the files I asked for?"

Mathew spread out a bundle of manila folders on top of Paul's desk. "These are the contracts and specifications on all our major current projects outside territorial U.S.A. I believe that's what you wanted."

Quickly, Paul scanned through the dozen or so folders but couldn't find what he was looking for. "I was particularly interested in the file on Project Galveston," he began, "but it doesn't seem to be here."

"Galveston?" Mathew repeated. "You're the second person within the last few days to express an interest in Galveston. Mrs. Molloy also asked me something about Galveston, and I told her I'd never heard of it before in relation to the Molloy Company."

Over the weekend in Southampton, one of the discrepancies Nora had asked Paul to "clear up," as she put it, was Mathew Rowley's denial of any knowledge of Project Galveston. There was no contesting the existence of the project in South Vietnam. Both Lee and Andy Sinclair had verified it.

How then was it possible that Charles's right-hand man was unaware of it?

Paul put it to him. "The Project Galveston that I'm concerned about has nothing to do with the city in Texas. Apparently Father merely used an old file title when he was searching for a name that wouldn't reveal the true nature of the scheme. It's to be a huge U.S. military installation in Southeast Asia."

"Military? Then in all probability, the specifications are either Secret or Top Secret, would you say?"

"That seems more than likely."

Momentarily, Matt had looked uncomfortable, as if Paul had questioned his competence. But now he relaxed. "Then that explains why I know nothing about it," he declared. "Do you remember back in the 1950's during the Korean War when we were invited to submit bids on a military installation near Seoul? The Pentagon insisted that everyone here at the office who would have access to the plans be screened by the FBI for security clearances. Remember, Paul?"

Yes, Paul did remember. Because later he ran into one of his old professors at Yale, who told him that the FBI had been snooping around campus, asking about him.

"Your father got a Top Secret clearance," Matt continued, "and so did you and Lee, which means that you have access to Confidential, Secret, or Top Secret material. But for reasons I was never made privy to, my clearance was restricted to Confidential material, nothing higher. Your father was a stickler about such matters, so apparently he kept all the material relating to this Project Galveston in the safe in his office, not in mine."

So the explanation was as simple as that. Matt hadn't been concealing anything, after all, when he denied knowledge of the project. Or more specifically, when Nora had asked if he knew anything about "the gentleman from Galveston," as Charles's caller was identified on the night of his death.

"Then do I take it that the plans for Project Galveston are now in Father's safe?" Paul asked.

"Either that, or in General McFadden's safe. I don't believe you've met him yet. He's based in Washington." He waited, then added, "But I'm sure your brother would have duplicate copies. Or Mr. Sinclair."

For reasons so complicated that he himself scarcely understood them, Paul preferred to discuss the matter with Andy rather than with Lee.

"All right, Matt. I'll give Andy a buzz right now." As Mathew rose from his seat to retrieve the unneeded files on Paul's desk, Paul reminded him of their luncheon engagement. The day before when he suggested it, Matt had seemed overwhelmed, because from the time that Paul joined the firm till the day he walked out in a huff, they'd never been particularly friendly. And certainly they'd never known each other socially.

But the day before, Paul wasn't yet aware of Matt's very logical explanation for having been kept in the dark about the military installation in Vietnam, and realizing he might have to pry information from him, he recalled one of his father's famous dictums: "When you want to learn something from someone who doesn't want to tell you, use plenty of sugar." It had seemed to Paul that Matt would be more susceptible to sugaring during lunch than at the office.

As Mathew turned to leave, something else occurred to Paul. "Say, why don't I book a table at the Four Seasons, Matt? Would you like that?"

Paul had a feeling that in spite of a very respectable salary, Matt probably ate most of his lunches on stools at one of the eateries along Lexington or Madison Avenue.

Matt seemed dazzled by the suggestion. "Yes, that would be splendid. I've never been at the Four Seasons."

If Mathew knew nothing about Project Galveston, he nonetheless was a reservoir of office gossip. And Paul hoped that if he sugared him adequately, just by chance he might learn something worthwhile.

And one thing that could be said of the Four Seasons was that there was sugar there aplenty.

After Matt left, Paul buzzed Andy's office but found that he wasn't in and wouldn't be back until midafternoon. So Paul asked his secretary to dial a number in California, using an outside line, and as he sat listening to it ring, he tried to conjure up Emmy as she left her loom in the loft of the cathedral-ceilinged living room and made her way down the stairs to the kitchen.

"You'll never guess what I've been bequeathed," he said the second she picked up the telephone.

"I give up. What have you been bequeathed?"

"My father's Brooks Brothers dress shirts, highly starched." He laughed again, but this time there was a trace of melancholy to it.

Emily understood at once, and also perceived the sadness. "I don't think that was very nice of him," she observed.

"So who ever said that my father was a nice man?"

"He knew it would hurt you to be called a stuffed shirt. Anyway, it's an unfair description of someone who took a simple, straightforward moral position on an issue and refused to budge." She waited, then asked, "What are you going to do with them?"

"My stuffed shirts? What would you say if I really stuffed them, then hung them over the fireplace, like they do moose heads and such?"

"No, because that would give them an importance they don't deserve. You don't have even one dress shirt, Paul. I would suggest that you keep them in a drawer, and if you're ever invited to a really gala party that requires black tie, you'll have something to wear."

"But I don't own a dinner jacket, a pair of black shoes, or even a black tie."

"Who knows? Maybe someone who loves you as much as your father did will leave them to you in his last will and testament."

Somehow, he felt all the sourness, all the hurt feelings drain from him. She was quite correct. His father's gift had a cruel edge to it, but her solution was perfect. He would merely accept it as a useful addition to his wardrobe.

"All right, I'll stick them into my suitcase and bring them home with me." He waited, then asked, "How's Spot?"

"Gurgling in his bassinet next to me while I finish my rug."

"Does he miss me?"

"Yes, but he wishes we could agree on a name for him. With a name like Spot, he'll be sitting up and begging at the table before he can crawl."

It was meant to be temporary. The truth of the matter was that they couldn't agree on a first *or* last name, because when the baby was born, Emily was still uncertain about Paul's readiness for marriage. Any minute, she expected his family to intrude and end their idyll together under the towering live oaks on the hillside in Sonoma County. She knew all about his difficulties with his father and his renunciation of the past, but she wasn't convinced that the break was permanent. And if his family ever succeeded in recapturing him, which she feared, it would be much more painful for her to lose a husband than a lover.

The baby was now six months old and still unnamed or legitimatized. They had very nearly decided on a wedding date when Paul's father died and he was summoned back to the East Coast.

"Before I forget," Emily added, "those people in Glen Ellen who owed you money for designing their pool house finally sent a check. So we're not broke anymore."

Emily knew all about the trust fund money that Paul refused to spend, and quite agreed with the position he took. The fewer Molloy tentacles in his flesh meant the less likely it was for him ever to be drawn back to the family and away from her.

And there was no doubt in Emily Nakamura's mind that she could never fit into the Molloy establishment in New York City. By no stretch of the imagination could she ever be a conventional corporate wife, hosting little dinner parties for other corporate wives. Culturally, a universe separated her from Sally Molloy, who belonged in New York. Emmy was an artist and she was Oriental. Neither money nor position interested her.

But, as she had just pointed out, as romantic as poverty could sometimes be, it was no fun to be threatened by Pacific Gas and Electric for nonpayment of bills, so whenever Paul did get a check for services rendered at the architectural firm in Santa Rosa, it was a special occasion. It proved that they didn't have to rely on money from the Molloys, and that he would never have to return to New York. The firm—Nakamura, Linden, and Molloy—was just beginning to establish a reputation, and until their work became better known, there were bound to be lean times.

"Is everyone being nice to you, Paul? More important, are you being nice to them?"

Emily had never met anyone in his family, though she knew each and every one of them intimately from having listened to Paul's admittedly biased characterizations. She knew by name virtually all the Molloy servants, past and present—nursemaids, cooks, gardeners—and all the chief officers at Molloy Company headquarters. But she was very much aware that Paul tended to look at most of them, particularly his siblings, with a somewhat skeptical eye, more inclined to see their shortcomings than their virtues.

"I'm being very charming to everyone," Paul assured her.

"Have you determined yet if Matt Rowley lied to your mother?"

Over the weekend, when he called from Southampton to explain why he was compelled to remain in New York for an entire month, Paul had repeated Nora's suspicions to Emily.

"He's clean," he replied. "He had a perfectly logical explanation for not knowing anything about Galveston. I've just talked to him here at the office."

There was momentary silence. Then: "The office? Why would Matt still be at the office? I thought you told me Lee was going to give him the sack."

My God, what a memory she had! Moreover, she had an uncanny talent for remembering only the most significant details about people she'd never met. When he spoke to her from Southampton, Paul had mentioned Lee's threat, then had forgotten all about it.

Certainly, Matt didn't give the appearance of an employee whose services were about to be terminated. Had Lee changed his mind during the past few days?

"I'm having lunch with Matt today. I'll try to feel him out. If Lee decided to let him go, it's most unusual for him to have second thoughts about it. Which reminds me, I have to book a table at the Four Seasons."

"Is that expensive?"

"Sinfully. I may have to hock my stuffed shirt to pay for it if they don't accept my credit card."

"I'm afraid for you, Paul. I hope you don't get too used to luxuries, because then you'll never want to come home."

"Nothing could keep me away. Nothing. I owe everything to you, Emmy. When I met you, I was coming all apart, and you put me together again."

"You did most of that yourself, Paul. Deep down, you're a very strong man. Just like your father, I think."

"And I've called you to listen to this abuse?"

"You are, Paul. And you know you are. But that's okay, so long as you come home."

"I'll come home."

"I'll be waiting."

All his life, Paul had known aggressive, brittle, nonstop-talking New York girls who left little or nothing to the imagination. But Emily Nakamura was serene and elusive, subtle and understated.

He'd met her at a time when he was down and out. Out of money, out of basic human emotions. Out of touch with his family and his past. When he fled to California after the quarrel with his father, he carried nothing with him that would remind him who he used to be. Like the early pioneers who were forced to throw their possessions from wagon trains to survive the long journey, Paul abandoned his old identity.

He knew one person in all of California, Pete Linden, who'd been in his class at Yale School of Architecture, and as luck would have it, Pete had just resigned from an architectural firm in San Francisco to set up his own shop in Santa Rosa along with Steve Nakamura, a Berkeley graduate.

"Wait'll you see what Steve's been doing," Pete said to him. "It'll knock your socks off. He's taken the best from Western architecture, the best from Eastern architecture, and he's created something that is totally Northern Californian. Gorgeous stuff."

Their office in Santa Rosa hadn't even opened yet, and the day that Paul drove up, the place looked deserted. It was unfurnished and locked from the inside. In the far corner, he saw a girl, her back toward him, working pensively at a loom. He tapped at the window for some time before the sound broke through her concentration, and when she turned, he had to catch his breath.

There was such a *stillness* about her, none of that frenzy he associated with New York girls.

After Paul explained who he was, she told him that she was Steve's sister and was just using the place temporarily for her loom.

"Could I see what you're doing?" he asked.

"You probably won't like it. It's not working out exactly the way I wanted it to."

It was a rug, and the wool was a kind of light terra-cotta color washed with the faintest suggestion of blue. There was no ornamentation at all except, at its top right-hand corner, a flash of darker blue that could have been a bird startled into flight. Or a spirit, a soul. It was nonrepresentational, yet almost more moving than anything Paul had ever seen before.

"I took the design from a third-century vase I saw in a museum in Tokyo," she told him.

It had the same stillness and repose about it that she herself had.

Months later, after he and Emily were living together and she was already pregnant, they attended a cocktail party in Belvedere given by one of Pete Linden's former associates. Emily made a spectacular entrance. Compared to her, all the other women seemed dull and banal. She certainly made a deep impression on at least one other guest, a local psychiatrist, who chatted with the two of them, then with Paul alone after Emily left to greet friends of her brother's.

Out of the blue, the shrink said to Paul, "I'll bet you anything that you're estranged from your family."

Paul nearly dropped his tequila. But with remarkable composure, he responded, "What makes you think that?"

"Oh, it's just a little theory I have. Nothing very scientific, mind you. But in my line of work, I've found that men who are drawn to . . . well, exotic women are generally trying to escape from something they don't like about themselves or their pasts. I'm treating a patient now—this is just between the two of us—a Harvard man from a distinguished Bostonian family who married a Puerto Rican who never graduated from high school. I've also treated a young man with a long history of homosexuality, scion of an old and respected family from the Eastern Shore of Maryland, who surprised everyone by marrying a native of Bolivia who speaks almost no English. Both patients held their fathers in deep scorn."

Paul's throat felt constricted. Nonetheless, he managed to protest, "I've known Harvard men from distinguished Bostonian families who married girls from Beacon Hill, and also homosexuals from rich southern families who never got married at all, in spite of the fact that they had, both of them, ambivalent feelings about their families, particularly their fathers."

"As I say, my observation is most unscientific."

Feigning only minor interest, Paul inquired, "Were they successful or not, the two marriages?"

The shrink nodded sadly. "As successful as most California marriages. One succeeded, one didn't."

When he revealed no more, Paul pressed, "Which was the happy one?"

The psychiatrist watched Paul's discomfort as he answered, "Not the Harvard man and the Puerto Rican girl, I'm afraid," intimating that Paul's union with Emily didn't stand much of a chance.

Paul worried about it, afraid that the man had seen something in him that he himself was unable to see.

As long as he remained with Emily in their private little eyrie perched on a Sonoma County hillside, no harm could come to their relationship. But once removed from that paradise and reestablished among his New York family, there was a chance he could be tempted by that old sorceress, the past, and overwhelmed by a sense of fealty. Because of that, while part of him hoped to restore the love he'd once felt toward his father, another part wanted to keep him his mortal enemy.

Thus far, his feelings toward Emily had proved durable. But when his mother begged him to unravel the circumstances surrounding his father's death, she had appealed to the very nub of his Irishness. In times of trouble and sorrow, Irish families closed ranks and fought to the death to preserve their solidarity. It was how they had survived centuries of abuse and hardships.

Having spent less than a week in New York, Paul could already smell trouble like a bad stench in the air. And it had taken Emily's reminder for him to perceive it. Only days before, Lee had passionately advocated the firing of Matt Rowley, but Matt was still very much in evidence.

What did Matt have on Paul's brother?

NINE

Quentin Potter leaped from his chair as Nora Molloy was
ushered into his office, dressed in widow's black, her face
veiled.

"An honor and a pleasure," Charles Molloy's personal
counsel said respectfully as he helped her into a chair.

"Thank you, Mr. Potter." Nora relaxed the grip the silver
fox fur had on her neck, then sat back.

"I am always at your beck and call, Mrs. Molloy, so it came
as something of a surprise when you asked to meet me here
at my office. I could quite as easily have gone to your apartment to save you this inconvenience."

"It is no inconvenience, Mr. Potter."

In point of fact it was, but Nora had thought it prudent
to make her request face to face at the offices of Potter, Stevenson, and Potter, where the information she sought would
surely be available. She had no doubt but that her husband's
former counsel would resist giving it to her.

"I trust that everything thus far has been handled to your
satisfaction," he declared.

"I'm more than satisfied."

It had been Nora's suggestion that the beneficiaries of
Charles's estate be notified individually and impersonally, and
although the will was available for public scrutiny at probate
court, only John Phipps had availed himself of the opportunity. The unusually generous bequest to Christine Lawrence
had caught his eye, and he brought it up with Caitlin, who
quizzed her mother.

"Who is this Christine Lawrence?" Caitlin had asked.

Nora hoped that a little fabrication wouldn't jeopardize
her spiritual destiny. "She's the widow of an old friend of

Charles's, and when her husband died, he left nothing but debts. Charles has been helping her out discreetly for a number of years and also left her a little something to ensure an old age free from want."

It was plausible enough because Charles had helped numerous friends or friends' wives and families after fortune had dealt them a bad blow. Moreover, he'd left sums of money to half a hundred other people, including aged housemaids put out to pasture years ago, hotel keepers in Badgastein and Paris, and even the colored shoeshine man at the Molloy building on Park Avenue who had polished his shoes every morning for the past twenty years.

So Caitlin didn't pursue the matter. But Nora felt compelled to. Now that Paul had agreed to try to ferret out answers to questions of a business nature, she'd decided to take the initiative and delve into the personal relationship between her late husband and the woman mentioned in his will.

"I should like to get in touch with Christine Lawrence," she said resolutely to Quentin Potter.

His jaw sank. "I sincerely urge you not to."

"I was confident you would. But I've made up my mind, and since you appear to be the only one with Miss Lawrence's address—you mentioned that she lived on East End Avenue, but I find no name under that listing in the Manhattan directory—I should be grateful if you could reveal it."

"You may live to regret it, Mrs. Molloy. As I've explained, for the past eight years on the first day of every month I've mailed a check to this . . . this Lawrence woman. I have never met her personally, however, and know nothing about her. If you contrive to meet her, you may very well incite her greed. She should be more than content with your late husband's generous bequest, but if heated words are exchanged between the two of you, it's possible that she'll press for a larger settlement."

"It's a risk I shall have to take."

"I'm sure I've had a good deal more experience than you, Mrs. Molloy, with common and vulgar women—during the course of my work, I mean to say. On more occasions than I care to recall, I've had to . . . negotiate with actress types or chorus girls who've threatened to annoy families of clients of mine. They can be a very truculent lot, these women."

"But human beings, nonetheless, so I'm sure that Miss Lawrence will hear me out. I must see her and confront her, to settle my mind."

"Then I shall accompany you."

"I would prefer to go alone, thank you."

Potter knew better than to protest, particularly in view of the fact that he was still employed by the Molloys to serve as executor of the estate and would be handsomely rewarded for it. So he consulted his files, then copied the address and gave it to Nora, saying, "For your sake, I hope the meeting won't be acrimonious."

Nora shared his hope.

She asked Jean-Claude to drop her off at the apartment of a friend who lived on Gracie Square, where she'd often visited. But today, instead of asking the doorman to ring Mrs. Cavanagh's apartment—Nora knew she was in Boca Raton— she waited until the car had driven away, then proceeded south toward East End Avenue on foot.

It was a comparatively new building, one of those white-bricked palaces that looked more suitable for Los Angeles than New York. As she approached the canopied entrance, a short, bloated man wearing sunglasses in spite of the gray day made his splay-footed way to a waiting limousine, almost certainly a rented one. If the other tenants in the building, including Christine Lawrence, were equally déclassé, then her worst suspicions would be confirmed. Miss Lawrence would turn out to be an opportunistic woman who'd taken advantage of an old man.

But after the doorman had helped the cigar-smoking tenant into the Carey Cadillac and returned to his station, Nora realized that she had already jumped to the wrong conclusions, at least in part, because when she asked, "Could you tell me if Miss Lawrence is in?" he looked momentarily puzzled.

Then he corrected her, "*Mrs.* Lawrence, did you mean?"

Nora was taken aback, but managed to nod in agreement.

"Is she expecting you?" he inquired.

No, she wasn't, Nora explained. "I was in the neighborhood, and just on impulse I thought I'd drop in."

"And whom should I say is calling?"

Nora couldn't help but wonder how Christine Lawrence would react when she heard her name. "I'm Nora Molloy," she said.

"One minute, Mrs. Molloy. I'll see if she's in."

Nora waited as he disappeared to one side of the entrance and buzzed an apartment, then tapped his foot on the marble floor as he listened to it ring. She studied a huge tree that stretched nearly two stories high, and for the life of her couldn't tell if it was real or a plastic facsimile. If the former, certainly it led a joyless life in these artificial surroundings, never knowing rain, never seeing sun.

"Just as I thought," the doorman said on his return. "Mrs. Lawrence isn't in. I was pretty sure she wasn't because I haven't seen her around for the last few days. She generally walks her poodle."

Her poodle? That was a bad sign. Was she one of those neurotic New York women who went everywhere clutching rheumy-eyed poodles in their arms? Into department stores, Gristede's, bakeries, banks?

"You wouldn't know when she's due back?" Nora asked.

No, he wouldn't, but he had a slip of paper and a pen in the event that Nora would care to leave a message. "I can put it in her mailbox." He bent his head around the corner and scrutinized the boxes set in the wall. "No one has emptied her mailbox for the last couple of days, so she must be out of town."

Nora had no intention of leaving a message. But she wanted to give something to the young man for his troubles. Neither too little nor too much, as either would be remembered. A five-dollar bill would do nicely.

"Thank you, ma'am," he said, forgetting her name—which was precisely her intention—the minute he slid the fresh bill into his pocket.

Charles Molloy had often combined business with lunch at the Four Seasons ("my flashier business associates," he described them, "the ones I wouldn't dare bring to the Union Club"), and because he tipped lavishly for good service and good food, he was well esteemed by the staff and management. However, when Paul called earlier that morning for a reservation, his name wasn't recognized, and as a result, when he and Matt Rowley arrived, they were told that there would be a delay for a table.

Paul didn't mind waiting outside the entrance to the Pool Room, but Matt bristled. "Excuse me," he said, striding into the room in search of the headwaiter.

The effect was instantaneous. Seconds later, the headwaiter appeared before Paul, visibly humbled. "My apologies, Mr. Molloy, for the dreadful mistake. Your table is ready."

Without further ado, they were ushered to a table set for four, helped into their chairs as if they were royalty, and handed the menus with great ceremony by the man who then backed away, head bobbing up and down, the way servants did in the presence of their betters.

Paul was vastly amused. "Whatever did you say to the poor man?" he asked when they were alone.

"Only that the Molloy Company spends thousands and thousands of dollars here on expense account lunches every month—I know because the bills go through my office—and that we never wait for tables. If it had happened to your father, that headwaiter would be looking for a new job."

Yes, more than likely. Charles had always enjoyed the trappings of wealth and position. Money purchased comforts, and when he was shortchanged or treated shabbily, his wrath knew no bounds.

Matt looked about the opulent room, undeniably impressed. "I've never eaten here myself, although I've had a sandwich at the Brasserie. I can't begin to tell you the number of times I've reserved a table—this very one—for your father. The headwaiter recognized my voice at once."

"I'm glad that at least one of us has clout," Paul remarked, earning appreciative laughter.

As Matt concentrated on the menu, Paul observed him. For a man born and raised in rural Georgia, he was remarkably urbane. Both his navy blue suit and his monogrammed shirt were hand-tailored, and his hair had been impeccably trimmed. His nails shone from a recent manicuring, and his face had a healthy glow to it, thanks to a sunlamp.

He certainly didn't give the appearance of a glorified secretary, as Lee always referred to him. More like the chairman of the board. By contrast, Paul felt positively scruffy in his old blue blazer, wrinkled gray trousers, and down-at-the-heel cordovans.

Paul was intrigued.

When his luncheon guest looked up from the menu, Paul asked with genuine interest, "How did you ever come to work for the Molloy Company, Matt? All I can remember is that in one year Father had three different secretaries and fired them. Then miraculously you appeared, and you've been with us ever since."

Matt had invented his own title, assistant to the president, and seemed displeased to be reminded that his predecessors had been mere secretaries. "It was no miracle, Paul. It was hard work that got me there. I'd been in New York for three years, ever since I graduated from high school and took a Greyhound bus out of town the next day. I clerked at a bookshop on Fifth Avenue while I went to night school, learning how to type and take stenography, because a teacher once told me that executives were a dime a dozen in New York, but what was scarce as hen's teeth was a really good office manager. I finished top in my class at typing school about the same time your father fired secretary number three, but at first he wouldn't even interview me. He said he didn't want any damned male secretary, to use his memorable description, but I persisted, and at last he agreed to see me. "When I walked in, he said, 'Well, at least you don't wave your ass around like my last three witless secretaries. Can you type and take dictation?' I said I could. 'Can you handle all the trivial matters that plague me six hours out of a ten-hour workday, and are you willing to put in ten hours next to someone as mean and vile-tempered as I am?' I told him that my daddy was the meanest man in the world and used to give me a kick first thing every morning, so I was used to that. 'Okay,' he said, 'I'll hire you on a trial basis. Two weeks. If I don't like you, out you go.' "

Matt laughed at the recollection. "In two weeks' time, he couldn't live without me. He called me in and said I could stay. I told him I would on two conditions: twice the salary he gave his last three victims, and a new title to fit the job I was doing. I'm probably the highest-paid administrative assistant in New York City, but I'm worth every penny of it, and your father knew it."

Now would come the sugary part, even treacly. "I've always been very impressed by your abilities, Matt, just as Father was. But what I've never been able to understand is why you didn't go farther than you have. You could have been a vice president by now."

"About three years ago, the year before you left, I almost quit," Matt replied. "By then, I'd taken my bachelor's degree from NYU, going to night school, and I had this crazy idea that I wanted to go to Harvard Business School. I was sort of old to be entering graduate school, but I'd had a lot of practical experience in business by then, and it's just what they like, so I was accepted. I went to your father and asked for a two-year leave of absence to get my MBA. His response was just sort of apoplectic. I rarely have occasion to use that word, but in this case it's appropriate. Mr. Molloy begged me to stay. He said that any fool could get an MBA, but that I was irreplaceable and he'd pay top price to keep me around. He didn't want my mind addled by the Harvard Business School."

"I'm glad he talked you out of it," Paul said. "I'm confident that everyone at the office wants you to remain at your job." Everyone except Lee, he might have added but didn't.

"Thanks. I have no intention of resigning."

Matt's tone was so militant that Paul was sure Lee had discussed his resignation with him sometime during the last few days, but he needed to learn more.

"I see no reason why you can't perform the same services for Lee as you did for my father," he said, hoping for a response.

Matt was about to answer when their waiter appeared at the table and requested their order. As a rule, Paul preferred a California-style lunch—a light salad or perhaps a sandwich on whole wheat bread garnished with bean sprouts—but didn't want to inhibit his guest, so after Matt ordered mussels in garlic sauce followed by roast rack of lamb, he did the same, also choosing a nice California cabernet to go with it.

After their waiter left, Matt needed no prompting to resume their conversation.

"I've already reached an agreement with Lee," Matt said. "I told him that I'd stay on as general office manager—that would be a new position—but that I would prefer for him to employ his own assistant when he moves up to the presidency."

Paul had the very distinct feeling that Matt had given Lee an ultimatum when Lee attempted to fire him. It was a most interesting area indeed, and Paul wanted to explore it.

"You don't particularly admire my brother, do you?"

Matt chose his words with the utmost care. "Let's say that I'm willing to admit that Lee has many, many virtues. But he's not Charles Molloy's son. You are, Paul."

Paul felt obliged to come to a beleaguered brother's defense. "In all my life, I don't think I've ever met anyone who's actually disliked Lee."

"Oh, I like him. Don't get me wrong. He's a very charming fellow. But he lacks vision and judgment. He's way, way beyond his depth. Do you know what your father once called Lee? Ordinarily, I'd never repeat a thing like this—one of the reasons Mr. Molloy and I worked so well together was that I know how to respect a confidence—but since things have changed since your father's death, I will. He said that Lee was minor league. He meant well, he tried hard, but there were limits to what he could do." Matt waited. "He said you were major league, Paul."

Yes, it was like his father to employ baseball terminology when he wanted to define a personality. And, yes, it would hurt Lee to the very core if he learned of it.

"The fact remains," Paul began, "that Lee will be assuming most of the responsibilities at the firm previously held by my father. I don't figure in the scheme of things at all. You may not be aware of it, but Father cut me out of his will before he died as a result of my stand on the Saudi contract."

"I'm aware of it," Matt said with feeling, "and I think it's terribly wrong."

"If you intend to remain with the firm—and you've just told me that's your intention—you'll have to learn how to work with Lee."

"Your father never meant for Lee to become president and chairman of the board."

"Oh, but he did. His last will and testament leaves no ambiguity on that score. Lee may very well be minor league, but he's a major stockholder. He owns twenty percent of the Molloy Company's stock."

Matt's face was anguished. "Your father never meant that to be. I know for a fact."

"Fact?" Paul repeated. "What fact can be more compelling than his last will and testament, in which I was disowned? Unless, of course, there's something you know that I don't know."

Matt set his lips firmly. If he'd planned to elaborate, and it was unlikely, the appearance of their mussels in garlic sauce interrupted him. Afterward, as they ate, Paul attempted to direct the conversation back to Lee, but his guest adroitly avoided picking up the threads.

"Terrific lunch," Matt said at its conclusion. "We must do it more often."

Matt liked his tailored suits and custom-made shirts, and being able to strike terror into the hearts of headwaiters. He had no intention of relinquishing his privileges and power.

Moreover, Paul had seen the momentary indecision in his eyes, just seconds before. A fashionable New York barber could trim his redneck's hair and a manicurist could labor over his hands till they looked as if they'd never known dirt, but for a brief moment, like the opening of a camera's shutter, Matt's eyes revealed the honest and hungry farmboy he'd once been, not what he'd become, and Paul clearly saw that he was lying.

Along with Paul, Andy Sinclair had also been invited to break bread with the Phippses at their Park Avenue apartment—an act of mercy, Caitlin Phipps described it, referring to the fact that after more than ten years of marriage, Andy and his wife, Barbara, had decided to call it quits, and she had fled home to Grosse Pointe, leaving her about-to-be-divorced husband at loose ends in New York.

Paul had been surprised to hear of the domestic problems, because of all people he knew, none was more responsible and rock-solid than Andy Sinclair, a loving husband and dutiful father of two enchantingly beautiful children. Why the divorce was about to take place no one seemed to know, and Barbara Sinclair, who might have clarified things, had already left the area. For his part, Andy simply wasn't talking.

But Paul was relieved to find him at the Phippses because he always dreaded being with his brother-in-law John, and Andy would make it less painful. For reasons Paul couldn't quite fathom, Caitlin's husband had enjoyed a luminous and incandescent youth. He was best friends at Harvard with the magical Tom Molloy, who had no time for fools, but had become dour and pompous in middle age. "Stuffy" was how his son Jake described him. Others were less charitable. It was Charles Molloy himself who said about his son-in-law, "If a man could die from the lack of a sense of humor, the way one can die from a vitamin deficiency, I wouldn't give John more than a few weeks to live."

Still, to his credit, John hadn't allowed himself to be sucked ·into the Molloy corporate empire, but preferred to make his living as a Wall Street lawyer. An unaggressive and unimaginative one, Paul had heard. His own family, one of the poorer branches of the Phippses, had much less money than they once had, so that Caitlin's husband contributed little more than his salary as a lawyer to help maintain their style of life. Needless to say, Molloy money paid for most of their expenses, but like many men who are sustained by their wives' largesse, John pretended not to notice where all the luxuries came from and who paid for them.

He'd also recently started to drink more than he used to, a habit Caitlin didn't actively discourage because she thought that liquor might make him less morose. But if anything, it served merely to depress him more. And the effect he had on others could be deadening.

He'd lost his trim figure and litheness, and his face was splotchy and puffed. "What are you drinking, Paul?" he asked after the customary greetings at the door, then made it impossible for Paul to choose by adding, "I'd recommend this admirable twenty-year-old single-malt scotch. Here, I'll pour some for you." As if to prove Paul's contention that lawyers considered it a challenge to monopolize a conversation, both in and out of the courtroom, he continued to speak as he walked toward the liquor cabinet. "I hear that your mother has induced you to remain in New York for a few months. I take it you're staying at the River House? You're welcome to stay here, Paul. There's plenty of room, what with the children both at college. You could use Jake's room. What would you say to that?"

Paul was about to answer, but his brother-in-law finished pouring a vast amount of ancient scotch into a tumbler, then turned to say, "I don't know why not. Don't you think that's a capital idea, Caitlin? It would be just like old times. The three of us could stay up half the night chatting about our callow youth."

"Your callow youth, not mine," Paul objected.

Diplomatically, Caitlin suggested, "I'm sure Paul would prefer his privacy."

Undeterred by his wife's attempt at tact, John droned on. "Have you heard what my wife is plotting to do this summer? She's thinking of letting the house in Southampton for the season and going up to Martha's Vineyard. Isn't that the damnedest thing?"

"It's only a thought," Caitlin apologized.

"There's no one on Martha's Vineyard except that loud, brassy crowd of New York Jews," he went on. "I don't know why she wants to spend the summer with them when we have a house in Southampton. She knows I won't be able to visit half so often because I refuse to fly and it's a long trip by car."

"I thought a change might do us all good," Caitlin said by way of explanation. "Mother won't be in Southampton, you know. She plans to be in Europe for most of the summer. She's thinking of going back to Ireland."

If she did, Paul knew, it would be only her second visit since leaving Ireland in 1916. After the war—in either 1945 or '46, Paul wasn't sure—she and Charles made a trip to Ireland, but they never discussed it for reasons the family assumed were very personal. On all the other occasions that she and her husband traveled to Europe—virtually every summer except during the war—they had deliberately avoided Ireland, as if the experience of returning was too painful for them.

"Do we have relatives there anymore?" Paul asked his sister.

"It's doubtful. Maybe third or fourth cousins, but that's all." She waited before continuing. "I think Mother wants to see it all again, one more time, because Father's death reminded her of her own mortality."

Andy interjected, "Reminded all of us," looking—significantly, Paul thought—in Caitlin's direction.

"Well, elephants may return to their birthplace in their old age, and even my blessed mother-in-law," John began crustily, "but Paul sure as hell won't. I don't understand why you hate our fair city so much. Why, the last time I visited Los Angeles, there was a poisonous yellow cloud hovering over the place, and when I breathed the air I knew what it was like to commit suicide in a carbon monoxide-filled garage." He swept his hand through the air in front of him, apparently to clear it, and in doing so he upset his drink. It splashed over his trouser legs.

With resignation, as if she'd done it often before, Caitlin handed him a napkin, then said, "Darling, Paul doesn't live in Los Angeles. He lives north of San Francisco."

"All the same to me," he retorted. "Beatniks all over the place from what I hear. Isn't that what they call them? Beatniks? Why, if I had my way, I'd line them all up and shoot every last one of them."

"But darling," Caitlin began, "I thought you were reserving that carnage for Democrats."

"Most of those twisted, perverted Beatniks *are* Democrats. Useless people. That's what I say!" He gestured with his arm and once again upset his tumbler, then began patting his kneecaps with the damp napkin.

"Yes, darling, we hear you," Caitlin said soothingly, but Paul discerned an iciness to the word "darling." She lifted the glass from her husband's hand. "I think we've had enough to drink before dinner. We don't want to spoil our appetite, do we?"

"Speak for yourself. I'm perfectly capable of deciding how many drinks I can or can't have, thank you." He reached out to reclaim his glass, and as Caitlin tried to retrieve it, he pushed her violently aside.

Paul saw his sister's bottom lip begin to tremble. "Excuse me," she said. "I'd better check on things in the kitchen."

Andy's fists were clenched tightly. "I think I'll see if there's anything I can do to help." He rose from his chair and followed her.

"You ready for another one?" John asked after they'd gone. When Paul declined, he once again filled his tumbler. "Shocking news about Andy and Barbara," he said, returning to Paul. "I just can't understand it. They seemed so happy."

"People change, if you'll pardon the banality," Paul suggested.

"Do they ever! All you have to do is look at me." Glassy-eyed, he surveyed himself, insofar as it was possible. "I'm forty pounds overweight, and it's hard for me to climb a flight of stairs without groaning. Back when I was in college, I was a member of the wrestling team and I could run three miles without feeling it. What's happened to me, Paul?"

"Well, if I were diplomatic, I'd say you're getting old. But I'm not, so I'd say you drink too much." He removed the glass from his brother-in-law's hand, and this time John didn't protest.

"Almost everyone I know drinks too much. Isn't that the damnedest thing, Paul? The best of my generation was killed off in the war, and those of us who survived are now sitting around drinking ourselves to death. Am I getting maudlin?"

"Yes, a bit."

"There isn't a week that goes by that I don't think of your brother Tom. I loved him. Did you know that? Not the way a man loves a woman, but I loved him. I would have done anything to keep him alive. Why is it, Paul, that the sweetest and the fairest are always first to be struck down by the gods?"

"I pass."

Paul had loved Tom, too. So had Lee. And most of all, so

had Charles. If Tom had lived, would the family have disintegrated the way it had?

"Rumor has it on the Street," John began, referring to the only street that mattered among New York businessmen, Wall Street, "that you Molloys may be in for some stormy weather."

"We Molloys welcome stormy weather. Don't you know by now that tempests bring out all our Celtic strengths?"

"I also hear that McFadden is promising government contracts that he can't deliver."

Momentarily, the name didn't register, then Paul remembered that General Cyrus McFadden, U.S. Army retired, was a chief executive at the Molloy Company.

"I haven't met him yet," Paul remarked. "I understand he's in Washington for a while."

"He's based in Washington," his brother-in-law corrected him.

"What function does he perform?"

"He's one of the few people who has Ike's ear. He was a member of Eisenhower's personal staff when he was commander in chief, and after McFadden retired a few years ago, he cast about for ways to supplement his government pension, and your father hired him to serve as liaison for the Molloy Company in Washington."

Cynically, Paul suggested, "So maybe there's justification for wars, after all. Without them, there wouldn't be retired admirals and generals to plead private industry's cause in the nation's capital."

"Don't misunderstand. McFadden is a real patriot."

"Patriots have always scared me. They're like those exhibitionists who unzip their flies in front of little old ladies in the park. They give the viewer little in the way of an alternative."

"Aptly put, but I think irrelevant in the case of Cyrus McFadden. He's not a fanatic, any more than Eisenhower is. He's a very sensible, trustworthy man who knows almost everything there is to know about the nation's defense, and if you'll pardon the inversion of the Republican National Committee's election button four years ago, Ike likes him."

Paul weighed it, then said, "I think I'd feel more comfortable if McFadden were a Democrat. I don't like to see important things like defense contracts get bogged down in party politics."

"Well, we owe our boom to Eisenhower," John observed, "and everyone wants to see it continue, Republican or Democrat. It won't hurt the business community any if we start gearing up for another war."

Paul felt a sudden chill. "Do you think one is inevitable, John?"

"Oh, absolutely. The Communists are up to mischief in Southeast Asia, and I don't have to tell you how vitally important that part of the world is to our interests. If we let South Vietnam sink, we might as well torpedo the Philippines at the same time, because they'll be the next to go."

It was bound to sound naïve, Paul knew, but perhaps his brother-in-law was too sloshed to notice it. "Do we really care what happens to the people of Vietnam or the Philippines?" he asked.

"Don't be absurd," John replied. "This country is ruled by self-interest, as every country in the world has been since the beginning of time. Why should we be any different? You hear people say that if the Cold War comes to a boil in Southeast Asia, we'll have to fight to preserve liberty. But that's *our* liberty we're talking about, not the real or imagined liberty of some semisavage a half-world away who wouldn't know his liberty from a hole in the ground."

"You don't think," Paul began cautiously, "that some people in America might be predisposed to another war just to keep the economic boom going, do you?"

"Leftist twaddle!" his brother-in-law exploded. "That's your typical Communist view of American businessmen. War mongers, they call us in Moscow and East Berlin. In their cartoons, we're drawn as Devil-like creatures with black cigars in one hand and an atom bomb in the other, mothers and their babies cringing with fear in front of us. It's all propaganda. Of course, the Russians don't like to see an American military buildup. They'd be happier if we were pushovers." Under the burden of emotion he was feeling, John seemed to sober up. "There were a lot of things your father and I disagreed on, Paul. But on that matter we agreed. If being prepared to fight a war is going to make us look like militarists, then by God, that's what we'll look like. It's preferable to being beaten and enslaved."

Charles Molloy's argument exactly. Almost word for word. Paul had listened to it so often that he could recite it verbatim.

But was it right or wrong? Who could tell? Providentially, Paul was still in basic training when the Second World War ended. Yet Tom and Robbie had both been killed. Would they be alive today if American isolationists hadn't prevented the rearming of the nation in the late thirties? Was Franklin D. Roosevelt a warmonger? Or a peacemaker? Would Adolf Hitler never have marched into Poland if the Molloy Company had been employed to build a behemoth of a military installation, a Project Galveston, in England or in France in the 1930's before the Wehrmacht was ready?

Paul hated the idea of war. Despised it. Yet he'd come to understand his father's passion for preparedness as a deterrent. But during the past two years, the firm's involvement in arming the nation had grown to such an extent that the company had its own liaison in Washington to bend Ike's ear. Now something called Project Galveston was to be the biggest peacetime military investment in the nation's history. Money, untold sums of it, would be going into it.

And it wasn't merely that money could corrupt people that worried Paul. In the end, all that could be lost was cash. What concerned him far more than that was that once a huge military installation had been built, there would be no reason not to use it. To justify it, a war that perhaps was only probable would become inevitable. And lives, not dollars, would be lost.

"I hope to meet General McFadden next week," Paul said. "I know that he's working on a government project that means a lot for the company, so I'd like to think that our bid will be accepted. What's the competition, or don't they know anything about that on the Street?"

"McFadden would be the authority, but from what I hear it's a consortium. Texas, Colorado, and California outfits have gotten together to work on this one because it's so big. They stand a good chance of getting the contract, the grapevine has it, particularly now that . . . ."

Now that Charles Molloy was dead, John might have said but didn't.

Paul could see why it was so important for Lee to complete what his father had begun. It was a tremendous undertaking, this Project Galveston, and for Lee to win it would be a feather in his cap, a test of manhood. Businesshood, too.

"Where the hell is the ice?" John complained, rising to replenish his drink.

"I'll get it," Paul volunteered.

Empty ice bucket in hand, he pushed open the door to the kitchen, and as he did, Caitlin looked up with surprise, her face flushed, somehow radiant. Only inches away stood Andy, and as Paul entered, Lee's best friend quickly began to skewer a wine bottle with a corkscrew.

Paul had the most peculiar feeling that he'd interrupted something terribly intimate. Because he loved them both, he was buoyed by it—how daring of Caitlin to spend the summer on Martha's Vineyard to get away from her husband! Paul was willing to bet that Andy would be there most weekends—but at the same time he was gripped by sadness, because in the next room sat a man who had no inkling of what was about to happen to him.

"I've just come for some ice," Paul stammered.

When Paul arrived at the River House apartment, Jean-Claude opened the door, still dressed in the black suit and tie he'd worn while serving dinner earlier that evening, but wearing slippers on his feet. One was gray, one was black, and his breath smelled of brandy.

"Good evening, Mr. Paul," the old man said. "Your mother would like to see you before you retire. She's in her bedroom."

As Paul stepped into the foyer, he saw how tired Jean-Claude looked. "Why don't you call it a a day, Jean-Claude?"

"Oh, no, Mr. Paul. That would never do. Mr. Charles was always very particular about that. I shall have to lock up after everyone else has turned in for the night."

Paul's father had never been able to sleep unless he knew he was securely locked in, protected from brigands and rogues. In spite of his age, Charles's faithful servant intended to go on performing his duties.

Paul found his mother sitting up in bed, an unopened book on her lap. After kissing her and sitting on the edge of the bed, he said, "Jean-Claude has been into the brandy again."

"Poor fellow, he's getting to be very forgetful, too. He misplaces things, then finds them days later."

"He has more than enough money to buy a little house in the country for himself; Father saw to that. So wouldn't it be a kindness if we could get him to retire?"

"Work is all he has, Paul. Without it, he would die. I don't mind if he gets into the brandy or loses things. I'll soon be dotty myself."

"That's most unlikely."

"Inevitable, you mean. It's the price one pays for longevity. I'm probably half dotty already, because I've been sitting here thinking about events that occurred forty years ago, things I'd secreted away at the back of my mind and forgotten till now." She laughed to herself. "I've been thinking of my mother, Paul, and the one-room cottage where she raised ten children. Often we had nothing but potatoes and buttermilk for our supper, but we were happy. I wonder what she would make of all this?" She extended an arm to indicate the sumptuous apartment around her.

"She'd be proud of you. You and Father worked very hard to get what you have."

"My mother and father worked much harder and got nothing. No, I take that back. They had children who loved them. And as for these possessions around me, they're nothing compared to the love of my children. I haven't always been successful. I failed with Megan, I nearly failed with Eddie. But the others—you and Caitlin, Deirdre, Mary, and Lee—are my riches."

"But families wear out, like old watches or shoes. Megan and Eddie got slightly different genetic cocktails and have had to make do with them."

"Eddie is shallow. He lives only for pleasure."

"Yes, I know. And Megan is nutty as a fruitcake."

"But harmless to others. She does damage only to herself." Nora sighed. "Oh, I *am* getting old. Your father's death has reminded me just how temporary a hold we have on life. There are so many things I have to do before my time comes."

Paul looked up in surprise.

"Money can pervert people," she went on. "Change them like a crippling disease. It changed your father, these past few years. I could see it."

"It's something I can't comprehend. If a man has enough to meet his needs, what drives him to want more?"

"It's a lust, and in time the lusting after money becomes an end in itself, I'm afraid." She waited, then added, "I'm worried, Paul."

"About Father?"

She nodded. "He wasn't himself these last few months. He was distracted. Business was all he could think of. His company. His legacy. And in the end, perhaps his mausoleum." She sought out her son's eyes. "Have you learned yet what caused your father's death?"

"The coroner said a faulty valve in his heart."

"No. Something caused that valve to stop and send a clot of blood to his brain."

What could Paul tell her? That Matt Rowley hadn't lied to her when he said he had no knowledge of any gentleman from Galveston? Or that, somehow or other, Lee was moved by compassion alone to keep a man on his executive staff whom he made no secret of despising? Yet if Paul could see no clarity or design in what he'd learned, how could he expect his mother to?

Instead, he said, "What if I should discover something about Father that we don't want to know?"

Nora sat up ramrod straight. "Then you have learned something?"

"No, not yet. I'm just reflecting. What if I uncover something that would be better left concealed? I mention this only because you and I seem to be the only ones pursuing this. I can't very well open any can of worms if I'm in California. If you like, I can leave first thing in the morning."

Nora carefully considered the implications before reply-ing. "I want you to stay until you've learned something. And if it proves to be detrimental to your father's reputation, then so be it." Momentarily, she closed her eyes, then reopened them. "Your father was an honest and moral man, Paul. I can't be-lieve that there *is* a can of worms."

"For your sake, and mine, I hope you're right."

Minutes later, he left the room, quietly closing the door behind him. As expected, Jean-Paul was snoring in his chair in the foyer.

Gently, Paul touched him. "I'm going to bed now, Jean-Claude."

Jean-Claude sprang to his slippered feet, listing a bit, then straightened his bent shoulders. As Paul began to walk toward his bedroom, he turned to face Jean-Claude, deep in thought. "There's something I've been meaning to ask you."

"Yes, Mr. Paul?"

"The night Father died in Southampton, he received a telephone call. Do you remember that?"

"I do, Mr. Paul," he replied without hesitation, "only too well."

"When you announced the call, Mother says she distinctly heard you say it was 'the gentleman from Galveston.' Is that correct?"

With apprehension, as if perhaps he was about to be ac-cused of some dereliction of duty, he replied, "That is correct."

"What I want to know is, was it the first time Father had received a call from that gentleman? Can you remember?"

Clearly, the old man was confused. "Pardon, Mr. Paul?"

Paul rephrased the question. "Had there been other calls from this 'gentleman from Galveston'?"

"Oh, yes. There were many."

Paul's heart quickened. "Did he ever identify himself by name? Did he ever tell you who he was?"

Once again, Paul thought that he'd lost him. Momentar-ily, the old man appeared baffled, as if faced with a contradic-tion his tired old head couldn't resolve.

Then, slowly, comprehension flooded his eyes. "But Mr. Paul," he began, "there has been a misunderstanding. That was merely how I was asked to announce the calls. It was at Mr. Charles's own request. But you see, it wasn't a gentleman at all who was calling. It was a woman."

TEN

After having had lunch with Ted and his roommate every day from Monday through Friday for two weeks, Kathleen went to their apartment one Sunday and prepared what she called her gastronomical triumph: Greek Stew Molloy. It was steeped in red wine and cloves and made the kitchen smell like an Egyptian whorehouse, Ted claimed.

"How would you know?" she asked.

"I've always had a very vivid imagination."

"Well, it makes sublime eating," Clay sighed. "If you can't earn a living any other way, you can always be a cook."

"My grandmother was, before she got married," Kathleen explained. "In fact, she taught me how to make this stew."

"Well, here's to your grandmother for preparing you for life," Ted proposed, holding up his glass of jug wine. "It's my considered opinion, based on years of experience, that all women are essentially indistinguishable in bed. It's in the kitchen where their true distinction expresses itself."

Kathleen felt her color rise. "Surely some women must be equally distinguished in both areas."

"Hear! Hear!" shouted Clay. "I propose a toast to the well-rounded woman. But before we drink to it, may I point out that my roommate's experience has been confined to the kitchen. So whatever he may think of a woman's accomplishment in bed, it's mere speculation."

"Spoilsport! Here I am, trying to impress Kathleen with my worldliness, putting on my Errol Flynn act, and you have to ruin it all."

"If I'm not mistaken, Errol Flynn prefers members of his own sex," Kathleen timidly suggested.

"He does?" the two Harvard undergraduates said more or less in unison.

"So does Tyrone Power."

"My other role model! What's a man to do? Anyway, how come you know so much about the sleazy side of life, and here Clay and I were under the impression you were a nice, respectable Radcliffe girl."

"My cousin Jake keeps me informed. He's at Princeton. I mean, he was at Princeton. One day in an elevator in New York, he was propositioned by Montgomery Clift, he thinks."

"Thinks he was propositioned or thinks it was Montgomery Clift?" Ted asked.

"No doubt about the latter. And just a little bit about the former. You see, Jake had a dinner date, so he had to turn him down."

Baffled, Ted asked, "So is he at Princeton or isn't he?"

"Well, yes, he is. And no, he isn't." Kathleen attempted to explain the whole deplorable story about Jake's deception, still not uncovered by his parents.

"I don't envy him if he's at Princeton," Clay said. "Or was at Princeton. It's the most conservative of all Ivy League colleges. For a long time, that was where the southern gentry sent their sons to be educated. I may be wrong, but I think it was the last of the Ivy League colleges to admit Jews, and probably the last to admit Negroes. If your cousin is having an identity crisis, it couldn't have been much fun to have it at Princeton."

"I've always wondered what it would be like to be on the outside of things," Kathleen said, "the way Scott Fitzgerald was when he was at Princeton. Or—"

"Or the way I feel," Clay interrupted, "here at Harvard. I wish I could say I'm reacting the way Fitzgerald did, that Irish Catholic in an Anglo-Saxon Protestant community. He looked at the people around him with envy and yearning, and he wrote about them that way, too. But as for me, I react with rage most of the time."

Kathleen protested, "I can see why you'd have a reason to be full of anger if you *weren't* at Harvard. But you're here. You've made it."

He shook his head in denial. "Sometimes if I'm walking through Harvard Yard and I don't have my book bag with me, I can feel people look at me with suspicion, wondering what I'm doing there."

"That's your imagination, Clay," his roommate suggested.

"No, it isn't. Last fall after some guy at Wigglesworth had a lot of camera equipment stolen, a cop stopped me when I was walking through the Yard and asked to see my student ID."

"But that's understandable," Kathleen remarked, "after something was stolen from one of the dorms."

"But the cop didn't stop white kids going through the Yard. Just me."

Instinctively, she reached across the table and covered his hand with her own. It was a simple, honest gesture, and she saw at once that he was moved.

So was Ted. "It isn't easy, being in the vanguard. You get it from both sides. Whites distrust Clay because he's broken down barriers. Negroes distrust him because they think he's sold out. Anyone else would have thrown in the sponge long ago."

"If I weren't everyone's symbol, I probably would have by now. But too many people are depending on me."

"Do you ever wish," Kathleen began, "that someone else was here in your place and you could just relax and be yourself and stop being a symbol?"

"All the time. But the only way I can leave is either to graduate or flunk out. If I flunk out, people will say, 'Well, what could you expect from a darky?' And that's why I have to stay and graduate."

Clayton had a paper due the following day, so shortly afterward he excused himself and went off to the library. "Swell dinner, Kathleen. See you at lunch tomorrow."

"See you tomorrow," she said without hesitation.

After he left, Kathleen began to clear the table, carrying dishes into the kitchen. "Just to show you how democratic we are around here," Ted said as he followed her, "we'll reverse the usual roles, and I'll wash and you can dry."

As he splashed steaming water from the tap into the sink,

he added, "I consider it penance for having been such a boor and making that crack about women in bed. I could see right away that you didn't like it."

"I know it may come as a shock, and it probably sounds like what the tart said in the *New Yorker* cartoon when she climbed onto the rich banker's lap, but I *have* led a pretty protected life."

"That's apparent. But you don't have to apologize for it. Have you ever . . . loved any man?"

"My father, whom I never saw. My uncle Paul, who always used to ignore me when I was a little girl. And my grandfather."

"You have a thing for older men."

"I didn't plan it that way. It just happened. I can't seem to get interested in boys who talk about nothing but football games or last weekend's beer bash."

He dipped the three wine glasses into the sudsy water, then began to wash them. "I used to go steady with a girl," he said at last.

"Steady" was an ambiguous word. It could mean anything from a regular Saturday night date to regularly shacking up with someone in a motel. "How steady?" she asked.

"Pretty steady. She goes to Smith, and I met her freshman year. For a while she used to come here every weekend or I'd go to Northampton. But then last year, we started going different ways. She didn't like Clay and said I was using him to show the world how progressive I was."

"Are you?"

"I don't think so. She also said I was crazy to get mixed up in the civil rights movement when it had nothing to do with me. She wanted your typical, average, ordinary country club sort of guy, and I wasn't it. So we split up. But it hurt, let me tell you. I don't have casual relationships with people. It's a total commitment or nothing. When it was all over, I hated myself for misjudging her, and letting her misjudge me. I couldn't let it happen again. That was one of the reasons I didn't get back to you right away after I met you at the dance. I was still hurting."

To give her hands something to do, Kathleen redried the wine glass she'd just dried.

"She wouldn't believe it," he continued, "if she knew someone like you was here helping me do the dishes. Last time I talked to her, she said I'd probably wind up with some crazy anarchist from Boston College who spends all her spare time making bombs."

"I wouldn't be any good at it. I'm more the Greek stew type."

He pondered it momentarily. "But don't you honestly think that we all have obligations to change things in society that are immoral or unjust? I mean, you don't have to be an anarchist to do that." Suddenly, something occurred to him. "What are you politically, anyway?"

It was a minute before she could answer, and when she did, she hedged. "I'm not sure I know. When I left home, I was an Eisenhower Republican."

"He's an amiable ninny!" Ted exclaimed. "A tool of big business, whether he knows it or not. They put him in power, and they're keeping him there. Now that he can't run for re-election, they'll throw their support behind that satanic Richard Nixon."

Kathleen couldn't help but wonder what her grandfather would have made of this young man. A dangerous revolutionary, he probably would have said.

"I really don't think it makes that much difference which party is in power," she said at last. "If the country could survive Harry Truman—a party hack with a small mind, my grandfather called him—it can survive Mr. Nixon."

He looked at her with dismay. "You're not going to work for his campaign, are you?"

"He has to be nominated first."

"Oh, he'll get it. No doubt about that. The big guns in the Republican party will see to it."

"And who will the big guns in the Democratic party choose?"

"For one thing, there are no big guns. And even if there were, they wouldn't be able to do the choosing. It's going to be an open convention, and it's my guess that Adlai Stevenson will get the nomination."

Smiling, she began, "To paraphrase you, he's a tool of labor and civil rights groups. They put him in power and want to keep him there. And if he can't win, they'll throw their support behind that satanic John Kennedy."

"Now you're making fun of me."

She was sorry if he saw it that way. "I just don't think it's fair to characterize people like Richard Nixon as satanic because you don't like the way they look. Do I have to remind you that some people thought Abe Lincoln was the Devil incarnate?"

He was dumbfounded. "So you *are* going to work for Nixon's campaign."

"I didn't say that. But it's very possible that I will."

He was furious and made no effort to conceal it. "Even if you know that people like Dick Nixon and his Republican friends don't give a rat's ass about people like Clay Gibson?"

"So prove to me that Adlai Stevenson or John Kennedy or any of their Democratic friends *do* give a rat's ass."

He wrung his hands in the soapy water, frustrated at her stubbornness. "It's a matter of approach, Kathleen. At least the Democratic party gives the illusion that they're concerned about minorities."

"But that's all it is, an illusion. In the long run, a good, healthy economy is going to do more for minorities than all your desk-pounding Democrats in Washington." She was only repeating what her grandfather had often told her.

He stood back from the sink to survey her. "And I thought we had something in common."

"I'm sure we do. But that doesn't mean we have to think the same way politically, does it? Can't I have my opinions and you have yours?"

At last he relented. "You're right. That's very intolerant of me. It's the old story all over again. You become a liberal because you hate people who are narrow-minded, but unless you're careful you become as narrow-minded as they are." He jutted out his chin. "So I'll have to learn to live with you conservatives—so long as you admit that Dwight Eisenhower is a senile old fool who's a captive of big business."

She watched his lips rise in a grin. "I'll do that if you agree that Adlai Stevenson is a pompous, ineffectual old bore who should probably be teaching in some midwestern college rather than trying to run for the presidency again."

"So what about John Kennedy?"

"Too glamorous to be President. Playboy type."

"You'd be happier if he looked a bit satanic?"

"Yes, I would, frankly."

"I don't understand you."

"I don't understand *you*."

He reached out and grabbed the dish towel from her hands, then stood back and snapped it against her thighs. She shrieked and in retaliation scooped up a feather duster lying on the counter top and plunged it into his soft underbelly.

In a minute they were chasing each other around the kitchen, thrusting and parrying.

Suddenly, both of them were laughing, and when she stopped, Kathleen saw him watching her in a most peculiar way.

She asked, "Why are you looking at me like that?"

"I'm trying to make up my mind about something."

"What?"

He leaned over and kissed her on the neck beneath her ear. "About that."

She shuddered as his lips met her skin, and when he saw the effect he produced, he rested his hands on the small of her back, drawing her close to him, then he kissed her on the lips. He held it a long time, opening her mouth with his tongue, and when they'd finished, both of them were breathless.

Kathleen stayed in the apartment all Sunday afternoon, feeling very, very adult. It was the first time she'd ever really been alone with a boy, and there was no one around to censure her.

"When I touch you," Ted said at one point, "it's like you're jumping out of your skin."

"I feel that way." Not merely out of her skin, but out of everything she found so constricting. And partly because being alone in an apartment with a boy was so forbidden, it was also irresistible. When he began stroking her breasts beneath her sweater, she knew she should pull away or ask him to stop, but it was hard to find the words.

"You'll wear away the cashmere," she said at last.

"I know a way we can avoid that."

"Un-unh. I know that line. It's what Anna Karenina listened to, and look where it got her."

"But she didn't have the advantage of a Radcliffe education. She was your typical high-strung, irrational nineteenth-century woman."

"If you keep that up much longer, you're going to have a typical high-strung, irrational twentieth-century woman on your hands."

"Could you put that in writing?"

Late in the afternoon, Clay returned and pretended not to be too surprised to find them lying on the living room sofa, face to face, but Kathleen was embarrassed. He volunteered to go out for a pizza and some beer, but after he examined his wallet and Ted counted the change in his pocket, they found they didn't have enough. So Kathleen gave him a twenty.

After supper, Ted walked her to the library and sat across from her at one of the long tables in the main reading room, in what he said would be a study date. Neither did much studying. Every now and then, his foot reached out and stroked her leg. And whenever Kathleen looked up from her book, she saw him watching her.

"Oh, am I lucky!" he whispered to her at one point.

"Shhhhhhh."

"You love me, don't you?"

"*Shhhhhhhhhhhhh!*"

Later, he walked her home to the dorm and they stood outside in the softly falling snow, clutching one another, dreading the minute when Mrs. Foxworth would start blinking the lights to remind her girls that curfew was about to begin. Kathleen's lips were raw from kissing, all her nerve ends ached.

"Listen," Ted whispered in the darkness. "Clay has to go home next weekend. Why don't you come and stay with me in the apartment while he's gone?"

There! He'd said it. If it wasn't exactly a proposition, it wasn't romantic love à la Petrarch, either.

"Spend the weekend with you?" She pulled away from him. "Ted, you know perfectly well I can't do that."

"Why not?"

Why not indeed? "Well, for one thing, if I check out for the weekend, I have to let my housemother know where I'm going. She's a martinet in that respect."

Ted was appalled. "My God, Kathleen. You're twenty years old. It's none of your housemother's goddamned business where you spend your weekends!"

"Yes, it is," she replied calmly. "You see, she serves *in loco parentis.* In case your Latin's rusty, that means in place of my parents. And if Mrs. Foxworth would disapprove of my spending the weekend with you, it's nothing to what my mother would do. She'd call out the National Guard, don't you think she wouldn't."

He was clearly suffering. "And you'd let her?"

Kathleen wanted to spend the weekend with him. Wanted it more than anything she'd every wanted. But to do so, she would have to renounce everything her mother had ever taught her about private morality.

Luckily, at that moment, Mrs. Foxworth's lights began blinking nervously.

"I love you," he called after her as she broke away and ran blindly into the lobby.

When she reached her room, she found her roommate taking off her storm coat and shaking the snow from her hair. Her eyes were filled with disapproval as she asked, "Who was that?"

Kathleen hadn't seen her return to the dorm in the darkness, but it was obvious that Carolyn had seen her and Ted.

Lamely, Kathleen replied, "Just a boy I know."

Carolyn pounced on it at once. "Just a boy you know! Well, that's the understatement of the year! My God, Kathleen, you two were only a step away from . . . from coitus!"

At any other time, Kathleen would have been amused to hear the word coming from Carolyn's lips, but one look at her roommate's face told her that she was deadly earnest. What had Ted been doing to her in front of the dorm? He'd been embracing her, perhaps . . . well, fondling her insofar as it was possible to fondle anyone in a heavy polo coat. But certainly they hadn't come anywhere near coitus.

But then Kathleen realized that Carolyn must have perceived the rapture Kathleen was experiencing as Ted stroked her. And for someone like Carolyn Biddle, who once boasted that she wouldn't mind at all being a spinster for the rest of her life, it must have been shocking.

"Don't be such a prude," Kathleen complained. "It was all perfectly harmless."

"Harmless, was it? Why, Kathleen, he was . . . digging himself into you, leaning you against the wall. You, of all people. Ever since we were at Rosemary Hall, we've poked fun at girls like Diane Crocker, who could never keep her pants on. And here"—Carolyn struck her forehead with her hand at the enormity of it all—"you're turning out to be just like her!"

Kathleen was close to tears. "Well, I'm sorry if I've offended your delicate sensibilities." She turned, ready to flee down the hall, but Carolyn grabbed the sleeve of her coat.

"Kathleen, listen to me. Don't you realize what's happening? You've been under a terrible strain these past few weeks, ever since your grandfather's death. You're so ready to let yourself go and have a little fling."

"It isn't what you think."

"I can only tell you what it looked like. I saw you out there in front of the dorm. All week long, you've skipped lunch because you said you had to study at the library. And tonight you skipped supper. Then the next thing I know, you turn up on the steps with this boy I've never even seen before. Is he a student . . . or what?"

"He's a student," Kathleen answered almost inaudibly. "His name is Edmund Burke Birmingham, and he's from New York City. His father owned a saloon, and his mother runs a restaurant." Carolyn's eyes opened wide with horror, as if she were watching a particularly grisly accident. Kathleen decided that she might as well give her something more to fret about. "He works at Eliot House dining room as a porter and shares an apartment with a Harvard senior named Clayton Gibson, who's a Negro." She had to catch her breath. "Now would you care to call the nearest insane asylum to have me committed?"

Carolyn was ashen-faced. Not since one of the girls in the dorm who'd been in Europe for the summer had passed around a pack of erotic playing cards from France did Kathleen's roommate look so close to fainting. Now, shattered by what she'd just learned, she sat down on the edge of a chair.

"Does your mother know?" she asked at last.

"And why, might I ask, is it any concern of hers?"

"For the same reason it's a concern of mine. We care about you, Kathleen. We don't want anyone to hurt you. Or exploit you."

Ah, so that was it. By now, it was rather common knowledge around the dorm that Kathleen was one of the chief beneficiaries of her grandfather's will. There'd been no coverage in the Boston press, but predictably the New York *Daily News* had run a few paragraphs on the subject to titillate its working-class readers.

"I think it's more likely that I'd be exploiting him," she retorted. "He's been very nice to me, Carolyn. And so far as I know, he's not even aware of Grandfather. Do you intend to mention this to my mother?"

"I'm not spying on you."

"It wouldn't be beyond her to ask you to."

"But I'm not. If you don't want me to mention it, I won't. But I'm worried, Kathleen. This just isn't like you."

If it wasn't, what was? "I don't intend to do anything rash," she heard herself say. "I've just met him, and I like him a great deal. You may be right: I'm ready for something like this to happen to me. But if it does, then I'll go into it with my eyes wide open and I'll accept the consequences. But I don't want my mother, as well-meaning as she is, to meddle. Promise me you won't say anything to her, at least for a little while."

Reluctantly, Carolyn promised. She didn't approve, but she had no intention of setting up obstacles to prevent Kathleen from seeing Ted Birmingham.

"I'm sorry I was cross," she said afterward. "I didn't mean to be. We've been best friends for so long and have always confided in one another. I guess I just felt left out of things when I saw you out front with someone I didn't even know existed. If you like him, then I'm sure I'd like him too, Kathleen."

Well, maybe yes, maybe no. Ted inhabited a world so vastly different from Carolyn's that she might find him more than a bit alarming.

It was a very long time before Kathleen could get to sleep that night, and when at last she did, she woke up twice before dawn, and each time Ted's face was next to hers, and she could feel him inside her.

Next morning, she was late for her course in Russian lit, and her professor, a bushy-eyebrowed Slav who always brought his West Highland terrier to class with him, scowled as she took her seat. And in her eleven o'clock class in Puritan lit, unable to follow what was being said about transcendentalism, she stopped taking notes entirely.

On the margin of the paper, she wrote "Ted," then "Edmund." Then "Edmund Birmingham," decorating the words with lavish care, like a medieval scribe.

Mindless. She'd been made mindless. How was it possible that she, of all people, wanted to sleep with someone she scarcely knew?

After class, he was waiting for her, and when she saw him slouched against the wall, she ran up and kissed him on the cheek.

"Hey, how come I deserve that?" he asked in surprise.

"I just felt like it, that's all."

As she fell into step next to him, he said, "So what about this weekend?"

"Can't you think about anything else?"

"Frankly, no. And neither can you." He turned to look into her face. "You'll have to decide, Kathleen, if it matters what your housemother, or your real mother, or anyone else thinks about you. You can't lead your life to please someone else. It's your life, not theirs."

"I know," she said lamely. "But I need more time. What you're asking me to do is a very big step. Once it's done, it can't be undone. And I don't want to do anything . . . that I'd be ashamed of afterward."

"Do you honestly think you'd be ashamed?"

"No."

"Why do you think I'm asking you, for crying out loud? I could have gone all the way yesterday afternoon in the apartment. You know I could have. But I don't want it to happen that way. I want you to know what you're getting into. I don't *want* you to be ashamed afterward. Don't you see?"

She reached over and slid her hand into the pocket of his army surplus parka, next to his own hand. "I understand, Ted. But I need a little more time to make up my mind."

Impatiently, he cried. "God, I should have ravished you yesterday!"

"I don't think you mean that."

He squeezed her hand inside his pocket. "You know I don't, Kathleen. It's just . . . you're driving me half crazy. You're all I can think about. I didn't understand a single thing in my chem class this morning." He yanked his hand free and pulled a notebook from his book bag, opening it for her to see. "Look. You see what you're doing to me?"

All over an otherwise wordless page he had written "Kathleen" in ten or fifteen different kinds of scripts.

"That's very childish," she said sternly. "If you don't pay attention in class, you'll flunk out."

"I know I'm going to flunk out," he said, closing his notebook.

"If you were mature, you'd be able to handle emotional situations like this without letting them upset your life."

"Oh, cripes, I agree. One hundred percent. I'm being childish."

"It's a sign of weakness, Ted. If you can't get your emotional life in order, how do you ever expect to get through med school?"

"God knows, maybe I won't. I never thought anything like this could happen to me."

Without another word, she opened her notebook to her morning's entries, then held it up for him to see.

"What's this?" he asked, squinting. Then as he perceived all the variations of "Ted" and "Edmund Birmingham," he began to laugh.

At lunch that day, Ted deliberately kept his distance, as if he didn't want his body to influence her decision. Didn't touch her. Didn't kiss her. And afterward, he walked her solemnly back to campus, scarcely uttering a word. He had already made his case, and it was now Kathleen's decision.

All afternoon she bumped into people, stumbled over curbs. On several occasions, she passed girls from her dorm, and when they waved at her, it took all her powers of concentration to remember who they were.

Her instincts told her that there was no retreating and that she would spend the weekend with Ted. Then, having decided that, she clearly heard her mother's voice ask: *So what happens to you on Monday morning, Kathleen?*

She was so distracted when she returned to her dorm late in the afternoon that the girl on duty at the reception desk had to shout her name twice to attract her attention.

"Kathleen, you have a guest. I told him that visiting hours don't begin for another hour, but he insisted on waiting. He's in the lounge."

Had Ted come over to plead his case again? Most unlikely, because he was due at Eliot House to help serve the evening meal in fifteen minutes. Probably instead it was a friend of her mother's who'd been conscripted to call on Kathleen while passing through Boston. Some intolerably dull and middle-aged Greenwich type. It wouldn't be the first time.

With resignation, she entered the lounge. The first thing she saw was a huge bouquet of red roses, three dozen at least, then the smartly dressed, Saville Row–tailored man who was holding them as he stepped forward and presented them.

"My compliments. I hope I haven't arrived at an inopportune time," he began. "But business has brought me to Boston for a few days, and when I remembered that you were at Rad-cliffe, it occurred to me that I might be able to persuade you to have dinner with me tonight." His smile was wise, gentle, comforting. "Provided you can remember who I am."

Relieved that she now had a legitimate excuse to postpone her decision about the weekend just a bit longer, and at the same time exhilarated at seeing someone who'd made a pro-found impression on her at their first meeting, she heard her-self say, "You're Stephen Olivari, my father's friend."

ELEVEN

"*F*ather Joseph!" a frail and gaunt Rafael Banuelos cried from his wicker chair beneath a grape arbor outside his small stucco house near Salinas. "You have come to give succor for our cause, have you?"

It was several days after the accident on Van Ness Avenue, and Father Joseph had driven to Monterey County with Susan Grainger. He leaned over to take Rafael's leathery hand and found it limp, without its customary firm grip. "I would be happier, Rafael, if you'd let me treat you to a decent dinner tonight—a thick steak with home-fried potatoes and a glass or two of lusty zinfandel. What's this I hear about your going on a fast?"

"Oh, yes, is *verdad,* Father Joseph. Our friends the ranchers pretend not to hear me even though I shout from morning till night, or see me even though I seldom stray beyond their field of vision. So to attract their attention, I have begun a fast, like the great Mahatma Gandhi. Today is my eighth day without food. I am very determined."

Behind him hovered two dark-eyed, ancient women dressed all in black, as if in mourning. In the shade of a nearby live oak, several barefooted, brown-faced children stared with awe at the gray-haired man in the chair.

Father Joseph asked, "And what if the ranchers' greed proves to be stronger than your determination?"

Serenely, Rafael replied, "I have no fears. If that is to be, then it is to be." He looked up at the young woman standing next to his visitor. "Surely I must be delirious already. Is that not one of God's angels you've brought with you, Father?"

Father Joseph made introductions. "Rafael, this is Susan

Grainger from San Francisco, who's expressed a keen interest in your cause."

It was more than hyperbole. It was a downright lie. During the ride from the city, Susan had reaffirmed her interest in the only subject that mattered: herself. Moreover, she'd fulminated against Christianity, knowing that it would offend her host—"God is irrelevant," she insisted. "Don't you see? It's just a symbol, and it's outlived its usefulness"—and was particularly scathing in her condemnation of Roman Catholic priests, whom she described as little more than magicians trying to pull miracles out of their hats like rabbits.

"God, give me strength," he prayed silently, wilting under her attack. At one point, he considered stopping the car and putting her out on the shoulder to hitchhike home, but in the end rejected the idea because it would only add fuel to her antagonism toward everything he stood for.

As for the object of their excursion—visiting the leader of the Chicano field hands to try to set up a voter registration drive among his people—Susan immediately questioned the motives of someone who appeared to be as self-sacrificing as Rafael Banuelos. "He's not for real," she said as they drove toward Salinas. "If you ask me, he's probably just another con man."

But now that she'd met him face to face and saw how weakened he was from his fast, she seemed much less sure of herself.

Father Joseph began, "What have the ranchers offered you so far, Rafael?"

With a tired smile, he answered, "They've offered to provide me with free transportation from here to Tijuana. They would like to dump me across the border. I have told them that I am not a wetback but American-born, and they say that if I can't provide documents to prove my citizenship, my fast will have been for nothing, because the ranchers will have me deported."

Susan appeared interested. "If you were born here in America, surely there must be records somewhere."

"There are no records if you are born in a field. I was

born near Hollister, where my mother and father were working in the lettuce fields. There was no doctor, only a midwife, and no record was ever filed."

"School records?" Father Joe asked. "Wouldn't they show your place of birth?"

"We had no schools when I was small. Our families moved from one part of California to another, following the harvests. There was no time for education. When I was five years old, I was working side by side with my mother and father."

"What about census records?" Susan suggested. "There would have been one in 1930, 1940, and 1950. And census takers are required to record the names and place of birth of everyone living in a particular area at a given time."

He shook his head sadly. "Then, as now, the ranchers do not welcome visitors at their labor camps. We have checked the census rolls without results. For all practical purposes, I do not exist. Even my mother—poor woman, she died last year—was a nonperson, although she, too, was born here in California, in San Diego County."

Father Joseph marveled at the ingenuity that powerful and rich Californians employed to remove irritants from their beautiful state. He expressed the hope that perhaps some record might be found in Sacramento. Then he said, "You know why we're here, don't you, Rafael?"

"Aaron Golden called me to say that you want to register my people as voters. I told him what I shall now tell you: The ranchers will not permit you into their camps."

Susan complained, "But I don't understand why it would make any difference to the ranchers."

The wizened old man looked at her again, perhaps perceiving the languor and frivolity he'd missed the first time. Patiently, he explained, "The ranchers are most reluctant to let the rest of the world know how we're forced to live. You see, that is one of the issues in our long dispute." He smiled bravely. "We are braceros. We plant and harvest the crops here in Monterey County. Without us, there would be no ranchers. We have made them rich men. And in return for that, all we ask are the basic necessities of life. A clean place to sleep. A place to cook our meals. A place to wash ourselves."

"But the ranchers maintain that they already provide adequate facilities," Susan pointed out.

"Adequate for whom? For the chickens that have previously lived in them?" He waited to gauge the look of disbelief on her face. "Oh, yes, often my people are housed in former chicken coops. Without electricity. Without running water."

"But if the conditions are so terrible," she resumed, "why do your people stay? Can't they get another job? After all, no one is forcing them to live that way."

"My people know no other trade except using their backs and hands to pick crops. As I say, most of us have received no education because the ranchers fear an educated bracero more than they fear drought or floods. We have no other place to go."

Rafael motioned for one of the old crones to pour water from a pitcher into glasses for himself and his guests.

"You don't think the ranchers will allow us into the labor camps to register voters?" Father Joe asked.

"If necessary, they will keep you out at gunpoint. I have tried for some time to get a newspaperman into one of the camps, but without success. I had hoped that this fast of mine might generate a little publicity for the cause, but thus far the only newspaper to give me any coverage has been the Carmel *Pine Cone*, a weekly generally devoted to reporting the results of bridge tournaments."

"I'd like to see one of these camps for myself," Susan said. "Is that possible, Rafael?"

"It's not impossible, but it could be dangerous. Roy Bannister is the largest rancher in Monterey County, and he has a camp only a few miles away from here." Unsteadily, he began rising from his chair. "I must prepare you, however. In the event we should be able to get in, it won't be a pretty sight."

"I'm tougher than I look," Susan said. "When I was in college, I went to Spain one summer and traveled everywhere by third-class coach. Nothing could surprise me."

"Oh, I think a few things could," Rafael warned her. "These camps aren't third-class. They are sixth- or seventh-class. Unfit even for chickens or pigs, and with no more of the creature comforts than you'd find for those poor beasts." As he walked shakily toward the car, he continued, "I told Aaron Golden that I would vote for any man who would pledge to install indoor toilets at our labor camps. And do you know what he said?"

"I can guess."

"He said that while he couldn't guarantee that it would receive top priority in the Democratic party platform, he was sure that John Kennedy would give it serious attention. And if necessary, he would even ask Bobby to supervise the job."

Laughing softly, he was helped into the backseat of the car. "It is as simple as that," he went on once Father Joseph and Susan had slid into the front seat, "this election of 1960. The ranchers will be voting Republican to protect what they already possess, as is only natural. We braceros, on the other hand, will be voting for something we don't yet have. It will be people with many, many bathrooms pitted against people with none."

Rafael sat in the backseat, wearing not a sombrero but a baseball cap and sunglasses, watching as Father Joseph steered the old Ford over a well-maintained asphalt road in the rolling foothills of the Gabilan Mountains. On either side were endless fields of strawberries, dotted here and there with workers whose hoes chopped at the soil methodically, their backs bent from the effort.

"Many of my people have permanent spinal deformities from having spent most of their lives working in the fields. Some are nearly bent in two."

He instructed Father Joseph to turn off the main highway and onto a dirt road that rose gradually as it made its way into the hills. Almond trees were in flower, and the air was heady with their fragrance.

"Paradise," Susan mused.

"Even paradise has its hells," the aged Chicano replied. "Here amid all this earthly beauty, Roy Bannister has built his prison for his laborers. Go slowly, Father Joseph, or we shall raise dust and attract notice. The entrance is just up here a bit behind that grove of trees, well hidden from the road—for good reason."

Another one hundred feet, and Rafael instructed him to pull the car under the limbs of the live oaks to shield it from anyone standing at a higher elevation.

As they proceeded on foot, they soon encountered a twelve-foot-high wire chain fence and a conspicuous sign.

PRIVATE PROPERTY. NO TRESPASSING.
VIOLATORS WILL BE SEVERELY DEALT WITH.

R. BANNISTER

"How severely?" Susan asked. "I wish he'd be a little more explicit."

"His men are armed with rifles, and they've been known to shoot at trespassers."

"Yes, I'd call that very severe," Father Joe opined. "But is it legal in this county to tote rifles and shoot people at will?"

"The excuse that Bannister gives is that it's necessary for his men to be armed at all times because there's always the possibility that they could run into a rattlesnake. The fact of the matter is that most of the rattlers were cleared out years ago. To put it bluntly my people in the fields simply respond more readily to orders when they're given by someone carrying a rifle." He motioned for silence, then pointed to a clump of bushes behind which there was an opening cut in the fence.

"Very hospitable, this Roy Bannister," Susan whispered as she slid through.

"He's gone to a lot of trouble to preserve his privacy," Father Joseph added.

Ahead of them was a long, narrow one-story building without windows. Directly beneath the eaves, however, the weathered boards had been slit from one end of the structure to the other, about a foot deep. It was covered with wire.

"My God, it *is* a chicken coop!" Father Joseph exclaimed.

"Was. The chickens perished and were replaced by field hands, who are heartier. Come with me. Miss Grainger, perhaps you would like to hold your handkerchief to your nose."

"I'm quite all right."

As they entered the doorless portal, the stench from the

latrine at the far end was overpowering, permeating the sleeping quarters. Everywhere, huge and voracious black flies swarmed, and it was necessary to saw the air to protect their lips and eyes.

Except for dusty light coming through the openings near the roof, the room was in darkness, and after the brilliant sunshine, it was a minute or two before their eyes could adjust to the gloom. When at last they could see, they perceived fifty or so cots lined up from one end of the room to the other, only inches away from one another. Beneath them, the floor still showed stains from chicken droppings, as did the walls. Here and there, the workers had hung crucifixes or photographs— here a child, there a woman—but otherwise the room was bleak and oppressive.

"Oh, the heat!" Susan cried.

"It's nothing today. In summer, when the temperature outside is a hundred and ten," Rafael told her, "in here it goes up to a hundred and twenty or a hundred and thirty."

Father Joseph was stunned. "How is it possible that one human being could inflict this on another?"

The elderly Chicano shrugged his shoulders. "I have long since stopped trying to understand my fellow men. From time to time, I have considered turning my back on this world, climbing the highest mountain and living there alone. But then someone warm and loving touches me, and I am reminded that cruelty is an aberration. Most men would never subject their fellow men to such indignities as you see here before you."

Just then, booted footsteps could be heard on the floor behind them, and an angry voice called out, "Okay, you greasers, why ain't you in the fields?"

When Father Joseph turned, he saw two men standing inside the doorway, peering into the semidarkness, apparently expecting to find malingering workers.

But as they recognized who it was, the man pointing the rifle exclaimed, "Holy shit! Damned if it ain't the king of the greasers himself!"

The other walked forward. "Mr. Bannister, he's going to

be mighty pleased to learn that you've volunteered for another jail sentence, Banuelos. It is real accommodating of you."

As the man with the rifle approached them, he was able for the first time to make out the Roman collar on Father Joseph's neck. "Looks like you brought your spiritual adviser with you this time, Banuelos. A goddamned priest! And what's this? A lady?" He reached out with his rifle till its muzzle touched Susan.

Father Joseph intervened. "We're public-spirited citizens who've come to begin a voter registration drive among the field hands."

"Sure as hell fooled me," the man with the rifle replied. "I would have took you for trespassers. I can see maybe why the greaser here can't read the signs we got up all round, but you"—he stroked Father Joe's turned collar with his rifle—"and Miss Public-Spirited here must know how to read. Or *do* you?" He let the rifle slide down Father Joseph's torso till it reached his groin. "Always wondered if you guys had dicks or a hole down there."

Rafael rushed at him, holding up his fists to beat him on the chest. "You have no right to talk to a man of God like that!"

In one swift motion, the man tilted the rifle and cracked its butt against the side of the old man's head.

Rafael's eyes opened wide with astonishment, then as pain swept through his body, he crumpled to the ground.

"You're going to regret this," Father Joe warned him as Susan ran to Rafael's side.

"You're wrong. *I'm* the one arranging all the regrettin' around here, and I got news for you. In an hour, you'll be settin' in the county jail regrettin' you ever stepped foot on Mr. Bannister's place."

One of the braceros must have seen Rafael, dazed and bloodied, being led into the deputy's car, along with a priest and a young woman, because by the time they reached the courthouse in Monterey, a small crowd had gathered there on the steps.

Even before the car door was opened, a very efficient-looking dark-haired woman in a neatly tailored suit stepped up and demanded of the deputy, "My client has been injured and needs medical attention immediately."

"Aw, come off it, Antonia," the deputy replied. "He just fell down while resisting arrest. I assure you, he's going to be all right."

She would have none of his placating. "Unless you're qualified to give a medical diagnosis, I'm not the least bit interested in your opinion. And my name is not Antonia. To you, it's Miss Fernandez."

"Aw, Antonia!"

Through the opened window, she exchanged rapid-fire Spanish with Rafael, then said, "Father Cassidy, Miss Grainger. Rafael tells me that you can vouch for everything he's said. One of Bannister's goons hit him without provocation while you were attempting to register voters. Is that correct?"

"More or less," Father Joe answered. "But I guess we were trespassing. They had a sign up forbidding it."

"If you were attempting to register voters—or preparing to register them, as Rafael tells me—no sign in the world could keep you out. Roy Bannister's camps aren't fit for human habitation, but nonetheless they're legal residences for the workers, and you have every right in the world to call on them. Have either of you been hurt as well?"

Father Joseph turned to Susan, who said, "I'm all right. But I think we should get Rafael to a hospital immediately. He may have gotten a concussion."

Bannister's man, still toting his rifle, said, "Soon as we book him on trespassing charges, you can do anything you want with the greaser."

Father Joe could see the rage and fury in Antonia Fernandez's eyes. For a moment, it looked as if, like Rafael, she might attempt to attack the man, but then she regained her self-control.

To the sheriff's deputy, she said very calmly, "This man has assaulted my client with a deadly weapon, and I intend to press charges against him, and his employer, Roy Bannister, for attempted murder."

* * *

Afterward, Father Joseph couldn't imagine what might have happened if Miss Fernandez hadn't materialized. If Bannister's men had treated Rafael with disrespect, everyone at the police station fell over backward trying to be nice to his legal counsel. They were terrified of her.

"People—even Americans," she said at one point to Father Joe and Susan during the booking, "can sometimes be reprehensible. But American law is beautiful. Every morning when I wake up, first thing I do is bless American law."

While Rafael was rushed off to the hospital by ambulance, Bannister's man filed trespassing charges against him and his two guests, and Antonia Fernandez filed attempted murder charges against Bannister's man. A preliminary hearing was scheduled for both charges two days hence, and in the meantime Mr. Bannister posted bail for his worker, and Miss Fernandez did the same for her clients.

"You're also my clients now," she said to Susan and Father Joseph, "whether you like it or not. I'm very, very good, and I work for cheap wages. In fact, for Rafael I work for nothing at all."

As they were leaving the station, a young man carrying a camera darted around them, snapping photographs.

"Hey, Miss Fernandez! Who clobbered Banuelos? Is he hurt badly?"

"We're going to the hospital now. I've filed attempted murder charges against Roy Bannister's henchman."

"Bannister says Banuelos was trespassing on his property, and when Bannister's employee attempted to make a citizen's arrest, Banuelos slipped and fell. Is that true?"

"Absolutely false," Antonia Fernandez answered, "and these two people here can vouch for it, because they were there. My client has just completed his eighth day of fasting, and I assure you he was in no condition to resist arrest."

"Fasting?" the young man repeated. "You mean he's on a fast?"

Father Joseph stepped forward. "Rafael Banuelos has gone on a fast to protest the inhuman and barbarous conditions under which the field hands of California are forced to live."

"First I heard of it," the young man said. "Who are you anyway?"

"My name's Father Joseph Cassidy."

"And are you a part of this movement?"

Father Joe's throat was dry, and when he spoke he was breathless. "Yes, I am."

He turned to Susan. "And you, miss? Are you a part of it, too?"

Father Joseph saw the indecision on her face, then she looked across at him and met his eyes. "I am."

After they left the station, the journalist offered to give them a lift to the hospital, and during the ride he could talk of nothing but the amazing story he'd stumbled onto. He was agog. In a land of plenty such as America, where most people overate, the idea of giving up eating in order to promote a cause was staggering.

The journalist dropped them off at the emergency treatment area, saying that he would like to wait with them but that he wanted to get back to San Jose to file his story.

While they sat outside the emergency ward, Antonia Fernandez mused, "The ranchers are their own worst enemy. All week long, poor Rafael has been waiting for a newspaperman to cover his fast, but no one was interested. By this time tomorrow, it will probably be picked up by the wire services and sent all over America—just as Roy Bannister is preparing to send his first crop of the strawberry season to the East Coast."

"Will shoppers boycott his products?" Father Joseph asked.

"Until now, it was only a hope. But with this publicity, there's a very good chance they'll support us. If they do, in a few weeks' time, strawberries will be rotting in Bannister's fields."

The prospects seemed to enliven them, all three, even though Father Joseph and Susan had never met the man whose inhuman labor practices they were protesting. It was a most peculiar feeling, having such power. For months, Father Joe had been worrying about his stained-glass windows at St. Brendan's, the targets of local vandals, yet hadn't been able to correct the problem. Now, in just one afternoon, he had participated in something that could, before it was over, cost a man millions upon millions of dollars simply because he refused to be humane.

"What about this Roy Bannister?" he asked. "Is he really the ogre he appears to be?"

"Not at all," Miss Fernandez answered brightly. "In fact, he's a very charming and likable fellow. He's on the school board in Monterey and is always involved in projects to help the community. But he *is* a businessman—the largest landowner in the county, I believe—and he doesn't look upon the braceros as human beings with human needs but as implements he has to use in order to make farming profitable. If he could replace them all with machines, he'd do it like a shot, but since he can't, he's stuck with them. But he wants to keep his labor expenses to a minimum, so when we come along and begin yelling about decent wages and housing for his workers, all he can see are dollar bills that he'll be losing."

"If they're the Bannisters I know," Susan volunteered, "they can well afford it. I used to date one of them when I was at UCLA."

"Oh, they're rich all right," Miss Fernandez replied, "but one of the reasons they're rich is that Roy Bannister is so stingy when it comes to doing things for his Mexican-American workers. He has Spanish blood of his own—a lot of the old colonial California families do—but he doesn't believe in sharing the wealth. He sees Rafael as a Communist."

"You said a little while ago," Susan began, "that you love American law. Why is it that American law can't solve the workers' problems? Why does Rafael have to go on a fast?"

Almost wistfully, she answered, "American law is one thing. American justice is another. In this state—in fact, in most states—judicial appointments are for sale. They're either given to men who will render politically correct decisions, or to men who are owed a favor. Gringo justice, we call it. Invariably when a rancher is brought to court, a judge rules in his favor. That's why Rafael has begun this fast. He hopes to appeal not to men's politics or intellects but to their emotions."

Father Joe asked, "How long does he intend to keep up the fast?"

"As long as injustices persist. Or as long as his old heart can stand the abuse he's giving it." She waited, then added, "Two years ago, he had a heart attack that almost killed him. When he survived, his doctors told him that he would have to lead a quiet, well-ordered life. They said nothing about getting hit over the head with a rifle or going without food."

A young doctor, dark-haired and dark-eyed, rounded a corner and bore down on them. As he did, Antonia Fernandez stood up to greet him.

"Gilberto, how is he?"

"Lucky he has a thick skull," her friend answered smiling, "but I want to keep him here for another day or two. He's suffered a bad concussion and is very, very weak. He tells me that he hasn't eaten in eight days." He shook his head in disbelief. "Is he trying to change the world again?"

"When has he not?" She proceeded with introductions. "Gilberto, these are two friends of Rafael's from San Francisco, Father Joseph Cassidy and Susan Grainger. Dr. Garcia is living proof that wetbacks can contribute a great deal to society once they're dry behind the ears. Gilberto's mother and father worked in the fields alongside my own parents."

He shook their hands heartily. "It's always a pleasure to meet friends of Rafael's who've thrown their support behind his cause."

Father Joseph could have backed off then and there. Miles away, he had pressing spiritual duties to perform. He was a simple parish priest, not a revolutionary. Why, then, didn't he protest?

He couldn't hedge on his commitment because Susan Grainger wouldn't let him. Almost sarcastically, as if revelling at the prospect of a Catholic priest embarking on a course of action that might cost him his job—his vocation, his faith—she said to the young Hispanic doctor, "Father Joseph and I both believe that it's the mark of a true Christian to help those who are worse off than we are." She smiled at Father Joe, challenging him. "Isn't that right, Father?"

TWELVE

*P*atrick Cassidy waited for Jimmy Hoffa to make his move on the Oakland waterfront, but nothing was stirring. First thing every morning, he called his East Bay union chiefs from his office on the Embarcadero to ask if any attempt had been made to tamper with union members, and each day he was reassured that no Teamster official or representative had arrived on the scene.

It worried Pat. Either Hoffa's men were infiltrating the Oakland work force so stealthily as to go unobserved, or the Teamsters had given up their hope of seizing Pat's Longshoremen's Union.

But late one afternoon, he received a visitor.

"A Mr. Costa from Detroit to see you," his secretary announced after having buzzed him at his desk.

"I know no Mr. Costa from Detroit."

"He says he's out here on vacation and simply wants to see you for a few minutes to relay good wishes from a mutual friend of yours."

By no stretch of the imagination was James Hoffa a friend, but Pat nonetheless agreed to see Frank Costa.

He was a surprisingly dapper and well-groomed middle-aged man, with none of the Damon Runyon characteristics Pat tended to associate with Chicago or Detroit union men. He wore a college ring—Dartmouth—and a Phi Beta Kappa key dangled from his vest.

"Mr. Cassidy," he began, "we've heard so much about you in Detroit. It's an honor to meet you."

Pat wasn't quite ready to share his enthusiasm. "You say you're on the West Coast for a vacation and just dropped by to say hello?"

"Well, yes and no." He waited for Pat to offer him a chair, and when it wasn't forthcoming, he said, "Would you mind if I sat down?"

Pat nodded, then watched as his visitor sat in a chair across from him, briefcase on his lap.

"I'm with Johnson, Leland, and deGeorge of Detroit, in their corporate division, and we've been engaged to represent a local businessman, shall we say, who has interests here on the Coast."

Bluntly, Pat rephrased it, "You people have taken the job that was offered to and turned down by Sheldon Hawkins here in San Francisco."

Costa appeared a bit flustered, but managed to say, "I know nothing about that. I've been sent merely to . . . well, extend felicitations from Mr. Hoffa—"

"I can do without his felicitations, thank you."

"—and to ask you to consider a little proposal he's empowered me to relay to you."

"The answer is no, but you might as well spell it out anyway."

Costa chose his words with exceeding care in order to avoid any hint of illegality. "Mr. Hoffa is most concerned about the state of America," he began.

Pat had to resist laughing.

"Traditionally, labor unions have endorsed a presidential candidate who, in their opinion, will best reflect the views of American labor. Mr. Hoffa would like to see a united front this time, and is prepared to go to great lengths to ensure one. He would like to know your . . . feelings about Hubert Humphrey."

There was little doubt but that Humphrey was labor's candidate in the coming election. Far more than Adlai Stevenson, he was a New Dealer and went to great pains to address the issues affecting working men and women.

"Hubert Humphrey is a good-hearted, decent, but absurd little man," Pat answered. "Those are my feelings."

"Then you have no plans at this time to support Mr. Humphrey's presidential bid?"

"Even if he's nominated at the convention in Los Angeles, it's doubtful that I could generate much enthusiasm for him. As you know, I am a delegate to the convention."

"Oh?" Costa said with mock surprise.

"In fact, it's altogether likely that I'll chairman the California delegation, and at the present time I can't say that there's much support for Humphrey."

"We think that Humphrey, who is our first choice, can get the nomination on the second or third ballot. If not Humphrey, then Stevenson, who is our second choice."

"Who can predict these things?"

Pat's visitor shifted his weight in the chair. "Well, that is one of the reasons I'm here. Mr. Hoffa happens to think that these things *can* be predicted if steps are taken to prevent . . . let's say, an outsider from getting the nomination. That's why he would like you to commit the California delegation to another candidate during the crucial first ballot."

"There is no way in the world anyone could pledge the support of the California delegation for someone like Humphrey."

"We weren't thinking of Humphrey. We were thinking of Governor Edmund Brown."

Patrick screwed up his face. "Come again?"

Costa explained the strategy. "We believe that what has to be prevented is an impetuous and emotional choice. As you know, Stevenson hasn't even declared himself as a candidate yet, so it's doubtful that his forces can muster enough support between now and July. Hubert Humphrey may not perform well enough in the primaries to be a strong candidate, but we're of the opinion that if we can prevent an outsider from getting the nomination on the first ballot, Humphrey might be able to get it on the second or third. That's why we're appealing to you to hold the California delegation to its favorite son candidate, Governor Brown."

At last, Pat understood what was being plotted. "Does Jimmy Hoffa hate Jack Kennedy that much?"

"I don't follow you, Mr. Cassidy."

"Ever since Bobby Kennedy has threatened to put Hoffa

in jail, the Teamsters have been after the Kennedys. And now you're attempting to influence the Democratic convention in Los Angeles."

"I'm afraid you're jumping to conclusions. We are merely interested in getting a strong prolabor candidate on the ticket next November."

But of course. Why hadn't Pat seen it sooner? "And you want either Hubert Humphrey or Adlai Stevenson because they'll be prolabor? Baloney! You want them because you know damned well that Richard Nixon will be able to beat them! And what you're really afraid of is that he won't be able to beat John Kennedy."

Pat pressed the button on the intercom to alert his secretary. When she answered, he said into it, "Mr. Costa will be leaving now. Could you show him out, please?"

Costa pushed back his chair. "Before I go, could I say that we are prepared to guarantee peace on the waterfront here on the West Coast—"

"If Hoffa's men try to muscle in, I'll stop them."

So that was to have been the bargaining point: peace on the Oakland docks in exchange for holding the California delegation to Governor Brown through the first ballot at the convention. Suddenly, Pat was furious. "Listen, when you get back to Detroit, I want you to give your boss *my* felicitations. Tell him that if I had any doubts beforehand about supporting John Kennedy, they've vanished now. Jimmy Hoffa will have to find another way to stay out of jail—though I'm not the least bit surprised that he expects cooperation from Richard Nixon. Good afternoon, Mr. Costa."

After his visitor left, Pat sat at his desk, basking in victory, sure that Hoffa wouldn't attempt to seize control of the Oakland docks in retribution. He had hoped to use that threat in order to sway Pat, but there was no way he could be intimidated.

Or at least he convinced himself that there was none. However, at five to six that afternoon, just as he was preparing to leave for the day, his secretary handed him an important-looking letter. On the envelope were the words PERSONAL. TO BE OPENED ONLY BY ADDRESSEE.

"I think someone is trying to tell us that it's confidential," she said, "so I didn't open it, Mr. Cassidy."

He was relieved that she hadn't because of the savageness of its threat. In childlike block lettering, it read:

MR. CASSIDY,
WE UNDERSTAND THAT CONGRESSMAN CONROY IS PLAY-
ING AROUND WITH BROADS AGAIN. WE WOULDN'T WANT
HIS WIFE TO KNOW THAT, WOULD WE?—UNLESS WE CAN
GET ANOTHER BED READY FOR HER IN TOPEKA, KANSAS.
SUMMERS ARE VERY HOT THERE, SOMETIMES ENDLESS.
YOU THINK WE SHOULD TALK? WE'LL BE IN TOUCH.

Pat read it again and again with clenched fists. Whoever had written it knew precisely where he was most vulnerable. Mimi was so very fragile, had such a tenuous hold on life. Any shock to her uncertain self-esteem could well be catastrophic.

Was this one of Hoffa's contingency plans in the event that Pat didn't buckle to his earlier threats? Or was it utterly unconnected?

How many people had known that Congressman Conroy had a woman passenger in his car that night? Not more than a handful. The Berkeley student who'd been in the VW. And the two patrolmen. In the torrential rain, no gawkers had been drawn to the scene out of perverse curiosity.

If the note was from Hoffa, as Pat believed, the information must have been relayed to him by one of the three.

Cornelius John Joseph Murphy.

Just to repeat the melodic Irish name to the officer on duty at the San Francisco Police Department headquarters summoned up joyful memories for Pat. Con's wife, Marie, had been Eva's best friend, and the Murphys were close neighbors of the Cassidys in the Richmond District. Their son Kieran had been Joe's best buddy through grade school and high school, a friendship that was deflected only when they went their separate ways: Joe into the seminary, Kieran to George-town University.

Then there was shared sadness that brought Con Murphy

and Pat close together. Marie had been first to die, of cancer of the liver, and afterward Eva and Pat more or less adopted Con, trying to ease his grief. Two or three nights a week he had supper with them, and on weekends they took little trips down the Coast Highway to Big Sur or all the way to San Simeon, the Hearst extravaganza that loomed like a fairy-tale castle on its hillside, or north to Mendocino. And when Eva died, there was Con, stepping in to shore Pat up and get him through the devastating days of loneliness.

It was peculiar, Pat thought, how men in their first burst of young manhood had friendships with other men so deep and profound that they would die for one another, then soon lost interest as they were gripped by a passion for women. Yet once again in old age, when passions died, friendships were rediscovered. A man could be comfortable with another man in a way he could never be even with a loving wife.

Con Murphy had much more than twenty years on the force and could have retired long before, but police work was in his blood. Kieran was with the consular corps, most recently posted to Lima, Peru, and Con seldom had a chance to see his grandchildren. As he himself said, he had a choice of drinking himself to death, as Irish widowers sometimes did, or throwing himself into his work as never before. He chose the latter course.

He had a desk job now, which was a relief because he was overweight and gouty, and an imposing title: supervisor of metropolitan traffic. As soon as Pat was informed that he was in, he made his way upstairs to his office.

Con greeted him at the door. "Patrick, me lad!" he cried. "It's to be hoped you're not here on business."

"Well, yes and no."

"Yes, you would like a ticket fixed? Impossible, even for an old and dear friend. Or are you still having trouble with cars blocking your driveway on Lake Street?"

"I'm still having trouble, but your man at the Richmond station has been most accommodating. He sends out a tow truck and tows them away in a matter of minutes." As Pat was led to a chair, he said, "I hate to bother him."

"You're not bothering anyone. It's a revenue producer. Every time a car blocks your drive and has to be towed away, the police department earns another forty dollars, because that's what it costs to get the car on the streets again." He smiled his irrepressible Celtic smile. "What can I do for you, Pat?"

"It's about the little accident my son-in-law, Congressman Conroy, was in about a week ago. Would you have the accident report on hand by any chance?"

"I can get it." He began to rise from his chair.

"And also, while you're at it, could I have the home addresses of the two patrolmen who signed the report?"

Con's ample white eyebrows shot up his forehead. "I hope that none of my men did anything to bring dishonor to the force."

Patrick reached into his coat pocket. "I've known you for three quarters of my life, Con, and I've always been candid with you—except once. If I had been more consistent, perhaps I would never have received this letter." He handed it to him across the desk.

As Con read it, his eyes became narrower and narrower. "An extortion attempt, that's clear," he said when he finished. "But the reference to Mimi and Topeka, Kansas, eludes me."

Sighing, Patrick explained, "That's the lie I was telling you about." He paused. "Mimi had a nervous breakdown after my granddaughter was killed in Washington. She spent most of one year at the Menninger Clinic in Topeka."

Con Murphy's mouth opened as if he was about to say something, but he couldn't find the words.

Pat continued, "Robert and I decided that Mimi had gone through more than enough. First the accident, then the breakdown and the long recovery. As a congressman's wife, she's considered public property by the men and women of the Fourth Estate. Had they known what had happened, they would have had a field day with the story. So instead Robert's office announced that she was in the south of Ireland doing up a house they'd purchased shortly before Sara's death."

It was another minute before Con could respond. "I'm so sorry, Pat. So damned sorry. I had no idea."

"It was the only time in my life I've deceived you. But almost no one knows the true story, to this day. We wanted to protect Mimi."

Con read the letter again. "Oh, the vile sons of bitches who sent you this! Why would anyone want to profit from someone else's personal tragedy?"

"Not only why, but how? I can't prove it, but I have a feeling that the Mob may be involved. Earlier today, I spoke with someone claiming to represent Jimmy Hoffa's Teamsters Union."

"Hoffa!"

"Hoffa's representative—and I have no reason to suspect that he was anything other than what he claimed to be—had a proposition for me that I was forced to reject. I'm not particularly vulnerable to attack, Con. The Longshoremen's Union here on the West Coast is healthy and free from the Mob's influence. I hope to keep it that way till the day I retire. So when threats were made that the Teamsters might try to usurp my union, I didn't react with the terror that was expected. I sent Hoffa's man on his way. Several hours later, this letter arrived."

"How could the Mob have learned about Mimi and the Menninger Clinic, Pat?"

Pat shook his head. "If we approach it that way, we could spend the next five years looking for an answer. I think we have to start with what we know, and that is that the letter-writer possessed the knowledge that my son-in-law, Congressman Conroy, was in an automobile accident, and at the time"—it was extremely difficult for Pat to utter the words—"he was with a young woman here in San Francisco when Mimi and everyone else was under the impression he was still in Washington."

Con's eyes darkened. "Robert is cheating on his wife?"

"He denied it. But what else could he do when confronted by his wife's father? I was there. I saw the woman—at a distance, mind you, but I saw her. It was the wildest night of the year, Con. Do you remember? We had five inches of rain in as many hours."

"Yes, I remember. It was a very dirty night."

"Had the accident happened in good weather, there would have been a crowd, but the sidewalks were deserted, and everyone in cars simply wanted to get home as fast as they could. Joe was with me, but apart from us I can't believe that anyone except the two police officers and the Berkeley student could have known that Robert and his young woman friend were in an accident."

Con pondered it. "I was on duty that night. I called you from here, remember? And later on I read the accident report when it was dropped off by . . . by Officer Martinez, I think it was."

"Yes, that was the name of one of them. The other one was directing traffic around the two cars."

"I read it right away because I was anxious to see if Robert or anyone else had been seriously injured. It should be in the files. Gimme a minute, Pat. I'll be right back."

As Con left the office, Pat tried to remember how Officer Martinez had handled the situation that night. He had definitely known the identity of Robert Conroy because at one point he addressed him as "Congressman." And he seemed to have been genuinely grateful when Robert haᴅ commended him, saying that he would bring his efficient work to the attention of the chief. It was little more than a politician's twaddle, but Martinez had been flattered.

In a few minutes, Con returned with the accident report and a legal pad on which he'd scratched a few notes.

As he took his seat behind the desk and placed his reading glasses on his nose, he said, "Here we go. Patrolman Hector Martinez responded to the call, arriving at the scene of the accident at eleven-fifteen. He was assisted by Patrolman Peter Trevino. I checked their dossiers." He looked down at his legal pad. "Martinez has been on the force for over six years, he's married, has two children, and lives in Novato. Last year he received a citation for capturing an armed suspect during a holdup attempt in the Tenderloin. He looks squeaky-clean to me."

Pat concurred. It was doubtful that anyone would risk a wife, two kids, and his ranch house by selling information to the Mob.

"What about Trevino?"

"He might bear scrutiny."

Secretly, Pat hoped he was clean. At least 30 percent of his union membrs were Italian-Americans, hard-working, decent, honest people. Yet because of the activities of a few men involved in organized crime, they received a very bad press. Pat despised stereotypes, but the minute he'd heard Trevino's name, the thought occurred to him that he might have an uncle, a cousin, a friend connected with the Mob.

"Trevino has been on the force for less than two years. He's unmarried, went to high school in North Beach, and has a couple years at San Francisco State." He waited, then added significantly, "He doesn't live in North Beach anymore. He lives in Sausalito." His eyes met Pat's.

Of all the contributions that Italian-Americans had made to San Francisco, and there were many, none was more important than the institution of the family. Italian-American families were incredibly close-knit. Members couldn't bear living too far from their kin. It was why North Beach and Fisherman's Wharf remained largely Italian.

Why had Trevino left a warm, lively, loving Italian community and moved to Sausalito? From a distance, that seagirt village on Marin's green hills looked impossibly romantic. But up close, much of it was glitz.

Con Murphy continued, "I noticed that he has a permit to park his car in the lot here, so just for the hell of it, I ran a check on the permit."

"Is there something unusual about a patrolman parking his car in your lot?"

Con waited. "Only when it's a Porsche."

Pat nodded. It was an expensive car for a rookie cop, just as Sausalito was definitely out of the low-rent district. Fast cars didn't necessarily mean that their owners preferred fast company, but if he was sketching a profile of someone who might have Mob connections, he'd be much more inclined to make him a Porsche owner than a Ford owner or, God forbid, a Gremlin owner.

"I think I'd like his address in Sausalito," Pat heard himself say.

"You got it." Con indicated the sheet of legal writing paper. "Also his folks' address on Columbus Avenue. If Trevino is up to something unsavory, some of his old neighbors might be able to help you."

Pat put it bluntly. "Are there many crooked cops on the force?"

His old friend shrugged his shoulders. "What can I say? We're human. We're very careful, but every now and then a bad article gets through. But in Trevino's case, he was highly recommended for the Academy. An uncle of his, George Trevino, is a precinct captain and a legend around here. The best. If young Trevino is up to hanky-panky, it's going to hurt."

In fact, Pat had met Captain George Trevino. He'd helped clean up the numbers racket and the whoring down at the Wharf. He was an honest man.

"What do you have on the guy who was driving the other car?" Pat asked.

Con read from the accident report. "Osborne C. Ashley II. He gives his occupation as graduate student at the University of California at Berkeley. Just a minute. I've asked someone to check him out with the Berkeley police." He picked up his telephone and dialed a number. "You have anything on Osborne C. Ashley yet?" he asked, then listened intently, making a note or two. "That's all?"

When he hung up, he said to Pat, "I never fail to be impressed by college students in their search for ways to offend society. O. C. Ashley is so clean he doesn't even have any outstanding parking tickets, and in Berkeley that makes him one in a thousand. He does have a police record, however, but it's not exactly what you'd expect from someone involved with the Mob. A year ago, he was arrested on Sproul Plaza carrying a sign that said BULLSHIT."

He waited for the smile to break on Pat's face. "He's also smart. He has an IQ over one hundred fifty, he says. It's on his police record."

"For the love of God, since when did they start giving IQ tests at police stations—even in Berkeley?"

"They didn't. But the guy over there we talked to happened to remember it. I guess one of the arresting officers complained that it was a pretty ignorant thing to do, walk around with a sign that says BULLSHIT, and O. C. Ashley II volunteered that he was a member of Mensa and then mentioned his IQ. I guess he was trying to tell them that it *was* smart to walk around with that sign."

"So what do you think, Con? How smart was it?" Pat asked, twitting him.

"Offhand, I'd say there are probably better things to do, though I expect that makes me old-fashioned."

Pat reached over and gripped him by the shoulder. "It makes two of us old-fashioned."

As Pat prepared to leave, Con asked, "Should we send the letter down to Criminal Investigations?"

"Let's wait till I see Trevino. I'd just as soon . . . well . . . I'd just as soon—"

"I understand," Con interrupted, knowing that his old friend didn't want strangers' eyes to read of Mimi's misfortune. "Let me know what we can do to help, Patrick."

"Definitely. I'll keep in touch."

The sun had begun to set by the time Pat drove through the Presidio and onto the Golden Gate Bridge. It was one of the last great thrills in the world to soar above that azure bay into those tumbling green hills that would soon turn golden under the Northern California sunshine. Every time he drove over the bridge, he felt goose pimples at the back of his neck, and as he reached the Marin side and began to climb the grade toward the dark tunnel that pierced the mountain, all he could think was that if God created this, He deserved an Academy Award. The impression was reinforced when he emerged from the tunnel and saw Sausalito aflame with the setting sun. He coasted down the Waldo grade, remembering all the times he'd done so, Eva at his side marveling at the experience.

Oh, it was a fine place for delusions, California was. You could spend months searching, and you'd never find a *memento mori*. Even a headstone was a rarity. In San Francisco when you died, you were interred outside the city limits, down in South San Francisco among Mexican-Americans, who had a greater tolerance for reality and death.

It was a good time to call on Trevino. He'd be home from work by now, Pat figured, and it was a little too early to start thinking about dinner. He turned off Bridgeway Boulevard and wound his way up a precipitous hillside toward the address he'd been given, but when he arrived at the gray-shingled house, the Porsche he expected to find parked in front was nowhere to be seen.

It was a four-unit apartment house, Pat discovered, and P. Trevino was listed as an occupant of apartment three, along with R. Gustafson. When he rang the bell, however, there was no answer, so he rang the button next to "Manager," as the card read, who resided in apartment one.

In a minute, a youth with sun-bleached blond hair and a deep tan, and wearing a white T-shirt and faded Levi's, looked onto the porch, then opened the door. He was barefooted.

"Are you the manager?" Pat asked. "I'm looking for Peter Trevino, but there doesn't seem to be any answer."

"I'm not the manager exactly. I'm just looking after the place for the owner. I'm an actor."

Pat was tempted to say: Around here, who isn't? But he resisted the temptation. "Do you know what time Trevino generally gets home?"

"He's been home. But he went out again. You see, he holds down two jobs. I don't know what he does during the daytime, but most nights he's a bartender."

So Trevino was moonlighting. With two salaries, one from the police department, the other as a bartender, it was possible that he could afford a car like a Porsche.

"What's he like anyway?" Pat asked.

Suddenly, the smiling face was suspicious. "Why do you want to know?"

A little dissembling was in order. "I work for a credit-rating company. Trevino is trying to get a loan, so we have to update his credit rating. How much does he pay for rent here?"

"He's got the one-bedroom apartment, and right now it's renting for one hundred a month. It's the cheapest apartment in the building because it has just a teeny-weeny view of the bay."

"Does Trevino lead . . . an ordinary sort of life?"

The young man brushed a lock of hair from his forehead. "Well, for around here, it's pretty ordinary. He and his friend never give parties, if that's what you mean. They're very outdoorsy. On weekends, they sail. Or they go backpacking."

"What's the friend do?"

"Insurance business, I believe. Real nice type. In fact, both of them are."

If Trevino and his girlfriend pooled their incomes, buying a Porsche or renting an apartment in Sausalito needn't be a terrible burden. In a way, Pat was disappointed not to find him living alone, giving parties two or three times a week, and throwing money around like mad.

"What time does his girlfriend generally get home?" he asked.

The actor-manager scowled. "I wasn't aware that he had one."

"But I thought he was living in a one-bedroom apartment with a girlfriend."

"No, he's living with a friend. Ronnie Gustafson. They've lived together for the last couple years, I think. Right now, they're saving up their money to buy a cabin up on the Russian River, so Ron works two jobs, too. They both get home around midnight."

Pat felt almost ashamed for having pried. It was all too obvious why Trevino wasn't living near his parents in North Beach. He lived with a lover, and since the lover happened to be another man, he wasn't too keen on his family finding out, not to mention his coworkers on the police force.

"Well, okay," Pat said, backing away. "Thanks."

"What should I tell Peter when I see him? About the credit rating, I mean."

What indeed? Of all things, Pat didn't want to strike terror in someone who probably felt beleaguered already because of his sexual orientation. Even if the SFPD was more emancipated than most police departments, Italian-American families weren't—not yet, not in the year 1960 anyway. Maybe sometime they would understand, but right now Pat suspected that Trevino was under a lot of pressure from home, and he didn't want to add to it.

"Just tell him that everything's okay, and that there'll be absolutely no trouble. No trouble at all."

"Will do," the actor-manager replied. "Watch your step when you leave. The second step from the bottom needs replacing. Dig an inch or two into the soil around here, and all you can see are termites. California is built on termites. I wouldn't be a bit surprised if they're the ones that are causing all the earthquakes, and all that about the San Andreas fault is just so much bushwa."

"You might have something. Thanks again."

"No trouble. Anytime. I'm an actor, you know. I'm just doing this while I'm waiting for a good role."

Patrick next visited the address in Berkeley that O. C. Ashley II had given the police. A bad-tempered woman dressed in a housecoat and wearing plastic curlers in her hair answered the door and told him that she'd never heard of anyone named Ashley. He didn't live there now and never had.

Having reached a dead end, Pat saw no alternative but to call it quits for the day.

THIRTEEN

Stephen Olivari was gently prodding a giant, diabolically ugly crustacean on the plate before him. "Who would think that beneath this sinister facade lies a gastronomic adventure of the highest order?" he remarked to the young woman seated across from him in the dining room of the Copley Plaza Hotel. "One can almost forgive New England for its witch-hunters and its slave-traders. We are forever indebted to Maine's humble lobstermen. And to think that I haven't been back to Boston to enjoy one *in situ* since 1938!"

As he began to dismember the clawed creature, Kathleen Molloy asked, "Why has it taken so long?"

"The war, for one," he sighed. "Then when it was over, guilt because of my role in it. Two years ago, in 1958, I very nearly returned for the twentieth reunion of my Harvard class, but then I remembered that some of my former classmates would shun me—as your uncle John did at your grandfather's funeral; I noticed even if everyone else was too polite to—and that others, whom I once loved, wouldn't be there at all because they died in the war. I couldn't bear to think that I was even indirectly responsible for the death of old friends"—he paused to meet her eyes—"like your father. Tom and I were roommates, you know, freshman year."

Kathleen, who had ordered steak Diane at least partly because it required less athletic dexterity to consume than a lobster did, rested her knife and fork on her plate. "No, I didn't know," she admitted, excited at the prospect of learning about her father when he was young. "How did it happen that you two were assigned to the same room?"

"I would like to believe that it was a fortuitous accident, but I know better. We were the only two Catholics in Hollis

Hall. I remember that on the third floor, there were two Jews, also roommates. I can only guess that the director of residence halls considered it reckless to mix people with different points of view."

"Things have changed," Kathleen offered, "quite a bit."

"I hope for the better."

"Oh, yes." She resumed eating, then stopped again. "What was he like—my father?" she asked.

Stephen smiled at the recollection; then, as he'd done at the funeral, seemed to look over her head into the past. "Tom was wildly good-looking, I suppose you know, the way only an Irishman can be with Celtic and Norman blood. He was lithe and graceful, generous and kind. Magical! He had such insight into people, such understanding." He shook his head, then laughed. "I remember the very first time I met him. I'd just arrived in New York two days before from Genoa, and I was feeling very ill at ease. My father was Italian, you know, and my mother was an American. Until I came to Harvard, I had spent most of my life in or near Rome. My father decided that I should have a car during my freshman year, so he ordered one, and I collected it after I landed in New York. It was a red Cadillac convertible, and I thought it was the most gorgeous car I'd ever seen. What my father forgot, however, was the Puritan austerity of my classmates. That first day, it was parked outside Hollis Hall, and as Tom came bounding up the stairs, surrounded as always by friends, one of them said, 'Who but a dago would drive a vulgar car like that!' The minute your father stepped into the room, he realized at once that I'd heard. Later, when we were alone, he apologized for his friend's bad taste. For a long time, I couldn't forgive my father for having inflicted that car on me. But Tom made me realize that it was a kindness. My father knew I'd be snubbed at Harvard because I was Italian and Catholic, and while my car wouldn't buy me friends, at least it would be a consolation."

"And was it?"

"Tom and I must have put twenty thousand miles on that car freshman year alone, running up to Marblehead, where I kept a sailing boat at the Corinthian Yacht Club. I've renewed my membership every year since then, for sentimental reasons, though I've never used it. If you ever want to get away from Cambridge for a sail, be my guest." He waited, then added cautiously, "Tom and I also used to spend a lot of time around Scollay Square, but perhaps I shouldn't mention that."

"But how wonderful! Was it as seedy and disreputable then as it is now?"

He chuckled to himself. "Raffish beyond imagining. But you *did* ask me about your father, and I'm telling you. He was an exceedingly human person, Kathleen, and loved to enjoy himself. Some of my classmates weren't very human at all."

In 1960, Scollay Square was commonly known as Boston's center of vice. To learn that her father may have made use of one of the ladies of the night who frequented the area added a dimension to his character that had been missing till now.

"When I was little, I could never see my father as flesh and blood. He was always larger than life," Kathleen confessed. "I used to sit and stare at his photograph for hours and hours, crying my head off because he was so . . . beautiful and brave. Somehow, I never thought of him riding around Scollay Square in a red Cadillac whistling at all the tarts."

"He was a very vital, very manly sort of fellow."

"Did you know my mother?"

"Much less well. Tom didn't meet her, if I recall, until senior year. And before then—this I probably shouldn't tell you—he had an affair of the heart with a young working-class girl. What *was* her name? Peggy something, I think."

Kathleen was fascinated. "He loved her?"

"Completely and utterly. In fact, almost up to his wedding day, we were all afraid that he might go running back to her. It wasn't . . . an intellectual thing. It was entirely emotional. In most other ways they simply weren't suited to be man and wife. I think she was a secretary or something."

Defiantly, Kathleen said, "If he loved her, he should have married her."

"Don't misunderstand. He loved your mother too, but in a different way. She was, among other things, the great catch of the season. Perhaps not quite so earthy as this Peggy."

"Not the least bit earthy," Kathleen suggested, laughing.

Then she became serious. "Do you think it's wrong to let your-self be ruled by your emotions? Or is that a stupid question?"

"I don't find it stupid at all. But I'm not sure I know the answer. I think we have to listen to our hearts, then weigh what we've heard with our minds."

"It's easy to say that. But when you're faced with a terri-ble, terrible dilemma, it's hard to do."

"Surely *you* have never been faced with a terrible, terrible dilemma."

"Now you're poking fun at me."

"Not a bit. It's just that you look so happy, so well ad-justed, without a care in the world."

In misery, Kathleen confessed, "Well, I'm not. In fact, I don't know what to do, and I don't have anyone to con-fide in."

"That can be corrected immediately. Tell me all about it."

And to her astonishment, she did. Told him everything about Ted Birmingham, how she'd met him, how their friend-ship grew. And the delicate state it was in at the present time.

"And you say he knows nothing about you or your fam-ily?" Stephen asked.

"Nothing. He's never asked. I don't think that sort of thing interests him. Money and all that. He's working his way through school, at least partly. He's a member of CORE—that's Con-gress of Racial Equality—and he and his roommate are very active in the civil rights movement."

"Has your mother met him? Or your grandmother?"

Kathleen threw up her hands. "Heavens, no!"

"Why heavens no?"

"My mother would probably think that he's a Bolshevist or an opportunist. My grandmother . . . I don't know about her. She would be appalled by what Ted's proposed. I mean, spending the weekend with him and everything."

"Are you going to spend the weekend with him?"

"I'm still trying to decide."

Stephen, who had devoured his lobster, now stared thought-fully at its remains, and said, "Then there is just one solution. I must meet this young man of yours."

Someone to provide guidance!

"You say that you have lunch with him and his roommate every day? So tomorrow, you shall bring a guest."

"And afterward, you'll tell me what to do?"

Wisely, he shook his head. "Afterward, you'll know what to do."

On the way back to her dorm, Kathleen contemplated the man seated next to her in the taxi. It was a blustery, brutally cold evening, yet Stephen's face had a warm glow to it—the week before, he'd been skiing, he told her—and he was wearing a double-breasted navy blue blazer, a white shirt with rep tie, gray flannel trousers, and no overcoat, as if proclaiming to the world that he generated his own heat.

She couldn't help but compare him with Ted, who always seemed to be shivering, as if he were coming down with a cold or getting over one. When they met, would Ted resent Stephen for his worldliness and wealth? Would Stephen dismiss Ted as a tiresome and brash juvenile involved in the civil rights movement for reasons of self-aggrandizement?

They would hate one another, she was sure of it.

Suddenly, she realized that she didn't really know that much about Stephen, so when there was a break in the conversation—he'd been commenting on the inevitable changes that had occurred in Boston in the last twenty years—she asked, "Are you married, Stephen?"

"How could I not be?" he answered, smiling.

"But it's not compulsory, even in Italy."

"No, but we Italians look upon marriage as a necessity and a convenience. We must have wives to attend to our creature comforts, care for our homes, raise our children—"

"Children!" she exclaimed. "You have children? How many?"

"Twins, a girl and a boy, Francesca and Georgio, born nine months to the day after our marriage. Then five years ago when no one expected it, a third, another girl, Alessandra. As shocking as it may seem, the twins are almost your age."

It *was* shocking. Because here she was next to a sensuous, dashingly handsome man old enough to be her father, yet somehow or other he just wasn't like what she imagined a father would be.

"What about your wife?" she persisted. "Were you madly in love with her when you married her?"

"I scarcely knew her," he replied. "You see, my father-in-law is also an industrialist, and at one time a fierce competitor. Many years ago, he came to me with a proposal to merge our two companies. I was skeptical at first, reluctant to trust him, so he said, 'Stefano, just to prove to you that I am an honest man and will not cheat you, you may have one of my daughters.' He had eight. So I chose the best-looking one of the lot, we merged our firms, and everyone has been very happy since then."

"But how unromantic—if you didn't love her!"

"I didn't love her when I married her, but I love her now, insofar as I understand the meaning of that word. Our love has matured as we ourselves have."

When they arrived at her dorm, they made arrangements for their meeting the following day, then Kathleen thanked him for the lovely dinner and the good company and dashed to her room.

There, she called Ted at the apartment and told him about the change of plans. She'd be bringing along "a dear friend" to have lunch with them the next day.

Not surprisingly, he was disappointed. "I was under the impression that you were going to spend the weekend with another dear friend of yours—me!"

"Can't we talk about that tomorrow?"

"Oh, dammit, I knew you were going to back out."

"Ted, I never agreed to it. It was your idea."

"I thought you wanted to."

"I do," she said, then was surprised at what she'd said.

He considered it a commitment. "There, you see. You admit it. So why are you creating all these obstacles? This 'very dear friend' of yours and everything."

She begged him, "Please, Ted, don't make me feel like a whore."

He must have gotten the message, because when he spoke

again, his voice was soft, gentle. "I'm sorry, Kathleen. I guess I thought . . . well, that we loved one another. And now you don't seem to be too sure anymore."

"I'm sure," she insisted, then immediately qualified it by adding, "but I want to be absolutely sure. Will you promise to be nice to Stephen tomorrow?"

He mimicked her tone. "Yes, I'll be nice to Stephen tomorrow."

He was being so absurdly petulant that she couldn't help but laugh, and in another minute he did the same.

The next day, Kathleen skipped her eleven o'clock class in Puritan lit and went shopping instead. Stephen would expect something more than the slapdash lunches they generally prepared for themselves, she decided, so she went to the butcher and bought thin scaloppines of veal, then to the grocery for mushrooms and tagliatelli, greens for a salad, out-of-season and very expensive strawberries for dessert, then to a liquor shop for some Marsala to cook the veal in and a nice Bordeaux to serve with it.

When she reached the apartment, she found that it was in an impossible mess. Ted had neglected to mention to Clay that they'd be having a guest for lunch. Deliberately, she was sure, to create the very worst impression.

"Oh, God!" she said when she saw the disorder in the living room. She quickly explained the situation to Clay, and with his help she began to get the place organized, superficially anyway. There was no vacuum cleaner, so she used a broom on the filthy living room rugs, removed the dirty plates that were perched on top of the furniture, and washed them. She set to scouring the bathroom and kitchen sinks, and because there was no toilet cleaner, she poured a healthy dose of Rinso into it, scrubbing it with the broom.

"I could have cleaned the place," Clay said apologetically, "if only Ted had told me we were having company."

"Ted wants Stephen to see him at his worst. He doesn't intend to like any of my bourgeois friends, as he calls them." She was angry, partly because of Ted's motives, partly because she was running late and there was still a good deal to do to get the meal on the table.

"I'll help you fix lunch," Clay suggested. "What do you want me to do?"

While she pounded the thin slices of veal on the kitchen counter, Clayton rinsed the salad greens under the tap, then shook them in the colander.

"How will you be getting home this weekend?" she asked.

"Home?" he repeated, as if he didn't quite follow her. Then: "Oh, home. Well, I guess I'll be taking the bus."

Ted arrived a few minutes later, running up the steps, pushing open the door, and yelling, "So where's our dear, dear friend?" In spite of the fact that Kathleen had asked him to dress nicely, he had deliberately set out to look sloppy in nearly threadbare tan cords and a surplus army shirt badly in need of both washing and ironing.

"You look terrific," Kathleen said sarcastically.

"I knew you'd approve." He rubbed his chin, which he hadn't bothered to shave that morning, then began to make his way to the bathroom.

"I gave Stephen the address," Kathleen called after him, "but I didn't tell him it's the second floor, so could you look out the window for him, Ted?"

"Soon as I pee." He waited. "I mean, if that's all right. If it isn't too gross, considering our dear, dear friend's imminent arrival."

As Kathleen began to slice mushrooms and shallots into the buttery pan, Clay asked, "Is he important to you, this Stephen Olivari?"

Until now, she wasn't sure, "Yes, very," she answered. "He was a friend of my father's. And I want him to like Ted."

"Don't tell Ted that. Because if you do, he'll do everything possible to get Stephen to loathe him. He'll consider it a challenge!"

Ted was peering out the window at the street below. "Someone dressed like a fop just got out of a cab in front of the house. Is that our guest?"

"Oh, God!" Kathleen cried.

But surprisingly enough, in view of the fact that he knew he was under scrutiny and was offended by it, Ted was remarkably civil. In fact, he walked down the outside steps to meet Stephen, arm extended. "Hi, I'm Ted Birmingham, Mr. Olivari."

"Please call me Stephen."

"Come on in. We've had the kitchen staff working all morning. Hey, guys, Mr. Olivari is here."

So that was how it was going to be, Stephen concluded. Ted was going to keep a safe distance.

But Clay was much more agreeable, and Kathleen saw at once that at least he and Stephen would get along.

"I've brought some wine," Stephen said, handing two bottles to Ted. "I didn't know what we were having, so I chose a white and a red."

The white was champagne, which received the expected reaction from Ted. "Jesus Christ! Champagne!" he exclaimed. "For lunch! If that isn't decadent, I'd like to know what is."

"Just put it in the refrigerator to cool," Kathleen said rather crossly.

"I'm not having champagne," Ted boasted. "I'm having beer. Anyone joining me?"

No one did. He removed a single Budweiser from the refrigerator, leaving the champagne on the kitchen counter. As Stephen and Clay drifted into the living room, Kathleen whispered, "Please, Ted, don't be a bore."

Angrily, he confronted her. "You're going to chicken out, aren't you? You're not going to spend the weekend here with me."

"I told you, I haven't made up my mind yet."

"But that's why you have that . . . that"—he pointed his beer bottle in the direction of the living room—"that piss-elegant guy here, to check me out first. Isn't that right? You're afraid to make up your mind by yourself."

"I'm not, Ted. It's just that . . . I don't know."

He put the bottle down and took her in his arms. "You want me. You know you do."

As he held her, mouth locked to hers, her knees began to

buckle and she was breathless. "Please, Ted," she implored him, pulling away. "Couldn't you go into the living room and be nice to him while I fix our lunch?"

"Sure, I'll be nice. I'm always nice."

He swaggered into the living room and found Stephen and Clay standing in front of the bookcase.

"This reminds me of my own digs, senior year," Stephen remarked to Clay.

"Oh, does it?" Ted interrupted. "When were you here, Mr. Olivari?" He just would not give in. He would hold on to that formal surname if it killed him.

"I left midway through my senior year, in 1938," Stephen told him. "I had to return to Italy."

"Son of a gun!" Ted exclaimed. Then he yelled into the kitchen, "Hey, Kathleen, did you hear that? Mr. Olivari was in Italy during the war." He turned to face Stephen. "I suppose you were in the army, were you?"

Calmly, Stephen replied, "Yes, I was conscripted."

Ted drank from his beer bottle, wiping his mouth with the back of his hand. "I could never understand how so many people allowed themselves to be manipulated. I mean, everyone knew that Hitler's Germany and Mussolini's Italy were fascist states. Why didn't you protest, for God's sake?"

With surprising composure, Stephen answered, "I fought for Italy, which was my homeland, not for Mussolini. I was just a young man, no older than you are, caught up in events beyond my control. There were millions more like me."

They heard a popping sound from the kitchen, and seconds later Kathleen appeared with the foaming champagne bottle wrapped in a towel. In her other hand was a tray with four glasses, an ice cube at the bottom of each.

"I've done the unpardonable," she explained. "I've used ice cubes to cool the champagne. But I thought . . . well, something to drink might relax all of us." She glared at Ted.

"Thanks, but I'm sticking with beer," Ted said, cupping his beer bottle with his hand, as if to protect it from contamination as Stephen poured champagne and raised his glass in a toast. "To youth."

"*Prosit*," Ted added, touching his beer bottle against their glasses of bubbling champagne, "as I think they used to say in Nazi Germany."

Kathleen heard herself groan.

At the kitchen table, Ted utterly ignored Stephen, as if he weren't even there. What few comments he made were directed either at Clay or Kathleen, and once when Stephen addressed a question at him, he pretended not to hear.

Clay tried to compensate for his bad behavior, however, and soon he and Stephen were in an animated conversation about civil rights. He and Ted hoped to travel to Georgia at Easter break, he said, to help desegregate lunch counters in the South.

"A noble cause," Stephen observed, "but in the end, prejudice is a personal matter. We all discriminate. When we choose our friends, we discriminate against those we don't want as friends."

Ted heatedly contested the point. "All right, I admit governments can't force us to like someone we don't want to like. But there are certain rights of the individual here in America that have to be guaranteed, no matter what we think of them." He slammed his empty beer bottle on the table. "I don't think we can say, Well, liking or disliking people is a personal matter and can't be legislated. That's no justification for making Negroes ride at the back of buses. We're not talking about liking or disliking. We're talking about fundamental human rights."

"Oh, yes," Stephen admitted, "I agree. But in the end, I think there are better ways to serve minority classes than to win them seats at a lunch counter."

Until now, Kathleen and Clay hadn't dared to interrupt, but now Kathleen asked, "What is it, Stephen?"

It was a minute before he replied. "I think colored people have to advance educationally and professionally at the same time as they advance socially. If the latter is attempted alone, it will inevitably end in failure."

"And how do you accomplish that, Mr. Olivari?"

"I suppose that the aim must be to get them into the middle class, one way or another. Give them good jobs for which they've been trained. Pay them adequate wages so that they can buy nice houses and cars and afford to educate their children. I see it as an economic thing, not a social thing. Once colored people are economic equals, where they have their lunch won't be quite so important anymore. They won't bother with lunch counters. They'll be able to drive their cars to a restaurant and order hamburgers, like any other American."

He received support from an unexpected quarter. "I think Stephen is right," Clay volunteered. "No amount of demonstrating is going to correct old injustices until we have self-respect. And we can have that only if we have jobs that will allow us to enter the mainstream of American life."

"But that is so goddamn *utopian!*" Ted protested.

"I don't see why," Stephen answered. "In fact, one of the reasons I'm visiting America at this time is to study the possibilities of opening an automobile assembly plant near Jersey City, which has one of the largest concentrations of Negroes in America. We at Olivari Industries owe much to America, and to the Marshall Plan in particular, which helped us rise from the ashes after the war. Now perhaps we can return the favor by helping you Americans."

Ted seemed impressed. Perhaps also because by then the beer had its desired effect, he was much less combative. Only one incident toward the end threatened to spoil things. When Kathleen brought in the dessert, Ted declined rather theatrically.

"I can't eat strawberries," he insisted. "Don't you know, Kathleen, that Rafael Banuelos has been on a hunger strike in California? It would be immoral to eat them."

"But I've already paid for them," Kathleen explained. "The growers have already got my money, so what difference does it make?"

Stephen came to Ted's rescue. "I think what Ted is trying to say, Kathleen, is that it's a matter of conscience. The gesture itself is a small one—rather like trying to desegregate lunch counters—but also a very noble one. So I think, if it's all the same to you, that I'll skip dessert, too."

Later, when his taxi arrived, Kathleen walked Stephen down the steps to the street.

"I'm sorry that Ted was so abominable to you," she said apologetically.

"Oh, but I found him delightful, Kathleen. You mustn't apologize."

"Delightful? He was rude and ill-mannered."

He looked down at her face. "But don't you see? He knew why I was there. I was the older generation brought to judge him, because you were afraid of your own judgments. Most other young men would have been fawning and ingratiating, but Ted refused to be. I liked him enormously."

"You did?" she cried joyously.

"Listen to your heart, Kathleen, and no harm will come to you." He kissed her gently on the forehead. "Call me on Monday—when your weekend is over."

The next morning at the breakfast table at Briggs Hall, Kathleen informed Mrs. Foxworth that she would be spending the following weekend with her mother in Greenwich, but that Friday after she signed out, she carried her overnight bag to Ted's apartment.

By Sunday, she was madly, overwhelmingly in love with him. Before she left, she agreed to go to Atlanta with him during spring break.

FOURTEEN

*F*ather Joseph knew that a summons from the archdiocese office—and a rap across the knuckles—was inevitable.

The morning after his return from Salinas with Susan Grainger, the *Chronicle* carried a front-page article on Rafael Banuelos's fast and his altercation with one of Roy Bannister's men. Accompanying the story was a three-column-wide photograph showing Susan and Father Joseph standing in front of the Monterey courthouse as Rafael was being removed to a waiting ambulance.

Every since, Father Joe waited to be called on the crimson carpet of Bishop Moriarity, who ruled the archdiocese like a Medici prince. But no call came. Instead he heard from Susan, who informed him that she was about to set up shop, as she described it, and begin groundwork for the voter registration drive among the braceros. "Also," she added, "to be of any help I can to Señor Banuelos. The experience might be amusing."

"It might be much more than that, Susan."

"Don't count on it, Father. I have a very short attention span. This won't be the first time I've thrown myself behind a cause, only to walk away from it a day later. I'm warning you: I'm too superficial to be reliable."

"Why don't you let me do the deciding?"

"Because your views are colored by Christian charity, and that makes them false and unreal."

"You refuse to admit, even for a minute, that you might be a very decent human being?"

"Not even for a minute. Once a whore, always a whore." She paused, remembering something. "Which reminds me—if my friend and procurer should come looking for me . . ."

The reference was obviously to the young man who'd been with her in Hillsborough.

"Procurer, Susan? Isn't that going a bit too far?"

"Procurer of pleasures. Procurer of cocaine. Procurer of my daily ration of male meat, as he would delicately put it. I'm trying to sneak out of town without his finding out, and he may try to get in touch with you to learn where I've gone. I'm sure he noticed the photos in the papers that morning. By the way, you looked very, very swashbuckling."

"I was afraid of that." Bishop Moriarity preferred his parish priests to look pink-cheeked and cherubic.

"If he calls you and asks, don't tell him where I'll be staying."

"I don't know where you're staying."

"Hidden Valley Motel in Carmel Valley. I couldn't bear spending the night at a local fleabag in Salinas. And the Hidden Valley has a swimming pool."

"You do believe in roughing it, don't you?"

"I told you I had money, Father Joseph. I didn't say I had character."

"You may discover some yet."

"I wouldn't know what it looks like. So I would appreciate it if you could refrain from trying to improve me. I'm going to hang up right now before you start saying a prayer for me."

"I already have."

"Merde!" After the oath, she relented somewhat and said softly, "Cheerio, Father."

"God be with you, Susan."

Father Joseph sat in the confessional box twice that day and later on made calls at the hospital to visit parishioners who were ill or dying. Between listening to confessions and making sick visits, he called Vinnie Chan at the Citizens for Kennedy office on Folsom and asked her to set up a meeting the following night for volunteers willing to participate in voter registration in the city, the East Bay, and in Monterey County.

She'd received several other obscene anti-Catholic, anti-Kennedy telephone calls, she reported, but she had devised a way of coping with them. After they hurled abuse at the candidate and his church, she would simply say, "Thank you for taking the time to call. And bless you."

"It shuts them up right away," she boasted.

Shortly after vespers, the call came from the archdiocese office. Father Declan picked it up and took the message, then ran into Father Joseph's study all aflutter. "Bishop Moriarity would like to see you. Immediately."

Father Joe consulted his watch. It was just seven-thirty. Bishop Moriarity was a celebrated gourmet who always sat down to table at eight. If Father Joseph timed his arrival with the after-dinner liqueur, the bishop's disposition was sure to be mellower than it would be if he was interrupted during the entrée.

Sure enough, when he arrived at the bishop's residence a little after nine, Bishop Moriarity was sipping amaretto. He placed his glass on the table next to him as Father Joseph leaned over to kiss his ring.

"Your Eminence," Father Joseph said respectfully as he stood to full height.

"It's so good to see you," the bishop replied in the rich brogue of County Waterford. "We have not had a chat for some time, Father Cassidy. Please help yourself to the liqueur, the essence of almonds. I trust that you're not rabidly temperate in such matters."

Father Joe poured himself a small glassful. "My models are probably more Greek than Judeo-Christian," he replied. "God's bounty was meant to be enjoyed, but sparingly. I've always believed in moderation in everything: in drinking, in eating"—he paused significantly—"and in the practice of one's faith."

It was an invitation to combat, and Bishop Moriarity at once accepted the challenge.

"But moderation also in the zeal with which we promote earthly causes, wouldn't you say, Father Cassidy?"

"I would have to agree."

His superior held up his tumbler. "To your health then," he toasted, drained much of it, then sat back savoring the almond-flavored liqueur. "I've been following your work at St.

Brendan's with much interest," he began. "You have strength-
ened a dwindling parish remarkably well. A difficult parish. A
changing one in which people don't know which way to turn.
If I'm not mistaken, you've increased the number of parishioners by nearly fifty."

Some, of course, were provisional members who engaged
in devotion with something less than zeal. Many of the Negroes in the neighborhood had been drawn out of curiosity,
but had left or were about to leave because there seemed no
place for them in the services.

"I've introduced some innovations," he answered, "not always with success. If we are to maintain St. Brendan's, it's going
to be necessary to try new approaches to attract new worshipers as the neighborhood changes. But, sad to say, in attempting to appeal to our new neighbors—by offering folk singing,
for example, and guitar music as part of the service—I've
sometimes simply managed to alienate our old ones. So that
the increase in the number of parishioners you've just referred to is a bit deceptive. By adding fifty new worshipers, I
may lose fifty or more old ones."

Bishop Moriarity shook his head solemnly, then refilled
his glass from the decanter. "It is confounding, Father Cassidy. One scarcely knows what to make of it, all this animosity
between races. Love thine enemy, our church has always pro-
claimed."

"While at the same time destroying its own enemies," Father Joseph suggested.

"True, to promote our faith, sometimes we've had to es-
pouse methods that have not always been gentle."

"Diplomatically put, Your Eminence." Father Joe said
brightly, trying not to think of all the victims of the Inquisition, the Jews chased from one corner of Europe to the other,
Moorish infidels beheaded for not converting to Christianity.

"But on the whole we have been benign." He sipped his
amaretto. "It is sometimes difficult for young priests, such as
you, to perceive the wisdom of the church in these matters.
But in the end, we must remember, you and I, that we are
servants of God, not people. There is a difference, Father Cassidy. We are ephemeral creatures, our passage on earth only

the blink of God's eye in eternity. Our cares, our problems are unimportant in the long run."

"But surely God is love," Father Joseph protested.

"Yes, and every time we stand before an altar, we celebrate that love. It is our function, our duty. It is not our job as servants of God to become involved in minor social matters."

There it was. No mistaking it. Bishop Moriarity was about to ask Father Joseph to extricate himself from the voter registration drive and his commitment to the cause of the field hands of Monterey County.

"I humbly beseech you to search your conscience," Bishop Moriarity continued, "and your vocation as well. It is admirable, Father Cassidy, that you have been so stirred by social inequities that you would like to help alter them. But it is inappropriate for a Roman Catholic priest. It is the work of others, not us. Our concern is the spiritual well-being of our believers, not whether they are registered to vote in an election, or whether they have comfortable beds or a flush toilet."

Perhaps because he saw the depth of disappointment on Father Joseph's face, Bishop Moriarity decided upon another approach. "It's not generally known," he began, "but I shall be retiring at the end of this year."

There was no way Father Joe could conceal his surprise. "But you're a comparatively young man, Your Eminence." How old in fact was he? Early seventies, Father Joseph guessed, a young age for a bishop to put himself out to pasture.

"I am dying," Bishop Moriarity continued. "No, no, please don't commiserate, Father Cassidy. We're too mature for that and have delivered far too many funeral masses. Death is the reward of all living creatures, and while we would like to extend our lives as long as possible, sometimes our bodies fail us. My doctors tell me that I have an inoperable growth in my throat—from smoking cigars all my life or singing masses, who can say which?—and when I leave this archdiocese in December, I should like to be remembered as a man who steadfastly defended the faith from corruption, from both within and without."

He paused till Father Joseph's eyes met his. "I don't want

to be remembered as the bishop who permitted his parish priests to stray from their true vocations and become involved in social or political revolutions. If people are in want, God will attend to their needs, Father Cassidy."

But God didn't register voters, Father Joseph wanted to say. Instead, he began, "The voter registration drive can be justified, Your Eminence. It's to give people a voice in government who've never had one before. As for helping Rafael Banuelos and his workers in Monterey County, who could be better qualified than a Roman Catholic priest to help ease the sufferings of Roman Catholics?"

"For their suffering they will be rewarded, I assure you."

Earlier when Father Joseph had said that he believed in moderation in everything, he meant everything. Including suffering. A little bit went a long way. While a modest amount could be instructive, even ennobling, too much of it merely beat down a man, extinguished his spirit. To hold out the promise that things would be squared away later on, in the life hereafter, was asking a great deal. Couldn't suffering be distributed more democratically? Some to Roy Bannister, for example, as well as to the braceros?

If God forsakes his people at their time of need, Father Joseph wanted to say, who will fill the gap?

Bishop Moriarity misapprehended the reason for his silence. Thinking that he had acquiesced, he said, "I knew you would understand. Before you leave, join me, Father, in prayer."

Osborne C. Ashley II had lied about more than his address, Pat discovered almost three weeks after the accident when he finally ran him to ground in the Berkeley flatlands.

He wasn't a grad student and hadn't been for some time. He was one of those perpetual students who liked the shelter and ambience of a university town but lacked the self-discipline ever to complete a degree.

Pat was finally able to obtain his correct address at U.C.'s administration office, where he still owed a lab fee for an undergraduate course he'd taken several years before. The door of the apartment was answered by a huge, bovine woman enveloped in a Hawaiian mumu. Behind her the room was furnished in a starkly utilitarian way—sleeping bags, pillows, blankets—and over everything clung the sweet, decaying smell of marijuana smoke.

"Ozzie's at his stand on Telegraph Avenue selling his stuff," the woman explained in what Pat supposed was Berkeley Esperanto.

"Stuff?"

"He makes bracelets and earrings in silver, stuff like that, and sells it on the street."

Pat found him standing next to his portable tray on the avenue's busiest block. He was dressed like a frontiersman in a Kit Carson leather jacket with rawhide streamers dangling like spaghetti al dente from his arms. With his bushy beard, cowboy boots, and faded Levi's, he couldn't have been more readily identifiable as anti-Establishment if he'd had a printed sign on his forehead.

He was anything but overjoyed to see Pat. In fact, if it hadn't been for the silver gewgaws laid out on his tray and the cumbersome high-heeled boots he was wearing, he might have hightailed it down the sidewalk.

Instead, he asked with annoyance, "What do you want, man? I already talked to Conroy's insurance agent. I'm getting seven hundred bucks to fix up the Beetle, which is more than it's worth. I don't have any gripes, if that's why you're here."

"That's not why I'm here." Pat went right to the matter at hand. "You didn't by any chance send me a letter recently, did you?"

"Me send you a letter?" At the first pronoun, he punched at his chest over his heart; at the second, he pointed his finger at Pat. "Hell, man, I don't even know who you are."

"But you do know who was driving the Mercedes that collided with you."

"Oh, sure. That was Congressman Conroy. I hate his guts."

"Would you mind telling me why?"

"Last year, some of my friends and I organized a group to try to save the sea otters."

Pat wasn't sure he'd heard correctly. "The what?"

"Sea otters. You know who I mean—those little mothers with the whiskery faces who float around on their backs, tummy up, off the Pacific coast. The salmon fishermen don't like 'em because they eat salmon, among other things, and they kill 'em every chance they get. So we went to Congressman Conroy's office to get him to sign our petition to save the sea otters, but he said he was too busy. That's why I hate his guts."

Well, if you needed a reason to hate someone, it was probably as good a one as any. It was doubtful, however, that it would drive O. C. Ashley II to attempt extortion. "And you don't have any other ax to grind?"

He seemed offended. "Man, I am *opposed* to axes. I am opposed to rifles. Even firecrackers. I am a pacifist."

A bit of a fruitcake, too, Pat decided, but probably harmless. Yet he was vaguely conscious of an edginess, almost fear, in this friend of the sea otters.

"Why are you afraid?" he asked, and the minute he had, Ashley confirmed it, his eyes darting in his head.

"Who says I'm afraid? I'm pissed off, man, because you're interfering with free enterprise. I'm just trying to make a buck here, selling my wares, and who wants to come up and look at my trinkets with you here? You look like you're fuzz."

"I assure you I'm not."

"Well, if there's nothing else you'd like to know, you'll excuse me while I go back to my business."

Just then, a frenzied-looking youth with longish hair and an unkempt beard rushed up and whispered loudly, "Hey, Ozzie, I need an ounce of your best."

The Wild West figure in the leather jacket crumpled, snapping his eyes shut.

"That's all right." Pat reassured him. "Go ahead and complete the deal. I sometimes smoke recreationally myself." He neglected to say that his smoking was limited to Havanas, when they were available.

Furtively, Ashley removed a small pouch from beneath his tray of jewelry, handed it to his customer, and accepted a fistful of bills.

After he left, Pat asked, "Now would you care to tell me why you were so antagonistic toward Congressman Conroy after the accident?"

Sighing, Ashley replied, "Man, I was shitting bricks. All I

wanted was to get away from there fast. I'd just made a run into the Tenderloin to collect some Colombian Gold. My glove compartment was filled with it, man! If those cops had searched my car, I'd be in the slammer now for dealing. I didn't give a rat's ass if the congressman was hosing that broad of his in the car. I just wanted to get things moving and make dust as fast as I could!"

Pat was convinced that he was telling the truth. The man had some scruples. Anyone who could go to the defense of endangered sea otters was not going to try to make a buck on someone else's sexual weaknesses. Osborne C. Ashley II hadn't written the letter, nor had he sold his information to someone who had.

"Okay," Pat said in conclusion. "Nice talking to you."

"Peace." He made a little steeple of his two joined hands.

"Peace," Pat repeated, dispensing with the architecture.

A more than customarily distraught Father Declan warned Pat that Father Joe might not return to the parish house for hours, because interviews with Bishop Moriarity sometimes lasted till dawn, particularly if His Eminence was in a sentimental mood and decided to play his recordings of Irish ceili music or show slides of his annual summer visit to County Waterford.

But as luck would have it, the bishop was fatigued and turned in early, so Father Joseph arrived home at shortly before eleven.

"I take it that the bishop doesn't like your choice of friends," Pat said as soon as his son entered the study, referring to the *Chronicle* article with the photograph that showed Father Joe beside a bloodied and dazed Rafael Banuelos.

Father Joe flung himself into a chair. "Bishop Moriarity has built a career out of not rocking the boat. In most matters, he's an ultraconservative, so I wasn't the least bit surprised to find him speaking out against activism."

"And what was your reaction?"

"I'm not sure I know yet."

During the drive back to Oakland, Father Joe had weighed and reweighed the bishop's request that he refrain from political activities. The church was vibrant and healthy today, two thousand years after its founding, because it resisted change. It was timeless, unalterable. And while now and then the winds of modernity blew out of the Vatican allowing for variations of ancient methods, what could never be the subject of reinterpretation was a priest's vow of obedience.

The Vatican ruled; priests obeyed without hesitation.

"There will be no church," Patrick insisted, "unless it acknowledges that people's needs have changed."

"Not their spiritual needs, Dad. They remain unaltered."

"Then the church will have to acknowledge that priests have changed. Men who never leave the cloistered walls of the Vatican can't begin to understand what priests in the fields of our Lord have learned, and that is that the church has obligations to help its believers in nonspiritual matters as well if that help is denied them by everyone else."

Father Joe conceded the point, but then suggested, "Who is to say that Rafael can't accomplish his goals without the aid of a meddlesome parish priest from Oakland?"

"A priest from Oakland—or anywhere else—will add dignity to his cause, Joe. As it is, the church has abandoned these people, just as society has. What can Rafael Banuelos's braceros think if the church turns its back on them at a time like this?

It wouldn't be the first time, Joe was tempted to say but didn't. During the Troubles in Ireland, the hierarchy condemned acts of violence of patriots attempting to throw off the yoke of British rule. In the early days of Nazi Germany, the Roman Catholic Church declined to speak out, even in that most Catholic of German provinces, Bavaria.

Yet it wasn't because the Vatican endorsed fascism or colonialism, Father Joseph knew. It was that one of the tenets of Catholicism was acceptance of earthly travail. Whether one was ruled by a dictator or by an occupying army was irrelevant. God alone ruled Catholics, and temporary inconveniences could be borne with.

"What are you going to do?" Patrick demanded.

Father Joseph was undecided. He was a Roman Catholic, there was no doubt about that. Once one believed in the notion of divinity, then Catholicism seemed to him the most appropriate way to give voice to it. It expressed the awe human beings felt toward God. Life. Death. It had grandeur and majesty, unlike some forms of Christianity that seemed to have been devised by accountants, joyless and vengeful. For Father Joe, Catholicism gave meaning to meaninglessness, hope to the hopeless.

"Bishop Moriarity has asked me to return to my parish duties," Father Joseph answered.

"I didn't ask you what Bishop Moriarity wants you to do. I asked you what *you* intend to do."

"I can't challenge him, Dad. The church doesn't allow for defiance."

Patrick raised his voice. "But it will have to if it wants to survive! A medieval church served a medieval society. If the Vatican and its small-minded Bishop Moriaritys persist in being medieval, it will lose its believers, Joe." He waited. "You will have to decide which is more important. God or Bishop Moriarity. You'll make the correct choice, I know. Because you're a loving, caring man, born to serve. But you're also an American, and the concept of blind obedience is repugnant to all Americans. You should know that. But what I haven't told you"—he paused again, perhaps reluctant to tell him now—"is that I had a hell of a job trying to persuade Bobby Kennedy that you were the right man to head the Citizens for Kennedy here in Northern California."

Father Joseph was shocked. If his father had begged Kennedy to give him the job, he'd never forgive him.

"It's not what you think," Pat continued. "You see, the Kennedys realize that their Catholicism could come between them and victory this November. They're very much afraid that people will believe that a Roman Catholic candidate can be ruled by the Vatican. It's that blind obedience issue again. They like to think that their Catholicism has been tempered by their being Americans, and it's their hope that the electorate won't vote against their religion. Yet if a bishop of the Church now demands that a working priest desist from activities that the church considers inimical to its aims, and if that priest obeys blindly, he is giving ammunition to all of John

Kennedy's enemies—precisely what Bobby Kennedy wants to avoid."

Father Joe squirmed in his chair. No matter which course of action he chose—compliance or defiance—he would be forcing an issue he would just as soon had never been brought up.

On the way home, Pat brooded over the letter that might threaten his daughter's sanity and the matter of conscience that could threaten his son's vocation.

Yet Joe was no pushover, of that he was sure. It wasn't for nothing that he was a Cassidy. Other babies' first words might be "Mommy" or "Daddy" or "doggie," but Joe's had been "Why?" perhaps because he'd heard it uttered in his home so often.

Why did things have to be the way they were?

Joe would make up his own mind, would never succumb to ultimatums. If the church insisted that he refrain from activism, he would try to convince the church that it was wrong.

Yet Pat was also very much aware of Mimi's warning that perhaps he wanted Joe to be the sort of priest he himself would have been, had he chosen that vocation. Was it as simple as that, he wondered. Did he secretly yearn for Joe to storm the very ramparts of the Vatican because he himself could never accept the status quo?

Quite possibly. And because of that, Pat vowed not to interfere. He'd said his last word on the subject. From now on, it was Joe's show alone. He could succumb to Bishop Moriarity's request, or he could fight back.

As for the letter, he couldn't help but think that he'd reached a dead end. In spite of the writer's pledge that someone would get in touch, no one had. When he first read it, it had seemed to Pat that if he could discover who had passed on the information about Robert's accident, that person would lead him to the letter writer.

But all three witnesses seemed to be above suspicion: Peter Trevino, Hector Martinez, and now Osborne Ashley II.

No one else could have known of the accident.

Then, just as he pulled off the Bay Bridge and began to

make his way toward Market Street, he remembered that there was indeed someone else. So instead of continuing toward Van Ness, he joined the late-evening traffic on Market, then turned up steep Taylor Street to Nob Hill.

There had been a gala ball that night at the Fairmont Hotel for the benefit of the de Jong Museum of Art, and as a result there was a good deal of activity in the lobby. At such events, San Francisco's society dug into their private safes for their diamonds and emeralds and dressed in their Paris gowns, and it was said—Pat was no authority—with better taste than New York's rich.

Pat surveyed the glittering crowd as they passed to and fro in the lobby, on their way to the ballroom or their waiting limousines. He was in luck, because if there had been no ball, chances are his only close friend on the staff at the Fairmont wouldn't have been on duty. But as it was, he found a perspiring, exhausted Jeremiah Foster in his assistant manager's office, waiting for the throng to go home so that he could do the same.

"I should never have gone into this damned business," Jerry Foster complained as Pat entered. "Look at the time! Midnight, and I haven't had my supper yet."

"It'll taste better the longer you wait," Pat comforted him.

"At this time of night, it'll be easier to drink it than consume it, and that means Agnes will have a pout on her face when I come home tipsy. Why are you abroad at such an unseemly hour anyway, Patrick?"

"I have a request, Jerry."

"So long as I don't have to get out of my chair to fulfill it, consider it accomplished."

Pat explained what he needed. "I'd like to have a look at your guest register. Not today's but . . . let me see . . . it was the night of the choir concert at Grace Cathedral, about three weeks ago."

"I remember that night," Jerry volunteered, "because we had a number of people in the dining room who requested early dinners in order to make the concert. Let me check my calendar." He leafed through a desk calendar until he found the notation he was looking for. "The concert was March twenty-first, and that means the register is right here behind me." He reached behind him and withdrew an enormous ledger from its shelf. "Could I ask why you want to see it?"

"It's personal, Jerry. But I assure you that I have no sinister intentions. I simply need a name."

A name, he might have added but didn't, that Robert Conroy certainly knew but would not divulge, any more than he had disclosed the true nature—Pat was certain of it—of his relationship with that woman.

"Well, we have to be discreet," Foster went on. "I don't have to tell you, do I, Patrick, that this human vessel of ours is flawed. We're subject to weaknesses of the flesh, and from my long experience I'd say that the weaknesses become more pronounced as the day wears on and people begin thinking about bedding down. Who are you looking for, and at what time approximately would he or she have checked in?"

"When I said I needed a name, I meant just that. I have no idea who she is, Jerry. As for the time she checked in, let me backtrack a bit. The choral concert at Grace Cathedral ended at eleven, I believe, and my son Joe and I went directly to my house on Lake Street. Probably arrived by eleven-fifteen or so. We left almost immediately, because there had been an accident, and most likely we got there between eleven-thirty and eleven-thirty-five. The party in question was dropped off at the hotel between . . . oh, I'd say between midnight and twelve-thirty." It couldn't have been later, Pat knew, because by one o'clock Robert was driving into the garage on Pacific Avenue.

"Well, let's see what we have here," Jerry said as he started reading the entries. "At five after midnight a Mr. and Mrs. John Doe arrived from Fresno, California. They had a reservation but no baggage, so they paid in advance."

"It's to be hoped that the Does of Fresno enjoyed their evening out on the town, but no, they're not who I'm after."

"Then we have a Mr. Solomon Lefkowitz of Two-oh-eight Coventry Boulevard, Shaker Heights, Ohio, who lists his business as dress manufacturer."

"No, it wouldn't be Mr. Lefkowitz either."

"Ah, perhaps this," Jerry said as his finger traced the next name. "At twelve-fifteen a Mrs. Christine Lawrence of Eight-seven-six East End Avenue, New York City, checked in. Under profession she lists public relations. She left first thing the next morning."

FIFTEEN

"*I* may know who she is," Nora Molloy announced to an astounded Paul, seated across from her in a downy, chintz-covered armchair. "The woman who called Charles that night may be a Mrs. Christine Lawrence."

Paul never failed to be impressed by his mother's imperturbability. Even now as she repeated the name of the woman she believed to be her late husband's mistress, she seemed so strong, so brave, so understanding and forgiving.

It was with reluctance that Paul had told her about his late-night interrogation of Jean-Claude and the revelation that Charles's mysterious caller, "the gentleman from Galveston," wasn't a man at all, much less a gentleman, but a woman. He'd expected his mother to be distraught because of its implications, but then very coolly and serenely she had provided him with the woman's name!

He'd returned to the River House apartment for a few minutes after having spent the last hour and a half with a vice president of Morgan Guaranty Trust, where Charles had done most of his personal banking. Paul wanted to have a look at the records of his accounts to see if anything unusual had transpired within the last year or so. Large sums withdrawn, that sort of thing.

Because while Nora believed that the woman who had called Charles on the night of his death had been his lover, Paul was more inclined to think that she may have been extorting money from him for some past indiscretion.

The only thing that bothered him, that was somehow out of sync, was her reference to Galveston when she'd identified herself to Jean-Claude. It had to be significant in view of the fact that the Molloy Company had bid on what Charles called the Galveston Project, a mammoth military installation in a country Paul had scarcely heard of, South Vietnam.

But a cursory examination of the Morgan Guaranty Trust records had shown nothing out of the ordinary. The Morgan representative who'd helped Paul so readily, believing him to be an heir to the Molloy fortune, had, however, provided some useful information. He'd advised Paul to make inquiries with his father's accountant, and when Paul asked who it was, he replied that Charles had used the senior accountant employed by the Molloy Company because it was his opinion that the staff in his accounting department was underutilized.

But after Paul telephoned to make an appointment with Ernest Squires (was there an accountant section in *What to Name Baby* books?), he stopped at his mother's apartment to reveal what he'd thus far learned, only to be told the name of his prey.

"But how did you know about this woman?" Paul demanded.

Patiently, Nora explained how Quentin Potter had called the day after Charles's death to reveal that every month for the past eight years, Potter had been sending a more than generous remittance to a woman named Christine Lawrence, who lived in a co-op apartment on East End Avenue. Moreover, his last will and testament included a two-hundred-thousand-dollar bequest to her, not a huge sum but more than went to most of the family retainers.

"Why didn't you tell me before now?" Paul asked.

"Because, quite truthfully, I didn't see any correlation between this Christine Lawrence and the extraordinary circumstances surrounding your father's death. I thought"—she faltered—"Well, I thought she was some silly young thing Charles had picked up and was having a fling with."

"Father? A fling?" Paul repeated incredulously.

"Well, what else could I have concluded? It never occurred to me to quiz poor Jean-Claude about the gender of the caller that night. After all, he clearly said that it was 'the gentleman from Galveston.' "

"Do you honestly think that Father could have done something like that?"

It was painful for her to answer. "I didn't think so, but I wasn't sure. I'm well past my prime, Paul. Long in the tooth, as they say. Your father was a very . . . sensual man when he was young. And something peculiar happens to such men as they age. Somehow or other, they want to experience just one more rapture, and that's when they do something absurd and have affairs with twenty-year-old girls. I was afraid that your Father . . ." She couldn't complete her thoughts.

Oh, yes, Paul had heard of them too, men in their mid-sixties or seventies who suffered cardiac arrests while performing the act of love with some mindless, gum-chewing twit just out of high school.

"If this Mrs. Christine Lawrence used the word 'Galveston' in identifying herself when she called Father," he began, "it's because she was in some way connected with the military installation that's about to be built in South Vietnam. I'm meeting General McFadden for the first time later this afternoon. He seems to be more closely involved with Project Galveston than anyone else, and he may shed some light on the matter."

The man Lee Molloy escorted into Paul's office seemed to be holding a lungful of air in his chest to add to his stature. But because he was short and bandy-legged, his posture made him look top-heavy. He stood rigidly at attention while Lee made the introductions.

"Paul, I don't believe you've met General McFadden yet—Cyrus McFadden. He's our liaison in Washington. General, this is my younger brother, Paul, who, as the expression goes, listens to a different drummer. He's with us for just a few weeks before returning to California, where he's an architect."

If the word "architect" didn't tell General McFadden everything he wanted to know about Paul, the word "California" did. Artistic, offbeat, unstable.

"I missed you at your father's funeral," the general began. "A truly great man. It's a terrible loss to the business community and to America."

Paul had listened to so many variations of this platitude

during the last few weeks that he no longer commented on them.

Instead, he said, "Well, General, why don't you sit down and brief me on Project Galveston. Tell me exactly where we stand."

Even in a chair, General McFadden's back remained ramrod straight. "As you perhaps know," he began, "I'm based in Washington. From sources I'm not at liberty to divulge, I've learned that of the twelve firms that have bid on Project Galveston, there are three serious contenders. One of them is the Molloy Company. The three front-runners have each submitted a cost-plus bid. I trust that you're familiar with the term, Mr. Molloy."

Paul was. Many of the Molloy Company's most profitable postwar ventures had been completed on the basis of a cost-plus contract. Briefly, it meant that the firm would construct the project at cost—all buying under the careful scrutiny of the General Accounting Office—allowing only a thin margin for profit.

He also knew, however, that through cost overruns—unexpected costs, once the project had begun—tremendous profits could be made. Because of overruns, a project anticipated to cost one hundred million dollars could wind up costing three hundred million, much of the additional two hundred million resulting in profits for unscrupulous contractors.

Lee now volunteered, "The Molloy Company enjoys an enviable reputation for not employing cost overrun devices to jack up our profits, and that is definitely an asset."

Paul asked, "Who are the other two leading contenders?"

"The most threatening—literally, they're nipping at our heels—is a brand-new company created for this project alone, although I'm sure you'll recognize the three partners. They're the Lazlo and Logan Company of Denver; the Smith, Curran, and Wiseman Company of Houston; and the R. C. Martinson Company of San Diego. Each brings a unique expertise to the partnership, and even though they've never worked together before as a team on an installation as huge as this one, I see their new company—the L.S. and R. Company, they call themselves—as very formidable competition."

"I don't know about the other two partners," Paul observed, "but Smith, Curran, and Wiseman is first-rate."

"Oh, they're good," Lee agreed, "but the fact that they've teamed up with the other two firms to create a new outfit to work on this project means, quite simply, that lots of things will have to be ironed out. As for paperwork and management, not only will everything have to be done in duplicate, but in triplicate—which means delays and cost overruns. Under the circumstances, I just can't believe that the Department of Defense is going to accept a bid from the L.S. and R. Company."

"Ordinarily, I'd be inclined to go along with that assessment," General McFadden began, "but this new firm has many, many friends in high places, particularly Smith, Curran, and Wiseman. And in the awarding of contracts such as this, friendships and politics play a very vital role."

Paul demanded, "Why shouldn't a firm be judged on its merits alone?"

Lee reached across the desk to pat his brother sympathetically on the shoulder. "Oh, Paulie. You people out in California are living in a dream world. In the real world, half the companies in America doing business with the government would have filed for bankruptcy long ago if merit alone determined who wins contracts. Jesus H. Christ, I can't begin to tell you how many asses I've personally kissed in Washington since we started doing government business. And in three quarters of the cases, all I got for my trouble was a case of chapped lips. Let me tell you, I've wined and dined some of the most personally revolting people you could ever meet, I've played golf with them, I've danced with and felt up their overweight and generally bad-breathed wives. All for one reason: to help us win a contract. Merit, shit! Merit has nothing to do with business, Paulie. That's a badge you get when you're a Boy Scout."

Maybe so. Paul had heard Charles Molloy himself say that in business the Ten Commandments had little relevance. It was the eleventh that made the difference between success and failure: when necessary, thou shalt kiss ass.

"Who's the other front-runner?" Paul asked.

"It's an international firm with headquarters in Paris, though largely German-owned and German-staffed. They're very big in Asia, having recently completed projects in Thailand and Pakistan, so they're familiar with the territory. Their chief liability is that on a military installation such as this one, the Department of Defense couldn't award the contract to foreigners without the risk of a lot of flak from the public here at home, If it weren't for that, I'd say that Otto Baumann & Company would be our strongest competitor. As it is, I think it's the L.S. & R. Company."

"And when is a decision likely?" Paul asked.

"Sometime after the first week in May."

As they concluded their meeting, Lee was summoned to his office to take a telephone call. During his absence, Paul asked General McFadden if the name Christine Lawrence had ever popped up in his work connected with Project Galveston.

"Name doesn't ring a bell," he replied. "Is she a lobbyist or something like that?"

Paul had the feeling he wasn't telling the truth. "I don't think so," he said, then asked, "Are you, by the way?"

General McFadden answered importantly, "I'm liaison for the Molloy Company in Washington. Let's put it that way."

It was after seven in the evening and Paul was still seated at his desk, listening to cleaning women in the hall outside shouting at each other from time to time in a language that might have been Polish or Hungarian. Laid out before him were records of the Molloy Company's financial activities for the past three years—the copious grist that would ordinarily have been abridged in annual reports, but because the firm was privately owned, there were no annual reports.

As Charles Molloy had said often enough, he reported to God. Period. No one else, thank you.

Most of the figures Paul read were unfathomable or impenetrable, as if the sole purpose in recording them was to confound and confuse. In view of the fact that the only eyes to see them, apart from the Molloys themselves and their senior executives, were those of Internal Revenue Service auditors, their deliberate complexity was perhaps forgivable.

Paul had hoped to find some clue, some tiny mistake that would lead him to a serious irregularity, but thus far all the debits and credits, the expenditures and income realized seemed . . . *seemed* more or less in order, except perhaps to the trained mind of a bookkeeper. And in that respect, Paul was willing to admit that he was well out of his depth.

His peripheral vision picked up a dark shape in the doorway, and when he looked, he saw Mathew Rowley standing there, dressed in a stylish oxford-gray overcoat.

"You're working late, Paul."

"You too, Matt."

"I've been clearing out my old desk, getting ready for the move tomorrow to my new office. It will be a corner room with windows facing in two directions."

"You're getting up in the world."

"Progressing laterally, I'd say. I'm just down the hall from the old office. I'm losing a lot of authority in taking this new position, but at least I'm getting a better view. What are you working on?"

As Matt approached the desk, Paul held up a page from the huge ledger he'd appropriated from the accounting department. "If they gave prizes to amateurs in bookkeeping, I should get a gold star at least. It's difficult for me to follow most of this. But every now and then, something catches my eye. Here, for example. According to this, last year the company spent a little over a half-million dollars on public relations. I wasn't even aware that we had a PR department."

"We don't," Matt volunteered.

"Then what the devil does this entry mean?"

Matt read the entry thoughtfully. "I think I know what that is. Your father farmed out the public relations work."

"Farmed it out?"

Matt nodded. "We don't have an in-house PR department, so he employed an outside agency. I've forgotten its name. But if you like, I could find it for you."

"That would be much appreciated."

When Matt left, Paul contemplated the necessity for a firm such as the Molloy Company to engage the services of a public relations office. The Molloys' product, engineering and construction, wasn't purchased by the public, so there was really no need to relate to it. Or did the entry mean something quite different?

When Matt returned, he seemed irritated. "Someone has apparently gone through your father's desk, because the private directory he kept there seems to be missing."

"Directory?"

"Telephone directory. Addresses. That sort of thing. You see, we kept two directories here. One was in my office, so that when Mr. Molloy buzzed me and asked me to call someone for him, I'd check the directory, make the call, then put it through to his office. But he had another directory that he generally kept in the middle drawer of his desk. Sometimes he'd buzz me and simply give me a number and ask me to put the call through to him when there was an answer."

Not for the first time that day, Paul was puzzled. "And what does that have to do with public relations, Matt?"

"I was just about to tell you. Once he gave me a number, apparently taken from his private directory—you know, of course, that he never bothered to memorize numbers if he could help it—and when I placed the call, I distinctly recall that the person who answered at the other end identified it as a public relations firm."

"I see," Paul began. "But you say that the directory has disappeared?"

"At least it's not where Mr. Molloy generally kept it. But I think he had a duplicate that he carried around with him. It might be in his effects at the apartment."

Hadn't his mother mentioned finding such a directory on Charles's desk in Southampton the night of his death? Paul had the distinct recollection that she had. As soon as Matt left, he would give her a call.

In the doorway, Matt shifted his weight from foot to foot. "One thing I wanted to ask you, Paul, was if it would be all right if I took a little vacation, say for two weeks, before I actually begin my new job. I've cleared it with your brother, who seemed to have no objections. But I wanted to ask you, too. You see, when I was married last year, we were very busy here at the office, and I hated . . . well, I hated to take the time off for a honeymoon. So my wife and I settled for a weekend in Cape May, New Jersey. I owe her a honeymoon, and I thought this would be as good a time as any."

In astonishment and admiration, Paul shook his head. "You actually gave up your honeymoon, Matt, just to accommodate my father?"

"Well, that may be an exaggeration, but he always used to say that he couldn't run his business without me. And I enjoyed working for him, Paul. He was like . . . a father to me." His voice wavered.

"To all of us, Matt, for better or worse."

Still, Matt hadn't finished. "I hope you don't think too harshly of him, Paul, for cutting you out of his will."

"He had reasons."

"Do you know that he went out to California to see you once?"

Paul was shocked. "For God's sake, when?"

"No one was supposed to know. I don't believe even your mother knew. And your father made me swear I'd never tell, but . . . well, it just seems to me that you should know. I made the reservations for him. He flew out one day and flew back the next. When he got home, I asked him if he'd seen you, and he said no, but that he'd rented a car and driven out to where you lived. A light was on inside, but he didn't go to the door."

"I wish he had."

"So do I, Paul."

After Matt left, Paul continued to sit at his desk, staring at the ledgers in front of him. He was about to pick up the telephone and dial his mother when a gray-haired woman stuck her head into the room and asked in pidgin English if she could clean it. Paul didn't want to hold her up, so he gathered together the financial records and put them in his filing cabinet, then walked down the hall to the very end.

The door was closed, and a new name had already been inscribed in a brass plate: LIAM F. MOLLOY, CHAIRMAN.

Paul opened the door and entered the darkened room. The curtains at the huge wall-to-wall windows were drawn, but here and there light filtered through from nearby skyscrapers. Instead of flicking on the ceiling lights, he stared at the eight-foot-long mahogany desk before which he'd stood on so many occasions, often with quaking knees.

Behind the desk, neatly arranged on top of a cabinet, were photographs of the family, taken at various times over the years. Tom was there, first in knee pants, then in his RAF uniform. Robbie was next to him. Lee. Mary. Eddie. Deirdre. Kathleen. Even much-maligned Megan. But there was no photograph of Paul.

Banished from the family for reasons of pride.

In spite of his name and new title on the door, Lee apparently hadn't occupied the office yet, because everything on the desk was as it had been the last time Paul had been summoned there by his father. Charles Molloy liked a clean and orderly desktop. Apart from a silver-framed photograph of Nora, forever his inspiration, he kept nothing on it except the necessary tools of his trade. Pencils, pens, paper clips.

All around him, Paul could feel his presence, as if he were in the room that very instant. Then came the recollection of those terrible words hurled at one another during their last meeting.

"If you think so little of me as that, I see no reasons for us to continue this discussion."

"Or begin any other."

Paul sat in the well-worn leather chair behind the desk and dialed the number at the River House. When Jean-Claude picked it up, Paul asked if his mother was available.

A minute later, Nora said, "Yes, Paul?"

"I'm at the office and I've just learned something that may or may not be significant. Father apparently kept a private directory of telephone numbers. The one he kept in his desk doesn't seem to be here, but Matt Rowley just told me that he had a duplicate that he generally carried around with him. Didn't you tell me that you found one in his study in Southampton the night he died?"

"Yes. It was next to the telephone."

"Is it still in Southampton?"

"No, I picked it up and brought it into New York with me. Why is it important, Paul?"

"I want you to look up a number for me."

"It'll take me a minute to find it. I put it in one of my dresser drawers."

While Paul waited, he pushed a button on the desk, then swiveled the chair as the massive curtains drew back electronically to reveal the midtown skyline, blazing with lights, everywhere around him slender towers piercing the night sky. God knows, maybe it was understandable that anyone who looked down at the world from this perch on the thirty-first floor would feel something more than human, larger than life, disdainful of criticism.

"Paul?" Nora asked at the other end. "I've got the directory here in front of me now."

"Look under the *P*'s, would you?"

"*P* as in Peter? Just a minute. My eyesight is fading. Even my reading glasses don't help much anymore. Ah, here we are. The *P*'s. Now what name do you want?"

"It isn't a name. It's simply P-R."

"P-R?" she repeated. "Well, let's see what we have. Paulsen. Perry. Phillips. Pine. Powell. Here we are. P-R. Is that supposed to be someone's name, Paul?"

"It's P-R for 'public relations.' Is there an address and telephone number?"

"No address, but there's a number. Here, let me hold it up to the light. Do you have a pencil? It's 555-4052. Did you get that, Paul?"

"Yes, I've got it, Mother."

"Why did Charles use just the initials, do you think? It's a most unusual way of listing a number. It's like instead of writing 'Gristede's' or 'D'Agostino's,' just writing 'Groceries.' "

"Yes, it *is* unusual. And I won't know for another minute or so why he didn't write the full name."

"If you find out, will you tell me, Paul?"

"I will, Mother."

After she hung up, Paul waited to compose himself before dialing the number she'd given him. If his hunch was right, he'd have to have his wits about him when the party at the other end answered.

It rang once. Twice. Three times.

When it was picked up, Paul caught his breath. As he listened to the voice, it was a second or two before he realized that it was a recording.

"Wells and Lawrence, Public Relations. Mrs. Lawrence is not available at the present but will return your call at the earliest convenience. Would you kindly leave your number after you hear the beep . "

SIXTEEN

*D*aily, Father Joseph expected to hear from Susan Grainger and learn that she wouldn't be able to continue with her work registering voters in Monterey County, because . . . well, because she had a party to attend at Lake Tahoe, or one to give in San Francisco. Or because she had a headache. Or a hangover. Or was bored. Or . . .

For weeks he heard nothing from her. It was Aaron Golden who finally propelled him to check on her progress, or lack of it.

"Father Joe, we're counting on you," Aaron said late one night when he called from Washington. "We expect you to have God looking down on us when we meet in Los Angeles for the convention."

"He may look, but don't expect Him to participate. Carrying placards around or leading one of your so-called spontaneous demonstrations isn't His forte."

"You mean we can't even get Him to wear a little button on His lapel with the candidate's picture on it?"

"Not even that. Among other things, God doesn't have a lapel."

"Yeah? Well, whadayaknow! So how are you, Father Joe? How are we doing on the voter registration drive?"

Father Joseph explained that teams of volunteers were being sent into the disadvantaged areas of San Francisco—the Mission District and Haight-Ashbury—as well as Oakland and other East Bay communities. Another team was working in the San Jose region, and a third, led by Susan, had just begun its efforts in the farmlands of Monterey County.

"You're letting Grainger work for us?" Aaron asked

doubtfully. "I know the type. Bored rich girls. We'd rather have her dough than her time."

"Listen, Aaron, she needs something like this to give her life a sense of purpose."

Scornfully, he said, "When you're as old and jaded as I am, Padre, you'll realize that there are a heap of people in this world who *have* no sense of purpose in their lives. She'll just mess things up, I know she will."

"I have faith in her."

"Faith? You'd have faith in anyone. Even Al Capone, Even Eva Braun. Next you'll be telling me you have faith in Republicans."

"But I do."

"Stop! I don't want to hear it. Talk about something else. Is Rafael Banuelos still fasting, or did he give it up?"

"He's gone without food for weeks, Aaron. Do you mean that the newspapers back East aren't covering it?"

"Well, you know journalists, Padre. When the news first broke, it got headlines here, but soon got pushed off the front page. I guess Americans don't like to read about guys who are fasting. It makes us feel guilty while we're gorging ourselves with food."

"Is there any chance that the Kennedys will lend their support to Rafael's cause?"

Aaron sputtered with indignation. "Haven't we already gone over that, Father? That isn't done in politics. If the Kennedys get too palsy-walsy with Banuelos, we'll lose the support of all those Central Valley Okies who distrust anyone whose last names have more than one syllable. We can't afford that."

"I think we owe Rafael and his braceros something."

"Couldn't we convince him to start eating again?"

"It's important to him, Aaron. The boycott isn't going to work unless there's a dramatic element to it. You say that people feel ashamed to eat while Rafael starves. Well, let them. We're not asking them to give up filet mignon, just strawberries."

"So what the hell do you want John Kennedy to do?"

Father Joe had hoped that Aaron would know. Or perhaps the candidate himself. "Couldn't he . . . well, simply stop putting strawberries over his cornflakes every morning?"

"Are you mad? The candidate can't reveal that he has cornflakes for breakfast! If he did, he'd have all the raisin bran fanatics in the world on his neck, and the Wheaties people, and the Rice Krispies partisans—"

"Oh, Aaron!"

"All right, already," he replied. "I'll see what I can do. But I can't promise much. You're the one who's in charge of miracles, not me. I'm just your ordinary, loud-mouthed smart Jewish kid from New York who always memorized everything my teachers told me to, so I got a scholarship to Harvard. If I hadn't, I'd probably be a tailor, just like my old man."

"If you were a tailor, you'd put Brooks Brothers out of business."

"Well, maybe. Being a failure is definitely not my style. I don't know how to be quiet or modest. I *am* pretty good at my trade. But don't expect me to change human nature, Padre. I know those Central Valley Okies, and I'm afraid of them. If we rub them the wrong way, we're going to lose California's electoral votes."

"If you waffle on this one, you deserve to lose them—and the election, too. If you want the Chicano vote, then you'll have to give them something in return, I don't know what. Obviously, it has to be handled discreetly, but somehow or other the Kennedys will have to put their feet in the water if they ever expect to learn how to swim."

"Apt," Aaron opined. "Very apt. I'll bring it to their attention. In the meantime, register as many Chicanos as you can, Father."

"I'll do my best. And maybe you could do without strawberries."

"No problem. I never have breakfast anyway. All I have is coffee and a bagel. I better hang up now. I'm calling from a public booth and I'm out of change."

"What would you do, Aaron, if suddenly you found yourself rich?"

The Kennedys' political strategist laughed to himself. "I'd probably become a Republican."

"And what if you wake up one morning and found that all the pain and suffering was gone in this world, and everything was perfect?"

"I know for sure what I'd be. I'd be dead."

An iron bedstead had been moved into the cramped living room of the tiny house near Salinas, and the shades had been drawn. In the dim light, candles were burning on a table beneath a garish, dime-store rendition of the Virgin Mary.

"How goes it, old friend?" Father Joe said to the figure lying in the bed beneath a single sheet.

Rafael Banuelos's voice had weakened considerably during the weeks of his fast, and when he replied, Father Joe had to bend over his chest in order to hear.

"It is good of you to come, Father. Please sit down. You are most welcome in my house."

Father Joe pulled up a rush-bottomed chair next to the bed. "How much longer do you intend to persist in this fast, Rafael?" he asked, holding his bloodless hand.

"The ranchers are still shipping strawberries to New York and Boston because people are still buying them. When they stop buying, the ranchers will succumb. Then, and not before then, will I end my fast."

"And what if your tired old body lets you down, Rafael? What if you should succumb before the ranchers?"

"But that is out of the question. I can't do that, because then my people would have no one to lead them, and the ranchers would win."

"If that's the case, then I think you should stop the fast at once."

The old man's face had the bluish pallor of a face recently embalmed. He shook his head, saying, "A little longer. The ranchers are beginning to despair because some orders have been canceled. If only many orders could be canceled, the berries will begin to rot in the fields, and our cause will have triumphed." His eyes opened and closed.

Next to him, on the other side of the bed, Susan Grainger fanned his face with a folded newspaper. "He's very tired and very weak," she said as if Rafael couldn't hear her.

"I'll only stay a minute."

Father Joseph had come to Salinas to tell Rafael that he wouldn't be seeing much of him anymore, that his parish duties would henceforth be taking most of his time. Little by little, in the coming weeks, he planned to return to the peaceful, noncontroversial life of an Oakland priest, extricating himself gradually from the Citizens for Kennedy movement.

But as he sat looking at the wasted body of Rafael Banuelos, he couldn't force himself to say the words.

"He sleeps most of the time," Susan whispered, leading Father Joe out of the room on to the porch.

Once they were alone, he asked, "Is he receiving any medical attention at all?"

"Antonia's doctor friend in Monterey comes out twice a week to have a look. Most of the local doctors wouldn't go near him for fear of offending the ranchers."

"And what does Antonia's doctor friend say?"

Susan sat on the top step of the porch stairs, leaning over to rest her elbows on her kneecaps. "Rafael is a strong and determined man. But he has a weak heart. His body can't take much more of this abuse." She turned to him. "Can't you do something?"

"I asked him, just now, to give up his fast, but he refused."

"Not that, dammit! He never will, don't you understand? If the ranchers don't give in, he'll die. You know he will."

Father Joe admitted reluctantly that Rafael would indeed fast to the death. Lamely, he began, "I can give him spiritual consolation, but that's about it. I can't do much more than that."

"He doesn't need spiritual consolation. He needs help to end this boycott once and for all. And the only way that's going to happen is if the ranchers agree to his three demands: The braceros must be paid the minimum wage, no children under fourteen can be employed in the fields, and adequate housing must be provided for them."

"I've spoken to Aaron Golden and asked if the Kennedys can't be persuaded to do something."

"And what did he say?"

"He's your quintessential politician, Susan. An East Coast academic, but a born politician. And he knows that it would be poison for Kennedy to make any sort of statement before the convention. But he promised to bring it to his attention."

Susan was near tears. "A fat lot of good that's going to do." She stood up and looked away from Father Joe into the fields. "When I was very little, my mother and father were still married, and my mother used to make me say my prayers every night before I went to bed. Once I asked her why I was praying, and she tried to tell me about Jesus Christ. I never really got the hang of it. After the divorce, my father seldom mentioned Christianity because he was an atheist. So I grew up without any faith. But now I think I understand what it's all about. I'm not sure *you* do, Father, or that church of yours. But *I* do. It's self-sacrifice. Whether it's for the salvation of mankind or for the success of a boycott of agricultural produce, it's self-sacrifice. Rafael has taught me that."

At last, she turned to look at him again. "I suppose it isn't much of a discovery. Infantile, in fact. But I hadn't expected it. Am I wrong, Father?"

"I'd say you're very, very right, Susan. What you've discovered is a simple truth that seems to escape even most theologians."

"In all my life, I've never seen anything like it," she continued. "Rafael is prepared to die for his cause. I didn't think there were people like that. Most of the people I've known have spent their lifetime consuming one another, then spitting out the bones. To sacrifice themselves for someone else? Unheard of!"

"So now that you know, Susan, where do you go from here?"

"I don't know." She laughed stridently. "Maybe to the madhouse, where my mother wound up."

"It doesn't have to be that. You have a talent for helping people, I can see it. Rafael admires you. So do his people."

"All we're doing is using them, Father. I'm almost ashamed of what I've done. I've talked them into registering to vote for the first time in their lives. Most of them didn't even know they were eligible to become a part of the democratic process. I should be proud of myself, but I'm not."

"What would it take for you to feel proud?"

She deliberated before replying. "I'm not sure I know. But it would help if I knew that there was a reason for all this. Rafael has his cause. But I'm not sure it has anything to do with the kind of President we do or do not elect."

"Oh, but I think it does. Because a President sets the tone of a nation. Establishes an attitude. The right President can heal wounds, rectify old wrongs. Can unite a divided country. I may be wrong, but I think we have a better chance with someone like John Kennedy than any candidate since Roosevelt because he has both intellect and compassion."

Almost angrily, Susan said, "There's a man dying in that bed in there. Why can't your Kennedy or your God start showing some compassion right now?"

He touched her gently, reassuringly, on the crook of her arm. "They may, Susan. They may."

"You can tell both of them—your God and your candidate—to start looking at the clock. Because Rafael can't live for another week."

The minute he turned the corner and pointed the old Ford down the quiet, tree-laned street toward St. Brendan's, Father Joe knew that the very worst had happened.

Parked in front of the rectory was Bishop Moriarity's black Cadillac, and waiting behind the wheel was his driver, an attractive young man just out of the seminary.

An anxious and apprehensive Father Declan met him at the front door. Whispering, he explained, "His Eminence was just driving by, he said, and asked if you were in. I was so flustered, Father Joseph—forgive me—before I knew what I was doing, I told him that you'd gone down to Salinas to see that Mexican fellow. It made him very, very agitated. He's in your study." He bent over and said into Father Joe's ear, "He's fuming."

"Well, a little fuming may do His Eminence good. Might burn off some of those calories."

Father Declan was horrified at the irreverence. He clapped his hands together in despair like a mountainy Irishwoman who'd just been told that her cow was dead.

The Buddhalike figure of Bishop Francis A. Moriarity filled an upholstered Victorian gentelman's chair in the study. As Father Joe entered, he peered darkly over his shoulder at Father Declan, lurking behind, and said perfunctorily, "That will be all, Father Declan. You may close the door."

The assistant curate backed from the doorway, head bowed, then silently shut the door.

"Forgive a tiresome old man for calling on you unannounced," Bishop Moriarity began. "But I was in the neighborhood having a delightful lunch with Mrs. J. Wells Ambrose, Jr., in the hills of Berkeley. A most generous woman. Her philanthropy will allow us to complete the steeple on our cathedral this year, and I'm pleased to report that she practices a similar largesse in laying food on her table. Added to which she was kind enough to make me a gift of a whole case of the exquisite 1956 chardonnay she served with our meal. I've brought a bottle for you and Father Declan."

Awkwardly, knowing what was coming next, Father Joseph thanked him for his thoughtfulness.

"I trust you've been in the parish making sick visits," Bishop Moriarity continued. "Or perhaps preparing the wee babes of the community for baptism, is that it? Or instructing would-be converts to our true and only church? One never has a moment's rest, does one, Father Joseph, as we toil, you and I, relentlessly in the fields of our Lord."

Without hesitation, Father Joseph declared, "I spent a few hours with Rafael Banuelos in Salinas."

"Salinas?" he repeated with mock surprise. "Am I to understand that St. Brendan's parish in Oakland has been expanded to include a sleepy and rural community in far-off Monterey County?"

"I'm well aware that it lies beyond my parish and my parish duties."

"Ah!" his visitor cried. "Of that you are aware. I'm most relieved to learn that, Father Joseph, but in view of the fact that during our recent conversation on the subject, I made it quite clear that we at the archdiocese office were opposed to a geographical enlargement of your parish, I confess that I'm puzzled that you disregarded our wishes in this matter."

Father Joseph tried to control his temper. "Rafael Banuelos is on a fast in order to bring national attention to the plight of his braceros."

The bishop nodded. "Yes, I have read something to that effect."

"I've known him for many years and consider him a friend. I wanted to help him in every way I could, both as a friend and as a priest."

Bishop Moriarity nervously tapped his ringed fingers on the arms of the chair. "But in so doing, you neglected your parish duties. While I have been here, Father Joseph, three women of your parish dropped by to have their holy medals blessed. Were we to turn them away from the door?"

"Father Declan is capable of blessing medals, Your Eminence."

"But surely you have been assigned to St. Brendan's to attend to such matters, have you not? At no time were you instructed that your duties were to include participating in the boycott of . . . of some agricultural product—artichokes or some such thing."

"Strawberries, Your Eminence."

"What it is, is inconsequential, Father Joseph. What is important is that today you were not engaged in priestly duties."

"But I think I was." Almost as the words slid off his tongue, he regretted them.

Bishop Moriarity furrowed his formidable forehead. "Then I fear we disagree on something so fundamental that the punishment I'd planned to give you now seems painfully inadequate. Instead"—he made his way to the long window overlooking the garden where Father Declan was mindlessly puttering with the flowers—"instead I think the time has come for you to reflect anew on your faith, to search the depth of your soul, and find your way back to the path from which you've strayed. You will recall, I'm sure, that during your seminary days, a period of 'grand silence' was observed from evening prayers until the following morning, a time of rich reflection when all earthly cares were forgotten. Sometimes, Father Joseph, we priests need reminding who we are and why we are here." He waited until Father Joe's eyes met his. "Because of that, as of the second week in May, you will be relieved of your duties here at St. Brendan's and assigned, for a period of twelve months or longer, to St. Anthony's Benedictine Monastery in Logansboro, Tennessee, where all who enter take a vow of perpetual silence. Good afternoon, Father Joseph."

"But Your Eminence!"

"God be with you, Father," Bishop Moriarity said, sailing from the room.

SEVENTEEN

*T*he evening news report on television showed a pensive Bobby Kennedy walking through a crowd of brown-faced braceros or sitting silently at the bedside of sunken-cheeked Rafael Banuelos. Afterward, he had no statement to make to the newsmen who'd followed him to the impromptu stop in Monterey County between scheduled meetings in Los Angeles and San Francisco. Nor did Kennedy headquarters choose to elaborate when given the opportunity, or announce that he was acting on behalf of the presidential candidate.

"The event speaks for itself," a member of his staff said.

Because of the darkness of the night and the reluctance of the visitor to show his face before the camera, some even charged that it wasn't Bobby Kennedy at all but an imposter.

No matter, it was the chief topic of conversation at dinner tables all over America that evening, and the next morning hundreds of East Coast wholesalers canceled orders of California strawberries.

"Tremendous!" Ted exclaimed the next day at lunch in Cambridge. "Just tremendous! It's the first time since Abe Lincoln that a presidential candidate has bothered to acknowledge that there are brown faces and black faces among the electorate. It's so brave, so daring!"

"It's grandstanding," Clay suggested. "You'll notice that the Kennedys' endorsement of Rafael Banuelos's boycott was mighty subtle. So subtle, in fact, that it's hardly an endorsement at all. It might have helped if we'd actually been able to *see* Bobby Kennedy's face. For all we know, it was a stand-in from Hollywood."

"The Kennedys were just trying to minimize the damage," Kathleen volunteered. "They wanted Banuelos to know that they were behind him, so they made it a very personal gesture. Do you realize what even that is going to cost them, Clay? It's going to cost them millions of votes, because people who are opposed to the boycott and what it stands for won't vote for John Kennedy after this."

"I still think it was very, very calculated," Clay insisted.

"In politics, is anything *not* calculated?" Ted interrupted. "But for all that, it was a human decision, not a political one, and I admire them for it."

"It's maybe a little too much like Eleanor Roosevelt and her do-gooding that my mom always talks about. Here was this rich-as-hell society lady who visited slum schools, smiling her head off, showing every tooth in her mouth, as the kids lined up to sing 'God Bless America.' Then she'd go home to the White House or her little palace in Hyde Park and write an inspirational column about it in 'My Day.' And the slum kids would have their suppers of rice and beans, no better off than they were before."

Kathleen's voice sounded tired. "Why can't you accept a small but honest gesture in the spirit in which it was made, Clay? Why do you always have to blame all your problems on white people, never accepting any of the blame yourself, and then when a white person does something nice, you belittle them?" Suddenly, there were tears in her eyes, and she pushed back her chair and rushed from the table.

"Hey, what did I say?" Clay asked when she'd gone.

"She's in a bad mood, that's all."

Clay indicated her unfinished soup and corned beef sandwich. "She didn't eat much either. Maybe she's coming down with something. Why don't you make her stay in bed this afternoon?" He bundled up in his parka in preparation for his one o'clock class, then made a horn of his hands and shouted in the direction of the bathroom. "I'm sorry, Kathleen. I didn't mean to upset you. I guess I'm a boor."

When she rejoined them, her face was colorless. "No, you're not, Clay. It's my fault. I don't feel so well."

"Probably the flu bug. It's all over the place."

After Clay had bounded down the stairs to the street, Ted suggested, "Why don't you sit down and let me do the dishes?

Sure you don't want any of your chicken noodle soup? I could reheat it for you."

"I'm not hungry."

As he carried the plates to the counter, he remarked, "There's a lot of Asian flu going around. Boy, that can sure knock you for a loop. I had it sophomore year and my temperature went up to a hundred and three."

When she continued to sit impassively at the table, he said, "What's wrong, Kathleen?"

She stared at the tabletop. "I'm not sure I'll be going to Atlanta with you." Spring vacation was to begin at the end of the week, and the Reverend King had scheduled the lunch counter sit-ins for the following Monday.

Ted wiped his hands on the front of his cord trousers and sat next to her. "Why not?"

It was some time before she answered, and when she did, it was as if she'd prepared a little speech. "Who are we trying to kid anyway? It's all such a sham. No matter what happens in Georgia during the demonstrations, we're not going to change anything."

"But we will, don't you see?" he insisted. "We'll be bringing the world's attention to the problem. Hell, as it is, half the people in America aren't even aware that Negroes can't eat at the same places as whites in the south."

"And the half that does, doesn't care. We can't force them to care, Ted, so why are we going to Georgia?" She sat up ramrod straight in the chair. "I'll tell you why. We're not doing it for colored people. We're doing it for ourselves. To prove to everyone how modern and liberal we are." She was almost breathless. "Do you know what my grandfather used to say? He said, show him a revolutionary and he'd show you a man who hates his father. He could have added: or a woman who hates her mother."

In all truth, Kathleen didn't hate her mother. But she didn't have much affection for her either. Nancy Romily was a cold, unemotional woman who didn't inspire strong feelings.

Ted's voice was husky from disappointment. "Do you honestly think that I'm involved in the civil rights movement simply because my old man drank himself to death? And that you are—*if* you are—because your mother is . . . Jesus Christ, I don't know what she is. You never even talk about your family."

Defiantly, she said, "So what would you like to know?"

"Anything you'd care to tell me."

She watched his eyes to gauge his reaction. "What would you say if I told you there was a great deal of money?"

He pinched up his nose with distaste. "What do you mean, a great deal of money? I don't know anything about money. If I have a couple bucks left over at the end of the month, I feel rich."

"More than that," she began, then added apologetically, "My grandfather was Charles Molloy."

Momentarily, the name didn't seem to register. When it did, Ted's mouth opened with astonishment. "You mean that robber baron was your grandfather?"

With more composure than she thought possible, Kathleen answered, "Chances are he would have considered you an adolescent whose mind has been addled by left-wing professors."

"I'm no addle-minded adolescent."

"I didn't say you were. I said my grandfather probably would have perceived you that way. And he wasn't a robber baron. He was a very smart businessman and a sweet, loving man."

Beginning to lose his patience, Ted demanded, "Will you kindly tell me what all this has to do with your sudden decision not to go to Atlanta with us? Are you having second thoughts about me, too? Is that it?"

In confusion, she shook her head. "I didn't say that, Ted."

"But you're thinking it, aren't you? I could tell yesterday that something was wrong. You seemed so remote when we were together."

Since their first weekend in the apartment, virtually the only time they could be truly alone was after they finished lunch. Clay had a one o'clock class on Mondays, Wednesdays, and Fridays, and Ted and Kathleen had two o'clocks on the same days. So for forty-five minutes, they made hurried, frantic love on the sofa in the living room or on one of the twin beds in the bedroom. On Tuesdays and Thursdays, it was slightly more relaxed, but there was always the possibility that Clay might return from the library or chem lab unexpectedly.

"Everything has happened so fast," she said by way of explanation. "I'm not sure anymore who I really am."

He cocked his head and said sarcastically, "And you think you may be just your ordinary spoiled rich girl, after all. Is that it? Is that why you're having second thoughts about everything?"

She was close to tears. "Now you're being cruel."

"And you aren't?" he shouted. "Hell, you've just told me you're not sure about me or anything else anymore. And you've told me your family is loaded. What am I supposed to do, Kathleen? Genuflect? I don't give a rat's ass about money. Don't you know that by now?" He was gulping for breath. "Or is it that you can't live without it? Maybe you've decided you don't want to give it up. Don't think I didn't see how palsy-walsy you and Stephen Olivari were, the day he was here. He's a part of your circle, but I'm not. I'm the one who has to bust open the piggy bank to take you to the movies. Maybe you'd like to spend the rest of your life with Olivari instead, traipsing around after him from Milan to St. Moritz to Monte Carlo. That would be *so* much more fun than going to Atlanta to protest against lunch counter segregation!"

"I'm fond of Stephen, I won't deny it. But that's all there is to it. You don't have to take a course in advanced psychology to realize that he's the father I never had."

"Sometimes women marry men for that reason, Kathleen."

"Well, I don't intend to."

"It's a very glamorous life, more than I could ever offer you."

"Don't you know the original meaning of the word 'glamour,' Ted? It's 'false magic.' I'm not impressed. You're the one I love, not Stephen, I swear to God."

If he was confused before, he was utterly confounded now. "Then why, all of a sudden, have you decided not to go to Atlanta with us?"

As tears flooded her eyes, she covered them with her hands.

"It's my grandmother," she began. "I don't want to hurt her."

Ted stooped next to her, holding her around the waist as she cried. Softly, he asked, "And would I hurt her? Is that what you're saying?"

She dried her cheeks with the back of her hand. "I haven't told her about you, Ted. Or Atlanta or anything. I'm closer to her than almost anyone else in the world. Why haven't I told her?"

The words were difficult to say. "Maybe you're ashamed of me."

"Or ashamed of myself because I don't know who I am. I know what my mother thinks I am, what my grandmother thinks, and what you think. But I don't know what I think, myself."

He dropped his head onto her lap, and she gently caressed his curly hair.

"Then maybe it's time for me to meet your grandmother," he said. "It might help you make up your mind."

When Kathleen called to inform Nora that there was a young man she'd like to bring to dinner the following Saturday night, her grandmother wasn't particularly surprised.

Ever since Charles's death, Nora was quite sure that someone or something had been shoring up her granddaughter emotionally. During the funeral and the long weekend at Southampton, Kathleen had shown genuine manifestations of grief that could sometimes, Nora knew, end in blackest, bottomless depression. Yet as soon as she returned to Cambridge, she re-embraced life with gusto. During their daily telephone conversations, Kathleen had given every indication that she was happy, yet she hadn't explained who or what it was that had caused this euphoria. Now she was about to bring a young man to dinner.

Kathleen planned to leave Cambridge a day before Ted, flying to New York on Friday after classes, partly because she wanted to spend an evening alone with her grandmother to prepare her—prime her—and partly because she hoped to distance herself a bit from Ted before the meeting. Ted would be driving to New York on Saturday, along with Clay, who had a ticket to a basketball game at Madison Square Garden Saturday afternoon. Both would be spending the night at Ted's mother's apartment.

Before leaving for the airport on Friday, Kathleen had another near-quarrel with Ted, this time over his wardrobe.

"I suppose I'll have to ask around Eliot House to see if someone'll let me borrow a suit," he complained.

"Why on earth would you want to do that?"

"Well, all I've got is a cruddy corduroy sport coat."

"Your cruddy cord sport coat will look fine."

He made an agonizing face. "Will I have to wear a tie?"

Ted may have been the most anti-tie man in the world. He ascribed most of mankind's torments—wars, cancer, madness—to the fact that men were throttled around the neck by a piece of ribbon.

"Would it kill you, just this once, to wear a tie?" Kathleen asked.

His pained look clearly indicated that it might. Still, he said, "I suppose not. Which one should I wear? The black knit or the red one?"

At a university where some students were known to boast that they possessed hundreds of neckties, Ted owned only two.

"The red regimental would probably look better."

He frowned. "Your grandmother will think I'm a Commie if I wear a red tie. I'll stick with the black knit."

She provided him with the address of her grandmother's apartment and the telephone number in the event that there was a last-minute hitch. If there wasn't, he was expected between seven-thirty and a quarter to eight. Nora generally sat down to table at eight-thirty.

"Eight-thirty!" he protested. "I'll be famished by then. I'd better have something to eat before I go. Otherwise, your grandmother'll think I'm a pig."

"At least she won't think you're a Commie pig."

Kathleen didn't look forward to the confrontation. In fact, dreaded it. Not because she was unsure how Ted would behave—he would be antagonistic—but because she didn't know how her grandmother would react.

* * *

As always when Kathleen stayed overnight at the River House apartment, at eight on Saturday morning Jean-Claude respectfully tapped at her door before entering with a tray containing freshly squeezed orange juice, a pot of tea, and *The New York Times*. While she drank the juice and sipped the tea, she quickly leafed through the paper, mostly ads—in the *Times*, news was a filler—then ran a comb through her hair, slipped on her robe, and went down the hall to have breakfast in her grandmother's room.

She found Nora Molloy sitting at a table before the long French windows overlooking the East River, and as Kathleen sat down across from her, Jean-Claude began to serve pancakes with maple syrup and tiny sausages.

"What would your young man like for dinner this evening?" Nora asked. "Or, put another way, is there anything he doesn't like?"

The idle rich, Kathleen wanted to say but didn't dare. Instead she told her grandmother, "My young man likes almost anything except liver. And his name is Ted, for Edmund. His full name is Edmund Burke Birmingham.

"So Irish."

"Oh, he's that, all right. And very, very contentious."

Nora supposed that it was meant to be a warning. Well, she'd had experience before with disputatious Irishmen and was sure she could handle this one. "I was considering Dover sole," she went on. "Annie does it so nicely. A homemade mushroom soup with sherry to begin with, and potatoes Duchesse with the sole. Then a baked Alaska for dessert." She waited. "Is there anything else I should know about your young man, your Edmund Burke Birmingham?"

"I love him, I think," Kathleen began, "even though sometimes he's maddening."

"And will he be maddening, as you call it, this evening?"

With a sigh, Kathleen answered, "Beyond a doubt. He's probably home, right now, practicing."

"Well, then, we must be prepared for him, mustn't we?"

By seven-forty-five, Ted still hadn't appeared, and Kathleen began to fidget on the Louis Sixteenth armchair in the large drawing room where her grandmother had decided to serve before-dinner drinks. Tapping the arm of the chair nervously, she said, "He's probably been held up in traffic."

Minutes later, she felt her heart leap as the bell sounded far away in the foyer, the doorman in the lobby buzzing to announce that a guest had arrived. Jean-Claude, whose hearing was in an advanced state of decay, instructed the doorman to send him up.

Kathleen listened to distant sounds as the door was opened and Jean-Claude awaited the arrival of the elevator. She heard voices, then Jean-Claude's shuffling feet as he escorted their guest to the drawing room.

"Clayton!" Kathleen cried, jumping to her feet.

Clay, who was nattily attired in a tweed sport coat, charcoal-gray trousers, a white shirt, and the red regimental tie that Ted had chosen not to wear, was full of apologies.

"Sorry we're late, Kathleen. Ted's still parking the car but asked me to run ahead and explain the delay."

Kathleen couldn't think of a single thing to say. Nothing. She was afraid to look at her grandmother.

But with remarkable serenity, Nora was striding from her chair toward her guest, arm extended, palm down. "How nice to meet you. I'm always delighted to meet any friend of Kathleen's. I'm Nora Molloy, Mr. Birmingham."

"It's Gibson," Clay corrected her. "Clay Gibson. Ted should be here any minute."

Momentarily, Nora was perplexed, staring at her granddaughter for an explanation. When none was forthcoming— in fact, Kathleen seemed more surprised than she did—she concluded that there were to be two guests this evening, not one. Discreetly, she said into Jean-Claude's ear, "I believe we'll need another setting at the table," then brightly addressed Clayton, "Come sit next to me. There's so much I don't know about the younger generation."

God, yes!

Kathleen was in a rage because she didn't know what was going on. When the bell sounded a second time in the foyer, she told Jean-Claude that she would attend to it herself.

Trembling with anger, she asked the doorman to send up their guest, then stood in the hallway outside the apartment door to wait for the elevator.

It glided to a stop, the elevator man pulled open the door, and there was Ted, a mischievous smile on his face.

As he stepped into the hall and the elevator's door closed behind him, Kathleen began to beat on his chest with her fists.

"Why did you do this to me?"

His expression became somber, and he made no effort to remove her fists. "I'm here to be examined by your grand-mother, aren't I? To see if I measure up to the Molloys' high standards? Well, there's no way in the world she can judge me without also judging Clay, because what he stands for is part of my life. I thought I'd make it easier for her. Bring it out into the open."

In a small, shaky voice, Kathleen said, "I'd so wanted her to like you."

He held her two fists in his hands. "If she doesn't like me because of Clay, chances are she wouldn't like me anyway, Kathleen. The reason we're all here tonight is for you to de-cide who you really are. I already know who I am." He squeezed her fists until they unclenched. "That's why I asked Clay with-out telling you. I said your grandmother invited him, too."

Nora didn't quite know what to make of it.

Initially, when she saw Clayton enter the room she mis took him for Kathleen's young man. Her reaction was much as it had been years before when her daughter Deirdre an-nounced that she had married Ben Stein. *What next?* was all she could think.

Then as it dawned on her that Kathleen hadn't expected Clayton either, she realized that Ted had plotted it this way for a reason. What was to have been an examination of him was instead going to be an examination of Nora.

She welcomed the challenge.

As Ted appeared at the entrance to the room with Kath-leen, Nora at once had to give her granddaughter high marks for choosing a very good-looking young man. More than that, he was utterly composed. Kathleen herself was so tense she was talking gibberish during the introductions, but Ted remained calm and sure of himself.

When Jean-Claude asked what everyone would be drinking, Kathleen hoped that Ted wouldn't insist on having a beer, and she was relieved when he asked for a white Dubonnet on the rocks. Clay chose scotch and water, and Kathleen opted for seltzer.

"Kathleen tells me that you're from New York," Nora said to Ted after they'd been served.

"I grew up on Eighth Avenue at Thirty-first." He could have concealed his origins by saying that his family lived in Chelsea—stretching the area a bit—or Clinton. There was nothing romantic about Hell's Kitchen; for generations it had been home to Manhattan's dockworkers and their families.

To Kathleen's astonishment, her grandmother asked, "Do the O'Connells still own the grocery store on Eighth between Twenty-ninth and Thirtieth?"

Ted leaned over in his chair. "They closed the store and moved to Yonkers about seven years ago. When I was a kid, I was a good friend of Paudie O'Connell's. We used to play stickball together. How do you know the family, Mrs. Molloy?"

Nora explained that she was originally from County Cork, as were Mr. and Mrs. O'Connell, and often she used to run into them at the Gaelic games in the Bronx, and also at Irish social and cultural events in the city. "Mr. O'Connell was an old IRA man," Nora concluded.

"Yes," Ted concurred, "it was always said in the neighborhood that Paudie's father collected money for the IRA."

"The IRA is the Irish Republican Army, isn't it?" Clay asked, then confessed, "I don't understand any of that mess in Ireland."

"Few people do," Nora answered, "even among the Irish."

Ted scrutinized her intently. "Do you think Americans should give money to the Irish Republican Army, Mrs. Molloy?"

Kathleen wanted to hide. Ted was baiting her, trying to reveal all her narrow-minded prejudices, hoping to show her for what she was; how could Charles Molloy's widow be anything but a politically and socially selfish archconservative?

But Nora refused the bait. "My husband and I disagreed on a number of things, one of which was the IRA. You see, I was present in Ireland in 1916 during the Rising and saw what violence did. But I also saw what it accomplished. Without it, in all probability there would be no free Ireland today. The IRA exists only because the six counties of Ulster are still part of Britain's colonial empire."

Ted persisted. "But isn't it understandable that Ulster is still part of Britain? After all, the majority of the population in the North isn't even Irish, ethnically speaking. They're of Scottish extraction and they're Protestants."

Kathleen knew only too well Ted's passionate views on the British in Ireland: They should be driven out, at gunpoint if necessary. What was he trying to draw Nora into?

"Quite right," her grandmother answered, "but we mustn't forget the minority. They are Irish and Catholic. If Britain were truly interested in maintaining a democratic state, she would guarantee the rights of the minority as well as the majority. But she doesn't. British troops are used to maintain the status quo, not to challenge it."

Good Lord, it was Ted's own argument! Kathleen had listened to it countless times.

"But I don't advocate violence to correct the problem," she continued. "Someday, in the near future, it's to be hoped that England's prime minister will have the courage to do in Ulster what President Eisenhower did in Little Rock, Arkansas, when whites prevented the integration of schools. It was a painful decision for Ike to make, but he made the right one. He sent in troops to protect the rights of the minority. If Britain could only have the wisdom to do that in the North of Ireland, there would be no need for the IRA."

Jean-Claude appeared at the doorway to announce dinner, and Kathleen welcomed the respite.

On the way to the dining room, Nora bent over to whisper to her, "Your young man is very earnest, isn't he?"

Kathleen nodded, both hating and loving the quality in Ted.

"But I don't find him maddening," Nora added.

* * *

Dinner was much more relaxed. There was even time for small talk. Clay was induced to give an account of the basketball game he'd seen that afternoon—Holy Cross versus St. John's—and Nora reminisced about the Hell's Kitchen she knew when, as a young girl, she first arrived in New York. Ted suggested that the next time they get together, they all go down to his mother's restaurant for a good Irish-Italian feed, which he described as corned beef and cabbage cooked in olive oil. Everyone marveled at Annie's splendid cooking.

Ted had his knee firmly against Kathleen's during most of the meal, and every chance he had, his hand dipped under the tablecloth to find hers. If Nora was aware of it, she didn't seem displeased.

After the first test Ted had put her through before dinner, Kathleen's grandmother was able to do what she did best: extract information from others. Long ago she'd concluded that the most esteemed of all hostesses was the one who did very little talking herself but managed to bring out conversation in guests. Nora listened as Ted spoke about his boyhood in Hell's Kitchen—he'd never talked about it even to Kathleen before—and Clay recounted what it was like to grow up in a small Hudson River Valley town where only a few other colored families lived.

As dinner drew to a close, Ted glanced at Kathleen before beginning, "A little while ago, we were discussing violence in the North of Ireland. You mentioned that it had its uses, at least in the past, but I wonder if the time hasn't come to try nonviolent protest instead?" His eyes met Kathleen's. "Clay and I are going to Atlanta next week to help the Reverend King in his peaceful demonstrations against segregated lunch counters. Some people think it's a waste of time because we won't accomplish anything. What do you think, Mrs. Molloy?"

Kathleen couldn't help but recall that at this very table, she'd listened to her grandfather denounce all acts of civil disobedience whose purpose was to undermine law and order. Anarchy could not be permitted, he said. If there were injustices, courts of law would have to correct them, not mindless mobs.

Nora reflected before replying, somehow knowing that her answer would be important.

"Several years ago, I was invited to say a few words to the graduating class at Marymount College, not because of my personal achievements or rare insight into human behavior but because my husband had made a substantial gift to the college. When I heard the topic they suggested, I groaned. It was 'What America has meant to me.' My husband had already declined the invitation to speak, but nonetheless he told me what I was to say. I was to describe how penniless Irish immigrants had come to this country, and because of its wonderful economic opportunities, they were now captains of industry and leaders of the nation. My husband firmly believed that America's business is business. And just as firmly, I disagreed. Not for the first time in our long life together, we went to bed without saying good night to one another."

Oh, yes, Kathleen remembered her grandfather's famous pouts. Sometimes if he didn't get his way, he would sink into silence for days.

"I told Charles that I would write my own speech," Nora continued, "and if he objected to what I said, he was free to walk out in the middle of it. It took me days to get my thoughts in order, and by the time the final draft had been typed, my daughter Caitlin, who was doing the typing, had stopped speaking to me, too. She said the speech was maudlin. Charles threatened to boycott it entirely."

Her young guests listened with amusement and interest as she continued. "In the end, I threw out the speech because it was all wrong. I hadn't said what I wanted to say, so when I reached Marymount I realized that I would have to ad-lib, and the best way for me to do that was to direct all my remarks at my captive husband, seated in the audience. He maintained that America's business is business. And I told him that America's business is *people*. Economic success is the least of it. I went on—chatted, really—to say that countless people came here from the Old World, where for years beyond number they'd waged wars against one another. Turks had massacred the Greeks, the Greeks massacred the Turks. Germans had killed the French, the French killed Germans. The Russians killed Poles, the Poles killed Jews. The English killed Irish Catholics, and Irish Catholics killed Irish Protestants. But in America, something wondrous happened. All these diverse people came together. They lived on the same blocks. They sent their children to the same schools. Sometimes they even married one another. After years of hatred and tribal carnage, in this country they were able to live together in peace." She waited before adding sadly, "With one exception."

Kathleen watched as perspiration broke out on Clay's forehead.

"I'm not an intellectual," Nora resumed, "but I don't have to be to know that the American experiment is still imperfect as long as millions of colored people are left out of it. Eight years ago, when I addressed the girls at Marymount, Negroes weren't much closer to the golden door than they had been a century before. But now they're knocking. And if we other Americans won't open the door for them, they have every right to start knocking very loud. To pound, if necessary. Even knock the door down. The protests the Reverend King is planning in the South are a part of that, and I assure you, they won't be a waste of time. If I were younger, I'd go to Atlanta with you."

The Congress of Racial Equality had scheduled its first lunch counter sit-in for noon on Monday, but it was midafternoon on Sunday by the time the small party from Cambridge left New York. All night long they drove, taking turns at the wheel, hoping that the Chevy's bearings wouldn't burn out. Shortly before dawn, they pulled off the road near Columbia, South Carolina, for a few hours' sleep.

Perhaps because they had driven during darkness, they hadn't perceived that during the night they'd left the North behind them and entered the South.

When they awoke from their naps, bones aching, they stretched their limbs and looked about them for a place to have breakfast before beginning the last leg of their journey.

It was Kathleen who spied the roadside restaurant about a quarter-mile away, one sign announcing EAT, another GAS.

After they had the tank filled and used the rest rooms, they parked in an area behind the restaurant next to a number of battered pickup trucks.

Inside, the four booths were occupied, but there were vacant stools at the long counter facing the kitchen. Kathleen took a seat, the boys on either side of her. A waitress at the other end of the counter stared at them with tired eyes, then made her way to one of the booths and whispered to a man wearing a Stetson hat, sipping coffee and smoking.

When no menus were offered, Ted stood up and helped himself to three and had just retaken his seat and distributed them when a voice behind him said, "I reckon you folks are in the wrong place. We don't serve nigrahs here."

The knuckles of Ted's fists were blue-white on the countertop. "Beg pardon?" he said needlessly, having heard perfectly well what had been said.

"I say we don't serve members of the colored race here. If you're hungry, there's a place about two mile down the road where I guess you could get something to eat."

Clay began to rise from the stool, but Ted motioned him to stay where he was. "We don't want to eat somewhere else." He turned to face the man. "We came in here to be served, and we intend to have breakfast." To the waitress, he called out, "Ma'am, my friends and I would like bacon and scrambled eggs for three. Grits if you have them, because we've heard so much about them—along with your famous hospitality. And three coffees, one with cream and sugar, two black."

The waitress looked anxiously at the man standing behind them, but didn't budge.

"I reckon you don't understand our local customs, sonny. I own the place, and I don't want your business."

"Well, that's too bad, because you've got it." Ted snapped his fingers at the waitress. "Ma'am, could you hurry up with that order?"

The woman crossed her arms in front of her as the room became eerily silent.

"I think I've just lost my appetite," Clayton whispered. "Why don't we get out of here?"

Kathleen agreed. "I think Clay's right. We're obviously not

going to be served, and if we stay, there's bound to be trouble."

Ted was furious. "Don't these crackers know that South Carolina is a part of the United States, goddammit!"

"Listen," Clay whispered, trying to reason with him, "we're out in the middle of nowhere, and it's six-thirty in the morning. If these guys jump us, no one's going to help us. I'm all for a fast retreat."

"That's cowardly."

"I think the situation calls for it. I hate to tell you, Ted, but until about thirty years ago, people like me were still being lynched around here. I don't want to get lynched over something as inconsequential as bacon and eggs."

This time when Clay lifted himself from the stool, Ted made no effort to reseat him. As he turned, the man in the Stetson hat saw the white *H* on the crimson sweater he was wearing.

"What's that *H* stand for?" he asked derisively. "That stand for Harlem?"

The letter Clay had won for running the mile on the track team was a badge of honor, proudly proclaiming that the bearer was a student at America's most elite university. But as he listened to this other interpretation, he crumpled.

"It stands for hope," Kathleen said as she rose to leave.

Ted was itching for a fight. She had to stand between him and their tormentor to prevent it. "We'll have breakfast somewhere else," she said soothingly. "And if we can't find a place we like, we'll stop at a grocery store and pick up some things and have a picnic."

As they made their way toward the exit, one of the men in overalls seated in a booth hissed, "Troublemakers."

Another said, "Look like them New York fellas who been registerin' voters over Batesburg way."

Outside in the early-morning chill, they shivered, smarting from their humiliation. Ted was all for returning to settle it once and for all.

"The mark of an educated man," Kathleen reminded him, "is to know when he's losing and to accept it gracefully. There was no winning back there. Maybe we'll win in Atlanta."

"It's all my fault," Clay began in misery. "I should have known better. It's been so long . . . I guess I just forgot what color I am."

"That ignorant, evil shitheel!" Ted cried.

"No, he's not," Clayton answered in the man's defense. "He was just doing what he's been conditioned to do, ever since Reconstruction days. You can't expect people like him to change overnight."

"I was ready to kill him," Ted went on.

"Oh, that would have been terrific. Just terrific. For the last two years, you've been drumming into my head that there's only one way to get rid of Jim Crow, and that's through peaceful protests. Gandhi's method, remember? So what do you do, asshole? You come down here, and on the first day you almost get in a fistfight."

"He provoked us."

"Hell, man, wait till this afternoon if you want to see provocation. They're going to lift us out of our chairs and drag us to the paddy wagons! What are you going to do then, Ted? Fight back? Hit someone? That'll be great. I'll be sure to send you letters when they put you in jail." He reached out and rested his hand on his friend's still-quaking shoulder. "We're here to make a peaceful, nonviolent protest. Now *say* it."

Through clenched teeth, Ted repeated, "We're here to make a peaceful, nonviolent protest."

"That's better. Now let's get out of here before they sic their German shepherds on us."

On the way to the car, Ted muttered, "I still wish I could have killed him."

"You would have been creamed before you threw your first punch. Did you see those guys in the booths? Mean. They were so *mean*, I almost pissed my pants." He opened the front door of the Chevy for Kathleen. "Hey, I liked that about hope."

Kathleen slid into the passenger seat. "What else could I say?"

"You made that man feel very small. I could feel him shrink."

Ted groused all the way to Atlanta, describing in minute detail how he should have pulverized the man. Kathleen made no attempt to silence him, knowing that it helped get the anger and frustration out of his system. In an hour or so, they would be expected to be nonviolent, no matter what happened to them, and it wouldn't be easy. In fact, it might be the hardest thing they'd ever have to do in their lives. At the lunch counter sit-in in Atlanta, vile names would be hurled at them, and they would be herded up like animals. During it all, they would have to accept the abuse, sustained by the teachings of Jesus Christ and Gandhi.

In the end, the protest at the lunch counter was something of an anticlimax. By the time they arrived, the police had been removing teams of nonresisting demonstrators all morning long and had grown weary of their task. As one group was led to waiting paddy wagons, another took its place, Negroes and whites of all ages, from all parts of the country, from every walk of life.

When it came time for the three from Cambridge to take their places at the counter, they joined hands until they were forcefully ejected. As they allowed themselves to be dragged away, they were aware that they were making history. And when they were taken to the police station and charged with disturbing the peace, it seemed to them an accolade of the highest distinction, finer even than graduating from college with honors.

"Hope," Clay said to his friends as they stood in the crowded station.

"Definitely," Ted agreed. "Hope."

EIGHTEEN

Mimi Conroy was nearly hysterical.

As hard as he tried, Patrick Cassidy could make nothing of what she was saying. Sobbing one minute, in a rage the next, she kept repeating her husband's name, then something about—was it possible?—a sweater and a pair of shoes.

"For God's sake, get hold of yourself!" Pat told her over the telephone. And once again, he listened to a stream of words from his daughter that seemed to make no sense. "Okay," he said at last. "I'll be right over. Stay where you are."

As he rushed from his office on the Embarcadero to his car in the parking lot, all he could think was that somehow Mimi's mind had begun to unravel again, and the one thing in the world he feared most, that she might have to reenter the Menninger Clinic, seemed a definite possibility. But this unexplained outburst he'd just listened to was vastly different from the bottomless depression she'd been thrown into after Sara's death. At that time, she scarcely spoke, barely acknowledged the outside world. Now she was in a rage, an absolute rage, and she was articulating it, but the trouble was that her father simply couldn't keep up with the torrent of words.

The inevitable afternoon gridlock on Geary near Union Square hadn't yet begun, and he made good time till he reached a section of the road torn up by the Pacific Gas and Electric Company in its remorseless disturbance of the city's tranquility. He had to wait while a huge machine ripped open the asphalt with desperate lunges of its claws; then a worker motioned for the backed-up traffic to proceed. By the time he turned onto Pacific Avenue, more than half an hour had passed, and he was worried because he hadn't notified the police or an ambulance to meet him at the house.

Owen was home from school, and that helped. The minute Pat entered the house, his grandson said, "Mom's upstairs crying, and I can't get her to stop."

"You stay right here," Pat urged him, "next to the telephone. We may have to get an ambulance."

"Is she sick again, Gramp?"

"I don't know. She could be. You stay here."

At the top of the stairs, he could already hear her sobbing, and at first he thought he might have to break down the door. It wasn't as easy as it looked in the movies. It meant a badly bruised shoulder and a mess on the floor. He knocked louder. "Mimi, it's your father. Let me in!"

At last her crying subsided, and he could hear her making her way across the room.

"It's locked," she said. "I don't know where the key is."

"It's probably on the floor. Stoop down and look for it."

He listened as she patted the carpeting on the other side of the door, then she stood up, inserted the key, and turned the cylinders.

"I'm all right now," she said, composing herself.

And he saw immediately that she was. Her eyes were red from weeping, but they weren't the eyes of a madwoman.

"Could you please tell me what's happened? I couldn't understand anything you said on the telephone."

"Close the door."

He did as he was instructed, first sticking his head out to give his grandson at the bottom of the stairs a sign that everything was under control. As he followed Mimi into the room, he noticed that a chair had been placed in front of the closet door, as if his daughter had been trying to reach for something on the top shelf. A small rectangular box was on the floor next to the chair.

Mimi sat on the edge of the bed, gulping deep breaths. "I was looking for a sweater. A cashmere sweater that belonged to Mother. I'd put it in a plastic bag with some other woolen things, along with mothballs, a year or so ago and forgot all about it. Today I remembered where I'd put it, so I got the chair to stand on while I took it down from the shelf. As I did, I noticed that box over there."

Pat scrutinized it from a distance. It was a Clark's shoe-box, its lid still on.

"I didn't pay much attention to it," she resumed. "I guess I must have thought that it might contain a pair of Robert's golf shoes or something. I removed the plastic bag, got the sweater from it, and was putting it back when I accidentally knocked over the shoebox. It fell onto the floor, and the lid came off."

Mimi walked across the room and picked up the box. She removed the lid and showed her father what was in it.

"My God!" Patrick cried.

"I never even knew there *were* thousand-dollar bills. But there are one hundred of them here."

"One hundred thousand dollars!"

Her voice broke as she asked, "Where did Robert get it, Dad? Where?"

Pat searched for an explanation.

Ever since discovering that the woman in the car with Robert that night was Christine Lawrence from New York City, he'd tried to reach her. All he knew about her was that her public relations firm seemed to be conducted from her private residence and was apparently a one-woman operation. Whenever he called, he left a message on her answering machine, but his calls were never returned.

As he looked down at the huge collection of bills, he knew instinctively that Christine Lawrence was somehow responsible for it being in Robert's house.

Still, he wanted to give his son-in-law the benefit of the doubt.

"Has Robert sold anything recently?" Pat asked.

"Not that I know of. There isn't that much to sell any-more. Most of the Conroy holdings have already been disposed of."

"Could he have converted stocks or bonds to cash?"

"We get a regular income on them, Dad. It's fluctuated a little bit, but not conspicuously during the last few years. I know that the money is still coming in because I've been using it for household expenses."

He took the box from her hands and slowly leafed through

the bills, almost caressing them. He'd never in his life seen more than five thousand dollars at any one time.

Mimi's voice was filled with grief. "Has he stolen it, Dad?"

Pat upended the box over the bed, spilling the green bills onto the bedspread. At the bottom of the box was a manila envelope, the usual eight-by-ten business size, folded in half, its shape distorted from having contained so many bills before they were transferred to the box.

In the upper left-hand corner was a name.

"Maybe worse than that," Patrick replied sadly as he read what was printed there:

THE MOLLOY COMPANY
340 Park Avenue
New York, N.Y.

After learning that Christine Lawrence was associated with a public relations firm that did business with the Molloy Company, Paul tried without success to get his brother to reveal the sort of work that was done for them.

Lee was seated in his new office, formerly his father's. He had now personalized it, however, and there could be no doubt that a new man was in charge, determined to leave his stamp on the firm. On the walls and the desktop were photographs showing his athletic prowess on the football field, the hockey rink, and the golf course. He looked to be a champion, and there were trophies to prove it, most dating from college and prep school days.

"Well," Lee said, draping a leg over his chair, "that was the old man's department, not mine. I didn't get involved in PR until about six months ago."

"But you must know what this Lawrence woman does, Lee. Hell, our records show that nearly a half-million dollars was spent last year on public relations. That's an astonishing sum for a firm that doesn't cater directly to consumers."

"I don't have to tell you, do I, that Father was always worried about our image. There are a lot of people out there in the world who distrust big business, Paulie. Consider us threats to the public weal and all that. So I wouldn't be a bit surprised that this Christine Lawrence simply tried to give us a fair shake in the press and on TV. Feed them information that would . . . ah, enhance our reputation."

"Have you ever met her?"

Lee paused a second before answering, "I have no recollection of it."

Suddenly, all of Paul's senses were alert. More often than not, those six words were used by people upon the advice of their lawyers in order to conceal the truth. Recollections were imperfect. Meetings could indeed be forgotten. Lee hadn't denied ever having met her, but had simply said he couldn't remember.

Part of him wanted to confront his brother, but Paul didn't have sufficient facts. Until he did, all he had to go on was instinct.

"If you have any questions about it," Lee continued, "why don't you get in touch with the woman?"

"I've been trying to do just that."

After returning to his own office, Paul left his name and number once again on Christine Lawrence's answering machine, but there was no response. He repeated the call every day for the next few days with similar results. Then one day he added that if his call wasn't returned within twenty-four hours, he intended to discuss various improprieties with a member of the district attorney's staff.

It did the trick. Less than an hour later, a most cooperative Mrs. Lawrence called to say that she'd just returned from out of town and would be more than happy to meet with him. Would four o'clock at her apartment be agreeable to him? Paul said fine.

When Paul left his name with the doorman at the East End Avenue building, he was told that he was expected and was sent directly to Christine Lawrence's apartment on the twenty-fourth floor.

The minute she opened the door, he realized at once that his father could never have had anything but a business relationship with her. She was a good-looking woman, but there was something cold and unfeminine about her, efficient and humorless. Her platinum-blond hair was pulled back severely from her forehead and laid neatly in coils at the crown of her head. Her eyes were unblinking, and she wore no jewelry. In one hand was a black cigarette holder that she held like a weapon.

"I would have recognized you anywhere," she said flatly. "You look very much like your father."

"People say that about my brother Lee, too."

"Oh, no, not a bit. I see no resemblance there at all. Come in, Mr. Molloy."

With that confirmation that Lee had lied to him, Christine Lawrence led Paul into a kind of white-on-white apartment: white wall-to-wall carpeting, off-white upholstered pieces, white walls. The place looked as severe as its occupant, and as unemotional.

"Could I give you something to drink?" she asked, but he declined, wanting to stay completely alert. He had a feeling that Christine Lawrence was seldom anything but that.

"I'm interested in learning precisely what you do for the Molloy Company." he asked.

"Did. Our services have been terminated."

"By whom?"

"I received official notification from your brother a few days after your father's death."

"All right, then I'll rephrase it: What *did* you do for the Molloy Company during the time you were employed by them?"

She smiled seraphically. "I take it that my answer to that will be considered off the record and not prejudicial to myself?"

"I won't repeat anything you tell me, if that's what you mean."

She leaned back on the white sofa and relaxed. "When he first came to me eight years ago, I didn't quite understand what your father had in mind. It was a bit out of my line, shall we say? He told me that he was a very successful businessman and that he owed his success to America. His parents, I understand, were poor Irish immigrants. In any event, he had definite notions of what he thought he should do for America in return for the bounty it gave him. Above all, he felt that the free enterprise system should be encouraged."

"That comes as no surprise," Paul interrupted.

"I shouldn't think that it would. The year was 1952, and Mr. Molloy and various of his friends had persuaded Dwight Eisenhower to leave the halls of academe at Columbia University to run for the presidency. Until then, no one knew precisely what Ike's political persuasion was, but Mr. Molloy and his colleagues helped . . . define Eisenhower's feelings. And needless to say, a great deal of their money went into electing Ike—though he probably would have won the election without anyone's help at all, because he was the stuff of dreams: a farm boy from Kansas who went on to become his nation's greatest war hero."

"I'm aware that Father worked actively on Ike's behalf during both presidential campaigns, '52 and '56. He made no secret of that."

"Quite right," Mrs. Lawrence agreed. "But his commitment went beyond President Eisenhower himself. Your father was a fervent Republican. He *believed* in Republicanism, and he thought it was the duty of businessmen to help preserve a Republican administration."

"He gave money?"

"A great deal of it. But for various reasons—some personal, some business—he preferred the gifts to be anonymous."

Paul was beginning to see the drift. "So he hired you to funnel money from the Molloy Company to—"

"To the Republican party and its candidates. It was generally cash because that way, the contributions were much more difficult to trace. And at no time were the gifts identified as coming from the Molloy Company. Your father was insistent on that count. At least *he* didn't expect favors in return for his largesse."

She might have added, but didn't, that Lee had. Paul did it for her. "When did my brother get into the act?"

Mrs. Lawrence inserted another cigarette into its sinister holder and lit it. "Oh, let me see. I would say . . . perhaps two years ago."

About the time that Paul had resigned from the company and fled to California.

"And Lee continued doing what Father had done?"

"Not exactly. Let's say that he saw an opportunity to expand operations." She waited, then once again sought reassurance. "This definitely *is* off the record?"

"It is."

"All right. So what we have is a neat little system designed to aid political candidates anonymously. By the way, the money your father left me in in his will isn't mine. It was his final gift to the Republican national party." She exhaled a bluish cloud of smoke. "I myself am apolitical. I have clients other than Republicans who also avail themselves of my services."

"Democrats as well?"

"Yes. I also do public relations work for members of the Democratic party. Your brother Lee became fascinated by all this. He came to me about . . . oh, seven months ago, I'd say, to discuss a project the Defense Department has been planning for some time in South Vietnam. He very badly wanted the project for the Molloy Company and asked me if there wasn't a way I could use my numerous contacts in both parties to help . . . ease the acceptance of the Molloy Company's bid."

Paul felt his stomach knot. "You bribed someone."

"Oh, but Mr. Molloy, must we use that vulgar word? And I must remind you that we agreed that this conversation can't be interpreted as being prejudicial against me. The fact of the matter is that since the system your father and I developed for making political contributions was so refined that no one would ever be able to trace the company's gifts, it wasn't too surprising that your brother seized upon the idea of employing the same system to influence a decision at the Defense Department."

"Whom did you bribe, Mrs. Lawrence, and what did it cost us?"

"I'm not at liberty to say. So far as I was concerned, I was paid a fee to do what I'd been doing for the past eight years: transferring a sum of money to a particular individual with total anonymity. That, by the way, is why your father called me 'the gentleman from Galveston.' "

"I'm afraid you'll have to clarify that."

"It's part of Texas lore. Not too long ago, a well-known

senator was reelected by a landslide after he'd spent a million dollars or more on advertising and promotion. He was reputed to be a comparatively poor man himself, so afterward, a member of the press asked where all the money had come from, and he replied, 'From a gent in Galveston whose name I can't rightly recollect.' "

"I don't see the connection between that, however, and the military installation in South Vietnam."

"There was none. Your father kept a record of his campaign contributions in a file labeled 'Galveston.' It was apparently on his desk during a meeting when the project in South Vietnam was being discussed. For reasons of secrecy, he wanted a code name for the project, so he reached over and picked up the file, and decided to call it Project Galveston."

For the first time, Paul began to grasp what had happened. He wasn't particularly astounded to learn that his father had made large but anonymous contributions to his party. It was quite common among businessmen; they preferred to back candidates who were sympathetic to them. But Paul still had trouble in believing that Charles Molloy was involved in bribing an influential public servant in order to win a military contract.

He put it to Mrs. Lawrence. "Was my father aware that a sum of money was offered to buy the vote of someone who was in a position to award the contract for Project Galveston?"

She answered without blinking. "When I undertook the additional assignment, it was my understanding that your father had approved the scheme. But later it became apparent that he knew nothing about it, and that your brother Lee had done it without his knowledge."

Yes, it made sense now. "You realized that the night my father died."

She nodded. "The night your father died, I called him from Los Angeles to tell him I'd dropped off a campaign contribution to someone he particularly admired. I also happened to mention that I'd made the connection we needed to secure Project Galveston and that the money would be delivered to our man the following night. Your father was furious. It came as a complete surprise to him, and he instructed me to stop everything immediately. Early the next morning, Lee called to tell me to go ahead with the delivery, as planned. I closed my telephone and answering service accounts in Los Angeles, did some business during the day, then left for San Francisco that night. Our connection flew in from Washington, I gave him the money at the airport, then he offered to drop me off at my hotel. We had a little accident on the way, but apart from that, everything went smoothly. The following morning, I went to Hawaii for a little vacation. I hope you don't think too badly of me."

"You killed my father, Mrs. Lawrence."

"No, your brother did."

By the time Paul got home to the apartment, he was physically sick. Gasping for breath, he managed to swallow two antacid tablets before his salivating stopped, and he was able to stand up straight in front of the bathroom mirror. He hurt all over. Ached from disappointment.

For a long time, he sat in his darkened bedroom, looking out at mid-Manhattan's dazzling skyline and trying to come to terms with what he'd learned. Maybe it would be best for everyone concerned if he left New York at once, before he could uncover any more ugliness.

At nine-thirty, he called Lee's townhouse on Beekman Place, but Sally said that Lee hadn't came home and she was worried.

So Mrs. Lawrence had done her last bit of public relating for her client. She'd warned Lee—probably the minute Paul left her apartment—that things had begun to unravel.

Well, Paul dreaded it, but he would have to see the thing through to the end. He told Sally to keep cool and was just about to leave the apartment to begin searching through the Third Avenue bars when the telephone rang in the guest bedroom.

It was Emmy calling from California.

His first reaction was that something had happened to the baby.

"No," she replied. "It's just that a man called here a little while ago who said he knows you. He met you at the dedication ceremonies of that new firehouse you and Peter and Steve designed in San Francisco. Patrick Cassidy? Does that ring a bell?"

"Yeah. Big man in the labor movement. Or used to be a big man in what used to be a labor movement."

"The Longshoremen's Union. That's the man. Anyway, he said he got to talking with you at the dedication ceremonies, and because your last name was Molloy and you were originally from New York, he asked if by any chance you were connected with the Molloys of the Molloy Company—"

"And I said yes. I remember him very clearly now. He'd met my father sometime or another. They were sworn enemies. Cassidy represented labor, Father represented management."

"Well, he wants you to get in touch with him as soon as possible. It's urgent, he says."

"Did he say what about?"

"Yes, but it didn't make much sense. He says he has one hundred thousand dollars that belongs to the Molloy Company, and unless he can get it back to you by tomorrow, some people are going to wind up in jail."

NINETEEN

*I*n the serene Japanese garden behind the Conroys' house on Pacific Avenue, Pat Cassidy sat staring as water trickled down huge boulders at the garden's end into a leafy, lily-filled pond. In the eternal spring of Northern California, the evening was mild and dry, the sky crystal clear. Inside, by himself in the living room, Father Joe stood looking through a front window at the street, deep in thought.

Surprisingly, the only one who had sufficient resources to cope with the emergency was Mimi, who was in the kitchen preparing a late supper because, as she said, if their world was about to disintegrate, the least she could do was to feed everyone a proper meal before it happened.

It was possible that Orientals were better prepared to face solitude than the Irish were. After looking at the waterfall for half an hour—never had falling water looked so restful before—Pat couldn't stand the loneliness anymore, and ventured into the living room in search of company.

Even if Joe hadn't recognized the footsteps, no one else had been in the closed garden or could enter through the garden doors. Still, his back remained stubbornly turned toward the room. A bad sign, Pat knew, when a priest refused to share his thoughts.

At last, Pat began. "What do it all mean? As my mother and father used to say. What do it all mean?"

Father Joe turned to face him. "Robert's career is over, isn't it?"

"We'll be lucky if we can keep him out of jail."

"You've talked to the people in New York at the Molloy Company?"

"I talked to one of the sons. He lives here in California—

Kenwood in Sonoma—and I met him a year or so ago. He feels as badly as we do. Apparently it was one of his brothers who offered the bribe."

"Where's the money now?"

"On its way to New York. It should arrive at Idlewild Airport first thing in the morning, and there'll be someone from the Molloy Company to collect it."

"When does it become a crime?"

"It's a crime right now, this very moment. It stops being a crime once the money is returned to the Molloy Company and once the House Armed Forces Committee meets without its chairman tomorrow morning, and the Department of Defense announces the name of the firm chosen to build a military installation in Vietnam."

"I don't see the connection. What does Robert have to do with the awarding of contracts?"

"I didn't see the connection at first either, but there is one, and it was worth a hundred thousand dollars."

Father Joe echoed what Pat had said seconds before: "What do it all mean?"

Both silently considered the matter, then Pat said, "It's astonishing how little we learn from history, Joe. It's as if each generation has to make its own discoveries, as if no one else had ever passed this way. The Molloys are Irish-Americans, the Conroys are Irish-Americans. Within this same century, both families lived in abject poverty under the heel of British rule. You would think that during those years of hardship and suffering they might have learned something about honor. But they didn't, and now both families will suffer again."

"Who was it at the Molloy Company who offered the bribe?"

"The older son—and inheritor of Charles Molloy's job as president and chairman of the board."

"What happens to him?"

"The same thing that will happen to Robert. A career is over. And there is no way now that the Molloy Company can accept the contract for the building of the military base, even if it's awarded on merit alone. I made that a condition when I talked to Paul Molloy. Robert is to announce his resignation from the House of Representatives tomorrow at eight. Lee Molloy is stepping down as president and chairman of the Molloy Company an hour or so later. By the second week in May, the Defense Department will have awarded the contract, but by that time the money will once again be in a safe at the Molloy Company. They'll need it when it becomes known that they've lost the contract."

Good people, all. But ruined now. Yes, it was confounding, Father Joe had to admit. Yet was it fair that they should merely be ruined, Robert Conroy and Lee Molloy? Wasn't additional punishment also necessary?

Still, as the crime had been committed by Irish-Americans, perhaps it was appropriate that Pat Cassidy's and Paul Molloy's notion of punishment be similarly Irish, without retribution.

Forgiving. Catholic. Compassionate.

"And Robert?" Father Joe asked. "After he resigns his seat in the House, then what?"

"He's a lucky man to have the wife he has, Joe. Have you watched Mimi since she realized what Robert has done? There was shock at first. Even repugnance. But then, God knows how, she found strength I didn't know she possessed. Robert is the one who will be coming apart, but she's going to hold him together, I know she will."

"So different from the last crisis in the family, when she went to pieces and Robert comforted her." Father Joe looked at his watch. "When is he due?"

"His plane arrives in about forty minutes." Pat went on, "He did it for Mimi and Owen, you know. There was just not enough money to maintain two houses and commute from one to the other. He saw that Mimi was thriving out here, getting better day by day. How could he tell her that they were having money problems? So when some woman named Lawrence came along and suggested that all he had to do to earn a hundred thousand dollars was to approve in his House committee a few pet Defense Department projects and in return the Defense Department would award a military contract to the supplier of the money, he jumped at the chance."

"Which means," Father Joe began, "that in addition to the

go-between—this woman named Lawrence—there's also some-one at the Defense Department who's guilty."

"Yes," Pat said, "and that's the saddest part of all. Because while Lee Molloy and Robert will never again be able to do harm, the generals still can, and so can this Lawrence woman and people like her."

The story of the world, Father Joe supposed. On the one hand, man's lust for mischief. On the other, a yearning to be good. More than anything else, greed and power could corrupt good intentions, make them evil and putrescent.

And men of God existed for one reason and one reason alone: to steer fellow men toward paths of righteousness, to try to prevent them from debasing themselves or others. Everything else was mere showmanship, as Aaron Golden would say.

Yet now, for having tried to bring out the best in men, Father Joseph was being rewarded with twelve months of solitary confinement.

"You look troubled yourself, Joe," Pat said to him. "You wouldn't by any chance be in need of a confessor?"

Father Joe smiled wanly but remained wordless.

"It's Bishop Moriarity, isn't it?" Pat persisted.

"Mimi says you knew it would come to this, didn't you? When you contrived to persuade Bobby Kennedy to put me in charge of the Citizens for Kennedy here in the Bay area."

Pat shook his head in denial, "Joe, the difficulties between you and His Eminence predate my meeting with Kennedy. You two have been on a collision course ever since you entered the priesthood. What has he done now? Has he asked you to give up your political activities?"

"Worse than that," Father Joe answered sadly. "As of May eleventh, I'm relieved of my parish duties and am to report to a Benedictine monastery in Tennessee for a year of silent reflection."

Pat was outraged. "And do you intend to follow his orders? Lock yourself up in a monastery simply because you've questioned Bishop Moriarity's infallibility?"

"He's my superior. In the archdiocese, bishops rule, priests obey."

"Can't you appeal?"

"There is no appeal. A bishop's ruling is final."

With sudden fury, Pat shouted, "Is it any wonder that non-Catholics fear Catholics! Blind obedience is what separates a fascist state from a democratic one. All Americans *question*, Joe. Americans are born questioners. How can you accept such a ruling as that? How can you walk away from Rafael Banuelos just as his triumph is beginning, after you've helped him achieve it? How can you hole yourself up in a monastery and pretend that you've never had anything to do with a voter registration drive that for the first time in history is going to give minorities their proper role in electing a President?"

"He wants me to reexamine my soul, Dad. He wants to test my faith. That's why he's sending me there."

"Your faith is as strong as his, if not stronger. The mindless repetition of prayers or endless genuflecting before plaster objects is not what the church is all about. You mustn't let Bishop Moriarity exile you to some God-forsaken place in the mountains of Tennessee."

Painful silence followed this impassioned plea. Then Father Joe began, "There's only one alternative. I've appealed to an authority higher than Bishop Moriarity for counsel. I'm now waiting for a sign."

Puzzled, Pat asked his son, "A sign, Joe? What kind of sign?"

"I won't know until I see it."

"And if you don't?"

Father Joseph could not find the words to answer.

After Paul left Christine Lawrence's apartment, she made two hurried telephone calls. The first was to Congressman Robert Conroy's office in Washington, where she learned that he had made a sudden trip to the West Coast. She then anxiously called the executive offices of the Molloy Company on Park Avenue.

When Lee's secretary answered, Mrs. Lawrence said, "Tell him it's the gentleman from Galveston."

Lee had been presiding over a late-afternoon conference attended by General McFadden, Andy Sinclair, and several others when his secretary tiptoed into the room and placed a note in front of him. Instantly, he rose from his chair. "I'm afraid you'll have to excuse me for a few minutes. Andy, could you preside over things while I'm gone?"

When he reached the privacy of his office and picked up the telephone, he was in a rage. "Dammit, the understanding we had was that you were never to contact me during office hours."

"I'm sorry, but I think the situation warrants it. I've just discovered that our friend in Washington who promised delivery on the . . . merchandise tomorrow has left for San Francisco and has no immediate plans to return."

Lee was stunned. "But he'll miss the committee meeting in the morning!"

"Exactly. Our friend has already been reimbursed for the merchandise, you know. But if he doesn't attend the committee meeting tomorrow, the merchandise can't be delivered."

Lee's temples throbbed as blood pumped wildly through them. "What are you saying?"

"I'm saying that it looks as if the proverbial cat is out of the proverbial bag. If this were a military situation, we should probably burn all our records and prepare to evacuate. For my part, I'm about to close the office and take a well-deserved vacation."

"But you promised me!"

Her voice was coldly impersonal. "I promised you nothing. I told you only that I had found a supplier of the merchandise you desired."

"But I've paid him, and now he's reneging!"

"Needless to say, when I gave him the money, I couldn't very well ask for a receipt. I don't have to remind you, do I, that I was prepared to extricate myself from this matter entirely after I spoke to your father in Southampton and learned that the offer had been made without his permission. But you insisted that we go through with it."

"We're counting on the contract. What's happened to our friend in Washington? What made him back out at the last minute?"

"I think I can answer that by saying that I had a visitor a few minutes ago. It was your brother Paul."

Lee's voice was so strident it was unrecognizable. "You told him?"

"I didn't have to. He already knew."

Suddenly, it was an effort for Lee to breathe. Christine Lawrence was saying something to him, but the words no longer seemed important. All he wanted to do was annihilate memory.

As he ran from the office, his secretary called out to him, but he pushed past her, and General McFadden and Andy Sinclair as he met them in the hall, then continued to the stairwell and ran down thirty-one flights of steps to the street.

That night at the River House, Paul briefed his mother.

It wasn't an easy story to tell, and Nora listened with horror. When she had sought Paul's help to root out the true circumstances surrounding Charles's death, in all her wildest dreams it hadn't occurred to her that as a result of it, her son Lee would be exposed as a man who attempted to bribe a U.S. congressman.

"Will he go to jail?" she asked.

Paul explained that if his brother's work could be undone before the awarding of the contract for the Galveston Project, it was possible that he might be able to escape punishment. Still, Lee's career was in shambles. No way in the world could he ever again hold a position of authority at the Molloy Company.

"He simply wanted to prove himself to his father," Nora remarked sympathetically. "Please don't hate him for it."

Paul didn't hate him. He pitied him. It would take all of Lee's considerable strength to rebuild his life. Surely, the family would help. There had to be some job at the firm that would enable him to use the gifts he had—personal magnetism, a smile for everyone—so long as it didn't involve making policy decisions.

As disappointed as Nora was to learn of Lee's downfall, she couldn't help but silently rejoice that her husband had been exonerated. At no time had she doubted Charles's loyalty and love. Oh, yes, for an infinitesimal second when Quentin Potter first made his allegations, she may have jumped to the wrong conclusion. But as soon as she had had time to reflect, she knew they were absurd. While Charles might have deceived the Internal Revenue Service—that had yet to be determined—in his zeal to serve the cause of Republicanism, she knew that he would never, never deceive his wife.

"Paul, your father always intended for you to succeed him as president of the company," she began. "I know that you and he had a serious difference of opinion, and I'm well aware that you've already declined an earlier offer. But for the sake of the family, won't you please reconsider and accept the job?"

Paul wanted to. When he first agreed to stay in New York to help unravel the mess that Lee had created, he was sure he would hate being back. But instead he came to love the excitement. Just this past week, the firm had been awarded a contract to build a new university in Abu Dhabi, and this time there were no restrictions on employing Jews. Looking over Andy Sinclair's shoulder at the preliminary plans, Paul's heart had leaped halfway up his throat. The project was to be built from scratch, everything from fountains to desks and chandeliers to be designed by the Molloy Company. Buildings that would affect the lives of thousands of students would be coming off the drawing boards. Looking at some of the first sketches, Paul yearned for a pencil to make his own statement.

But something prevented him. During that last tumultuous meeting with his father, he'd said that he would never return to the company unless Charles Molloy admitted his error in judgment over the Saudi deal.

His father never had.

"Let me think about it," Paul answered his mother. "First I have to find Lee. He's done another disappearing act, and this time Andy thinks he'll try to drink away all his problems in the gin mills along Third Avenue. Someone saw him head in that direction when he ran out of the office. Andy'll be here in a few minutes to help me start searching through the bars."

"What will you do when you find him?"

"Sober him up. Talk to him."

Gently, his mother took his hand. "You'll have to do more than that, Paul, or we'll lose him. He's made a terrible mistake.

The best you can do for him now is to tell him you love him, in spite of it."

Well, maybe it would help. God knows, he'd never told him before. Perhaps it was time for their youthful rivalry to come to an end.

Only a few years before, the grim tracks of the Third Avenue El had kept the avenue in perpetual darkness, fit for little other than seedy saloons and secondhand shops. Now that the tracks had been pulled down, many of the shops had been gussied up and turned into quality antique shops, and the bars no longer catered to the crowd of rummies who shuffled along the sidewalks from the Bowery all the way to the Sixties, but to young New Yorkers who lived in the neighborhood.

Paul was no authority on any of them, but Andy, who'd sometimes accompanied Lee on his nocturnal rounds, seemed to know the territory. There were three different kinds of saloons in the area, he said. In the first, a well-dressed, prosperous-looking junior executive set congregated, male and female, with the object of letting off a little steam and perhaps getting in a feel or two before the night was over. The second were bars frequented by New York's large homosexual community, and they ranged from rather preppy places where everyone wore Brooks Brothers suits to raunchy leather bars where the customers, who toiled at law firms or in publishing houses during the day, tried to look like hard-hat construction workers or World War Two bomber pilots at night. The third kind, Andy said, was a remnant of the original Third Avenue bar, where the great unwashed went to drink themselves into stupefaction.

"Don't bother with the chic places or the fairy bars," Andy told Paul.

If Lee had left the office on foot, chances are that he'd be within a twenty-block radius. Andy suggested that Paul go north from Fifty-first, trying each bar but skipping those that looked fashionable or queer. He would go south. They arranged to call Caitlin every half-hour to report if Lee had been found, using her as their go-between.

"If you see him first," Andy said as he turned to set off, "go easy on him, Paul. He's hurting."

Paul didn't need to be reminded.

It was close to eleven by the time Paul entered his first bar, just north of Fifty-first. It was one of the original articles, a real Irish saloon that smelled of beer and whose windows—and glasses—probably hadn't been washed since Thanksgiving. Everyone looked middle-aged and morose. He walked the length of the bar, stuck his head into the rest room in the rear, where someone had recently vomited into the urinal, and quickly left.

He was almost relieved to find that the next bar was filled with young men who looked clean and seemed to be enjoying each other's company. The bartender could have passed for the legendary kid next door and cordially asked what Paul would be drinking, but Paul replied that he was just looking for someone. As he made his way through the crowded, narrow aisle between the bar and the wall toward the rest room, he had the distinct impression that someone touched him, but he made no fuss. In the rest room all he saw were a lot of imaginative grafitti.

As he left, someone followed him out. "Gonna be a cold one tonight," the young man said.

"No doubt."

"I live just around the corner."

"Sorry," Paul said politely, "but I have to do some pub-crawling."

"Suit yourself. See ya around."

Well, you lived and learned, to use a familiar phrase. The young man who had just propositioned Paul seemed indistinguishable from half the executives at the Molloy Company, and looked more manly than many of them.

There were two or three saloons to every block, and apart from being yelled at once by a bartender—"Can't you read the sign?" he said pointing to the REST ROOMS RESERVED FOR PATRONS ONLY—Paul ran into no trouble. At one of the mixed bars, he stayed long enough to have a scotch and water, and while he was drinking it, a young woman came up and told him that he was cute.

"Thanks," he replied. "My wife thinks so, too."

"Oh, you're one of those pricks, are you?" she said, walking away in a huff.

My, my, women were getting almost as foul-mouthed as men. Back when he was at Yale and infrequently dating Smith or Vassar girls, most of them couldn't even say "copulate."

As he journeyed northward, the quality of the bars improved the closer he got to Bloomingdale's. More and more of them were filled with recent college graduates out for an evening of drinking and perhaps rutting. By the time he reached Daly's, he was ready for another drink.

It was one of the older pubs trying to adapt to a new life without the shadows of the El. The clientele was varied. There were several old codgers, one of whom had a huge Irish wolfhound at his feet, engaged in serious conversation in one corner. There was a preppy crowd in another. And at the bar were a good many young men who would probably gravitate to the all-male bars before the evening was over.

Lee was seated at the end of the bar, holding his head in both hands, staring at a drink in front of him.

Paul went directly to the telephone, dialed Caitlin's number and told her, "Lee's at Daly's Bar. Third Avenue and— I'm not sure, but I think it's Sixty-first. Tell Andy when he checks in. We'll wait for him here."

When Paul sat next to him, Lee didn't look up. Even when Paul ordered a scotch and water, his brother continued to look down at the bar.

"As always, the life of the party," Paul said at last.

Without looking up, Lee answered, "Get lost."

"What are you drinking?"

"I have no idea. Bourbon, I think."

"What are you trying to prove now? That you can get drunker than anyone else?"

"Yes. Everyone has to have a talent for something."

"You've got better talents than that."

Lee sipped from his glass, at last looking up to watch their reflections in the mirror behind the bar. "For screwing up," he said.

"No. You were only doing what Father taught you to do.

And it would have worked, too, if Conroy's wife hadn't found the money."

His mind was befuddled with the liquor, but Lee asked, "Is that what happened? I thought it was Mrs. Lawrence who double-crossed me."

"She did double-cross you, but that's not why the thing failed. Did you know that she was also working as a public relations consultant for the Teamsters Union?"

"What does that have to do with us?"

"Nothing. Except that after she delivered the money to Robert Conroy in San Francisco, they were involved in an automobile accident. Very minor. No one was hurt. But Conroy's father-in-law turned up, and she realized right away that he was coming to the wrong conclusions and thought that Conroy and Mrs. Lawrence were shacking up together. The father-in-law is Partick Cassidy, a labor leader, and Mrs. Lawrence knew that her boss at the Teamsters was looking for a way to get at Cassidy, so she sold the information to Jimmy Hoffa. A real nice woman."

Lee asked, "Do I go to jail?"

"Not unless you really want to. The money's on the way back to New York. Conroy is in California and will miss the committee meeting tomorrow, and all other committee meetings." He waited. "Who was our friend at the Pentagon who promised us the contract for Project Galveston in return for favors Conroy gave him?"

Lee slowly rocked back and forth on the stool. "I don't know. That was General McFadden's department."

"McFadden is out. We want his resignation first thing in the morning."

"You'll get it."

The words were difficult to say but had to be said. "Yours too, Lee."

"Done."

Lee drained his drink, then ordered another.

Consolingly, Paul began, "Only a few people have to know about this."

"I know about it."

"So you made a mistake. Everyone makes mistakes."

Vehemently, Lee denied it. "The old man never did."

"Oh, but you're wrong. He did. He caved in to the sheiks' demands when they told him that no Jews could work on that project in Saudi Arabia. He sold out his principles for money—although he wouldn't accept my assessment of what he'd done. That's why I quit. But after he did that, I can see why you thought that money in the right places could win us a contract. Father was your mentor."

When Paul looked at their faces in the bar mirror, he had to turn away in embarrassment. Tears were coursing down Lee's cheeks.

"He found out," Lee said almost inaudibly.

"He called you that night, didn't he? What did he tell you?"

"He told me to stop it before it was too late. And I told him I couldn't, because the money was already on its way to Conroy. He got crazy. Yelled at me. Just the way he used to when I was a kid and I fucked up. Then he hung up. I was sure I was going to be fired, but a couple of hours later Mother called to say that he was dead."

"Then he must have died right after he'd talked to you."

"No. He made another call. To Matt Rowley."

"Matt said he never talked to him that night. So he was lying."

"Yes and no."

"What do you mean by that?"

"You'll have to ask Matt."

Just then, Andy arrived and said that he had a taxi waiting outside. "We'll get you home, Lee."

"I can't go home. I'm too ashamed."

"Sally doesn't know anything about this and never has to," Paul told him.

"It doesn't make any difference. I know, and I'm ashamed."

Andy volunteered to put him up in the new apartment he'd acquired after his marriage split up, but it wasn't easy to dislodge Lee from the bar stool. All that liquor had made him self-pitying. What was the use of going home, ever? he asked. What was the using of living?

Reassuringly, Paul answered, "Because we'd feel terrible if something happened to you. We all love you."

Lee looked up.

"We all love you a lot," he repeated. "That goes for me, too."

Both of them were embarrassed by the sudden declaration, but the words seemed to soothe Lee.

"Where do I go from here?" he pleaded. "This time I really screwed up. I don't have anything. No job. Nothing."

Andy and Paul began to steer him toward the exit. "We'll find something for you to do. No wheeling and dealing this time, but something. Don't worry about it."

"I have to worry. I'm broke, buddy."

"Hell, no, you're not. You're loaded. You've got all that money Father left you."

"No, I don't," he answered sadly as they helped him into the taxi. "Ask Matt if you don't believe me."

Paul was sure he'd have to get Matt out of bed, but when he arrived at the Greek Revival house on West Twentieth Street, he saw a car double-parked in front and a woman walking down the steps holding a batch of clothes in her hands.

"Mrs. Rowley?" Paul asked, and when she replied in the affirmative he introduced himself. "Is Matt here?"

She was clearly annoyed. "Well, actually, we were supposed to leave for Montauk about four hours ago. We've rented a house there for a week. A sort of delayed honeymoon. Anyway"—even in the darkness, Paul saw her face flush—"we got occupied with something else, so we're getting a late start."

A little prehoneymoon bliss perhaps. Well, there was nothing wrong with that. Still, Paul never failed to be astounded at the partners some men chose. The new—or comparatively new—Mrs. Rowley had close-cropped hair like a boy's and a turned-up nose that missed being grotesque by only an eighth of an inch. That she might conceivably inspire love he could understand. Lust, never.

Matt had been checking things out on the second floor—faucets shut, lights off—and as he descended the staircase with two valises in his hands, he stopped in his tracks when he saw Paul standing in the hall. Then, as if he knew why Paul was there, he continued slowly to the bottom of the stairs. With resignation, he placed the suitcases on the Oriental rug.

"Wouldn't you know it?" he said, trying to be cheerful. "It looks as if once again I'll have to sacrifice my honeymoon for the Molloys."

"It will only take a minute, Matt."

To his wife, who was standing in the open doorway, he said, "Why don't you wait in the car, honey? I'll be right along."

"All right, darling, but please hurry. It'll be almost dawn by the time we reach Montauk."

After she left, Paul asked, "What happened, Matt? The night my father died." When there was no immediate response, he added, "I've talked to Lee. He's leaving the firm. Resigning."

The deep lines on Matt's forehead furrowed. "Because of what he tried to do to me?"

"I'm not sure I know what he tried to do to you."

Matt's voice quivered with anger. "He tried to *fire* me, that's what. He came to me and said my services weren't needed anymore. That's all I got—after devoting my whole life to Mr. Molloy and the firm!"

"How did you stop him?"

"He didn't tell you?" He waited for Paul to shake his head. "I had no choice. He was going to put me out on the street. How could I let him do that? I just got married. I'm paying for a house. I couldn't let him do that."

"You lied to my mother when you said you hadn't spoken to my father the night he died, didn't you?"

"Yes, but that wasn't the lie. I didn't speak to him. You see, that night, my wife and I were out and didn't get home till almost midnight. When your mother told me that Mr. Molloy might have tried to get in touch with me between ten-thirty and eleven, I remembered that I'd turned on the answering macnine before I went out and I'd forgotten to play it back that morning because of all the confusion as a result of Mr. Molloy's sudden death. So your mother asked me to check my answering machine to see if he'd left a message. I did; then I told her that there was none. That was the lie. When I heard that tape, something told me I'd better hold on to it for a few days. It was a spontaneous decision, and as it turned out, a stupid one. I didn't think about you or anyone else. Just myself. And once I made the decision, I couldn't change it. I knew that Lee has always hated my guts. I guess he thinks I'm not very manly. Well, there are different gradations of masculinity, like everything else. Anyone who thinks that there are just two sexes is fooling himself. There are hundreds of variations. But I didn't quite meet up to Lee's high standards because I was just an administrative assistant. A plain old secretary, he called me. And I had a funny feeling that he might try to give me the sack. So I held on to the tape."

"You still have it?"

"Here in the study."

Outside, a car horn honked as Mrs. Rowley complained about the delay. Matt opened the front door and yelled that it would be just another few minutes, then closed the door again and led Paul into a small, book-lined study.

"You might like to have a drink first," he urged Paul.

"That's okay. I've already had more than I need for one night."

Matt removed several books from a shelf, then reached in and withdrew a small black cylinder. The answering machine was next to the telephone on the desk, but before playing the tape, he turned again to Paul.

"I guess it was wrong, what I did. I loved working for your father, and I think he respected me. He was a good man. An honest man. When I heard his voice on the tape, I realized that something very terrible had happened because he was so upset. Why don't you sit down, Paul?"

Paul did as he was instructed. And as Matt inserted the tape, then pressed a button, Paul shielded his eyes with the edge of one hand. First there were clicks and muffled sounds of previous recordings, then came the clear and unmistakable voice of Charles Molloy.

"Matthew, this is Charles Molloy speaking. I have just learned something so heinous and revolting that I want you to prepare a codicil to my last will and testament and have it on my desk for my signature first thing in the morning. And in

the unlikely event that something untoward happens to me between now and then, I am sure that any court of law will accept my voice in lieu of my signature. Here goes." He cleared his throat. *"I hereby revoke any bequests granted to my son Liam Molloy made in my last will and testament, dated December 6, 1959. He is to get nothing. Repeat: nothing. Instead, all gifts previously bequeathed to him will go to my beloved son Paul, who warned me two years ago that once a pact is made with the Devil, there is no turning back. For my stubbornness and wrong-headedness, I beg his forgiveness. Being of sound mind and body, this is Charles A. Molloy, and God is my witness."*

TWENTY

On the day of the Democratic primary in West Virginia, a multimillion-dollar contract for the construction of a vast military installation in South Vietnam was awarded to the L.S. and R. Company of Denver, Houston, and San Diego, the largest Defense Department project ever begun during peacetime.

Only a very few critics expressed the view that peace was violated the minute the contract was let. If until then there had been no war in Southeast Asia in which Americans were actively involved, there was now.

Father Joseph read the news in the afternoon *Examiner*, the same issue that announced Robert Conroy's decision to support Sheldon Hawkins, Democratic assemblyman from Oakland, as his replacement in the House of Representatives.

Conroy had agreed reluctantly to the endorsement. It was Pat Cassidy who persuaded his son-in-law that it would be appropriate for him to make amends for his transgressions by supporting a candidate who might otherwise find it tough going to shift his power base from Sacramento to Washington. In spite of his illness—the *Examiner* was vague on the nature of it—Robert was expected to play an influential role in California Democratic circles for some time to come, and his endorsement of Assemblyman Hawkins was considered significant.

Afterward, Shelly Hawkins called Pat at his office and asked what he owed him for the favor.

"Well, the first thing you can do is trade in that pink Cadillac of yours for a nice gray Ford."

"It's white, not pink."

"Same thing. You'll never get anywhere in politics if you persist in driving around in cars that are better than your constituents'. Don't you know what John Kennedy did when his wife bought him a Jaguar for a Christmas present? He sent it back to the showroom."

"Does it have to be gray, for God's sake?" He waited. "Couldn't it be white?"

"Well, maybe off-white.

Aaron Golden had called Father Joe first thing that morning—unprecedented till then because the full daytime long-distance rate was in effect—to express his apprehension about the polling in West Virginia. "No one likes Humphrey," he said. "The man has as much charisma as your local pharmacist, but he's a Protestant. And most of those people in the hills of West Virginia are direct descendants of eighteenth-century Anglo-Saxon Protestant settlers who aren't materially much better off than their great-great-grandpappies were. Their one solace is their enduring faith in a Protestant God, and most of them have never even *met* a Catholic before. I'm afraid that Humphrey is going to win."

"And if John Kennedy loses in West Virginia, where does that leave us out here in California?"

It was agonizing for Aaron to say it. "It leaves us with a six-month lease on an office south of Market, and we won't be able to pay the rent."

"Those people in West Virginia may surprise us yet, Aaron."

"We may be asking too much of them, Padre. You can't unlearn hundreds of years of prejudice in just a couple of weeks. Personally, I'll be happy when it's all over. I spent most of last week in and around Charleston, and I didn't understand more than a few words anyone said. They talk a very peculiar lingo down there."

"I'm sure they found yours a little offbeat too, Aaron."

"God, yes. I was the most exotic thing they'd seen in a long time. One of them asked me if I was a Catholic, and I told him, no, I was a Jew. And I really don't think he knew what one was!"

Father Joseph had intended to inform him that he would be leaving Oakland and severing his connections with the

Northern California Citizens for Kennedy office, but didn't have the heart to add to the gloom being generated by the West Virginia primary.

Instead, late in the afternoon he dropped in at the Kennedy office on Folsom Street and found it jammed with volunteers. By then, twenty or so telephone lines had been installed, and each one was in use as calls were being made to voters asking them to support the candidate. Young people were departing, arms filled with campaign literature and voter registration information, and others were returning, arms empty, for fresh supplies.

"Are you giving out Green Stamps or something to every voter you register?" he asked Vinnie Chan when he finally located her in a crowded corner.

"Isn't it exciting? It's been this way all day long."

"I guess you haven't heard the news. Kennedy is going to get trounced in West Virginia. He doesn't have a chance. Even if he brings his entire family down there—sisters, brothers, nieces, nephews, cousins—there still couldn't be more than fifty Catholics in all of West Virginia."

"You underestimate Americans," she lectured him. "Haven't you ever read that old spiel on the Statue of Liberty? You know what I mean? The tired, the poor, the huddled masses, the refuse of the world. Boy, did we get the world's refuse! That's why people came here. Because they were considered garbage in their homelands. You don't think that descendants of those people are going to turn against a presidential candidate just because he practices a different form of religion, do you? No way! Here in America, we're the original Heinz 57 varieties. Those West Virginians aren't going to vote against John Kennedy because he's a Catholic, I know they're not." With her thumb, she indicated the crowd around her. "These kids know it too. Can't you feel it?"

Father Joe *could* feel it. The faces in the room were white, brown, yellow, and black, and not one of them looked despairing. Maybe, after all, they knew something about Americans that he didn't.

He was buoyed by them. As with Aaron Golden, he couldn't

bring himself to tell Vinnie that he wouldn't be back. Maybe he could send a letter.

When he had left the rectory in Oakland, Father Declan was in the process of packing Father Joe's meager possessions, sighing softly all the while. The office of the archdiocese would be sending a car around at seven the following morning to drive Father Joe to the airport, and until then he had nothing to do. Rather than returning to hang around the parish house, he decided to make one last trip to Salinas.

If he had never made a first one, Bishop Moriarity wouldn't now be banishing him to a year of enforced solitude and reflection. Still, Father Joe wanted to see and talk to Rafael.

When he pulled up in front of the tiny house, he was cheered when he saw his old friend once again sitting on a chair under the trees.

"So you have risen from your deathbed," Father Joe said by way of greeting.

"You haven't heard, Father?" Rafael replied. "The ranchers have succumbed."

"Moved by Christian charity?"

"Moved by rotting strawberries! Look around you in the fields, Father. Everywhere, the berries are rotting because people have refused to buy them. Now that the ranchers have expressed a willingness to negotiate, I've given up my fast."

"I'm happy for you, Rafael. I wasn't sure you could carry it off."

"Oh, I have much confidence in mankind, Father. In the end, goodness triumphs over evil. But sometimes it is necessary to give goodness a little kick in the behind to get it hopping. That's all I have done with my fast."

Father Joe was moved. Rafael had gambled his own life on his cause and could so easily have lost. Yet that hadn't deterred him.

"Have you won all the concessions you sought?" he asked.

"Not all, but most. The ranchers are willing to give us the minimum wage, and that is a beginning. They have promised to upgrade—that is a pithy American word, is it not?—the standards of our housing. And they have agreed to discuss future complaints with me and a group of democratically chosen spokesmen. A beginning."

In the background, Father Joe saw the women dressed in black who were part of Rafael's domestic retinue. But someone was missing.

"Has Miss Grainger left?" he asked.

"Just yesterday. A young man—a very violent young man—came here to take her away."

No doubt her old boyfriend and tormentor. So she had reverted to type, after all, just as she'd prophesied. Once again she was driving around in her burgundy Daimler with her procurer, as she called him. Once again leading a life of hedonism and debauchery.

Well, why should he be disappointed? She had warned him.

"She was very good to us," Rafael continued. "We shall miss her. She was a troubled woman when she first arrived, I could feel it. But I think she found peace here. I hope it will stay with her always."

Father Joe professed the same hope, but without much conviction. "I may be going away, too," he went on, "far away. And I may be gone for a year or more. So I've come to say good-bye."

"But who will baptize my daughter's newborn child?" he cried.

"Either my replacement in Oakland, or we can send someone from Monterey or Santa Cruz."

"It will not be the same, Father. We are very close to you. We braceros look upon you as our brother. You must come back. You belong with us. And until you return, *vaya con Dios*."

When Father Joe arrived at the rectory, he found an envelope on the hall table, and in it was his airline ticket to Memphis.

Father Declan stood contemplating him from the entrance to the parlor, wringing his hands. "The bishop's office called while you were out to say that your replacement will be arriving by midmorning tomorrow. His name is Hartmann. Father Hartmann. It sounds Germanic, doesn't it, Father Joseph?"

It certainly did. A little Prussian discipline might do the parish some good. On the other hand, it might do harm. Father Hartmann would no doubt get along very well with Bishop Moriarity.

"We'll miss you, Father Joseph," Father Declan sighed, on the verge of tears. "Mrs. Esposito has prepared a lovely meal for us this evening, although she's been weeping all afternoon in the kitchen. Will you be ready to sit down at the table by seven?"

Father Joe said that he would be there, but first he wanted to visit his church next door.

It was always locked at dusk as a precaution against vandals, so he had to fetch the key, a needlessly large, ornate, Gothic-looking device that fit the huge oak doors in front. The Middle Ages had seen Christianity rise to a lofty glory never to be repeated, and it was perhaps proper that Gothic architecture was employed even in California to express Catholic reverence and awe. Father Joseph couldn't help but remember how down at the heels the interior had looked when he was first assigned to the parish: pews scratched and in need of revarnishing, huge cracks in the nave's ceiling, peeling and lusterless statuary, and an organ so badly out of tune that it sounded like a dozen concertinas. Now everything had been polished and stained, patched, repainted, and tuned, and St. Brendan's Church was filled with a kind of majesty.

In the sacristy where the vestments of his priestly duties were kept, he knelt at the prie-dieu and bowed his head. After he prayed, he rose to wash his hands, murmuring, *"Da, Domine."*

At the vesting bench, he placed the linen amice over his shoulders and arranged the alb so that it fell gracefully to his ankles. He girded himself with the cincture, then took up the maniple, gently kissing the cross in the center as he placed it on his left forearm. He reached for the stole and rested it around his neck, took the chalice in his hand, and walked solemnly toward the altar, holding the sacred vessel in front of him.

Of course, Bishop Moriarity was right. Priests had no business meddling in social affairs. Their duty was to celebrate God and prepare people for the endless life after death, free from travail. Suffering always had been, and always would be, a part of earthly existence, and men of God were placed here to make it more bearable, not to attempt to correct it.

Yes, Father Joseph knew that. But he couldn't help but compare Bishop Moriarity and Rafael Banuelos. While one was more than content to accept suffering and injustice—all the while eating his plump lamb chops and sipping his French wine—the other had protested, nearly forfeiting his life in the process. Which of the two was the true holy man, the bishop who promised comfort and relief in the life hereafter or the humble bracero who was not content with such promises and wanted clean latrines and a minimum wage for his people right now?

More than heaven was necessary. Surely, that was a me-dieval solution, not a twentieth-century American one. In the New World, happiness and bounty were expected to be more fairly distributed during this lifetime, not the next, thank you.

Yet because of such dissident thoughts, Father Joseph was being exiled to a bare cell in a faraway monastery, removed from the people he longed to help. How could God, whose insight and understanding was superior to Bishop Moriarity's, permit it?

Now, more than ever, confused and tormented, Father Joseph needed reassurance. Some sign to tell him that his priesthood was worth fighting for. Some small sign that God was watching, listening.

At the altar, Father Joe offered the Host in his hands, uttering the ancient words *Hoc est enim corpus meum*, beseech-ing God's attention.

After a sleepless vigil, Father Joe arose at first light and said his prayers at his bedside as he'd done every morning since childhood. He showered, shaved, then dressed in a pair of casual slacks and a garishly colored sport shirt.

Father Declan must have heard him because he was wait-ing for him at the bottom of the stairs. "The archdiocese office won't be sending the car till seven," he reminded him, having the good manners not to remark on his wardrobe.

"I won't be needing it. Or the airline ticket either." He

handed his curate an envelope. "When the car arrives, could you give the driver this to pass on to His Eminence?" The envelope was unsealed, and the letter inside was addressed to the Most Honorable Bishop Francis A. Moriarity. It said:

> In all good conscience, I find it impossible to carry out your request that I disassociate myself from people's worldly sufferings. Because of that, I humbly and respectfully submit my resignation from the priesthood.
>
> Joseph M. Cassidy

The Chinese-American paperboy had pitched the morning *Chronicle* from his bicycle, but it had missed the front porch and landed in the rhododendrons. Joe Cassidy bent over from the stoop to retrieve it, then used his key to open the door.

He could smell hickory-smoked bacon. "Anyone home?" he cried, stepping into the hall.

"Here in the kitchen. I've been expecting you."

As Joe entered the kitchen, his father stood at the stove, his back toward him.

"Your old room is ready, aired out and cleaned. There'll be no charge for room and board while you cast around for some way to use your undeniable gifts. I'll fix breakfast every day; I don't like surprises early in the morning, so it's always the same. But I would expect you to help with the supper, since you're a better cook than I am. Some of your old friends from college have been asking about you, and I've told them it will probably be a few weeks before you get in touch. As for womanizing, as I believe it's called. I have no objection so long as you don't cohabit with anyone in this house while I'm around. If you marry, as you no doubt will, I'll expect a grandchild every second year." At last he turned. "Welcome home, Joe. How do you feel?"

"Empty," Joe said, slumping into a kitchen chair.

"That's an awful shirt you're wearing. It was out of style ten years ago."

"I'll have to do some shopping."

"Did His Eminence put up much of a fuss?"

Joe consulted his watch. It was a quarter to eight. "He should be reading my letter of resignation about now. I have a feeling he won't be displeased. He has a very delicate digestive system, I hear, and it's easily upset by priests who fail to toe the line."

Patrick set a plate of bacon and eggs with an English muffin before his son. "The Church of Rome will simply have to understand that in order to survive, it must adjust to modern times. Bishop Moriarity hasn't yet gotten the message—if he ever will." He placed a second plate on the other side of the table, then sat down. "What are your plans now?"

"I have none. Maybe in a few weeks, I may go over to Berkeley to talk to someone about graduate school. Law maybe. Social work. Something like that."

"You'll be good at anything you choose to do because you have a deep feeling for people. Next fall, Sheldon Hawkins will need all the help he can get to be elected to Congress, and I—"

Joe held his hands up, palms out. "My God, I hope you haven't offered my services to another political candidate. I'm afraid that my first candidate has already sunk out of view in the hollows of West Virginia."

"John Kennedy?" Pat asked in surprise. "Then you haven't heard the news this morning." He unfolded that *Chronicle* and placed it on the table. A banner headline read: KENNEDY WINS IN WEST VIRGINIA; HUMPHREY WITHDRAWS FROM RACE.

As Joe hungrily read the article, his father said, "Doesn't that make you feel good? Almost everyone predicted that bigotry was going to win in West Virginia, and look what's happened!"

It did make Joe feel good. The people of West Virginia hadn't listened to the hate-mongers after all, but had chosen the man they thought would make the best President.

"Every now and then," Joe began, "I'm actually pleased to be a member of the human race."

"You and me, too. But don't think that this means winning in November is going to be a piece of cake for Kennedy. It'll be uphill all the way, make no mistake, and the fanatics will be at our heels right up to the polling booths. I don't think West Virginia is a true sample, Joe. Those people knew that the eyes of the world were on them, everyone expecting them to vote on narrow religious lines. They're poor people, most of them, just barely eking out a living in coal mines, but they're proud. They didn't want to be seen as bigots. Next November, others may not be so self-conscious and will act out their prejudices in the privacy of polling booths, where no one can watch. It'll be a close one, I think, with a very exciting finish."

Joe was beginning to like politics. If Kennedy won in November, it would be a miracle, and that was something even religions couldn't easily deliver anymore. Sheldon Hawkins's old seat in the State Assembly would be up for grabs the following spring. Maybe the time had come for a former priest to toss his hat in the ring. Why not? During the first part of his career, Joe had helped people prepare for death. During the second half, as a public servant, perhaps he could enlarge the possibilities of their lives.

Thoughtfully, he said, "You know, even if we accomplish nothing else in this election, if we learn something about religious tolerance and if we can get Negroes and Hispanics involved in the American electoral process, I think we'll have accomplished one helluva lot."

"Absolutely," Pat agreed. "One helluva lot." He waited, smiling. "By the way, there's already a noticeable improvement in your language. Until now, I've always felt a bit uncomfortable, cussing in front of you—like you were going to rap me across the knuckles. But now I can relax."

When the doorbell rang, Pat said, "Finish your breakfast. I'll get it," then returned in a minute. "It's a woman to see you. She's in the living room."

Joe hoped it wasn't anyone from St. Brendan's because he was in no mood to offer explanations for his resignation, but he couldn't imagine who else it could be. Quite naturally, he'd told Father Declan where he'd be staying.

He found Susan Grainger standing in front of the fireplace. At first she was almost unrecognizable. In place of her customary stylish I. Magnin clothes, she was wearing a simple dark-blue dress, and her hair had been cut in a no-nonsense way. There was no lipstick, mascara, or powder on her face, which made the huge black-and-blue bruise beneath one of her eyes all the more conspicuous.

"My God!" Joe cried. "Did your boyfriend do that to you?"

She was remarkably tranquil. "It's unimportant. You see, he said I'd tricked him. Remember, he always threatened to kill any man who took me away from him."

"Sit down, Susan."

"I can't stay. I just wanted to drop by to tell you how grateful I am for everything. For rescuing this fallen woman, I mean. I stopped at the parish house in Oakland and they told me you'd be here. If it hadn't been for you, I'd still be the same useless, superfluous woman I was before I met you. Do you remember what you told me that first day we talked in Hillsborough? You said that if I was unhappy, the best way to get over it was to do something for people who were worse off than I was. Well, I did. And now I understand what you meant, and I think I understand your God, too." She drew a deep breath. "I'm going away. Leaving California and every-thing I hate about my life. I'm starting all over again some-where where no one knows me. I feel strong now, and I think I can do it. Thank you, Father Joseph. Thank you."

At last the sign. But an ambiguous one.

Or was it? Joe had helped someone change her life for the better without even once having appealed to her as a priest. No rituals were involved, no ceremonies. He'd found a woman who was suffering, and to save herself he advised her to do something for someone worse off than she was. It had worked.

Maybe it was the ticket for everyone. For humankind. Maybe even what Christianity was all about.

Suddenly, he felt very happy about himself and who he was, more Catholic than ever. Exciting times lay ahead. The possibilities were endless.

From the pulpit, Joe hadn't truly been able to reach Shelly Hawkins's constituents in West Oakland. From the Statehouse, perhaps he could.

Yes, the possibilities seemed endless.

* * *

In spite of the fact that there were no longer any obstacles to prevent Paul from assuming the presidency of the Molloy Company—his father had seen to that—he continued to hedge.

He wanted the job with all his heart, but there was Emily to consider, far off in their hilltop paradise in Sonoma County. Once she'd confessed that she didn't think she could ever live in New York City, where there were no redwoods, no sweet-scented eucalyptus, no vineyards. How could he ask her to make such a sacrifice? Every night when he called, he told her that he would be home . . . well, in just a few more days.

One afternoon, he was sitting at his desk when his secretary buzzed to announce a visitor. Even before she'd given a name, Emmy was standing in the doorway, clutching Spot in her arms.

Paul ran across the room to embrace them. "But I told you I'd be home in just a few more days!"

"No, Paul," she replied with infinite wisdom. "This is your home. I know that now, and you do, too. So instead of waiting for you to come home to us, we've come home to you."

The day after Paul became president and chairman of the board of the Molloy Company, he and Emily Nakamura were married at a Buddhist temple in Morningside Heights, a somewhat astounded Roman Catholic priest assisting in the ceremony. During it, Nora held her new Japanese-American grandson on her lap, and he howled robustly.

Afterward, Nora suggested, "Don't you think we could come up with a more Christian name than Spot?"

"We already have." Paul watched his mother's eyes glisten as he added, "Emmy and I would like to call him Charles Molloy."